Flaubert

Flaubert

HENRI TROYAT

Translated by Joan Pinkham

VIKING

VIKING
Published by the Penguin Group
Viking Penguin, a division of Penguin Books USA Inc.,
375 Hudson Street, New York, New York 10014, U.S.A.
Penguin Books Ltd, 27 Wrights Lane, London W8 5TZ, England
Penguin Books Australia Ltd, Ringwood, Victoria, Australia
Penguin Books Canada Ltd, 10 Alcorn Avenue, Suite 300,
Toronto, Ontario, Canada M4V 3B2
Penguin Books (N.Z.) Ltd, 182–190 Wairau Road,
Auckland 10, New Zealand

Penguin Books Ltd, Registered Offices:
Harmondsworth, Middlesex, England

First published in 1992 by Viking Penguin,
a division of Penguin Books USA Inc.

1 3 5 7 9 10 8 6 4 2

Originally published in France by Librairie Ernest Flammarion. ©
Flammarion, Paris, 1988.

Grateful acknowledgment is made for permission to reprint excerpts
from the following copyrighted works:
The Letters of Gustave Flaubert, selected, edited and translated
by Francis Steegmuller, Cambridge, Mass.: The Belknap Press of
Harvard University Press. Copyright © 1979, 1980, by Francis
Steegmuller. Reprinted by permission of the publisher.
Pages from the Goncourt Journal, edited, translated and introduced by Robert Baldick, 1962. By permission of the Oxford University Press.

LIBRARY OF CONGRESS CATALOGING IN PUBLICATION DATA
Troyat, Henri, 1911–
Flaubert/ by Henri Troyat; translated by Joan Pinkham.
p. cm.
Translated from French.
Includes bibliographical references and index.
ISBN 0-670-84450-0
1. Flaubert, Gustave, 1821–1880—Biography. 2. Novelists,
French—19th Century—Biography. I. Title.
PQ2247.T76 1992
843'.8—dc20 92–217

Printed in the United States of America
Set in Plantin · Designed by Francesca Belanger

CONTENTS

Contents

TRANSLATOR'S
NOTE

As the reader will find, this book is full of quotations from nineteenth-century French sources. Most of them are taken either from Flaubert's voluminous correspondence or from the contemporary diary of the brothers Edmond and Jules de Goncourt. In the present century, these fascinating literary documents have naturally attracted the attention of many English-language translators of varying talents, and in translating M. Troyat's biography, I have constantly consulted their work.

Mindful of the proverbial broken clock that is nevertheless right twice a day, at one point or another I have gratefully adopted a happy turn of phrase from even the least reliable of my predecessors. I owe special mention, however, to two excellent translators whose work I have (with permission) pillaged at some length.

The first of these is the late Robert Baldick, whose *Pages from the Goncourt Journal* (Oxford University Press, 1962) shows refreshing evidence of intelligence and judgment on every page. I have used his language without change for perhaps a dozen excerpts from the *Journal*.

The second is Francis Steegmuller, whose work on Flaubert—translations and biographical studies—spans what for most people would be a professional lifetime and has lately culminated in the Harvard University Press two-volume edition of Flaubert's selected letters. Justly acclaimed as a scholar, Mr. Steegmuller is also a superb translator highly esteemed by his fellow practitioners. Accordingly,

Translator's Note

I have lifted intact, or with only slight modifications, many passages from his versions of the Flaubert correspondence. I am happy to express here my gratitude for permission to do so and my pleasure at having had this opportunity to learn from a master of our craft.

I have also profited from Mr. Steegmuller's knowledge of the period. In a number of cases where I have provided a footnote explaining some point in the text, the information offered comes, in whole or in part, from him. This is indicated in the footnote by the notation (FS).

It is also my pleasure to acknowledge the generous assistance of Professor Andrée Demay of Smith College (retired). Her knowledge and skill have helped me solve many a problem and have saved me from more than one blunder.

—JP

Flaubert

Chapter 1

THE COCOON

The two young people liked each other and sought every opportunity to converse in private. Their mutual attraction was no secret to anyone. They were both well brought up and came from good families. Why shouldn't they be married? At the end of the year 1811, that was the question in the mind of Dr. Laumonier, chief surgeon of the Hôtel-Dieu, the municipal hospital of Rouen. He had taken into his home little Anne-Caroline Fleuriot, the daughter of one of his cousins (Dr. Jean-Baptiste Fleuriot), who had died in 1803. Anne-Caroline had lost her mother when she was a week old and her father at the age of ten. She had been raised by two former schoolmistresses from Saint-Cyr who kept a boarding school in Honfleur, but when the two women died she had been left alone in the world, and the Laumoniers had generously opened their arms to her. On her mother's side the orphan came of an excellent family in Normandy, the Cambremers of Croixmare, one of whose forebears had acquired patents of nobility thanks to his service in the judiciary. She was pretty, innocent, and sensible. These qualities had soon charmed Dr. Achille-Cléophas Flaubert, aged twenty-seven, who had been sent to Rouen to work under Laumonier.

The Flauberts were from Champagne. From father to son they had been veterinarians or horse breeders. During the Revolution Achille-Cléophas's father had been condemned to deportation for "lack of patriotism," but he had been saved by the downfall of

Robespierre. Achille-Cléophas had grown up in Nogent-sur-Seine, where his energetic father looked after the domestic animals of the whole region. Breaking with family tradition, the young man decided early on to become a doctor. After brilliant studies in Paris, he came out third in the competitive examination for hospital internships and joined the staff of the famous surgeon Dupuytren. The elder man soon became jealous of his pupil's exceptional gifts. Fearing that Achille-Cléophas might get in the way of his own career in Paris, Dupuytren had suggested he apply for a job in Rouen as instructor in anatomy under Laumonier.

At this time Rouen was a rich industrial city with a population of one hundred thousand, proud of its churches, factories, warehouses, and vast harbor installations spread out along the Seine, where ships of every nationality came to berth. Watched over by its superb cathedral, the city, with its academy, museums and schools, prided itself on being a cultural center of the first rank. When Achille-Cléophas arrived there, he had no sense of having made a change for the worse. Especially since from the outset his new chief, Laumonier, offered him his friendship, esteem, and confidence. He felt at ease in this family milieu brightened by the presence of the charming Anne-Caroline. Happy in his work, encouraged in his love, he spoke of his intentions to the man whom Anne-Caroline regarded as her father.

Laumonier approved of the marriage plan at once. But the girl was only eighteen, still a minor. The decision depended on the family council. This body, which included doctors, landed proprietors, lawyers, and members of the electoral college of Calvados, met to study the suitor's morality. After an investigation, it rendered a favorable verdict. The wedding took place on February 10, 1812, and the couple moved into number 8, Rue du Petit-Salut.

A year later, on February 9, 1813, Anne-Caroline gave birth to a son. He would be called Achille like his father and, God willing, like his father he would become a doctor. Even before he had shown his talents, his mother was proud of him. She was also proud of her husband, whose learning, dedication, and authority were the admiration of those around him. In 1815, two weeks before the battle

The Cocoon

of Waterloo, Dr. Flaubert succeeded Dr. Laumonier as chief surgeon at the hospital of Rouen. Another child was born, Caroline, but she died in infancy. Then came a boy, Emile-Cléophas, but he too lived only a few months. He was replaced by little Jules-Alfred, whose weak constitution led everyone to fear the worst. In the meantime, following the death of Dr. Laumonier on January 10, 1818, the Flauberts had moved into the hospital wing set aside as the chief surgeon's residence. It was a noble rectangular structure of gray stone, with two stories and high windows. A big room on the ground floor served as laboratory and dissecting room. For Achille-Cléophas was not content merely to treat patients and perform operations; his passion for knowledge drove him ever deeper into medical research. He was already celebrated throughout the region. His reputation and emoluments having grown over the years, for thirty-eight thousand francs he purchased a property just outside the city, in Déville-lès-Rouen, a little town half rural, half industrial, with a population of twenty-five hundred.

The property, enclosed by walls, included a courtyard, a garden, a slate-roofed residence, a chapel, greenhouses, a stable, cow shed, barn, and brick oven, all covering almost two hectares. It was to be the family's summer home. Delighted with his acquisition, Achille-Cléophas had a bust of Hippocrates set up in the middle of a flower bed. His wife was pregnant again. They were both hoping for a girl this time. But on Wednesday, December 12, 1821, in her room in the Hôtel-Dieu in Rouen, Anne-Caroline gave birth to another son. In spite of their disappointment, the parents pretended to rejoice over the birth. The new arrival was named Gustave. The baptism took place the following January 13 in the Church of Saint Madeleine. To show his anticlericalism, the father did not attend the ceremony. Six months later, while baby Gustave was kicking lustily in his cradle, his brother Jules-Alfred died in turn. The parents didn't let that discourage them. They wanted a large brood. The new bereavement was followed by a new pregnancy. And on July 15, 1824, little Caroline came into the world. She bore the same name as her sister who had died in infancy; she was two and a half years younger than her brother Gustave and eleven years younger than her other brother, Achille. Achille was already in school and outstanding for his diligence. For practical purposes, he belonged to the world of adults. Three surviving children out of six was a good average for the time. Achille-Cléophas thought they could leave it at that. To help with the housework he engaged a servant, Julie (her real name was Caroline Hébert), who from the beginning showed a preference for Gustave, who was then three.

Dr. Flaubert kept to a rigorous schedule. Winter or summer, at half past five in the morning he would leave his apartment in the Hôtel-Dieu and, candle in hand, enter the wards. His associates would follow him deferentially from bed to bed. He would operate steadily until noon and spend the rest of the day seeing patients. Notwithstanding his liberal opinions, which he made no attempt to hide, in 1824 he was elected to the Académie Royale de Médecine. His patients were grateful for his integrity and devotion, his colleagues admired him, the authorities respected him. In the eyes of little Gustave, he was a kind of omniscient deity with a blood-spattered apron. The whole world rested on his shoulders. He knew everything, could do everything, held sway over life and death. Often after Gustave and Caroline had played in the garden, they would climb up the trellis to a window on the ground floor that gave on the dissecting room. They would see their father bending over a cadaver, scalpel in hand. The inert, livid flesh, the deep incisions gave them the impression of a dismal butchery. But curiosity was stronger than repugnance. "The sun shone on [the corpses]," Flaubert was to write long after; "the same flies that were flitting around us and around the flowers would light on them and come buzzing back. . . . I can still see my father looking up from his dissection and telling us to go away."[1] From the time the children took their first steps in the world, their minds were filled with images of disease, decay, and death. Stretchers were carried by in the garden. Skeletal silhouettes limped down the paths on crutches. The faces of some of the inmates bore the expression of clinical idiocy, and Gustave amused himself imitating them, with their staring eyes and pendulous lower lips.

While his father's clothes smelled of the hospital, there was nothing frightening about his mother. But with her dark, melancholy eyes, her black hair, pale complexion, and lips that rarely smiled, she too was the image of suffering. Anxious, nervous, a bit obsessive, she trembled for her offspring. To be sure, her oldest child, Achille, showed encouraging signs of health and intelligence, but the other two had such delicate constitutions that it augured ill for their future. Gustave in particular seemed both hypersensitive and intellectually retarded. He was always withdrawing into a sort of stupor, his finger in his mouth, his eyes vacant, deaf to what was being said around him and incapable of uttering a correct sentence. It was his mother who gave him his first lessons, with anxious patience. He stumbled over words, balked at learning the alphabet, and his father was distressed to find him so lazy. This slow, dull-witted son was an irritation to him. He did not see in him, as in Achille, the worthy depositary of the family name.

Gustave understood this and withdrew more into himself. Since his mother, for her part, preferred the gentle Caroline, he felt rejected by his parents and turned passionately to friends. He had one whose affection filled him with happiness: Ernest Chevalier. Ernest was the grandson of old M. Mignot, who lived just opposite the Hôtel-Dieu. M. Mignot would sometimes take Gustave on his lap and read *Don Quixote* aloud to him. Thus, even before he could read himself, Gustave delighted in the imaginary feats of the famous slayer of windmills. He also listened wide-eyed and eager to the local folk tales whispered to him by the servant Julie. This fantastic universe collided in his head with the macabre sights of the hospital. On the one hand, the daring capers of the imagination; on the other, the foul-smelling everyday reality. Increasingly, dreams became the child's refuge from life. He hardly knew how to hold a pen, and already he hoped to become a writer. Like that Cervantes who had made up Don Quixote.

On December 31, 1830, when he had just turned nine, he confided his plans to his friend Ernest Chevalier in a letter whose spelling was somewhat unconventional: "If you'd like us to work together at writing, I'll write comedies and you can write your dreams, and since there's a lady who comes to see papa and always says stupid things I'll write them too." And a month later he wrote again: "Please answer me and tell me if you want us to get together to write stories, please tell me, because if you do I'll send you some notebooks I've begun to write and ask you to send them back to me, if you want to write something in them I'd like that very much." Subjects were piling up in his head. He listed them: *The Beautiful Andalusian, The Masked Ball, The Moorish Woman.* Mignot encouraged him in his first unsteady steps as a writer and even had hand-lettered copies made of a piece he had written in praise of Corneille, titling it *Three Pages from a Schoolboy's Notebook, or Selected Works of Gustave F.* . . . This school exercise was followed by a study on constipation, which, according to the author, was due to "a contraction of the shitarena hole." From the sublime to the scatalogical was only a step, and Gustave made a joke of it: "You see I was right in saying that the splendid explanation of that famous condition constipation and my eulogy of Corneille would go down to posterity. That is, down to the posterior," he wrote his friend.[2]

Having been to the theater with his parents, he was now seized with ambition to write for the stage. He enthusiastically scribbled one play after another and, with his sister, Ernest Chevalier, and later another friend, Alfred Le Poittevin, put them on for his parents and the servants. The performances took place in the billiard room. The billiard table, pushed against the wall, served as stage. Little Caroline took charge of the sets and costumes, while Ernest Chevalier was the stage hand, but they both acted as well. To keep the troupe supplied with material, Gustave turned out tragedies and comedies: *The Miserly Lover,* "who won't give his mistress any presents so his friend gets her," a "history of Henri IV," another of Louis XIII, another of Louis XIV. . . . At the Saint-Romain fair, held every October in Rouen, he saw a marionette show: the temptation of Saint Anthony struggling with the devil. He was thrilled by this performance. The memory of the saint's infernal hallucinations was to pursue Gustave all his life. Everything he saw, everything he heard, everything he read was a source of inspiration to him. Like most beginners, he copied others and thus without too much effort gave himself the illusion of producing.

The Cocoon

With the revelation of literature, his behavior began to change. The withdrawn, abstracted, ill-defined child of the preceding years was gradually discovering a reason for living. In the presence of his parents he still appeared dull and sluggish, but behind the mask was an intense inner ferment. The imaginary personages dwelling inside him drew him away from the world in which the grown-ups wanted to confine him. He hated everything that prevented him from indulging in the free play of his thoughts. The need to unbosom himself drove him to write one letter after another to his beloved Ernest Chevalier. They were signed: "Your best friend until death by God." Or: "Your dauntless dirty-minded friend till death." He was irresistibly attracted to this merry lad. Joys and disappointments, grandiose schemes and clumsy jokes—he wanted to share everything with him. It was no longer simple camaraderie but a passion for communion, a thirst for the other's presence. "You and I are bound by a love that can be called fraternal," he wrote to Ernest on April 22, 1832. "Yes, I who have deep feelings, yes, I would walk a thousand leagues if necessary to be reunited with my best of friends, for nothing is so sweet as friendship." Bursting with affection, he asked the apprentice of his uncle François Parain, a goldsmith and jeweler, to make two seals engraved as follows: "Gustave Flaubert and Ernest Chevalier, individuals who will never part."

In 1832 there was a cholera epidemic in France. A special wagon was designated for transporting the sick. The hospital was crammed with the dying. On the other side of the dining room wall, coughs and death rattles could be heard. Dr. Flaubert was overwhelmed with work. Gustave was not unduly upset by the grisly atmosphere. He was used to it.

For summer vacation in 1833, the whole family left by post chaise for Nogent-sur-Seine, the cradle of the Flaubert tribe. On this occasion Gustave visited Fontainebleau, Versailles, and the Botanical Gardens and saw "the famous Mademoiselle George" in *La Chambre ardente,* "a drama in five acts in which seven persons die." "She played her role to perfection," he told Ernest Chevalier with complete assurance.[3] That was all it took to rekindle his creative enthusiasm. Play or novel, the form didn't matter, as long as he could summon up the world of passions and the clash of swords. When would he be able to devote himself body and soul to his vocation? For the time being, in spite of the flame burning in his heart, he had to go back to the dismal boredom of school.

Chapter 2

FIRST WRITINGS, FIRST STIRRINGS OF LOVE

In the fall of 1831 Gustave entered the local lycée, the Collège Royal de Rouen, as a day student.* He was nine and a half. In March 1832 he became a boarder. This ancient establishment—it had opened its doors in 1595—was run according to strict military discipline. The professors wore the cap and gown with white facings. Each pupil had his own horn inkwell divided in two sections, one side for black ink, the other for red. They used goose quills that they trimmed with a knife. They all wore uniforms. There were no desks; they wrote on their laps. The classrooms were big and ill-heated. In winter the children shivered. Behind the professor's desk hung a black wooden cross. At the end of the day the boarders were back in their white beds, behind white curtains, in the dormitory lit by an oil lamp. "At night," wrote Flaubert, "I would listen a long time to the wind blowing mournfully. . . . I would hear the slow steps of the watchman making the rounds with his lantern, and when he came near I would pretend to be asleep and then fall asleep indeed, half dreaming, half crying."[1]

At 5:00 A.M. reveille sounded. The drum roll shook the walls. Immediately, the forty boarders would drag themselves out from under their covers grumbling, in a daze, and dress clumsily in the semidarkness. They would wash their faces hurriedly in the icy water

---

* The school is now called the Lycée Corneille, in honor of one of its most illustrious alumni.

9

of the fountain in the courtyard. Then, returning to the dormitory, they would stand at attention in front of their beds for the first roll call.

This tightly scheduled existence under constant surveillance was exasperating to Gustave. "From the time I entered school," he wrote later, "I was melancholy, restless, seething with desires. I yearned ardently for a wild and turbulent existence, I dreamed of passions and wanted to experience them all."[2] He hated being imprisoned, bound hand and foot, forced to march in line; he hated being young. And also being separated from Ernest Chevalier. The smallest events in the daily life of the little community called forth his bitter irony. Proudly, he wanted to be different from the others, scornful of easy pleasures, hostile to every form of official approval.

Already at the age of eleven he sneered when King Louis-Philippe visited his good city of Rouen. "Louis-Philippe, with his family, is now in the city that saw the birth of Corneille," he wrote Ernest. "How stupid mankind is, what fools the people are! . . . To run to see a king, to vote 30 thousand francs for a celebration, to spend 3,500 francs bringing musicians from Paris, to go to all that trouble, for whom? For a king! Ah, how stupid people are! As for me, I have seen nothing, neither the review nor the king's arrival, nor the princesses, nor the princes. Only, I did go out last night to see the illuminations."[3]

In another letter to his friend, written the following year when he was twelve and working, he said, on a novel about Isabeau of Bavaria, he made it even clearer that the human condition was wretched and ridiculous: "You think I must miss you a lot, yes, you are not mistaken and if I didn't have a fifteenth-century queen of France in my head and at the tip of my pen, I should be totally disgusted with life and a bullet would long since have delivered me from this crude joke called life."[4]

In spite of this childish misanthropy, he went on with his studies, for whatever they were worth. In class the pupils were saturated with Latin. Translation from Latin and into Latin, Latin composition, Latin poetry, Latin grammar, and commentary on Latin authors made up three quarters of the curriculum. The teaching of

First Writings, First Stirrings of Love

French was neglected. Anyway, Gustave received poor grades in that subject. Too much imagination and not enough spelling. He made up for it in natural history and especially in history. Under the guidance of an enthusiastic young professor, Pierre-Adolphe Chéruel, he devoured Michelet, Froissart, Commynes, Brantôme, Hugo, Dumas. During field trips with his teacher, he discovered the vestiges of the past in the city and its environs. The magnificence and violence of former centuries consoled him for the dullness of the present. With Chéruel's encouragement, he began writing a series of wildly romantic historical works, including stories and plays. Along the way he won prizes in history several years running. In 1834 he created for his schoolmates a handwritten review, *Art and Progress*, to which he was the sole contributor. That year the curriculum included—apart from Latin—fables and geography. The next year he started Greek, ancient history, English, *Télémaque*.* Then he discovered Beaumarchais, Voltaire, Shakespeare, Rabelais, Scott. . . . Each new thing he read made him more determined to be a writer himself. He was the disciple of all the great authors he associated with. His production at this time, of which almost nothing is left, became increasingly voluminous. He substituted quantity for quality.

But along with the first literary aspirations came the first stirrings of adolescent love. In 1834, while he was spending summer vacation with the family in Trouville, a quiet seaside resort where his parents had some property, he discovered the delights and torments of flirtation. Having made the acquaintance of the two daughters of the British admiral Henry Collier, Gertrude (aged fifteen) and Harriet (eleven), he promptly fell in love with them.† They exchanged a few squeezes of the hand, a few languorous sighs, a few kisses on the cheek, and then they had to part. "It was a sweet, childish feeling untarnished by any notion of possession, but for

---

* *Télémaque* [Telemachus] is a pedagogical novel composed by the quietist priest Fénélon in 1699 for the edification of his pupil the duc de Bourgogne, grandson of Louis XIV. —Trans.

† The girls later became, respectively, Mrs. Tennant and Mrs. Campbell.

that very reason lacking in energy," he was to write later. "Yet it was too foolish to be Platonic. . . . Need I say that it had been to love what the pale dawn is to broad daylight?"[5]

When school opened again, he went back to the cold classrooms, the communal life of the dormitory, the hastily done assignments. But in the midst of the humdrum routine of school life his guiding light was the thought of a body of work to be produced. The manuscripts piled up: *The Death of Marguerite de Bourgogne, A Journey to Hell, Two Hands on One Crown, A Secret of Philip the Wise, A Perfume to Breathe, The Woman of Fashion, The Plague of Florence, Bibliomania, Rage and Impotence, Norman Chronicle of the Tenth Century*. He who, later, would agonize over every sentence, let his pen race easily, rapturously, grandiloquently. In *A Perfume to Breathe* he confessed how delightful he found it to scribble words on paper: "Perhaps you do not know what a pleasure it is to compose! To write, oh! to write is to seize hold of the world, of its prejudices and virtues, and to sum them up in a book; it is to feel one's thought be born, grow, live, stand erect on its pedestal and remain there forever. So I have just finished this strange, bizarre, incomprehensible book. The first chapter I did in one day; then I went for a month without working on it; in one week I did five more and in two days I finished it." His philosophy, he said, was "gloomy, bitter, dark and skeptical." But as a reaction against this tendency to neurasthenia, he went in for salacious jokes and belly laughs. It was about this time that there appeared in his fantasies the character of "the Boy." This personage, invented by himself and a few friends, including a newcomer, Alfred Le Poittevin, was a sort of jovial monster, grotesque and Rabelaisian, whose function was to denounce provincial stupidity. Vulgar and never at a loss for words, he threw mud at everyone around him. For Gustave he provided the outlet for a tremendous rage against mediocrity.

Alfred Le Poittevin and Louis Bouilhet were the new companions with whom he held philosophical discussions and made plans for the future. Alfred Le Poittevin was five years his senior. Of a meditative turn of mind and inclined to melancholy, he nevertheless took a keen interest in petticoats. Louis Bouilhet too was attracted to girls. Between themselves they affected crude language and a virile cynicism. Gustave picked up their style and wrote Alfred a letter in the form of a school prize list: "Continuity of sodomite desire: first prize—(after me): Morel. Erection in pants: first prize: Morel. Solitary masturbation: prize: Rochin . . ."[6] The talk among comrades was all about "the cheesiferous cock," "the male organ," "pussies," "fucking."

For all the obscene language, Gustave dreamed with pounding heart of the ideal, inaccessible, supreme woman who would chain him at her feet. If he still contented himself with solitary pleasures and furtive caresses with comrades, through every pore of his skin he felt the call of true love, the love that unites two beings of different sexes in an ecstasy as strong as death. His flirtation with the little English girls in Trouville had left him with a sense of frustration.

The summer vacation of 1836 brought him back, with his parents, to the scene of his first flutters of the heart. In those days the journey to Trouville was quite a little expedition. From Pont-l'Evêque on, travelers had to take a path that carriages could not negotiate. They went on foot, their baggage being carried by horses. The seaside resort was only a humble fishing village. Two modest inns shared the visiting clientele, and six wooden cabins on the sand served as shelter for the few ladies who came to bathe. To entrust oneself to the movement of the waves was still considered eccentric. The Flaubert family stayed at the Hôtel de l'Agneau d'Or. Gustave, who was fourteen and a half, liked to go for solitary walks along the beach, his hair blowing in the wind. "At that time I was splendid," he wrote later. Very tall, very slim, with a bright complexion, light brown hair, green eyes, and a direct gaze, despite his youth he had the look of an athlete in top form. One morning as he was strolling on the beach, he saw a red cloak with black stripes lying on the sand and in danger of being swept away by the incoming tide. He picked it up and set it down farther off, out of reach of the waves. That same day at lunch in the communal dining room, he heard himself addressed in a woman's melodious voice. It was the owner of the cloak, who was thanking him for his gesture. When he looked at her, he felt faint. "How beautiful she was, that woman!" he was

13

to write. "I can still see those blazing pupils under black brows fixed on me like the sun. She was tall, dark, with magnificent black hair falling over her shoulders in braids. Her nose was Greek, her eyes burning, her eyebrows high and admirably arched, her skin glowing as if sifted over with gold. She was slim and delicate, and one could see azure veins winding across the brown and crimson throat. Add to all this a fine down that darkened her upper lip and gave her face a manly, energetic expression that would have made blond beauties pale beside her. . . . She spoke slowly; it was a modulated voice, musical and sweet."[7]

Every morning he went to see her bathing in the ocean. Standing on the shore, he would imagine the supple movements of the swimmer caressed by the waves. When she came out of the water, with her wet garments clinging to her thighs and breasts, he would be seized with a kind of vertigo: "My heart beat violently, I lowered my eyes, the blood rose to my head, I was suffocating. I felt this half-naked woman's body pass near me with the perfume of the waves. Had I been deaf and blind, I should have sensed her presence . . . I loved."

The object of this secret passion was named Elisa. She was twenty-six years old. Before so much beauty, grace, and assurance, Gustave was paralyzed with shyness. He felt himself too young, too mediocre to interest such a superior creature. But already he sensed that she would be the woman of his life, the one to whom he would dedicate his wildest dreams and whom he would portray under other names in his future works. Although he knew nothing, or almost nothing about her, he wanted to be faithful to her memory. The truth was that Elisa was not a person who had great respect for convention. On leaving the convent at the age of eighteen, she had married a young officer, Emile Judée. A short time later she had separated from him and, since then, had been living conjugally with a Prussian who had become a naturalized French citizen, the music publisher Maurice Schlésinger, thirteen years older than she.* She

---

* Maurice Schlésinger was to marry Elisa only in September 1840, after the death of Judée in 1839.

had just given birth to a baby girl, Marie, who, since the couple were not married, had been declared "of unspecified mother," on the birth certificate. Gustave would have liked to be in the child's place so as to bask in the warmth of his beloved. One day he saw Elisa uncover her breast to nurse the baby. He was overwhelmed by the sight of this nudity. "It was a full, round breast," he was to write, "with brown skin and azure veins that one could see beneath the glowing flesh. At that time I had never seen a naked woman. Oh, the strange ecstasy into which I was plunged by the sight of that breast! How I devoured it with my eyes, how I should have liked just to touch that bosom! It seemed to me that if I had placed my lips upon it, my teeth would have bitten it with rage, and my heart melted with delight thinking about the voluptuous pleasures that kiss would give. Oh, how long afterward I saw that palpitating breast, that long, graceful neck, and that head, with its black hair in curl papers, bent over the nursing child whom she rocked slowly in her lap, humming an Italian air!"[8]

Maurice Schlésinger, a "coarse, jovial man," took a liking to his mistress's timid admirer. Gustave went boating with them, accompanied them on their walks, even shared many of their meals. In September he attended a ball at the marquis de Pomereu's. But he was too young to dance. He watched the others, the adults—a humiliating situation that moved him to sarcasm. The closer the hour of parting came, the more it pained him not to be able to confess his love. And suddenly the vacation was over. The Schlésingers and the Flauberts packed their bags. The idyll came to an end on a deserted beach under a rainy sky. "Farewell forever!" Gustave wrote later. "She disappeared like the dust of the road that rose into the air behind her steps. How I have thought of her since! . . . In my heart there was chaos, an immense dull roar, madness; everything had vanished like a dream. . . . At last I saw the houses of my city. I returned home; everything there seemed deserted and mournful, empty and hollow. I began to live, to drink, eat, sleep. Winter came and I went back to school. . . . If I told you that I had loved other women, it would be an infamous lie."[9]

Back in school, he could not forget the enchantments of the

summer and decided to describe them in *Mémoires d'un fou* [Memoirs of a Madman]. Pen in hand, he relived with nostalgia the smallest moments of this amorous adventure, which was so important to him and of which Elisa, doubtless, had known nothing. Out of discretion, he named her Maria in his story. And he concluded: "Oh Maria! Maria, dear angel of my youth, you whom I saw in the freshness of my emotions, you whom I loved with a love so sweet, so full of perfume, of tender daydreams, adieu! . . . Adieu, and yet I shall always think of you! . . . Adieu! and yet when I saw you, if I had been four or five years older, more daring . . . perhaps! . . ."* This confession was dedicated to his new friend, Alfred Le Poittevin. Together they scoffed at women in obscene language, and together they dreamed of them.

---

* *Mémoires d'un fou* was completed in 1838.

Chapter 3

STUDIES AND DAYDREAMS

Alfred Le Poittevin left school while Gustave was still in the lower grades. But their friendship survived the separation and even grew stronger with the passage of time. Gustave felt deep affection and admiration for the older boy. He had a constant need for his approval. "I thought of you again," he was to write him a few years later. "I had a strange craving for you; for when we are far from one another, there is in each of us something that seems adrift, something indefinite and incomplete."[1] Alfred Le Poittevin's romantic pessimism found fertile ground in his young comrade. When they were together, they would urge each other on to depict violent emotions, macabre situations, horrible forebodings. Almost everything that Gustave wrote at the age of fifteen was relentlessly Gothic. In *Rage and Impotence* he tells of a man buried alive who devours his own arm. In *Quidquid Volueris* [As You Like It] his protagonist is the offspring of a Negro slave girl and an orangutan. In *Dream of Hell* he presents an old alchemist living in a ruined tower inhabited by bats, to whom Satan offers youth and love in exchange for his soul. But the alchemist has no soul; it is Satan who is swindled.

To take a rest from the great storms of passion, Gustave also liked to mine the satiric vein. Thus, inspired by Balzac's very popular *Physiologie du mariage*, he decided to write the physiology of an office worker. He titled it *A Lesson in Natural History: Genus Clerk*. It was a bold caricature, skillfully drawn, in which there appeared a "short, stout, pudgy, fresh-faced" personage who was in some ways reminiscent of the Boy. Now, it happened that Alfred Le Poittevin was at that time the editor of a local newspaper, *Le Colibri* [The Hummingbird], printed on pink paper and open to young authors. He offered to publish his friend's piece. Gustave was exultant: now he was an officially recognized writer. With feigned casualness he informed Ernest Chevalier: "My *Clerk* is to appear next Thursday, and on Wednesday . . . I shall correct the proofs." He awaited these proofs, the first of his life, with pride and anxiety. But he was still fifteen and a half and relished a good joke. While he began his letter like a serious author, he ended it like a merry schoolboy. He had just learned that the assistant headmaster had been surprised in a brothel and was to be summoned before the Academic Tribunal. He was jubilant: "When I think of the assistant headmaster's face when he was caught in the act, screwing, I shout out loud, I laugh, drink, sing, ah! ah! ah! ah! ah! and roar with laughter like the Boy, I pound the table, tear my hair, roll on the floor. That's a good one! Ah! Ah! What a joke, ass, shit! Farewell, for I've gone crazy over this news."[2]

That year he won first prize in both natural history and literature. But the satisfaction he took in these scholastic honors was as nothing compared to the happiness of having appeared in print in *Le Colibri*. In December 1837, a few days before his sixteenth birthday, he finished a "philosophical tale," *Passion and Virtue,* in which the heroine, Mazza, was a woman of stormy temperament whose dreams swept her away from the conventions of marriage and who in the end, disappointed by her lover, committed suicide: "She no longer believed in anything except misfortune and death. To her, virtue was a word, religion an illusion, reputation a deceptive mask, like a veil that hides wrinkles." Three months later it was a historical drama, *Loys XI,* in which Louis XI appeared as a friend of the people, whom he defended against the aristocrats and the wealthy. Then came a series of despairing meditations: *Agonies, The Dance of the Dead, Drunk and Dead* . . . all these works were permeated with the idea that cruelty and injustice dominate the universe and that life is not worth living since death is at the end of it. "Often I asked myself why I was alive, what I had come into the world for, and the only answer I found was an abyss behind me, an abyss ahead; to the right, to the left, above, below, everywhere darkness," he wrote in *Agonies*. Only a woman's love could console Gustave for his persistent melancholy. But no woman was interested in him. Still haunted by the memory of the beautiful and inaccessible Elisa Schlésinger, he finished the *Mémoires d'un fou*, a grief-stricken confession in the Byronic mode. In it he expressed once again his hatred for school, his contempt for humanity, his cynicism in the face of a meaningless life, his longing for death. "Woe to men, who have made me corrupt and evil, I who was good and pure!" he cried. "Woe to the aridity of civilization, which dries up and withers everything that grows in the sunlight of poetry and of the heart!" At the end of his course upon the earth, man could not even hope for rest in the abyss of eternity: "To die so young, without hope in the tomb, without being sure of sleeping there, without knowing if its peace is inviolable! To cast oneself into the arms of nothingness with no certainty that it will receive you! . . . Yes, I die, for is it living to see one's past as water that has flowed into the sea, the present as a cage, the future as a shroud?"[3] These dismal lamentations were followed without transition by the memoirs themselves, steeped in the charm of the first encounter with Elisa Schlésinger: "Here are my tenderest and at the same time my most painful memories, and I approach them with a wholly religious emotion. . . . It is a wide scar on my heart that will last forever, but as I prepare to retrace this page of my life, my heart beats as if I were going to disturb precious ruins."

For summer vacation Gustave returned to Trouville with the hope of finding there the woman who he dared not dream would one day single him out in spite of his youth and awkwardness. But she was not there. Without her, the village was dreary, the sea dull, the sky leaden, the people ugly and ordinary. Besides, it rained without letup. For two weeks Gustave moped in his room. "I heard the rain falling on the slate roof, the distant sound of the sea and, from time to time, the shouts of the sailors on the wharf," he wrote.[4] The constant thinking about Elisa brought on hallucinations. It seemed to him that he would never be able to love another woman. He was not yet eighteen, but his life was already over. And the one who was responsible for this disaster was completely unaware of the torments she was inflicting.

It was a broken, disenchanted adolescent who, in October 1838, entered his next-to-last year at the lycée. By good luck, his parents had agreed to his becoming a day student. That enabled him, he said, to smoke a cigar at the Café National while waiting for the bell to ring. Pleased though he was with this new arrangement, he was nonetheless impatient to leave school forever: "It is true that I am now a free day student," he wrote Ernest Chevalier, "which couldn't be better, until such time as I leave this goddamn blasted shitty nut house of a school entirely."[5] As a crowning sorrow, Ernest and Alfred, his two best friends, were now in Paris studying law. To console him for their absence, Gustave had only reading, writing, and memories. His current enthusiasms were Victor Hugo ("as great a man as Racine, Calderón or Lope de Vega"), Montaigne, and especially Rabelais and Byron. "Really," he confided to Ernest, "I have profound esteem for only two men: Rabelais and Byron, the only two who have written in a spirit of malice toward the human race and with the intention of laughing in its face."[6] He himself wrote in rapid succession *The Arts and Commerce, The Funeral of Dr. Mathurin, Rabelais, Mademoiselle Rachel,* and *Rome and the Caesars,* but above all he was working on a medieval mystery play, *Smarh.*

Inspired by both Byron's *Cain* and Goethe's *Faust,* this strange, prolix, exuberant work, in which dialogue alternates with narrative, presents the struggle of a peaceful hermit, Smarh, who, through his thirst for knowledge, is delivered into the service of the devil. The idea of the dizziness that overcomes a man pure in heart when he gazes into the abyss of supernatural knowledge had haunted Gustave from earliest childhood, ever since he had seen the marionette show of the temptation of Saint Anthony at the Saint-Romain fair. To break down Smarh's resistance, he places at the devil's side a ter-rifying and grotesque character, Yuk, who attacks the noblest as-pirations of the individual with insolent irony. Yuk, the author's spokesman, thinks the only reasonable attitude for a man to take is to denigrate everything, reject all ideals, laugh at the absurdity of those who still believe in something or someone. The morality play closes with a description of the end of the world and the triumph of Yuk. "It's something incredible, gigantic, absurd, unintelligible both to me and to everyone else," Gustave wrote Ernest. "I had to finish this mad enterprise in which my mind was stretched to the limit."[7]

While Gustave was doing battle with the figments of his imagination, his sober, level-headed brother Achille obtained his medical degree in Paris and soon after got married. Now, *there* was a fellow who didn't ask himself any questions, whose road was all laid out for him, whose parents were proud of him. Gustave no longer judged him: the man didn't belong to his universe. In October 1839, still having no clear idea what he would do later, he entered his last year at the Collège Royal. His philosophy professor, M. Mallet, recognized his gifts and gave him the top mark in composition. Gustave was secretly flattered, but as was only correct, with Ernest Chevalier he affected contempt for the honor: "What a farce! Mine the laurels of philosophy, morality, reasoning, good principles! Ah! Ah! clown! you have made yourself a fine paper mantle out of a seamless web of big, banal phrases."[8] But a storm was brewing at the school. M. Mallet was judged insufficiently strict with his pupils and was replaced by a certain M. Bezout. The students, who liked and respected M. Mallet, rebelled. To reestablish order, M. Bezout punished the whole class: he gave them a thousand lines of poetry to copy. Encouraged by Gustave, the students drew up a petition against their new teacher. The assistant headmaster chose three "mutineers" at random and threatened to expel them if they continued to disobey. Among the designated victims was Gustave Flaubert. He at once wrote a second letter of protest, which twelve of his comrades also signed. He felt himself an insurgent to the depths of his soul: he was fighting injustice, striking a blow against the stupid administrative authority, symbol of the whole bourgeois society. But the headmaster, to whom the assistant headmaster transmitted the letter, upheld the sentence. To avoid the disgrace of having his son dismissed for insolence, in December 1839 Dr. Flaubert withdrew him from the school.

Thus it was alone at home that Gustave prepared for his baccalaureate examination. To help him, Ernest, who was a year older, sent him the notes and papers he had written himself during his last year at the lycée. Gustave was exceedingly tired and discouraged. "You can't imagine a life like mine," he wrote to his friend on July 7, 1840. "I get up every day at 3:00 A.M. precisely and go to bed at 8:30; I work all day long. Another month like that to go; it will be lovely, especially as I have to hit the books even harder. . . . I've had to learn to read Greek, to memorize Demosthenes and two cantos of the *Iliad*, philosophy, in which I shall shine, physics, arithmetic, and a relatively harmless amount of geometry. All that is rough for a man like me who is better suited to reading the marquis de Sade than idiotic things like that! I expect to pass and then afterward . . ." Overworked, exhausted, lonely, he found it hard to be cut off from his friends and also to be cut off from women. He was tormented by waves of sensuality. In his private notebook he wrote: "So who will have me? It should have happened already; I have such need of a mistress, of an angel! . . . Oh, a woman, what a wonderful thing! . . . I love to dream of her contours. I love to dream of the charm of her smiles, of the softness of her white arms, the shape of her thighs, her attitude as she bends her head."[9]

The month of August wore on, with its heavy heat, its last cramming, its premonitory anxieties. At last on August 23, 1840, the baccalaureate exam. Passed! A great step forward in life! Gustave was eighteen. To reward him for his successful efforts, his father, who thought he was abnormally depressed and nervous, proposed that he take a trip to the south of France and Corsica. But the young man would be accompanied by a friend of his parents, Dr. Jules Cloquet, by the latter's elderly, unmarried sister, Mlle. Lise, and by an Italian priest, Father Stephani. In this way, the family thought, he would be shielded from temptations. Although he was irritated to have this trio of chaperones at his heels, Gustave looked forward with joy to the proposed change of scene. He bought notebooks in which to record his adventures on the trip. As a true man of letters, he wanted all the events of his life to find expression in writing. He had famous examples to inspire him: Chateaubriand's *Itinéraire de Paris à Jérusalem*, Alexandre Dumas's *Impressions de voyage*. Why not Gustave Flaubert's *Impressions de voyage*? Even before the journey began, he felt that he had changed his skin. He was no longer a studious schoolboy but a free man, perhaps even an adventurer.

Chapter 4

EULALIE FOUCAUD

The travelers first headed for the southwest. They visited Bordeaux, which Gustave described as "a southern Rouen," Bayonne, then Biarritz, where he plunged into the water to save a drowning man. Then on to Pau, where he received a blow to his pride when he read his travel notes to his companions and found them unresponsive. "Little praise and little intelligence forthcoming from them," he wrote. "I am annoyed; that night I write Mama, I feel sad; at table I can hardly restrain my tears."[1] The journey continued through the Pyrenees, to Toulouse, Nîmes, Arles. . . . "You cannot imagine what the Roman monuments are like, my dear Caroline, and the pleasure it gave me to see the arena."[2] On October 2 the little group found itself caught up in the gay crowd along the Canebière, the famous main thoroughfare of Marseilles. Then, Toulon and the embarkation for Corsica. A storm came up during the crossing. Gustave was sick with fear. To steady himself, he imagined he was back in his room in Rouen, or in Déville, the family's summer home. "I entered the grove, opened the gate and heard the sound of the iron latch striking the wood." Thus, although he longed for a life of danger and excitement, he secretly wished also to return to the peaceful, stable, protected home in which he had grown up. Daring and cautious by turns—the duality was to accompany him, he felt, throughout his life.

And now here he was in Corsica. His observant eyes took in both the beauty of the landscape and the peculiarities of the inhabitants. He inquired into the status of women on the island and was surprised at their blind submission to the will of men. "If the husband insists on keeping her pure, it is not out of love or respect for her," he wrote. "It is out of pride in himself, veneration for the name which he has given her. . . . The son, even as a child, enjoys more respect and authority than his mother." Back in Toulon he went into ecstasies over a palm tree, which symbolized for him all the splendors of the Orient. Already he dreamed of one day penetrating deep into those countries of sun, sand, and mystery. Meanwhile, they returned to Marseilles. Gustave now had only Dr. Cloquet for a companion. The priest and the old maid had returned to hearth and home. Alone with the easygoing doctor, Gustave felt more comfortable. They stayed at the Hôtel Richelieu, 13 Rue de la Darse, in the Canebière quarter. This establishment was run by a handsome Creole woman of thirty-five, Eulalie Foucaud, and her mother. Eulalie Foucaud had very dark hair, amber skin, a motherly look in her eyes, and decisive gestures and speech. On first sight of her young guest she was struck by his good looks. At eighteen Gustave was six feet tall, with broad shoulders, clean-cut features, and a curly blond beard. Years later his English friend Gertrude Collier was to recall him as he had been when they first met: "At that time Gustave Flaubert was like a young Greek. He was in midadolescence, tall and slender, lithe and graceful as an athlete, unconscious of the gifts which he possessed physically and morally, caring little for the impression that he produced and entirely indifferent to conventional manners." Another old friend, Maxime Du Camp, would give an equally glowing description in his *Souvenirs littéraires*: "He was as handsome as any hero. With his white skin and faintly rosy cheeks, his long, fine, floating hair, his tall stature, broad shoulders, thick golden beard and enormous sea-green eyes under black brows, his voice that resounded like a trumpet call, his exuberant gestures and ringing laugh, he was like one of those young Gallic chieftains who fought the Roman army."

Captivated by the inexperienced youth, Eulalie Foucaud drew him to her bedroom. "I was still a virgin and had never loved," Flaubert wrote in *Novembre*.

Eulalie Foucaud

I saw a face of ravishing loveliness. A single straight line, beginning at the crown of her head, passed along the parting of her hair, down between her great arching eyebrows, along her aquiline nose with its dilated, lifted nostrils like those in an antique cameo, divided her warm upper lip shadowed with blue down, and continued on down to her neck—her neck that was full, white and round. Through her thin dress I saw the shape of her breasts come and go in the motion of her breathing. . . . Without a word, she put her arm around me and drew me down to her in a mute embrace. I held her in my arms, I pressed my mouth to her shoulder, and blissfully drank in the first kiss of love. . . . With a movement of her shoulder, she slipped her arm from her sleeve; her dress fell away. . . . Suddenly she released herself, freed her feet from the dress, and leapt into the bed with the agility of a cat. . . . She stretched out her arms to me, she held me to her. . . . Her moist soft hand moved over my body, she kissed my face, my mouth, my eyes, and each of her urgent caresses made me swoon. She stretched herself on her back, and she sighed. . . . At length, abandoning herself to me completely, she lifted her eyes to heaven and gave a great sigh that shook her whole body.

Gustave was stunned by this embrace, overwhelmed with pride, happiness, and tenderness. When he confessed to Eulalie that she was the first, she murmured languorously, "So you are a virgin and I have deflowered you, poor angel!"[3] To take a souvenir of these miraculous moments, she fetched a pair of scissors and, leaning over Gustave, cut a lock of hair from the back of his head. Dumbfounded at his good fortune, he reflected with despair that he had a mistress and that soon he would have to leave her to go back to his parents. For four days the impetuous woman showered him with caresses. She found him a passionate and sensitive lover. When it came time for them to part, it was an unbearable wrench for both of them. They wrote to each other for eight months. To conceal this brief affair from his parents, Gustave recommended that Eulalie send her letters to his schoolmate Emile Hamard, in Paris, who would forward them to him in other envelopes. "To have possessed you and be deprived of you is fearful torture, a torture out of hell," she wrote. And announcing that she was soon to leave for America, she promised to resume their affair on her return: "I shall be able to press you in my arms with the same ardor and the same happiness, to cover you with delirious, voluptuous kisses, and to offer you again a gaze full of fire and desire." He, for his part, retained a burning memory of the adventure in Marseilles. But at the same time he was afraid that this beautiful, demanding creature would encroach on his private life. He was grateful to her for having initiated him into physical delight but also worried that too strong an attachment might threaten his tranquillity. He already felt the need to keep within himself a garden of meditation and dreams protected from the indiscreet assaults of a mistress. Unhappy to be parted from Eulalie, he nevertheless wondered whether he would have been happy if he could have kept her near him. In any case, to him she represented carnal love, while Elisa Schlésinger remained, in his memory, the symbol of ideal love. Even as he complained of loneliness, he had the presentiment that his life and work would be divided between these two types of women, one ethereal and inaccessible, the other tangible and usable.

From the time he returned to Rouen in November 1840, he felt that having lain in Eulalie's arms he had blossomed, gained assurance; that now at last he looked at the world with the eyes of a practical, blasé man of experience. While continuing to reply— with increasingly conventional politeness—to the letters from his Creole mistress, he wrote to Ernest Chevalier: "You say you don't have a woman. Upon my word, I think that's very sensible, seeing that I regard the species as rather stupid. Woman is a commonplace animal that man has over-idealized. The liking for statuary inclines us to masturbation; the reality we find disgusting."[4] Fed up with France, with Europe, with the whole civilized world, he dreamed of escaping forever to the Orient: "I'm disgusted to be back in this damned country where you see the sun in the sky about as often as a diamond in a pig's asshole," he confided to Ernest. "Someday I

Eulalie Foucaud

must buy myself a slave in Constantinople, a Georgian girl—a man who doesn't own a slave is a blockhead; is there anything more stupid than equality? . . . I hate Europe, France—my own country, my succulent motherland that I'd gladly send to hell now that I've had a glimpse of what lies beyond. I think I must have been transplanted by the winds to this land of mud; surely I was born elsewhere—I've always had what seem like memories or intuitions of perfumed shores and blue seas. . . . I have nothing but immense, insatiable desires, frightful boredom and incessant yawns."[5]

In spite of all his prejudices against the rules of Western society, he gave in to his father's wishes and agreed to study law. He would become a jurist, since the family wanted him to. Still, he didn't think much of the law: "It has always seemed to me that men's justice is more ludicrous than their evil deeds are hideous," he declared.[6] But Rouen had no law school. Only one solution: Paris. He would rejoin his friends there, and in particular Ernest Chevalier, who was finishing his studies to become a lawyer or magistrate: "So I tell you, my dear friend, that next year I shall be studying the noble profession that you are soon going to exercise. I shall go to law school, adding a fourth year so I can shine with the title of doctor. . . . After which, I may well go off to become a Turk in Turkey, or a mule driver in Spain or a camel driver in Egypt."[7]

On November 10, 1841, he enrolled in the Law School of the University of Paris. But he stayed on in Rouen. On New Year's Eve he sadly recalled the happy times when he and Ernest had waited together for the clock to strike midnight:

How we smoked, how we shouted, how we talked about school, about the assistant masters, about our future in Paris and what we would do when we were twenty! . . . But tomorrow I shall be alone, all alone, and as I don't want to start the year by looking at toys, offering best wishes and making visits, I shall get up as usual at four o'clock, do some Homer, smoke at my window and look at the moon shining on the roofs of the houses opposite. I won't go out all day and I won't pay a single call! I don't care if people take offense!

. . . As the ancient sage said, "Hide thy life and abstain." So people think that I'm wrong, that I should go out into society, that I'm a queer sort, a bear, a young man not like the others. No doubt I lead a sordid life, spending all my time in cafés, public houses, etc.—that's what the bourgeois think of me.[8]

Greatly troubled in mind, Gustave, the dyed-in-the-wool materialist, suddenly discovered that he was tempted by mysticism. He was ready to believe that "Jesus Christ had existed" and that it was sweet to "humble oneself at the foot of the cross," to "take refuge on the wings of the dove." It didn't last long. He was soon his old self again, with the cold despair of the atheist in his heart. The prospect of becoming a lawyer was even less attractive to him since he had matriculated. He felt as if he had fallen into a trap. He confided his thoughts to his former literature professor, Gourgaud-Dugazon: "I will pass my bar examination, but I scarcely think I shall ever plead in court about a party-wall or on behalf of some poor paterfamilias cheated by a rich upstart. When people speak to me about the bar, saying 'This young fellow will make a fine trial lawyer,' because I'm broad in the shoulders and have a booming voice, I confess it turns my stomach. I don't feel myself made for such a completely materialistic, commonplace life. On the contrary, every day I admire the poets more and more. . . . This, then, is what I have resolved: I have in mind three novels, three tales, each of them different, each requiring a particular way of writing. That will suffice to prove to myself whether I have talent or not."[9]

It was in this frame of mind that he prepared to leave for Paris. He was not a student who was thinking vaguely about a career as a writer, but a writer who was distressed at the idea of still being only a student. His head was buzzing with ambitious projects. Yet he was afraid that his hand would betray him. He wrote quickly, too quickly, with a kind of impetuous abandon. Was that really the way you constructed a masterpiece? Didn't you have to keep a closer watch on yourself? What he wanted was perfection. As long as he hadn't attained it, his literary efforts would remain in a drawer. As for the law, it was at most a subterfuge designed to pacify the family.

Eulalie Foucaud

Flaubert arrived in Paris at the beginning of January 1842. He was twenty years old and wanted to prove to the world that he was no longer a child but a man. He brought with him a secret vocation, a bitter philosophy, a taste for independence, and the religion of friendship. As soon as he was settled in the Hôtel de l'Europe on the Rue Lepelletier, he wrote his mother to allay her anxiety: " 'Everything is fine, everything is going well, everything is for the best possible,' as Candide says. I am now sitting in front of a good fire roasting my legs, I have just downed two cups of tea with brandy to neutralize the taste, and in a little while I am going to M. Cloquet's where we shall abandon ourselves to mad embraces. . . . I have slept well and am not at all tired. Farewell, I kiss you all. *Nota:* I have not been run over by an omnibus, my face has not grown thin and I have not lost an eye."[10]

Chapter 5

ELISA

After finding out about the curriculum, the class schedule, and the program of examinations for the first year, Flaubert went back to Rouen. He planned to work at home. But the law books repelled him from the start. "I don't do anything, not a damn thing, I don't read or write anything, I'm no good for anything," he announced to Ernest Chevalier. "And yet I have begun the Civil Code, of which I have read the first section (which I didn't understand), and the *Institutes* [of Justinian], of which I have read the first three articles (which I no longer remember). What a farce!"[1] One consolation: on March 2, drawing lots at the town hall, he came up with a good number, 548, which exempted him from military service. The army seemed to him as ridiculous an institution as the law. However, as summer approached, and hence the examination, he became more and more afraid of failing. In spite of intense application, he couldn't absorb the stern prose of the jurists. He gave vent to his bitterness in his letters to Ernest Chevalier:

To me, human justice is . . . the most ludicrous thing in the world. The spectacle of one man judging another would make me die laughing, if it didn't move me to pity and if I weren't at the moment forced to study the series of absurdities according to which he judges him. I can see nothing stupider than the law, unless it's the study of the law. I work at it with extreme repugnance, and it leaves me with no heart or mind for anything else.[2]

In April he made a short trip to Paris to register, as had to be done every term, visited Ernest, cast sidelong glances at the prostitutes between the Rue de Grammont and the Rue de Richelieu, then came back to Rouen and immersed himself in his studies again with loathing: "You ask me to write long letters; I am incapable of it," he wrote Ernest. "Law is killing me, numbing me, tearing me apart, it's impossible for me to work at it. When I have spent three hours with my nose in the Code, during which time I haven't understood a thing, I can't go on, I'd commit suicide (which would be most unfortunate, for I show great promise)."[3] On his father's advice, to get some relaxation, he took a swim in the Seine every day. At the end of June he went to Paris to regularize his position at the Law School, because while the students were not required to attend classes, they could not sit for an examination unless they had received a certificate from the professor whose course they were supposed to be taking. Flaubert had no doubt that he would obtain this document as a courtesy and meantime worked hard to prepare for his exam, which was set for August 20. Between cramming sessions he strolled around Paris and was bored. "If you knew how boring it is in Paris in summer and how one's thoughts turn to trees and waves, you'd be even happier than you are," he wrote his sister Caroline, who was staying with her parents in Trouville. "I've already been twice to the swimming schools. I shrugged my shoulders with pity. All idiots! Dirty water, with ridiculous brats or stupid old men splashing in it. There wasn't one who was fit just to watch me swim."[4] And a little later, also to Caroline: "I think I shall now be able to present myself [for the examination] at the end of August with some chance of passing; things are beginning to go a little better for me. . . . I am working like a real ditchdigger, and I go to bed at night with the brute satisfaction of the ox that has plowed well, of the imbecile whose fingers have writer's cramp and whose head is heavy with everything he has tried to cram into it."[5]

While he was driving himself like this, his chances of taking the examination in August were suddenly compromised. His professor of civil law, M. Oudot, "an idiot," had taken it into his head not to issue the necessary certificates unless the candidates showed him the notes they had taken in class. Flaubert, having no notebooks to submit, tried to procure some from his comrades: "But," he told his sister, "it's pretty hard. . . . So if he [M. Oudot] notices that they aren't mine, or if I can't get any that are good enough, my exam is going to be postponed to November or December, which would be a real nuisance, because I'd rather get it over with right away." That was exactly what happened. In spite of everything he tried, Flaubert failed to obtain his certificate and had to resign himself to not taking the exam until December. Disappointed, he packed his bags at once and took the coach to join the family in Trouville. There he abandoned himself to the pleasure of endlessly rehearsing memories of Élisa, breathing salt air, and lazing about all day. "I get up at eight, have breakfast, smoke, go for a swim, have lunch, smoke, stretch out in the sun, have dinner, smoke and go to bed again to redine, resmoke and rebreakfast," he wrote Ernest Chevalier.[6]

Back in Paris in November, after a short stay in Rouen, he found a little flat to rent at 19 Rue de l'Est. The rent was three hundred francs a year; he bought two hundred francs' worth of furniture. His classmate Hamard helped him get settled. Soon he renewed his friendly relations with Gertrude and Harriet Collier, the two young English girls he had known in Trouville, and with their little brother Herbert. Once in a while he would go to dinner at their house and linger at the bedside of Harriet, who was an invalid and always stretched out in her bed or on a sofa. He had little leisure time. "This is what my life is like," he wrote his sister. "I get up at eight, go to class, come home and have a very frugal lunch; I work until five in the afternoon, at which time I go to dinner; by six o'clock I am back in my room, and there I amuse myself until midnight or one in the morning. I hardly cross the water once a week to see our friends [the Collier family, on the right bank of the Seine]. . . . I have made a deal with the proprietor of a greasy spoon in the neighborhood to feed me. I have ahead of me thirty dinners all paid up—if you can call them dinners. . . . I surpass all the other regular customers in speed of eating. I affect a manner that is preoccupied, gloomy and casual all at once, which gives me a good laugh when I am alone again in the street."[7] Naturally, he railed against the style of the Civil Code, which he had to swallow in large doses: "The gentlemen who compiled it didn't offer much of a sacrifice to the Graces. They made it as dry, as hard, as stinking, as flatly bourgeois as the wooden benches of the Law School where we go to harden our buttocks while hearing it explained."[8]

In December Flaubert was so depressed that he made a quick visit to Rouen over Christmas to cheer himself up, not without having first recommended to Caroline and his mother that they be amiable and cheerful during his stay: "Suffer as much as you like from backaches, headaches, chilblains or bites, I don't care (I am even pleased, at heart), but manage it so that home is a pleasant place for me. . . . A little vacation with you will do me much good from every point of view."[9] His heart was bursting with affection when he was reunited with his beloved confidante Caroline, always in delicate health, with his melancholy, reserved mother dressed in black, and with his father, who didn't understand him, he felt, but whom he admired so much.

Somewhat refreshed by this period of immersion in family life, he returned to Paris just in time to present himself for the final examination for the first year of law school. It took place on December 28, 1842. He passed. In spite of his disdain for official approval, he was proud of his victory—especially because of his parents, who didn't have much confidence in his literary vocation and placed all their hopes on his achieving an honorable, lucrative position in society. Now he had to screw up his courage to continue his studies. But a more exciting project distracted him from the law books. He had undertaken to write a kind of personal novel, *Novembre*, inspired by Goethe's *Werther*, Chateaubriand's *René*, and Musset's *Confession d'un enfant du siècle*. Mixing autobiography with fiction, he portrayed the chronic despair, vague desires, contempt for the world, longing for the infinite, and obsession with suicide of an adolescent of eighteen who resembled him like a brother. Bursting with sap, this young man needs to lose himself in the flesh of a woman. He finds one: Marie, who is none other than Eulalie Foucaud. And he experiences the intoxication of possessing a woman for the first time. The Marseilles episode is related here in detail, in a tone of wonder and gratitude. Yet after a brief affair, the hero of *Novembre* flees from his beloved, with curious thoughts: "So Love was no more than that! So Woman was no more than that! Why, in God's name, are we still hungry after we have had our fill? Why have we such aspirations and such disappointments? Why is the heart of man so large and life so small? There are days when the love of the very angels could not satisfy him, and he wearies in an hour of all the caresses on earth." And a little further on: "Why was I so eager to flee? Did I already love her?" This fear of physical attachment to another being was very characteristic of Flaubert. He could not endure ties that would be a constraint to him in daily life. He did not want to be possessed by any passion. And then, there was his pure love for Elisa Schlésinger. If that feeling was to retain its quasi-mystical value, it must never come to fruition. And no sexual adventure would be allowed to disturb its reign for long.

With this new and intimate outpouring, Flaubert had the impression that he had done the best thing he was capable of. He was aware that *Novembre* represented definite progress over his earlier narratives. To be sure, in accordance with the fashion of the time, it still contained many long-drawn sighs, resounding denials, and bitter professions of faith. But the style was more sure, the canvas more solid. The truth was that while Flaubert had begun to write just to amuse himself and to imitate others, the game had become a vital necessity for him, and already he conceived of life only as a pretext for literature. Four years later, speaking of *Novembre,* he was to say, "That work was the end of my youth."[10] And indeed, he felt that he should no longer indulge in romantic descriptions of his moods. But what did one say to other people if one didn't talk about oneself? He wondered about it anxiously, even as he sat glumly over his law books. Holed up in his room, which was cold in winter and suffocating in summer, he envied "the young crowd with thirty thousand francs a year" who went to the Opéra or the Théâtre des Italiens every evening and smiled at "pretty women who would have us turned out of doors by their porters if we presumed to show up at their houses in our greasy overcoats, our three-year-old black suits, and our elegant spats."[11] For diversion he would see a few of his fellow law students and on rare occasions go to a brothel. "How can one complain of life when there is still a brothel where one can console oneself for love, and a bottle of wine with which to lose one's senses," he wrote Ernest Chevalier.[12] His friend Alfred Le Poittevin, informed of these escapades, congratulated him in the crudest terms: "What a picture, Léonie on her knees between your legs, intoxicating herself, no doubt, with the perfume of your cheesiferous cock. . . ." "I admired your coldness toward the woman you go bathing with [in the sea at Trouville]. Could it be that your male organ is quiet because the water is so cold? . . . Or are you exhausted by the ultra-frequent habit of masturbation?" "What do you do with yourself down there? . . . What a happy man you must be. . . . You trot your happy phallus around to visit the cunts of the Parisian whores as if you wanted to catch the pox; but it's in vain, the most maculate cunts give it back to you intact."[13]

But contrary to what Le Poittevin blithely supposed, it was not long before Flaubert contracted a venereal disease. He treated it as best he could. Sometimes he would seek refuge at the home of the Colliers, who welcomed him like their son. He was fond of Harriet, and he would often read aloud to her. But the Colliers, whose apartment was located near the Champs-Elysées, moved to the suburb of Chaillot, and Flaubert, discouraged by the length of the journey, came less frequently. "It takes me a full hour to get there and as much again to come back, which makes a good two and a half leagues on the pavement," he wrote Caroline. "When it's raining and muddy the trip is intolerable. My means don't permit me to take a cab, and my tastes don't permit me to take an omnibus. I only go there on foot and in dry weather."

Another house where he found a welcome was that of the sculptor James Pradier, nicknamed Phidias by his admirers. Flaubert was fascinated by Pradier's wife, the smiling, flirtatious, and notoriously unfaithful Louise. He saw her as a wonderful character for a novel. During a party at the sculptor's studio one evening he met his idol, Victor Hugo. He wrote at once to his "old rat," Caroline: "What can I tell you about him? He is a man like any other, with a rather ugly face and quite a common appearance. He has magnificent teeth, a superb forehead, no eyelashes or eyebrows. He talks little, seems to be on his guard, not wanting to let anything slip. He is very polite and a little stiff. I love the sound of his voice. It was a pleasure to observe him close up. I looked at him with astonishment, as if he had been a casket full of gold and royal diamonds, thinking of everything that had come out of this man who was now sitting next to me on a little chair and staring at his own right hand that had written so many wonderful things. . . . The great man and I did most of the talking. . . ." Clearly, for Victor Hugo this Gustave Flaubert with the tall stature and loud voice was a totally unknown young man who had a few notions about literature, nothing more. One admirer out of a thousand. "As you see," Flaubert concluded, "I go to the Pradiers' quite often. It's a house I like very much; one feels at ease there and it's just my kind of place. . . ."[14]

Still, it was at the Schlésingers' that he felt most at home. He had met them again in Paris and had become a regular guest, dining at their table every Wednesday. Thus he could spend hours gazing upon the face of the woman who a few years before, in Trouville, had revealed to him the torments and delights of an impossible love. At this time Maurice Schlésinger was a prominent figure in the world of the arts: as the editor of *La Gazette musicale,* he was much sought after by famous musicians. But while Flaubert accepted Schlésinger's invitations, he had no great liking for the man, whom he judged to be a scheming bourgeois climber. On the other hand, he was profoundly moved by the charm of Elisa, who had never seemed to him more beautiful or more desirable. She, for her part, showed an affection for him that was at once maternal and flirtatious. This equivocal attitude was exactly what he wanted from a woman. Doubtless he didn't even wish to make her his mistress. He placed her too high not to fear the disillusion he always felt after carnal possession. Distance between bodies guaranteed perfection of sentiments. The better to worship Elisa, he preferred to leave his desire unsatisfied. And she was grateful to him. Between these two beings who were irresistibly attracted to each other there developed an uneasy atmosphere of restrained impulses, forbidden dreams, burning chastity. He was baffled by her fidelity to a husband who was a mediocrity and who constantly deceived her. But at the same time, he admired her noble conduct. While now and again, at long intervals, he liked to climb into bed with a strumpet, he felt a rare pleasure in kneeling before an immaculate creature who made him suffer by refusing him. "In my youth I loved inordinately—loved without any return, deeply, silently," he was to write years later. "Nights spent gazing at the moon, plans for elopement and travels in Italy, dreams of winning fame for *her* sake, torture of body and soul, spasms at the scent of a perfumed shoulder, and sudden pallors when two glances met—I have known all that and known it well. Each of us has in his heart a royal chamber; I have walled mine up, but it has not been destroyed."[15] Flaubert was already thinking about celebrating this spiritual affair in a novel to be titled *L'Education sentimentale*. But while he was writing it, he also had to continue studying for his law exam. He was fed up with his life as an indigent student and, as usual, his thoughts turned toward home. After having spent Easter vacation in Rouen, he confided to Caroline:

> It feels like a fortnight since I left you all. . . . Now I am completely alone, thinking about you, imagining what you're doing. You are all there around the fire and I'm the only one missing. You are playing dominoes, shouting, laughing, you are all together, while I sit here like an imbecile with my elbows on the table, not knowing what to do. . . . I found on my table the blessed law books I had left there. I much prefer my old room in Rouen, where I have spent such pleasant, quiet hours, when I could hear the whole house stirring around me, when you would come at four o'clock to do history or English and instead of history or English you would chat with me until dinner time. To be happy in a place, you have

to have lived there a long time. It takes more than one day to warm one's nest and make oneself comfortable there.[16]

Not long after, he wrote Caroline again:

> I buck up my spirits, as the saying goes, and I need to buck them up every minute. . . . Sometimes I feel like pounding the table with my fists and making everything fly in all directions. . . . Evening comes, and I go off to sit down at the back of a restaurant, all alone and looking glum, thinking of the good family table surrounded by friendly faces, where one is in one's own home, in one's own self, where one eats heartily and laughs out loud. After which I come back, close the shutters so the light won't hurt my eyes, and lie down.[17]

The examination was scheduled for August. Flaubert had studied for it so intensively that he thought he had a good chance of passing. In the meantime he had met a young man of his own age who dazzled him with his refinement and his free and easy manners: Maxime Du Camp. The meeting had taken place in the lodgings of Ernest Le Marié, a former classmate of Flaubert's. Maxime Du Camp was to recount the circumstances in his *Souvenirs littéraires*. Le Marié was playing Beethoven's *Marche funèbre* on the piano when the doorbell rang. The next instant there appeared before them a young man with a blond beard and a hat cocked jauntily over one ear. Le Marié introduced them to each other: Gustave Flaubert, Maxime Du Camp. Gustave Flaubert looked at Maxime Du Camp with immediate admiration. In the presence of this elegant, fluent, rather vain personage he had a sense of inferiority. Maxime Du Camp had the style and wit of the authentic Parisian, while he himself was only a provincial lost in the big city. In any case, they had the same tastes and the same literary ambitions. They had exchanged only a few words before they realized they were going to get on famously. But Flaubert soon came to understand also that Du Camp would do anything to win renown, while he himself, by philosophical conviction and by temperament, scorned the bubble reputation. Flaubert was nevertheless impressed by the newcomer's youthful authority. They promised to see each other again and, indeed, a strong friendship was born that day between them.

The son of an eminent surgeon (a member of the Académie de Médecine), Maxime Du Camp was a lighthearted young man who had ample means and a wide range of interests, while Flaubert was an unfortunate student possessed by a single idea: to remain in the shadows and write. Relations between them were affectionate, even passionate. Which did not prevent them from being strongly attracted to women and comparing notes on their romantic adventures. While Du Camp had plenty of money, Flaubert, notwithstanding the assistance of his parents, had to scrimp on everything and couldn't help running into debt. In July 1843, a month before his examination, he asked his father for an extra five hundred francs and was roundly berated for it:

> You are a fool twice over, first for letting yourself be swindled like a real provincial, a ninny who lets himself be taken in by crooks or loose women whose usual prey must be morons or doddering old imbeciles, and thank God you are neither stupid nor old; your second mistake was not trusting me, not to have told me at once how and where the shoe pinched. I hope you will be franker in future, I thought I was sufficiently your friend to deserve to know everything that happened to you, good or bad. I am today remitting five hundred francs to the Railway Administration, you will go to collect them. . . . So pay your tailor, whom you are always talking to me about and for whom I so often give you money. . . . Goodbye, dear Gustave. Spare my purse a little, and above all be well and keep working.[18]

That same year, Dr. Flaubert dismissed from the hospital a medical student who had enrolled the year before: one of his son's former classmates at the Collège Royal de Rouen, Louis Bouilhet. Reason: the culprit had asked for wine at meals instead of cider and demanded permission to stay away from the hospital overnight.

Elisa

Thus, in his professional life as in his family life, Dr. Flaubert was the stern father. He hoped that Gustave, who was so scattered, so vulnerable, would pass his examinations. If not, what was to be done with him? But on August 24, 1843, Gustave failed. The examiners had given him two black balls and two red. Flaubert was devastated at the idea of having done all that work for nothing. His father tried to make the best of it and advised him to persevere in his study of the law. Flaubert, an obedient son, remained noncommittal, left for Rouen, and went from there to Nogent-sur-Seine, where he loafed about, daydreamed, swam in the river, and reacquainted himself with the pleasures of family life. Then back to Rouen again, a city which, he told Ernest Chevalier, he detested: "It has beautiful churches and stupid inhabitants. I loathe it, I hate it, I call down upon it all the imprecations of heaven because it witnessed my birth. Woe to the walls that sheltered me! Woe to the bourgeois who knew me as a child and to the paving stones where I began to harden my heels! Oh Attila, when wilt thou return, kind humanitarian, with four hundred thousand horsemen, to set fire to this beautiful France, land of trouser straps and suspenders?* And begin, I pray thee, with Paris first and Rouen at the same time."[19]

In December he was back in Paris. His brother Achille, who was now deputy chief surgeon at the Hôtel-Dieu in Rouen, came to see him and brought him, on request, "a white vest with lapels" and "two pillowcases." After Achille left, Flaubert found himself alone again and adrift as before. He spent Christmas Eve at the Colliers' and New Year's Eve at the Schlésingers' in Vernon. Everywhere he went he displayed an arrogant disgust for society. He even criticized openly the politics of "that infamous Louis-Philippe," which shocked certain influential personages among the guests. He told Caroline: "I am a bear and I want to stay a bear in my den, in my cave, in my skin, in my old bearskin, nice and quiet and far from the bourgeois of both sexes."[20]

---

* Trouser straps were passed under the soles of the feet to keep the trouser legs taut, as in women's "stirrup pants" that have been periodically fashionable in modern times.—Trans.

43

Flaubert

At last, on January 1, 1844, he returned to Rouen to spend a few days. But he promised he would go back to Paris on the fifteenth to register at the Law School again. An academic setback was never insurmountable. With a little luck maybe he would finally manage to get his degree and become a lawyer: it was his parents' dream and his own nightmare.

Chapter 6

THE BREAK

In the month of January 1844, the whole family was preoccupied with a serious matter: Dr. Flaubert had decided to build a summer cottage on a piece of land he owned in Deauville. His son Achille was to visit the property to inspect potential sites for the structure. For the journey he would use a rather uncomfortable cabriolet which his father had purchased the year before. Gustave, who was back from Paris, would accompany him and give his opinion. The two brothers left Pont-l'Evêque on a pitch-black night. It was Gustave who held the reins. Suddenly he felt a horrible dizziness and collapsed unconscious on his seat. In a panic, his brother drove him to the nearest house and bled him. After several veins had been opened, Flaubert came to. He was transported to Rouen. His father was perplexed: was it an epileptic seizure or a nervous malady?* He leaned toward the epileptic seizure and dealt with the illness accordingly. The treatment he prescribed was so severe that Flaubert came near dying of it. A seton was placed on the back of the patient's neck so as to drain as much blood as possible; he was forbidden meat, wine, and tobacco; he was purged unmercifully. Utterly exhausted, he wrote to Ernest Chevalier:

* The experts are still not agreed as to the nature of this illness. The most commonly held opinion is that it was epilepsy involving the left temporal-occipital lobe.

45

Dear Ernest, without suspecting it, you came close to going into mourning for the worthy who is writing you these lines. . . . I am still in bed, with a seton in my neck—a gorget even stiffer than the kind worn by an officer of the National Guard—taking countless pills and infusions, and above all plagued by that specter, a thousand times worse than all the illnesses in the world, called a *diet*. Know then, dear friend, that I had a cerebral congestion, a kind of miniature attack of apoplexy, accompanied by nervous symptoms which I continue to display because they're genteel. I very nearly croaked in the midst of my family. . . . They bled me in three places at once and I finally opened my eyes. My father wants to keep me here a long time and take good care of me; my morale is good, however, because I don't know what worry is. I'm in a rotten state; at the slightest excitement, all my nerves quiver like violin strings, my knees, my shoulders, and my belly tremble like leaves. Well, such is life, *sic est vita, c'est la vie*. I shall probably not be returning to Paris, except for two or three days around April, to give up my flat and settle a few odds and ends.[1]

And a week later:

Yes, old chap, I have a seton that keeps flowing and itching, holds my neck rigid, and is so irritating that it makes me sweat. They purge me, bleed me, put leeches on me; I'm not allowed to have anything good to eat, I'm forbidden to drink wine—I'm a dead man. . . . Ah, what a bloody bore! . . . My pipe! yes, my pipe, yes, you read correctly, my old pipe—*I'm not allowed to have my pipe!!!* I who loved it so, who loved nothing else! With cold grog in summer and coffee in winter.[2]

When his condition seemed to have taken a turn for the better, he went to Paris to register for Law School again. But immediately afterward the attacks resumed. They came almost every day. During one of these attacks Dr. Flaubert, who had just bled his son, was so worried at not seeing the blood flow from the vein that he had hot water poured on the patient's right hand. In the general panic, no one noticed that the water was boiling. Flaubert suffered a second-degree burn and almost fainted. All his life he was to carry the scar. The seton planted in his neck was another painful nuisance. He tried to accommodate himself to it. "This morning I shaved with my right hand," he wrote his brother. "Although with the seton pulling at me and my hand unable to bend, I had some difficulty. However, I still wipe my ass with my left hand. I've gotten used to it."[3] And to Ernest Chevalier he wrote: "Not a day goes by but from time to time there passes before my eyes something that looks like bunches of hair or Bengal lights." [4] When asked what he felt during these attacks, he said, "I have a flame in the right eye, I have a flame in the left eye, everything looks the color of gold."

The attacks were becoming more frequent, and Dr. Flaubert determined that his son should abandon his law studies and live a calm family life under constant surveillance. This decision corresponded to Flaubert's most secret desire. He had conceived such a horror of the law, of the legal profession, and of life in Paris that he almost welcomed his illness. Thanks to this infirmity, he thought, he was going to escape from all professional and social obligations and be able to devote himself to his work; he was going to detach himself from the life of his contemporaries to deepen his own life; he was going to become himself. And his parents wouldn't have a thing to reproach him for. A year later, aware that he had passed from one destiny to another, from one Flaubert to another, he wrote: "I have bidden an irrevocable farewell to the practical life. My nervous illness was the transition between these two states."[5] And a year after that: "I have had two very distinct existences. External events marked the end of the first and the birth of the second. It's all mathematical. My active life—passionate, full of feeling, of sudden conflicting emotions and different sensations—came to an end at twenty-two. At that time I suddenly made great strides, and my life became something else."[6]

Meanwhile Dr. Flaubert, as a wise paterfamilias, was planning to provide a retreat for his son, who was ill and could no longer be expected to succeed in any field whatever. He sold his land in Déville-lès-Rouen, which the new railway under construction was going to pass through, and for Fr 90,500 bought a country house in Croisset, a few kilometers downstream from Rouen. The family moved in gaily, even before the workmen had finished the remodeling. It was a charming eighteenth-century manor with a garden at the river's edge traversed by an avenue of linden trees.* The rooms were large and light, with views of the shimmering Seine through the leaves. Dr. Flaubert, who liked his comfort, furnished the house opulently. There were scrolled mahogany beds, walnut card tables, large upholstered armchairs, an elaborately inlaid clock, quantities of bibelots, a cellar furnished with fine wines, and, in a nearby shed, a carriage for the doctor and a boat for Gustave.

Deep in the silence of the countryside, Flaubert led a peaceful existence. He read, swam, and went rowing, but his mother was always afraid he might have a sudden seizure when he was away from home. She kept an eye on his comings and goings and was only at peace when he was shut up in his study. Liberated from his law courses, he had gone back to work on *L'Education sentimentale*. When he sat with pen in hand, he felt that at last he had discovered his path in life. Far from the backbiting of salons and the tinsel of honors, he had no wish to publish the numerous manuscripts that slept in his drawers. He, who in his earliest youth had dreamed of pushing himself into the first rank of writers so as to win recognition and applause, no longer wanted anything but the happiness of constructing a great work in seclusion and solitude. "I often doubt if I shall ever publish a line," he wrote later to Maxime Du Camp. "Do you know, it would be a fine idea for a fellow to publish nothing until he was fifty and then all at once, one fine day, to bring out his complete works and stop there. . . . An artist who was truly an artist, working for himself alone, without worrying about anything else—that would be beautiful; he might know immense joy."[7]

---

* After Flaubert's death, his niece sold this residence, which was demolished and replaced by a factory. There remains only a small pavilion that now houses a modest "Flaubert Museum."

The Break

He was encouraged in this idea by the fortunate circumstance that he was relieved of all material concerns. He didn't have to earn a living. Thanks to his father's prudent management, the family income would be sufficient to support him without his having to sell the products of his pen. He felt sorry for men of letters who were paid by the line, padded their articles, and courted the critics. When Ernest Chevalier successfully defended his doctoral thesis, Gustave congratulated him in mocking terms: "Bravo, young man, bravo, very good, very good, highly gratified, extremely happy, delighted, receive my congratulations, accept my compliments, be so kind as to receive my respects. . . . So much for the Law School. . . . Have you at least shit against the cornerstone of that establishment to mark your respect for it? . . . This calls for dancing unbridled cancans, wild polkas, titanic cachuchas. One must crown oneself with flowers and sausages, grab one's pipe and have 200,000,987,105,310,000 little drinks."[8] Similarly, he deplored the fact that his other friend, Maxime Du Camp, was interested in a cheap, worldly sort of literary success. The more Du Camp advised him to come out of his hole and make himself known, the more stubbornly he insisted on remaining in total obscurity. The one wanted to enjoy all the pleasures of life, the other refused to disperse his energies and fiercely defended his independence, isolation, and secret labor. His unsociable disposition was aggravated by his illness. Yet the attacks were becoming less frequent; his nerves were growing calm; at times he even thought he was cured. Disappointed in Maxime Du Camp, whom he judged far too superficial, he drew closer to Alfred Le Poittevin, whose character, he felt, was more in harmony with his own conceptions of art and life. "It is truly wrong for you and me to part, to disrupt our work and our intimacy," Gustave wrote him. "Each time we have done so we have found ourselves the worse for it. Once again, at this last separation, I felt a pang. . . ."[9] And a few months later, this passionate declaration: "No, I don't think of myself as one to be pitied when I remember that I have you. . . . If I were to lose you, what would I have left? What would I have in my inner life—that is, the real one?"[10]

This sudden affection of Flaubert's for Le Poittevin irritated

Maxime Du Camp. He was jealous because he was no longer Gustave's closest confidant and afraid that Le Poittevin's falseness and vulgarity would have a bad influence on his friend. There was no question that Le Poittevin's obscene letters stimulated Flaubert to write in the same vein, but in doing so, he was only indulging a masculine taste for crude jokes that had nothing to do with his deep feelings. Nevertheless, Du Camp insisted: "You, who have a rare intelligence, are aping a corrupt creature, a 'Greek of the Byzantine Empire' as he calls himself; and now—I give you my sacred word, Gustave—he is making fun of you and doesn't believe a word of what he has told you. . . . Don't be cross with me and write me that you love me a little."[11] And in the same letter, this cry from the heart: "If you knew how much I love you and how much it pains me to see you finding happiness where it does not exist!"

Pulled this way and that between two men who were contending for his trust, Flaubert felt that it was not necessary to see his friends in the flesh to enjoy the warmth of their attachment. Now the family lived sometimes in Rouen, sometimes in Croisset. Du Camp, having left France in May 1844 to travel in the Orient, returned in March 1845. At that time, Flaubert had already finished his first *L'Education sentimentale.** Unlike *Mémoires d'un fou* or *Novembre*, this work was not a violent outpouring of personal feelings. This time the author took the precaution of embodying his ideas and memories in fictional characters. Renouncing lyricism, he tried to show them in an everyday light, acting in a believable way, in a setting accessible to all. The heroes of *L'Education sentimentale* are two young men, two friends who are different in every respect. One, Henry, goes to study law in Paris; the other, Jules, stays in the provinces. Like

---

* Flaubert used the title *L'Education sentimentale* both for this obscure juvenile work and for the mature and justly famous novel he was to publish twenty-five years later. It is usually rendered in English simply as "A Sentimental Education." However, this translation—if it means anything—fails to convey the theme of both works: they deal with the "education" of the heart, which learns that romantic love is only an illusion. Francis Steegmuller has suggested "The Education of the Feelings" or, more freely, "The Story of a Romantic Passion."—Trans.

The Break

Flaubert and Ernest Chevalier, they write to each other. Living in a boarding house run by M. and Mme. Renaud, Henry is soon captivated by the charm of his landlady, who is, naturally, a brunette with "tawny skin and deep shadows under the eyes" and "shining black hair parted in the middle." After some preliminaries, Emilie Renaud and Henry fall into one another's arms. Their passion is so strong that the unfaithful wife and her young lover leave for America. But ecstasy is quickly followed by disenchantment. Henry cannot find work in New York and Emilie Renaud is bored far from the brilliant life of Paris. They go back to France and separate. The husband forgives his wife. Henry returns to the trivial pleasures of the capital. Jules, meanwhile, having been disappointed in his love for an actress on tour who has scorned him and swindled him, seeks a meaning to life in solitude, dreams, and writing. At first he is tempted by romanticism, but he soon discovers how false and overblown it is. He comes to believe that art should not express the author's judgment of his characters but should be above all impartial and impersonal. Beauty and truth are one. Refusing to yield to worldly ambitions, understanding that the artist's only reward lies within himself, Jules retreats into his work and keeps the world at a distance. Thus each of the two friends has had his "sentimental education." Henry, a frivolous climber who has, however, gotten over his illusions, is destined to win all the prizes coveted by the ordinary run of men: position, money, marriage, notoriety. He will succeed, but he will lose his soul by becoming a bourgeois like the others. Jules, the disenchanted hermit, discovers his raison d'être in meditation over a blank sheet of paper.

The models for Henry are both Maxime Du Camp and the Flaubert of the early days in Paris. Jules, on the other hand, reflects the present anxieties and hopes of his creator. He is Flaubert's spokesman and is presented as a wholly sympathetic character. As for Emilie Renaud, she represents a mixture of Eulalie Foucaud and Elisa Schlésinger. Beautiful, common, and enterprising, she gives herself to her admirer, while Flaubert was not so fortunate with Elisa. Thus the whole novel appears as a skillful transposition of Flaubert's personal experiences. Describing Jules's intimate thoughts, he writes: "Heedless of praise or censure so long as he has been able to render his thought as he conceived it, to do his duty and chisel his block, he cares for nothing else and does not greatly concern himself about the rest. He has become a great and serious artist, whose patience is never exhausted and whose dedication to the ideal never flags. . . . It is the conciseness of his style that makes it so mordant, its variety that makes it flexible." Is it not of himself that he is speaking, with obstinacy and pride?

Nevertheless, when he had finished *L'Education sentimentale,* he quickly came to recognize its weaknesses. To be sure, the characters are well drawn; certain scenes, like the ball or Henry's visit to the fashionable man of letters, sparkle with humor and accuracy; the analysis of the love between Henry and Emilie Renaud, then of its slow decomposition, rings true; the episode of the mangy dog that insists on following Jules in the night has a haunting power. But the work as a whole lacks cohesion: the two plots of which Jules and Henry are the protagonists unfold along parallel lines that never connect. When Emilie Renaud goes back to her husband, the story seems ended. The author prolongs it artificially when he sets forth Jules's esthetic theories.

Not for a moment did Flaubert contemplate publishing this latest work. But he was happy to have completed the undertaking. Looking at his manuscript, he felt the satisfaction of the creator who lets his arms drop after an exhausting effort. Once, despite his disdain for other people's judgments, he asked for his father's opinion. Dr. Flaubert was not overly pleased to see his son, who had abandoned the study of law for reasons of health, scribbling away all day long. Nevertheless, he settled into an armchair and listened to Gustave read, in his deep voice, the beginning of *L'Education sentimentale.* It was very warm. They had just had a copious lunch. Dr. Flaubert's eyes kept closing and at length he dozed off, with his chin on his chest. Gustave, offended, said, "I think you've had enough."

His father awoke with a start, began to laugh, and dropped a few words about the futility of the writer's trade. "Anyone who has the time can write a novel like Hugo or M. de Balzac," he muttered. "Literature, poetry, what use is it? No one has ever known!"

"So tell me, doctor," Gustave retorted, "can you explain to me what use is the spleen? You have no idea and neither do I, but it's indispensable to the human body, just as poetry is indispensable to the human soul."[12]

Dr. Flaubert shrugged his shoulders in annoyance and left the room. Between his elder son, Achille, a surgeon like himself, and Gustave, the dilettante, the failure, he had already made his choice. Gustave knew it and was hurt. Even though he felt a physical need to live in the warmth of his family, he realized they were alien to his essential concerns. Even those who loved him didn't understand him. But the important thing was that he was no longer disturbed with demands for a career and respectability. "One good thing, at least, will have come of my illness: I am allowed to spend my time as I please, which is a great thing in life. For myself, I can't think of anything in the world that is better than a nice, well-heated room, with the books one loves and all the leisure one wants. As for my health, it is better on the whole, but in these damnable nervous diseases, recovery is so slow as to be almost imperceptible."[13] There were times when it seemed to him that he had finally found his balance in the midst of the eddies of life, and others when he felt more unsteady than ever. But he would not have traded his anxious doubts for all the cheerful self-satisfaction of a Maxime Du Camp.

Chapter 7

BEREAVEMENTS

Caroline was going to be twenty-one. For the last few months she had been very responsive to the courtship of a former classmate of Gustave's at the Collège Royal de Rouen, Emile Hamard. He was a melancholy, tormented youth, and the girl's heart was touched by his unstable character. Flaubert, on the other hand, expected nothing good to come of a union between two such fragile creatures. Furthermore, he loved his sister too much to imagine that she could leave him. He felt that by taking an interest in another man she was breaking up their sweet complicity, betraying their childhood. But their parents seemed delighted at this prospect of matrimony and on March 1, 1845, a contract was signed before a notary. Two days later the wedding took place. Caroline was radiant. Gustave made an attempt at gaiety in spite of a secret feeling of sadness. The young couple would lack for nothing. Emile Hamard, a landowner, brought with him farms, rental properties, investment income, and a capital of ninety thousand francs. Caroline had a dowry of five hundred thousand francs and a rich trousseau.

The arrangements for the wedding trip were somewhat unusual. The couple were to be accompanied on their honeymoon by the bride's parents and her brother Gustave. Thus the family escort would watch over the first steps the lovebirds took in married life. The journey began with a train ride—the railroad line had just been completed—from Rouen to Paris. They took their places in an open car. The weather was cold and damp. Buffeted by the wind of the racing train, Dr. Flaubert contracted an eye ailment that soured his temper.

In Paris Gustave felt as if he were returning to his student days after a hundred years' absence. "Everywhere I went I was walking in my past, the way one climbs up a mountain stream with the water murmuring around one's knees," he wrote Le Poittevin.[1] He went to see the Collier family, who had moved back into their old apartment on the Champs-Elysées. Just as three years earlier, Harriet was ill and reclining on a sofa. The furniture around her was the same. Under the windows an organ grinder was playing a familiar tune, as in the old days. It seemed that in this immutable universe he alone, notwithstanding his twenty-four years, had totally changed: He hurried to the Schlésingers': they had left Paris. Then he went to visit Mme. Pradier, who had separated from her husband and whom all decent people condemned for her adultery. Seeing her in tears, he told her straight out that for his part, he approved of her: "I pitied the baseness of all those people who are baying after this poor woman because she opened her thighs to admit a prick other than the one designated by M. the Mayor."[2]

On April 3 the party left for Arles and Marseilles. To Gustave, this latter city was the unforgettable scene of his first experience of love. Was he going to have another encounter there with the dark and ardent Eulalie Foucaud? And how would it be when they saw each other again, now that illness condemned him to chastity? "I shall go to see Mme. Foucaud. . . . That will be singularly bitter and comical, especially if I find she has lost her looks, as I expect," he said ironically.[3] Escaping the surveillance of his parents, he went back to the Rue de la Darse. The Hôtel Richelieu was abandoned, the door nailed up, the shutters closed. "Isn't that symbolic?" he wrote. "The shutters of my heart, too, have been closed a long time now, its steps deserted; it was a tumultuous hostelry once, but now it is empty and echoing like a great tomb without a corpse."[4] Of course, he could have tried to find out from the neighbors the current address of Eulalie Foucaud, "that admirable big-breasted female who gave me such blissful interludes there." But he didn't have the courage. "I have," he said, "a strong aversion to revisiting my past." Love no longer had a place in his desires or even in his thoughts. Still, he complained bitterly about the way the great journey was proceeding. No doubt he was exasperated by the love-struck looks of his sister, who he thought was silly in her role of the young bride, and by the comments of his parents on the sites and monuments that they dutifully admired on faith. "The farther I go, the more I feel incapable of living the same life as everyone else, of sharing family pleasures, of warming to others' enthusiasms, blushing at what shocks them," he confided to Le Poittevin. "By everything you hold sacred, if you hold anything sacred—by everything true and grand—oh my dear sweet Alfred, I conjure you in the name of heaven, in my own name, never travel with anyone! Anyone! I wanted to see Aigues-Mortes and I did not see Aigues-Mortes, nor the Sainte-Baume with the cave where Magdalen wept, nor the battlefield of Marius, etc. I saw nothing of any of those, because I was not alone, I was not free. This is the second time I've seen the Mediterranean like a grocer on holiday. Will the third time be better?"[5]

The party traveled along the Côte d'Azur and then stopped in Genoa. There, in the Balbi Palace, Flaubert had an illumination in front of a canvas by Breughel, *The Temptation of Saint Anthony*. He wrote in his notebook: "Underneath the impression of merrymaking suggested by the details, the thing as a whole is crawling, seething, jeering in a wild, grotesque way. At first the painting seems confused, then it becomes strange to most people, funny to some, something more to others. For me it blotted out everything else in the gallery. I've already forgotten the other pictures."[6] And he wrote to Le Poittevin: "I have seen a painting by Breughel, *The Temptation of Saint Anthony*, which made me think of adapting the story for the theater. But it would take some other fellow to do it. I would gladly give the entire collection of *Le Moniteur*, if I had it, and a hundred thousand francs besides, to buy that picture, which most people who see it surely think is bad."

He confirmed in passing that he had no more interest in women: "Fucking has nothing more to teach me. My desire is too universal, too permanent, too intense for me to have desires. I don't use women as means to an end . . . I use them only as objects of contemplation."[7] In another letter two weeks later he returned to the subject: "It's a singular thing, the way I have drawn away from women. I am satiated with them, as those must be who have been loved too much. Or perhaps it is I who have loved too much. Masturbation is the cause of that: moral masturbation, I mean. . . . I have become impotent as a result of those magnificent effluvia that have seethed in me too furiously ever to flow. It is now two years since I last had coitus; and, in a few days, a year since I performed any lascivious act. I no longer experience in the presence of any skirt even the desire that springs from curiosity, that impels you to strip the veil from the unknown and look for something new. I must have fallen very low, since the sight of a brothel inspires me with no urge to enter it."[8] Actually, the diet and medication that Dr. Flaubert prescribed for his son had something to do with this indifference to sex.

For that matter, on the long journey everyone had problems of one kind or another: Caroline complained about her head and her back, Dr. Flaubert about his eyes, his wife of constant anxiety and Gustave of his nervous seizures (he had two, close together). As for Achille, who had stayed in Rouen to look after his father's patients in his absence, he was so exhausted by overwork that he begged his parents to return as quickly as possible. So the Flaubert clan started back, but by way of Switzerland. They took the Simplon Pass, and the coach rolled between two walls of snow. "We were up to our wheel hubs in it." In Geneva, Flaubert went for a walk on a little island where there stood a statue of Rousseau sculpted by Pradier and declared: "At the two ends of Lake Geneva there are two geniuses who cast shadows loftier than those of the mountains: Byron and Rousseau, two stout fellows, two sly ones who would have made very good lawyers."[9]* Back in France, the travelers stopped in Nogent to visit a few farms belonging to the family.

---

* An allusion to a remark made by Alfred Le Poittevin's father, who had said of Flaubert: "He's a sly one; he'd make a good lawyer." —Trans. (FS)

Bereavements

On June 15, 1845, they returned home to Rouen: "The port, the eternal port, the paved courtyard. And at last my room, the same surroundings, the past behind me, and as always, the vague impression of a more perfumed breeze."[10]

Caroline and her husband had remained in Paris to look for a suitable apartment and to buy furniture. Staying sometimes in Rouen, sometimes in Croisset, Flaubert tried to get used to this new life apart from his sister. He wrote her: "I cannot imagine not being sad because you are no longer with me, I was so used to your presence! Sometimes I feel in my mouth the need to kiss your good cheeks that are as fresh and firm as shellfish."[11] And to Ernest Chevalier: "Ah, dear friend, the house is no longer gay as in the past, my sister is married, my parents are getting old, and I am too; all of that wears one down!"[12] And to Le Poittevin: "My life seems to be arranged in a regular way now. Its horizons are less wide, alas!—less varied, especially; but perhaps it is the more intense for being restricted. . . . Normal, regular, rich, hearty copulation would take me too much out of myself, disturb my peace. I would be returning to active life, to truth in the physical sense, to common sense in short, and that has been bad for me every time I've tried it."[13]

As time passed, Flaubert's health improved. He studied Greek, read Shakespeare and Voltaire, swam, went rowing. Stendhal's *Rouge et le noir* came into his hands. "It seems to me that it is the product of a distinguished mind, a mind of great delicacy," he wrote to Le Poittevin. "The style is French. But is it *style*, true style, the old style that is unknown today?"[14] Maxime Du Camp came to see him in Croisset. A few days of excited talk about art, of jokes, plans, and boisterous male laughter, and the visitor was gone again. As for Ernest Chevalier, he had recently been appointed assistant public prosecutor in Corsica—another friend disappearing into the distance. The atmosphere of the house was growing heavy. "I notice that I hardly ever laugh anymore and that I am no longer depressed," Flaubert wrote again to Le Poittevin. "I am ripe. . . . Ill, agitated, prey a thousand times a day to moments of terrible anxiety, without women, without wine, without any of the tinkling distractions the world offers, I continue my slow work like the good workman who, with sleeves rolled up and sweat in his hair, pounds his anvil, indifferent to rain or wind, hail or thunder. . . . I think I have finally come to understand one thing, one great thing. That is that for people like you and me, happiness is in the *idea*, and nowhere else."[15]

Now he was gathering materials for an ambitious undertaking, a big opus: *La Tentation de Saint Antoine*. Underneath his apparent serenity he was tormented by anxiety. He doubted his talent. And as if that weren't torture enough, the outside world, which he wanted to have nothing to do with, intruded itself upon him every day with disconcerting violence. After his sister's marriage, it was his father's illness that occupied his thoughts and distracted him from his work. Dr. Flaubert suffered from a deep tumor in the thigh. He insisted that the necessary surgery be performed by his son Achille. After the operation the family was somewhat reassured: "No more fever," Flaubert wrote Le Poittevin. "The suppuration is stopping. And it is almost certain that no new lesion is forming in the thigh."[16] But a new lesion did form. Dr. Flaubert died on January 15, 1846. The family was in utter consternation. The pillar on which the life of the little group rested had disappeared. Everything was crumbling. Faced with so great a void, Flaubert suddenly understood how important this affectionate, dignified, and uncomprehending father had been to him. "You knew, you loved the good, intelligent man we have lost, the gentle, noble soul that has departed," he wrote Ernest Chevalier. "What can I tell you of my mother? She is grief incarnate! It is heartbreaking to see her. If she has not died, or if she does not die of it, it is because one cannot die of sorrow."[17] The entire city went into mourning. All the newspapers of the region praised the virtues of "one of the most illustrious surgeons in France," his learning, energy, integrity, and devotion to the cause of the poor. The day of his funeral, workplaces were closed. The longshoremen claimed the honor of bearing the coffin from the house to the Church of the Madeleine, a copy of the one in Paris, which the students of the deceased had hung with black. His two sons and his son-in-law Hamard were chief mourners. After the religious ceremony, many speeches were made on the parvis. A subscription was taken up to erect a statue to the great man. It would be executed, people said, by James Pradier.

As soon as the funeral was over, Flaubert had to attend to a hundred practical matters that he found exasperating. His father, who had had a good head for business, left an inheritance of around half a million francs. The family's future was thus assured. But difficulties arose with regard to Achille's career. A coalition of doctors at the hospital was opposed to his succeeding his father as chief surgeon. Gustave threw himself into the struggle: he went to Paris, pleaded for his brother, and won his case. Achille became chief surgeon of the first division of the Hôtel-Dieu, while his rival, Emile Leudet, was given the same post in the second. This promotion enabled Achille to move into the official lodgings that his parents had occupied until then. The Hamard couple came to live with him.

Caroline was pregnant. A week after the death of her father, she gave birth to a daughter, whom it was decided to name Caroline. Sadness and joy followed one another in the family. After a few difficult days, the young mother seemed to be rallying. Flaubert, reassured, went to Paris to look after the inheritance. But shortly after his arrival, he was called back to Rouen by an urgent letter from his mother: Caroline had puerperal fever. He rushed home by train and found the household in total disarray. His sister was rambling deliriously in a feeble voice. She no longer remembered her father and scarcely recognized the faces leaning over her bed. "Hamard has just left my room, where he was standing sobbing beside the fire," Flaubert wrote Maxime Du Camp. "My mother is a weeping statue. Caroline talks, smiles, caresses us, speaks gentle, affectionate words to us all. She is losing her memory. Everything is confused in her head, she didn't know whether it was I or Achille who had gone to Paris. What grace there is about the sick, what strange movements they make! The baby nurses and cries. Achille says nothing and knows not what to say. What a house! What a hell! . . . It seems that calamity is upon us, and that it will not leave until it has gorged itself on us. Once again I'm going to see the house draped in black; once again I'm going to hear the vile sound of the hobnailed boots of the undertaker's men descending the stairs.

I prefer to have no hope, but on the contrary to enter by anticipation into the grief that is to come."[18]

For yet a few days Caroline struggled against pain. Then, on March 22, 1846, at three o'clock in the afternoon, she passed away. They combed her hair, dressed her in her white bridal gown, surrounded her with bouquets of roses, immortelles, and violets. Gustave spent the night keeping vigil over the body. "She seemed much taller and much more beautiful than when she was alive," he said, "with the long white veil coming down to her feet." Beside himself with grief, he recalled over and over again scenes from the happy days they had spent together. Then suddenly he went to get the love letters Eulalie Foucaud had written him five years before. He reread them beside his sister's corpse, by the light of the tapers, in the funereal silence of the house. Everything around him was sleeping. The vanity of earthly joys: what was the good of living? With a heavy heart he put the useless pages back in their envelopes and wrote on the packet: "Poor woman, can she really have loved me?"

The next day he had molds made of Caroline's hand and face. Then came the burial. "The grave was too narrow," Flaubert recounted, "the coffin wouldn't fit. They shook it, pulled it, turned it this way and that; they took a spade and crowbars, and finally a gravedigger trod on it—just above Caroline's head—to force it down. I was standing at the side, holding my hat in my hand; I threw it down with a cry."[19]

At the end of March, Flaubert, his mother, and the baby had gone to Croisset. "My mother is better than she might be," Flaubert continued. "She busies herself with her daughter's child, sleeps in her room, rocks her, cares for her as much as she can. She is trying to make herself into a mother again. Will she succeed? The reaction has not yet set in, and I dread its coming." Another cause for anxiety: Emile Hamard was showing symptoms of mental derangement. There was no question of leaving the child in his guardianship. But he was determined to keep her. It took the threat of a lawsuit for the little girl to remain under her grandmother's protection. "I am crushed, numb, I need to resume a quiet life, for I am suffocating with grief and irritation," Flaubert concluded. "When shall I return to my austere life of tranquil art and long meditation?"

On April 6 little Caroline was baptized in the church of Canteleu. Flaubert considered the ceremony absurd. "The infant, the guests, myself, and even the curé, who had just had his dinner and was still red in the face—not one of us had any understanding of what we were doing there," he wrote. "As I looked at all those symbols that had no meaning for us, I felt as though I were witnessing a ceremony from some remote religion exhumed from the dust."[20]

So now he was launched upon a new life between a niece still in the cradle and a mother broken by sorrow but proud of taking her daughter's place at the orphan's side. This strange trio resided sometimes in Croisset, sometimes in Rouen, where the Flauberts had rented a little apartment for the winter, at the corner of the Rue Crosne-hors-la-ville and the Rue Buffon. "At least I have one great consolation," Flaubert declared, "one support on which I lean. It is this: I don't see what further misfortune can befall me."[21]

But this black year held in store for him a third unexpected blow. His great friend Alfred Le Poittevin informed him that he was going to marry Aglaé de Maupassant. (A few months later, Alfred's sister Laure was to wed Aglaé's brother Gustave.)* This sudden decision stunned Flaubert and wounded him like an undeserved betrayal. Not only was Alfred abandoning him for a woman, but he was also leaving Rouen for Paris. Again ties were being broken, again the surrounding zone of cold and absence was being widened. Some were snatched away by death, others by life. He alone remained where he was, unchanging, with his despair and his memories. He was so disappointed that he wrote to the friend who had just become engaged: "Not having asked me for advice, it would be proper for me to give none. So we won't speak about that. There are many things which I foresee. Unfortunately, I am farsighted. . . . Are you sure, oh great man, that you won't end up

---

* These two would become the parents of Guy de Maupassant.

becoming a bourgeois? I made you a part of all my artistic hopes. That's the thing that distresses me. Too late! Let be what will be. I will always be here for you. Remains to be seen whether you will be there for me. . . . No one wishes for your happiness more than I, and no one is more doubtful of it. Because in your very seeking it you are doing something abnormal. . . . Will we still share those *arcana* of ideas and feelings, inaccessible to the rest of the world? Who can say? No one."[22] And to Ernest Chevalier: "So there goes one more who is lost to me, and doubly so—first because he is marrying and second because he will be moving away. How everything disappears! How everything disappears! The trees are leafing out again, but for us, where is the month of May that will give us back the lovely flowers that are gone and the virile fragrance of the days of our youth?"[23]

Besieged by sorrow, cares, and painful reminiscences, he had only one defense: work. Eight hours of immersion in Greek, Latin, history. "I make myself drunk by reading these good old ancients whose art I'm coming to worship. I'm trying to live in the world of classical antiquity, and with God's help I'll manage to."[24]

Mme. Flaubert was busying herself about the house with the servant Julie, the baby had wet her diapers and was crying, and Gustave, bent over his books, was journeying in another century and dreading the moment when he would have to tear himself away to confront everyday reality.

Chapter 8

LOUISE COLET

Toward the end of July 1846, Flaubert went to Paris to commission a bust of Caroline from Pradier.* In the sculptor's studio there was the usual lively gathering of men and women from the world of the arts, who were smoking, drinking, playing dominoes, and chatting. As soon as he entered the room, Flaubert was struck by the ripe beauty of a woman. He who professed to like only brunettes was fascinated by her ash-blond hair, her direct gaze, her full, maternal bosom. Perceiving that he was stirred by the stranger, Pradier introduced him to her, saying, "Here is a young man to whom you might give some advice on literary matters."

She was thirty-six years old, he was twenty-five. Her name was Louise Colet and she took pride in her position as a poetess of recognized talent, in the free life she led, and in the countless love affairs she had had. Born on September 15, 1810, in Aix-en-Provence, where her father was the regional postmaster, Louise Revoil had demonstrated brilliant poetic gifts while still very young and had soon become celebrated in provincial salons as "the muse of

---

* It is now in the Carnavalet Museum in Paris, together with the bust of Flaubert's father.

the department."* In 1835 she had married the flutist Hippolyte Colet and the couple had settled in Paris, where the musician had been appointed a professor at the conservatory. There, she shamelessly exerted herself to obtain from prominent writers—Chateaubriand, Sainte-Beuve, Béranger—prefaces to her poems, recommendations to publishers, subsidies, and support for her candidacy for literary prizes. In 1838 she met the philosopher Victor Cousin and became his mistress. Later, when he was appointed Minister of Education, he helped her get government pensions. She had a daughter by him. On May 30, 1839, the Académie Française awarded the scheming beauty a prize for her poem *"Le Musée de Versailles."* Alphonse Karr immediately attacked her in his satiric review *Les Guêpes* [The Wasps], making fun of her pregnancy, which he attributed to *"une piqûre de cousin"* [the bite of a gnat].† In a blind rage, she went to his house to stab him with a knife she had purchased. He disarmed her, threw her out, and hung the knife on the wall of his study with a card reading: "Given me by Madame Colet, née Revoil, in the back." In the salons, some people made fun of her, others compared her to Charlotte Corday.** In 1842 Victor Cousin presented her to Mme. Dupin, who introduced her to Mme. Récamier's. The following year she received from the king's hands a gold medal as "a reward and an encouragement." To Pradier, whom she cultivated assiduously, she was "Sappho." He executed a bust of her that was a celebration of her charms. She knew she was beautiful, irresistible, and she once declared proudly before a group of friends:

"Did you know that they have found the arms of the Venus of Milo?"

"Where?" asked a guest.

"In the sleeves of my dress."

When Flaubert met her, she was still married to Hippolyte Colet

---

* "Department" in the sense of administrative subdivision of France. Aix-en-Provence is in the department of the Bouches-du-Rhône, in the southeast.—Trans.

† The pun on *cousin* is lost in translation. —Trans.

** Who had stabbed Marat to death in 1793. —Trans.

and kept by Victor Cousin, whose daughter she was raising. Her disordered life was known to all. But she braved public opinion, and the hermit of Croisset was captivated by her womanly courage. Having ventured out of his provincial backwater, he looked with all the emotion of a neophyte upon this superb creature to whom writing poetry was as natural as breathing and who derived many pleasures from her body. The day after their first meeting in the sculptor's studio, which had taken place on July 29, 1846, he paid a visit to Louise Colet and took her for a ride in an open carriage in the Bois de Boulogne. Two days later, after a second outing, she consented to go with him to his hotel. There, she proved a wildly uninhibited lover. He was shaken to his very bones; no doubt he was even a little frightened by her passion. In any case, he could not stay with her longer. He had to think of his mother, whom he had left alone in Croisset with little Caroline. Filial duty gave him a pretext for fleeing. Louise wept when he left. He swore to return soon.

As he had foreseen, his mother was waiting for him at the station in tears: she had suffered so from his absence. He consoled her and immediately returned in thought to Louise.

Twelve hours ago we were still together, and at this very moment yesterday I was holding you in my arms! Do you remember? How long ago it seems! Now the night is soft and warm; I can hear the great tulip tree under my window rustling in the wind, and when I lift my head I see the moon reflected in the river. Your little slippers are in front of me as I write; I keep looking at them. Here, locked away by myself, I have just put away everything you gave me. . . . I am not writing to you on my ordinary writing paper—that is edged with black and I want nothing sad to pass from me to you. I want to cause you nothing but joy, and to surround you with a calm, endless bliss—to repay you a little for the overflowing generosity of the love you have given me. . . . Ah, our two marvelous carriage rides! How beautiful they were, particularly the second, with the lightning flashes above us. I keep remembering the color of the trees lit by the streetlights, and the rocking motion of the springs. We were alone, happy: I kept staring at you, and even in the darkness your whole face seemed illumined by your eyes.[1]

In spite of the glowing memories of their love, he did not plan to return to Paris immediately: he couldn't bring himself to distress his mother, who needed his presence so. She kept him jealously under her thumb. Living with her, he was surrounded by the familiar warmth of the nest in which he had grown up, in which he worked. Louise must not encroach upon that territory. Nevertheless, he couldn't stop thinking about her with desire and remorse: "I see you lying on my bed, your hair streaming over my pillow, your eyes raised to heaven, your face pale, your hands clasped, pouring out wild words." But at this pitch of retrospective excitement, he had a sudden anxiety. Had she perhaps misinterpreted the causes of the physical failure he had experienced with her? "What a wretched lover you must think me! Do you know that what happened to me with you has never happened to me before? (I had been so exhausted for three days and taut as a cello string.) If I were the sort of man who has a high opinion of his own person, I should have been bitterly chagrined. I was, but for your sake. I was afraid you might suppose things insulting to yourself; other women might have taken it as an affront. They would have thought me cold, or repelled, or worn out. I was grateful to you for your spontaneous understanding, for not being surprised, when I myself was as surprised as if it had been something unbelievably monstrous."[2] But she demanded that he hurry back to Paris, and he equivocated: "I am shattered, numb as though after a long orgy; I miss you terribly. There is an immense void in my heart. . . . I cannot read or think or write. Your love has made me sad. I can see you are suffering; I foresee I will make you suffer. Both for your sake and for my own, I wish we had never met, and yet the thought of you is never absent from my mind."[3] She didn't understand this reluctance and took offense at his coldness as compared to her own ardor. To show him how great a sacrifice she had made by surrendering to him, she sent him some letters from her official protector, Victor Cousin. He was not particularly shocked. "Ever since we first said we loved each other, you have wondered why I hesitate to add 'forever,' " he wrote. "It is because I always sense what lies ahead. . . . I have a foreboding of immense unhappiness for you. . . . You think that you will love me forever, child. Forever—how presumptuous on the lips of a human being!" And he promised generously: "Later this month I'll go to see you. I'll stay a whole long day. Before two weeks are out—twelve days, even—I shall be yours." But let her not ask him to change his character or his way of life: "You tell me, for example, to write you every day, and if I don't you are going to reproach me. Well, the very idea that you want a letter every morning will prevent me from writing it.* Let me love you in my own way, in the way my nature demands, with what you call my originality. Force me to do nothing and I will do everything."[4]

Notwithstanding his explanations, she couldn't understand that at the age of twenty-five he had to have an excuse to leave the house. "My mother needs me," he told her. "She is distressed by my slightest absence. Her sorrow imposes a thousand unimaginable tyrannies upon me. Things that would be nothing to others are a great deal to me. I don't know how to say no to someone who implores me with a grief-stricken face and tears in her eyes. I am as weak as a child, and I give in because I don't like reproaches, entreaties, and sighs."[5] When Louise made so bold as to suggest coming to see him in Croisset, he panicked and did everything to dissuade her: "What's the good of thinking about such follies? It's impossible. The whole countryside would know of it the next day; there would be no end to the hateful talk."[6] Cut to the quick, she replied ironically, "So you are watched over like a young girl!" Undaunted, he continued to keep her at a distance. At his request, the many letters she wrote him were addressed to Maxime Du Camp, who forwarded them in other envelopes. When he went to see her in Paris, it was a whirlwind visit. They had hardly made love when

---

* He was to send her more than one hundred and twenty letters, most of which have been preserved. Louise Colet's replies, on the contrary, were destroyed, perhaps by Flaubert's niece Caroline.

he was off again so as not to alarm his mother. Louise upbraided him for hastening to leave her. He justified himself for the hundredth time:

> How can I stay? What would you do in my place? You always speak to me of your sorrows: I know they are genuine, I have seen proof; and I feel it in myself, which makes it the more convincing. But I see another sorrow, a sorrow constantly at my side, one which never complains, which even smiles, and beside which yours, however exaggerated it may be, will never be more than what a fleabite is to a burn, a spasm to a death agony. That's the vise I am caught in. The two women I love most have slipped a double-reined bit into my heart and hold me by it; they pull me alternately by love and by grief. . . . I no longer know what to say to you; I hesitate now. When I speak to you, I'm afraid of making you cry, and when I touch you, of hurting you. You remember my violent caresses, how strong my hands were, you were almost trembling! Two or three times I made you cry out. But be more reasonable, poor child that I love, don't grieve over things you only imagine! . . . I love in my own way, whether more than you or less, God knows. But I love you, come, and when you say that I may have done for common women what I do for you, I have done it *for no one*—no one, I swear it. You are absolutely the first and only woman whom I have ever been willing to travel to see —whom I have loved enough to do that for—because you are the first to love me as you love me.[7]

When he was away from Louise, he took delight in dreaming of her while gazing at her little slippers or the portrait—an engraving framed in dark wood—that Maxime Du Camp had brought him on her behalf. Perhaps he even loved her more when she was absent. When she was not there to offend him by some unkind remark, he would give way to tender feelings, let his imagination run, float between heaven and earth. Then suddenly he would wake up. Louise, more and more demanding, now wanted to have a child by

70

him. The very idea of it made his hair stand on end with horror, almost with revulsion. He berated her severely for her obsession: "In the sublime selfishness of your love you take pleasure in the thought that a child might be born. You desire one—admit it. You want a child as one more bond that would unite us, as a contract sealed by fate that would weld our two destinies together. Oh, it's only because it is you, dear and too affectionate friend, that I am not angry with you for wishing for something that would be so disastrous to my happiness! That I, who have sworn never again to join anyone's existence to my own, *I* should give birth to another life! . . . The very idea makes a chill run down my spine. And if, in order to prevent that life from coming into the world, it were necessary for me to leave it, the Seine is here, and I would throw myself into it at this very moment with a 36-pound cannonball attached to my feet."[8]

She was revolted that a man who claimed to love her could be so selfish. She bristled up and insulted him by letter. He retorted in kind: "Anger, for God's sake! Acrimony, abuse, stinging reproaches! What's the meaning of that? Do you like disputes, recriminations, and all the bitter daily wrangling that in the end makes life a real hell? . . . How can you love me if you regard me as such a contemptible individual?"[9] Since she insisted, with rage, with tenderness, on seeing him more often, he finally yielded and proposed that they meet in Mantes, halfway between Paris and Rouen, at the Hôtel du Grand Cerf. But he wanted to be back the same evening so as not to worry his mother: "We'll have a whole long afternoon to ourselves. . . . Are you pleased with me? Is that what you wanted? You see that when I can be with you I seize upon the smallest opportunity like a starving thief."[10] But far from rejoicing, she resented his granting her so little time and heaped insults upon him. "I who expected you were going to kiss me for the idea I had of our trip to Mantes!" he wrote. "Yes, of course! You are already reproaching me in advance for not staying there longer. . . ."[11] Finally she accepted the plan and he arranged a schedule: "Take the train that leaves Paris at 9:00 in the morning. I'll leave from Rouen at the same time."[12]

71

Flaubert

Their reunion was so happy, so ardent that instead of separating in the evening, as agreed, they spent the night together at the hotel. Since he had not warned his mother that he was staying over, when he saw her the next day Flaubert felt all the remorse of a guilty child caught in the act. There could be no question of admitting to her that he had a mistress. Quickly he invented an excuse for his tardiness. "I made up a little story which my mother believed," he wrote Louise, "but the poor woman was very worried yesterday. She came to the railroad station at eleven o'clock and lay awake all night fretting. This morning I found her on the platform in a state of extreme anxiety. She uttered no reproach, but the look on her face was the greatest reproach anyone could make." And as a lover conscious of his exploits, he declared: "Do you know that that was the most beautiful day we have had? We loved each other even better than before; we felt exquisite pleasures. . . . I was proud of what you told me, that you had never tasted such happiness. Your joy enflamed me. And I, did I please you? Tell me; it is sweet to me. . . . Before going to bed I wanted to send you, as I promised, another kiss, a faint echo of those which at this time yesterday rang so loudly on your shoulder when you cried: 'Bite me, bite me!'— do you remember?"[13] She, for her part, celebrated their union in delirious verses and sent them to him:

> Like an untamed buffalo of the American wilderness,
> Vigorous and superb in your athletic strength,
> Bounding upon my breast, your black hair flying,
> Tirelessly you infused life into me.*

* To turn these lines into regular, rhymed verse in English, it would be necessary in some places to choose different words. I have thought it preferable to preserve Louise Colet's exact language in a plain prose version. For interested readers, the original French is as follows:
> Comme un buffle indompté des déserts d'Amérique,
> Vigoureux et superbe en ta force athlétique,
> Bondissant sur mon sein, tes noirs cheveux épars,
> Sans jamais t'épuiser tu m'infusais la vie.
>
> —Trans.

Louise Colet

Taken aback by the comparison, he burst out laughing: "Come now, I make a sorry buffalo! And the rhyme *athlétique* that comes afterward isn't right for me. I am scarcely of a robust temperament. . . . For the rest, I thought there were some really fine things."[14]

He was more indulgent toward the next work she sent him:

> Your arm encircled my waist,
> Your neck bent toward my neck,
> And your pure, perfumed lips
> Hung on my lips.
> Two tongues in the same mouth
> Mingled their unctuous lickings,
> Our bodies, joined together, crushed the couch
> Under their passionate thrusts.*

Promptly losing all critical sense, he declared himself enchanted with this pennywhistle lyricism: "These are thrilling lines that would move stones, let alone me. Soon we'll do it again, won't we, challenging each other to quench our thirst. . . . Farewell. A thousand bites on your rosy mouth."[15]

Toward the beginning of their affair he was chilled by an alert: Louise felt faint at times, and her menstrual period was delayed. Was she pregnant? It would be such a catastrophe that the mere prospect of it made him retreat into his shell. But he was soon reassured and greeted the news with jubilation: "Since the event has turned out as I wished, so much the better! So much the better—that's one less unhappy creature on earth. One less victim

---

* Again, the original lines:
> *Ton bras enlacait ma ceinture,*
> *Ton cou vers mon cou se tendait*
> *Et ta lèvre embaumée et pure*
> *A ma lèvre se suspendait.*
> *Deux langues dans la même bouche*
> *Mêlaient d'onctueux lèchements,*
> *Nos corps unis broyaient la couche*
> *Sous leurs fougueux élancements.*
>   —Trans.

of boredom, vice, or crime, of misfortune beyond a doubt. My obscure name will die with me, and the world will go on its way just as if I had left an illustrious one. . . . Oh, how I kiss you! I am moved, I am weeping."[16] Another time he questioned Louise anxiously to know if "the Redcoats had landed." And on learning that it was so, he breathed a sigh of relief. The danger receded for another month.

In spite of this relentlessly negative attitude on his part, Louise still dreamed of possible motherhood. The union of two such exceptional personages as herself and Flaubert, she thought, must inevitably give birth to a genius. She was convinced that if he were faced with a fait accompli, his heart would soften. But the more time passed, the wearier he grew of her stormy passion. Everything separated these two beings who found themselves in harmony only in a bed. She was sentimental, he bitter and skeptical; she longed for the tempests of the high seas, he for the calm of the harbor; she placed love above everything else, while he considered it an agreeable diversion from his work as an artist; she wanted to see him every day, he fiercely defended his solitude and independence.

If he had not been living with his mother, Flaubert would have invented some other excuse for not meeting his mistress too often. Even Louise's conception of a writer's career was diametrically opposed to his. To her, writing was only a means of achieving fame. Attracted by the glitter of success, she demanded that he make an effort to "arrive." He vehemently rebelled against this worldly, commercial vision of the literary calling. "Fame! Fame! But what is fame?" he wrote her. "It is nothing. A mere noise, the external accompaniment of the joy art gives us. . . . But then, I have always seen you lump art together with other things—patriotism, love, what have you—a lot of things which to my mind are alien to it and, far from augmenting its stature, in my opinion diminish it. This is one of the chasms that lie between you and me. It was you who exposed it and revealed it to me."[17]

At one of their meetings he gave in to her request and read her a few pages of the manuscript of *Novembre*. She complimented him. But he was not deceived: "I don't know how I was inveigled into reading you something. Forgive my weakness. I couldn't resist the temptation to make you admire me. Was I not sure of success? How puerile of me!" He wondered if it were not out of simple feminine vanity that she wanted to believe in the talent of the man she had chosen for a lover. By crowning him, she crowned herself. In any event, he swore he did not and would never write for the public: "When I was a child, I had dreams of glory like everyone else, neither more nor less. Good sense sprouted late in me, but it is firmly planted. So it is highly doubtful that the public will ever enjoy a single line of mine; and if that does happen, it will not be for at least ten years."[18] And when she suggested that they collaborate on a book, he backed off: "It was a sweet idea you had, that we should write a book together. I was touched by it, but I don't want to publish anything. This is a stand I have taken, a vow I made to myself at a solemn period in my life. I work with absolute disinterestedness and without ulterior motive or concern. I am not a nightingale but a shrill warbler hiding deep in the woods lest I be heard by anyone except myself. If I do make an appearance one day, it will be in full armor; but I shall never have the assurance."[19]

Possessive, easily offended, intrusive, Louise was also jealous of Flaubert's past. He had made the mistake of telling her about Eulalie Foucaud. She resented his having loved another woman before her. In letter after letter she complained that she no longer received from him the marks of esteem and affection she deserved. She took him to task for not having kissed her when they parted, she complained that he had forgotten her birthday, she accused him of having slept with Mme. Pradier. Suffocated by her love and exasperated by her demands, he wrote to defend himself: "If despite the love that binds you to my poor self, my personality causes you too much pain, leave me," he replied. "If you feel that is impossible, accept me henceforth as I am. It was a foolish gift I made you when I offered you my acquaintance. I have passed the age when one loves the way you would like me to. I don't know why I yielded that time; you attracted me—me, who so distrust attractive things. . . . I shrink from everything that belongs to life; I have a horror of everything that lures me back and plunges me into it again. . . . I have within me, deep inside, a fundamental, intimate, bitter, and never-ending *boredom* that prevents me from enjoying anything and that fills my soul to bursting. . . . Adieu, try to forget me; *I* shall never forget you."[20]

Of course, on being invited to break off relations that were so painful to her, Louise refused. For that matter, he wasn't really thinking of a separation either. For both of them there was an element of playacting in these epistolary breakups and reconciliations. They stayed apart and picked at their sores; they put on a show for each other of a great love worthy to figure in the annals of the century. But while Louise was becoming more and more violently emotional, he was becoming more and more withdrawn. Although in the beginning he had been proud of inspiring such a passion, now he said he was fed up with living in a state of continual tension. This woman loved him too much. And she loved melodramatic scenes too much. Their meetings in Paris or Mantes were increasingly rare and brief. They would make love and insult each other between trains. After which they would write to each other all week long, offering explanations, justifications. Flaubert felt that under the barrage of recriminations, pinpricks, and bitter allusions, he was losing his identity. "Why have you tried to encroach on a life that does not belong to me and to change my whole existence to suit your love?" he wrote her. "It has pained me to see your vain efforts to shake this rock that makes your hands bleed when you touch it."[21] And then a sudden explosion:

> It is impossible for me to continue any longer a correspondence that is becoming epileptic. Change it, for pity's sake! What have I done to you [*vous*] (since it's *vous* now) that you should unfold before me, with all the pride of grief, the spectacle of a despair for which I know no remedy?* If I had betrayed your secret, advertised our liaison, sold your letters,

---

* Here Flaubert switches from the familiar *tu* form, normally used between lovers, to the formal *vous*, apparently because Louise has addressed him in this chilly manner. —Trans.

etc., you could not have written me things more atrocious or distressing. . . . You know very well that I cannot come to Paris. You want to force me to answer you brutally. I am too polite to do so, but it seems to me I have repeated it often enough for you to remember the fact. I had formed an entirely different conception of love. I thought it was something independent of everything else, even of the person who inspired it. Absence, insult, infamy—none of that can affect it. When two people love each other, they can go ten years without seeing each other and without suffering because of it.

In the margin opposite this passage, Louise noted furiously: "What is one to make of this sentence?" He concluded:

As for me, I am weary of grand passions, exalted feelings, frenzied loves, and howling despairs. I love good sense above all, perhaps because I have none.[22]

Actually, given his withdrawn personality, he would have needed a mistress who was motherly, indulgent, available, and self-effacing; instead, he had chosen a tigress. Now he could neither do without her nor get rid of her. To lay the groundwork for an honorable conclusion to their affair, he wrote fewer letters. But she continued to harass him until he lost his temper: "You ask me to send you at least a last word of farewell. Well, from the bottom of my heart I give you the most intimate and sweetest blessing that one can lay on someone's head. I know that you would have done anything for me, that you would do it still, that your love would have deserved an angel, and I am grieved that I was unable to respond to it. But is it my fault? is it my fault? . . . Loving peace and repose above all else, I have found in you nothing but agitation, storms, tears, and anger." He reproached her for having been cold to him one day because of a trifle; for having insulted him another day in public, at the railroad station; for having "sulked" during a dinner with Maxime Du Camp. "All the trouble has come from an original error. You made a mistake in accepting me, or else you would have had to change. But can one change? Your ideas on morality, patriotism, devotion, your tastes in literature—all of that was antipathetic to my ideas, my tastes. . . . *You* wanted to draw blood from a stone: you chipped at the stone and made your fingers bleed. You wanted to make a paralytic walk; all his weight fell back on you and he became even more paralyzed. . . . Adieu, imagine that I have left for a long journey. Adieu again, meet one who is more worthy; to find him for you I would go to the ends of the earth."[23]

A family problem was now added to the problems caused by the irascible Louise: Caroline's father, Emile Hamard, went mad. "Hamard has left for England, where I believe he is to stay a year," wrote Flaubert to Ernest Chevalier. "The poor fellow's mind is deranged; he has had more wind in his sails than he could handle."[24] And really, who on this earth *was* of sound mind? Flaubert wasn't sure how well balanced he was himself. As for Louise, she lived in a perpetual state of useless agitation, morbid suspicion, furious invective, absurd jealousy, and romantic desire.

In April 1847 Flaubert was offered an opportunity to escape from the clutches of the excitable bluestocking. Maxime Du Camp proposed that they take a walking tour of Brittany, "with stout shoes and with packs on our backs." Mme. Flaubert was worried about such a journey. But Gustave's health was no longer a cause for concern. The doctors who were consulted even declared that the exercise and the change of air would do him good. Somewhat reassured, his mother, sighing, helped him prepare for the expedition. She trusted Maxime Du Camp. He would watch over her son. Before leaving gaily with his friend for this masculine adventure, Flaubert wrote Louise: "Little by little time will pass, you will become accustomed to thinking that I no longer exist. The bitter things in your memory of me will fade, will soften by dint of being touched, and perhaps there will remain in your heart only something vague and sweet, as for an old dream that one still loves although one has it no longer. Then, when you have reached that point, I will return; perhaps I will be better and you more reasonable. . . . Adieu, adieu. If there were justice in heaven, it would grant you the happiness you have not found in me. What is there to drink in an empty glass?[25]

The most convenient route to Brittany led through Paris. On this occasion Flaubert could have made a last visit to Louise. He took care not to do so and contented himself with sending her an "ultimate" letter: "You want to know if I love you so as to settle things frankly once and for all. . . . That's too big a question to be answered by a yes or no. . . . For me, love is not and should not be in the foreground of life. It should remain in the back shop. There are other things in the soul which come first, which are, it seems to me, closer to the light, nearer to the sun. So if you consider love as the main food of existence: No. As a seasoning: Yes. . . . If you are hurt by this letter, if it's the 'blow' you have been expecting, it seems to me that it's not such a hard one. . . . Blame only yourself. You asked me, on your knees, to insult you. But no, I send you my affection."[26]

Thus on May 1, 1847, without having completely repudiated the angry woman, but with the feeling of having shifted his burden from one shoulder to the other, he took the train for Blois, together with Maxime Du Camp, "to go breathe free amid the heather and the broom, or beside the waves on the great sand beaches!"[27]

Chapter 9

TRAVEL AND
TRAVEL PLANS

The two companions had decided that when they returned from their travels they would write a book together recounting their adventures. Maxime Du Camp would do the even-numbered chapters and Flaubert the odd ones. Each of them carried a pocket notebook in which to record his impressions on the spot. Each was equipped with "a gray felt hat; a horse trader's stick ordered expressly from Lisieux; a pair of stout shoes (white leather, nails like crocodile teeth); ditto in patent leather (dress shoes for diplomatic visits, in case any are to be made . . .); a pair of leather gaiters to go with the heavy shoes; ditto in wool to protect our socks from dust on the patent leather days; a linen jacket (stylish stableboy type), a pair of inordinately large linen pants to be tucked into the gaiters; a linen vest, whose coarse fabric is redeemed by its elegant cut. Add to that another edition of the same costume in wool. Also, the perfect knife, two water bottles, a wooden pipe, three silk shirts, what a European needs for his daily ablutions, and you will have the outfit in which we presented ourselves in Brittany and in which we lived for several weeks, rain or shine. No ball gown was ever planned with more loving care or, what is certain, was so comfortable to wear."[1]

Flaubert felt well and didn't regret the decision to leave. His comradely relations with Maxime Du Camp were delightful after the scenes with Louise. Together they visited the châteaux of the Loire: Blois, Chambord, Amboise, Chenonceaux. . . . In Tours, however, Flaubert had a nervous attack. A doctor summoned in haste ordered "sulfate of quinine in large doses." The patient recovered and the journey was resumed. They entered Brittany.

Even though he cursed Louise, at every stopover Flaubert looked for a letter from her. On May 17, in Nantes, he wrote her: "Since you stubbornly persist in refusing to write and in living, so far as I am concerned, as if you were dead, I am forced to ask you for news myself. What are you doing and how is life for you? . . . Come, Louise, be kind again, don't despise me. For I don't deserve it. And don't forget me entirely, because *I* think of you often, every day. . . . If I see you again (if you think that would be safe for you), I will not be another man but the same one, with his good and bad qualities. If, on the contrary, this letter too remains unanswered, it will be a farewell, a long farewell, as if one of us had left for the Indies and the other for America." She answered him, but too coldly for his liking. So in Quimper, on June 11, he insisted: "My *vous* doesn't express what I am to you as well as *tu*. So I say *tu*, because I have a special and particular feeling for you, an exact name for which I am seeking but cannot find. . . . I walk beside the sea, I admire the bouquets of trees, the fleecy patches of sky, the sunsets over the waves, and the green seaweed waving under the water like the Naiads' hair, and at night I lie down exhausted in canopied beds where I catch fleas. There! Besides, I needed air. I had been suffocating lately."

In Brest, where the two friends arrived on foot "with our chests bare, shirts puffed out in the breeze, our neckties round our waists, and our packs on our shoulders," Mme. Flaubert and Caroline met them. Mme. Flaubert, an anxious mother, could wait no longer to see her son again. "The poor woman, being unable to do without me, has come to join me in Brest (as had been agreed anyway)," Flaubert wrote Ernest Chevalier, "and we have all traveled together over those parts of the route that had to be done in a carriage, reassembling and separating as we pleased."[2] In Saint-Malo, Flaubert thought with emotion of Chateaubriand, who at seventy-nine remained for him a model of literary and human success. He went to see the tomb that the illustrious writer had had built for himself on the Islet of Grand-Bé, facing the sea. "I send you, my dear friend, a flower that I picked yesterday at sunset on the tomb of Chateaubriand," he wrote Louise. "The sea was beautiful, the sky rose, the air soft. . . . The great man's tomb is on a rock, facing the waves. He will sleep with their sound, all alone, in sight of the house where he was born. I hardly thought of anything but him the whole time I was in Saint-Malo."[3]

July 29 was the anniversary of his first meeting with Louise. Absorbed in the kaleidoscopic journey, he forgot the sacred date. Louise wrote to reproach him for not having sent her flowers, which any gentleman in his place would have done. "Again tears, recriminations, and, what is more amusing, insults," he replied. "You declare that *I ought* at least to have sent you flowers on July 29th. You know very well that I don't acknowledge any obligations; you strike feebly because you try to strike too hard. . . . You ask me to forget you absolutely. I could make a show of having done so, but for it to be truly so, no. You have not been able to resign yourself to accepting me with all the weaknesses of my position, all the exigencies of my life. I gave you the depths of my devotion; you wanted the surface things too, the appearances, the little attentions, the constant comings and goings—everything that I have killed myself trying to make you understand I cannot give you. Let it be as you wish! If you curse me, I for my part bless you, and my heart will always be stirred at the sound of your name."[4]

In the letters that followed, the tone on both sides softened. The tour continued, sometimes on foot over impassable roads, sometimes by carriage. It lasted three months. Three months of sun, dust, rain, mud, healthy fatigue, and wonderful sights. Mme. Flaubert and Caroline, meanwhile, had returned to Croisset. But the country being "overwhelmed with a children's disease," they hastened to take refuge in La Bouille, eighteen kilometers from Rouen. Flaubert joined them there at the beginning of August. When Louise took it into her head to pay him a visit in the village, he was panic-stricken and, as was his wont, wrote that she must do no such thing: "As for coming here, you must not think of it. The village consists of a dozen houses on the quay. There is no place where we could see each other. Patience, then, my poor heart; this winter I hope to go spend a couple of weeks in Paris."[5]

In September, back in Croisset with his mother and niece, he dreamed of leaving again, but this time for the Middle East. "Oh, if you knew the desire, the need I feel to pack up and go far away, to a country where I don't understand the language, far from everything that surrounds me, everything that oppresses me! To think that never, doubtless, shall I see China, that never shall I fall asleep to the rhythm of camels' feet, that never, perhaps, shall I see gleaming in the forest the eyes of a tiger crouched in the bamboo!"[6]

In the meantime, he was working slowly and painfully on the account of his journey through Brittany and Normandy. He was worried about his health: "My nerves are no better," he confided to Louise. "Any day now I expect to have some quite serious attack. . . . Anyway, I don't give a f___, as Phidias [Pradier] would say." And a little later: "I had a seizure, about a week ago, and it has left me tolerably sick and irritable. . . . We (Maxime Du Camp and I) are busy now writing up our journey, and although the work doesn't demand great refinement of effects or a preliminary arrangement of material, I am so unaccustomed to writing and I get into such a bad temper over it, especially with myself, that I am always in trouble. It's like a man who has a good ear but plays the wrong notes on the violin; his fingers refuse to reproduce correctly the sounds he has in his head. So tears flow from the eyes of the poor fellow scraping away, and the bow falls from his fingers."[7] And again, also to Louise: "You inquire about our work, Maxime's and mine. Know, then, that I am exhausted from writing. The question of style, which is something I take very seriously, agitates my nerves horribly; I am in a constant state of vexation, eating my heart out over it. There are days when it makes me sick and gives me a fever at night. . . . What a strange obsession it is, to spend one's life wearing oneself out over words and sweating all day long to produce well-rounded periods!"[8]

Never before had Flaubert taken such care with the construction and music of his sentences. Here, for the first time, he proved himself a rigorous craftsman of the word. There is a striking contrast between the chapters written by Maxime Du Camp, whose style is correct and impersonal, and those written by Flaubert, which are bursting with emotion, color, and life. Among others, the pages on Combourg, on Chateaubriand's tomb, on the slaughterhouses of Quimper-Corentin are superb. But neither of the two authors had any intention of making these texts public. "As for publishing them, it would be impossible," noted Flaubert. "Our only reader, I think, would be the public prosecutor, because of certain reflections that might not be to his taste."[9]*

In his return to solitude, he had one great joy: the new friendship of a former schoolmate, Louis Bouilhet, who had once been a student at the hospital in Rouen but had abandoned medicine and founded a small school for lagging pupils who required special tutoring. Louis Bouilhet lived in dire poverty, was passionately interested in literature, and declared himself a partisan of "art for art's sake." He himself composed verses which Flaubert thought were excellent. But he was a self-effacing man, warm and modest, who had little confidence in his gifts as a writer. All week he worked eight hours a day coaching dunces in Latin to earn his living, but he had begun spending his weekends at Croisset. Soon he and Flaubert were inseparable. Thanks to Louis Bouilhet, the old house on the banks of the Seine echoed with fierce debates and laughter. Thus reinvigorated, Gustave felt less and less need to go to Paris. Especially since Louise, after a few days' lull, was again heaping shame upon him, accusing him of belonging to the tribe of "pleasure-seekers," "swearers," and "smokers." He replied with good humor: "*Smokers*, all right, yes: I smoke, resmoke, and oversmoke, more all the time; I'm smoldering with rage and smoke comes out of my mouth. *Swearers*, there's some truth in that too. But I do so much swearing internally that I should be forgiven the small portion of it that people hear. . . . He's a fine specimen, your *pleasure-seeker*! He

---

* Flaubert's text, titled *Par les champs et par les grèves* [Over Field and Strand], was published only after his death.

consumes more quinine than rum, and his 'orgies' are so noisy that people don't even know if he's still living in his own town, the one where he was born and where he resides."[10]

Although he declared he was disgusted with politics, he couldn't help taking some interest in the currents that were swirling over the country in the last weeks of 1847. The opposition faction was giving Louis-Philippe's government a hard time and holding protest banquets throughout France. On Christmas Day, at the urging of Louis Bouilhet and Maxime Du Camp, Flaubert attended one of these events in the suburbs of Rouen, in a great hall draped with tricolor flags. In spite of his hostility toward the king, he was struck by the mediocrity of the speeches that rained down on his head. "I am still under the influence of the grotesque and lamentable impression that this spectacle left upon me," he wrote Louise. "I remained cold and nauseated with disgust in the midst of all the patriotic enthusiasm aroused by the 'helm of State,' the 'abyss toward which we are racing,' the 'honor of our flag,' the 'shadow of our banners,' the 'brotherhood of peoples,' and other stuff in the same vein."[11] Nevertheless, it did seem as if all the hotheaded talk was paving the way for a real revolution. On February 23, 1848, Flaubert and Louis Bouilhet arrived in Paris to witness firsthand the demonstrations announced by the newspapers. There they found their friends Maxime Du Camp and Louis de Cormenin. The next day they were all present at the violent disorders in the capital. At first they were amused by the immense uproar; then, caught up in the game, they enlisted in the National Guard and for a few hours Gustave, armed with a hunting rifle, gave himself the illusion of participating in republican action. But his enthusiasm soon waned. Jostled by the crowd, he saw a red flag floating over a barricade, an orator struck down by a bullet, officers of the National Guard trying to interpose themselves between the troops and the people, the gleams of a conflagration crowning the city. People were shouting: "Down with Guizot!" Following them, Flaubert and his friends entered the Tuileries and watched with consternation as the palace was sacked. Then they made their way to the Hôtel de Ville. Joining the multitude that was milling about in the square, they heard the republic proclaimed. These images of collective madness fixed themselves in Flaubert's memory with photographic clarity. In the midst of the upheaval, he had confused thoughts of the description he might one day give of it. Now he looked upon everything he experienced, everything he felt, as something to write about. In any case, events were moving so fast that it was impossible for the mind to follow them: abdication of the king, installation of a provisional government, banking crisis, proliferation of revolutionary clubs, demonstrations and counterdemonstrations in the big cities, attempted coup d'état by the "Reds" . . .

Back in Croisset, Flaubert looked upon this chaos with a contemptuous serenity, a haughty mockery. "Well, it's all very funny," he wrote Louise. "The expressions on the faces of the discomfited [monarchists] are a joy to see. I take a profound delight in contemplating all the crushed ambitions. I don't know if the new form of government and the resulting social conditions will be favorable to Art. That is a question. But it cannot be more bourgeois or more worthless than the old. As for being more stupid, is that possible?"[12] To him, the gravest events should be considered from the point of view of the artist. No matter if the world crumbled, as long as writers were the better for it. The lines just quoted were in answer to a letter from Louise in which she informed him incidentally that she was pregnant. By whom? Certainly not "the official," as she called her husband, nor by Victor Cousin, nor by Flaubert, whom she had hardly seen these last months. In reality, while heaping reproaches on Gustave, she had not denied herself other lovers.* It was without question one of them who was the father. "Also, what's the point of all your preambles before telling me the *news?*" Flaubert wrote Louise. "You could have given it to me straight away without circumlocutions. I spare you the reflections it inspired in me and the feelings it aroused. There would be too much to say. I pity you, I pity you greatly. . . . Whatever happens, count on me always. Even if we should no longer write each other, even if we should no longer see each other, there will always be an indissoluble bond between

* The latest was a handsome, vigorous young Pole by the name of Franc.

us, a past whose consequences will endure. My 'monstrous person-ality,' as you so amiably call it, does not obliterate in me every last decent feeling—human feeling, if you prefer."[13]

A far more painful anxiety was troubling him: Alfred Le Poit-tevin was seriously ill. It was thought that his dissolute life had led him to this physical collapse. The doctors said his case was hopeless. He was only thirty-two. Flaubert, who was twenty-seven, considered himself to be "as old" as he. He went at once to his friend's side, in Neuville-Champ-d'Oisel. On April 3, 1848, the end came. "Alfred died on Monday at midnight," Flaubert wrote Maxime Du Camp.

I buried him yesterday, and am now back. I watched beside him two nights (the second time, all night), I wrapped him in his shroud, I gave him the farewell kiss, and saw him sealed in his coffin. I was there two days—very full days. While I sat beside him I read Creuzer's *Religions of Antiquity*. The window was open, the night splendid. I could hear a cock crowing, and a night-moth circled around the tapers. I shall never forget all that, or the look on Alfred's face, or, the first night at midnight, the far-off sound of a hunting-horn that came to me through the forest. . . . At daybreak, about four o'clock, the attendant and I began our task. I lifted him, turned him, covered him. The feeling of the coldness and rigidity of his limbs stayed in my fingertips all the next day. He was horribly decomposed; the sheets were stained through. We wrapped him in two shrouds. When it was done he looked like an Egyptian mummy in its bandages, and I was filled with an indescribable sense of joy and relief on his account. . . . That, dear Max, has been my life since Tuesday evening. I have had marvelous intimations and intuitions and flashes of untranslatable ideas.[14]

Flaubert also informed Ernest Chevalier:

He suffered horribly and saw the end coming. You who knew us in our youth, you know how I loved him and what pain this loss must have caused me. Another one gone, another one who disappears. Everything is collapsing around me; sometimes I feel very old. Each time a misfortune befalls you, you seem to defy fate to send you another, and hardly do you have time to think that it's impossible when new ones arrive that you didn't expect, over and over, without end. What a dreary business life is! I don't know if the Republic will do anything to change that; I doubt it very much.

This letter was dated April 10, 1848. The next day Flaubert stood sentry duty for the first time as a member of the National Guard. Two days earlier he had participated in a review on the occasion of the planting of a Tree of Liberty. He thought this ceremony—the patriotic songs, the bombastic political speeches, the address of the curé celebrating the "Christian republic"—was perfectly ridiculous.* He wanted to forget all the commotion, the long-winded orators. The center of his life was not in Paris, it was in Rouen. But Rouen too was in an uproar. Forty thousand workers had caught the fever from Paris and had gone on strike, demanding shorter hours and higher wages. To no avail: people in the provinces were more reasonable than those in the capital. In the general elections it was the moderates who triumphed. The public prosecutor Sénard, who headed the list of successful candidates, called upon the army to dismantle the barricades. Some thirty rebels were killed. In Paris the June Days of insurrection were followed by massive arrests. General Cavaignac became president of the council, replacing the Executive Commission, which had resigned. Order was reestablished. Flaubert was as indignant over the violence of the repression as over the fury of the revolt. He was neither republican nor conservative. He was as disgusted by the hotheads on the political left as by the timid souls on the right. His nervous seizures reappeared. He was worried about the future of his niece Caroline because Emile Hamard, who was back from England, was showing

---

* Flaubert was to recall the scene when he was writing Chapter VI of *Bouvard et Pécuchet.*

increasingly clear signs of mental derangement. He had become dangerous, announcing his intention to become an actor, squandering thirty thousand francs in one month, and demanding his daughter back. Mme. Flaubert was terrified and went into hiding with the child at the home of friends in Forges-les-Eaux. The proceedings to have Hamard committed dragged on. Finally a court decision ordered that Caroline would stay temporarily with her grandmother. "As for me, it's driving me mad too," Flaubert wrote Ernest Chevalier, "mad with grief. If he [Hamard] doesn't leave on a journey in a few days, as he intends, and if we are again exposed to his visits night and day, we shall emigrate to Nogent."[15]

During this time, Maxime Du Camp, who had received a bullet wound in the calf during the June riots in Paris, was decorated with the Legion of Honor by Cavaignac. There's one fellow, thought Flaubert, who knows how to navigate among the reefs and attain the highest official distinctions. So much the better if it makes him happy! As for himself, once again cloistered in Croisset, he had begun to write his *Tentation de Saint Antoine*. This time he felt himself swept along on a tide of inspiration, as in his youth. Totally caught up in his work, he hardly thought about Louise anymore. He knew that she had given birth to a daughter in June 1848.* When she sent him a letter enclosing a lock of Chateaubriand's hair—Chateaubriand had died the month before—he replied coldly: "Thank you for the gift. Thank you for your very beautiful poem. Thank you for the remembrance. Yours, G."[16] The axe had fallen. Louise was eliminated—at least for the time being, Flaubert decided. Nothing must disturb him in his difficult undertaking. But in November Maxime, the tempter, returned from a trip to Algeria and reawakened in Gustave the desire to escape to the warm countries. He talked about it when Maxime came to see him in Rouen in February 1849. Achille, the older brother, was brought into the secret and approved of the plan. There remained to convince Mme. Flaubert. "It won't be easy," said Achille, "but I'll try." At his first words on the subject, she was up in arms: so long an expedition,

---

* The child lived only a short time.

and in barbarous countries, might damage her son's health! Besides, she couldn't stand the idea of his being far from home for months. To dissipate her fears, they called upon their old friend Dr. Cloquet, who certified by letter that such a journey would be good for Gustave. Mme. Flaubert resigned herself to defeat. "Since it is necessary for your health, go off with your friend Maxime," she said. "I consent." Her expression, noted Du Camp, was "even icier than usual." Gustave reddened to the roots of his hair and thanked her. But having won his case, he was in no hurry to leave. First he wanted to finish this blasted *Tentation* that was draining all his energy. "Next October (don't be afraid of what's coming next, I'm not getting married, it's better than that), next October or at the end of September, I'm clearing out for Egypt," he wrote Ernest Chevalier. "I'm going to travel through the whole Orient. I'll be gone for fifteen to eighteen months. . . . I need to get a breath of fresh air, in the full meaning of the word. My mother, seeing that it was indispensable for me, has consented to the journey, and there you are. I can't help worrying about the anxieties I'm going to cause her, but I think it's the lesser of two evils. I haven't left yet. Between now and then many things can happen."[17] And to his uncle Parain: "My mother and I have agreed that in the time until my departure we won't say a word about this journey, for two reasons: first, because there is no point in her worrying ahead of time and being sad in anticipation; second, because since I have not yet finished my accursed *Saint Antoine* (for he's still dragging on, the little wretch!, although I'm losing weight over him), it would distract me and prevent me from working. You know, old companion, that the mere idea of being disturbed disturbs me, and I have quite enough of a job ahead of me without also having the Orient dancing on the end of my table and the dromedary bells tinkling in my ears over the sound of my sentences. So although the trip has been decided upon, we don't speak of it here; do you understand?"[18]

At the same time that he was working "like ten slaves" on his *Tentation de Saint Antoine*, Gustave was looking for a servant to accompany Maxime and himself on their expedition. Uncle Parain volunteered to hunt up this rare bird. According to Flaubert, the man was to set up and strike the tent, look after the weapons, horses, and baggage, brush the clothes and boots, do the cooking, wear "the costume that we see fit to give him," do without women, and renounce wine and alcohol. He would follow his masters on horseback and receive wages of fifteen hundred francs. One additional obligation: "In the interest of our security, he should maintain the greatest respect for us (especially in the presence of strangers). Of course he will take a back seat at all times, and when we are in the field he will sleep at the door of our tent."[19] Thus, curiously enough, this anti-bourgeois had a highly bourgeois conception of the relations between masters and servants. In any case, he had always considered equality an absurd principle. Everyone should stay in his place in society—the intellectual, the creator, at the top of the ladder; the worker, the clerk, the servant at the bottom. That didn't exclude mutual respect and even liking. In the end, it was Maxime who turned up the ideal servant. A certain Sassetti, "a splendid lad, Corsican, a former dragoon, who has already been to Egypt and seems to be a cunning rascal."[20] In the meantime, Maxime was getting together with a photographer to learn from him the rudiments of a trade that was still very new at the time. He meant tobring back photographs of his journey to illustrate the text of his recollections. Suddenly, on September 12, he received an imperious summons from Gustave: "I have just finished *Saint Antoine.* Come!"

The next day Maxime was in Croisset, where he found Louis Bouilhet, who had also been advised of the event. Flaubert needed their sincere opinions as to whether or not he should publish this work with which, for his part, he was highly satisfied. The reading was to last for four days, eight hours a day, each day divided into two sessions: from noon to four o'clock and from eight to midnight. Maxime and Louis promised to keep silent throughout the reading and to give their views only at the end. Before beginning, Gustave, tapping his thick manuscript (five hundred pages), cried in great excitement: "If you don't roar with enthusiasm, it will be because nothing is capable of moving you!" But after the first few pages,

Travel and Travel Plans

Maxime and Louis exchanged despairing glances. The monotonous text, in which expansive flights of lyricism substituted for action, struck them as totally uninteresting. The sentences were beautiful, the intention ambitious, and the result a crushing bore. There was no end to Saint Anthony's visions. To think that Gustave had worked for nearly three years on this big, overblown thing! After each session Mme. Flaubert would ask the two friends what they thought of her son's work. Embarrassed, they avoided answering. In the end, they took counsel together and decided to pronounce a stern verdict. When Flaubert, having finished the final reading, said, "Now for the three of us—tell me frankly what you think," the pitiless answer struck him to the heart: "We think you should throw it in the fire and never speak of it again." Flaubert shuddered under the blow and uttered a terrible cry. They had just torn from him a pound of flesh. Pitifully, he tried to argue, to defend his work. But the two judges were unshakable. Few were the pages that stood up to their criticism. In the end, they advised their stricken friend to turn his back on romanticism and attack a down-to-earth subject, as in Balzac's *Cousine Bette* or *Cousin Pons*, without rambling and digressing. "It won't be easy, but I'll try," mumbled Flaubert. They went on talking until eight o'clock in the morning. At that point the door opened and Mme. Flaubert appeared, wearing her usual black dress. She had come to hear the news. Her son informed her of the catastrophe. She had a strong reaction and shot a vengeful look at Maxime Du Camp and Louis Bouilhet. They sensed that she would never forgive them for having wounded Gustave. Then the three friends went out into the garden. Sitting on a bench, they continued to talk about the unfortunate *Saint Antoine*. Maxime and Louis tried to cheer Gustave up. They felt like two nurses at a patient's bedside. Suddenly Louis said, "Why not write the story of Delaunay?" Gustave raised his head, a gleam of joy came into his eyes, and he exclaimed, "What a good idea!"[21]

Maxime Du Camp was mistaken when he gave the name of Delaunay in his *Souvenirs littéraires*. In fact, he was referring to Eugène Delamare, an *officier de santé* who had been a student of Dr.

Flaubert's.* He had married a woman older than himself and after she died had remarried one Delphine Couturier, a young woman who was both a nymphomaniac and a compulsive spendthrift. She had deceived him, contracted debts behind his back, and finally committed suicide, leaving behind a little girl. A few months later, he too had died. The Delamares lived in the village of Ry, in the Rouen region. Their pitiful story was known throughout the surrounding area. By referring to it after hearing *La Tentation de Saint Antoine*, Louis Bouilhet reawakened Gustave's interest in an ordinary domestic tragedy. But it was only a spark. The fire didn't catch. Flaubert had no intention of immediately throwing himself into a novel of provincial life as he was advised to do. He felt that the failure he had just had called into question his whole future as a writer. What was the point in slaving to cover page after page with ink if he was incapable of constructing a work of quality? He was too devoted to excellence in literature to accept an approximation. Right now, the only thing he was counting on to help him get over his mortification was the expedition to the Middle East. Perhaps when he was removed from his usual surroundings he would regain the desire to write. He hoped so, but he was weary, disoriented, and besides, it grieved him to have to leave his mother. A bad writer and a bad son, he condemned himself across the board. It was in this frame of mind that he packed his bags. His mother was weeping. His heart was heavy. And yet he would not have given up the journey for anything in the world. Now it represented an unlooked-for opportunity to escape from himself.

* At this time in France the *officier de santé* was a licensed medical man who was not, however, a full-fledged M.D. and whose practice was subject to certain restrictions. The category was abolished in 1892. —Trans.

Chapter 10

THE MIDDLE EAST

If Flaubert was an incorrigible dreamer, Maxime Du Camp had practical sense for two. In order that they might enjoy official protection during their journey, he arranged for the government to charge each of them with a mission. He would carry out scientific research and photographic work for the Ministry of Education, while Flaubert would gather information for the Ministry of Agriculture and Commerce in ports and in stopping points along the caravan routes. Of course, even though their activities were approved in high places, they would not be remunerated. While Du Camp was determined to keep his word and bring back complete documentation on the countries they traveled through, Flaubert had no intention of sending the least report to the authorities.

Flaubert left Croisset on October 22, 1849, took his mother to Nogent, where she was to stay with friends, and, having settled her there, departed for Paris. Their farewells were heartbreaking. They couldn't tear themselves away from each other. Once again, Flaubert felt guilty in the presence of this statue of sorrow. "My mother was sitting in an armchair before the fire," he recalled afterward. "As I was caressing her and talking to her, I suddenly kissed her on the forehead, rushed for the door, seized my hat in the dining room, and ran out of the house. How she screamed when I closed the door of the living room behind me! It reminded me of the cry she uttered at the moment my father died, when she took his hand."[1]

At the station in Nogent he saw a priest and four nuns, which he thought a bad omen. In the train bringing him to Paris, as he was alone in the compartment, he let himself go and burst into sobs, with a handkerchief pressed against his lips. At every stop he wondered whether he shouldn't jump down onto the platform and return to his mother's side. She was so kind, so gentle, so understanding! She had not hesitated to disburse Fr 27,500 so that he might satisfy his whim to visit the Orient. Since the time he was a child, she had been at the center of his life, protecting him, nourishing him, warming him. And his only thanks were to flee as if he were fed up with her company. Overwhelmed with remorse, he drank four small glasses of rum at the Montereau station to numb his mind. In Paris he dragged himself to Maxime's apartment and grew even more upset on finding his friend was not home. When Maxime returned later in the evening, he found Flaubert lying on the floor in front of the fire. He thought he was asleep, came near, bent down, and heard stifled sobs. "I shall never see my mother again!" Flaubert blurted out. "I shall never see my own country again! This journey is too long, too far; it's tempting fate! What madness! Why are we going?"[2] Maxime, in a panic at this last-minute loss of nerve, gave him a good talking-to and finally convinced him. In the days that followed they said good-bye to their friends and the last night dined with Louis Bouilhet, Louis de Cormenin, and the critic and poet Théophile Gautier in one of the private rooms at Les Trois Frères Provençaux in the Palais-Royal. They talked about literature, art, and archaeology, and in the noisy, cordial atmosphere Flaubert somewhat forgot his apprehensions.

The next day, October 29, 1849, he informed his mother: "Everything is ready, we are leaving. The weather is fine; I am more gay than sad, more serene than apprehensive. The sun is shining, my heart is full of hope." That same day the two friends climbed into the stagecoach—there was as yet no train to the south—and prepared for an extraordinary adventure. From Lyons, Flaubert sent another letter to his "poor old darling," as he called her tenderly: "It feels like ten years since we saw each other."[3] Henceforth he would make it a rule to write to her almost every day—the way he had once written Louise Colet. He had a confused sense that he could never repay the debt of gratitude he owed her. In Marseilles he was seized again by the memory of Eulalie Foucaud and hung about in front of the hotel where long ago he had known his first hours of happiness in the arms of a woman. The hotel was still closed. In the street, a stream of indifferent faces passed. It almost made him doubt his memory.

On Sunday, November 4, at eight in the morning they boarded the packet *Le Nil*. Flaubert noticed from the outset that he was a good sailor. While Maxime and the servant Sassetti were both seasick, he remained cheerfully untroubled by the rolling of the ship. "I don't know what it is about me, but I am adored on board," he wrote his mother. "The watery element is so flattering to my physiognomy, it seems, that these gentlemen [the crew] call me Papa Flaubert. You see, my poor old dear, that things are off to a good start."[4] On November 15 the travelers arrived in Alexandria. "We landed amid the most deafening uproar imaginable," wrote Flaubert. "Negroes, Negresses, camels, turbans, cudgelings to right and left, and ear-splitting guttural cries. I gulped down a whole bellyful of colors, like a donkey filling himself with hay. . . . Except for those of the lowest class, all the women are veiled, and on their noses they wear ornaments that hang down and sway from side to side as on a horse's headband. On the other hand, if you don't see their faces, you see the bosoms of all of them."[5]

The two friends paid an official call on Suliman Pasha, "the most powerful man in Egypt," and another on Artin Bey, the Minister of Foreign Affairs, both of whom welcomed them with oriental graciousness, promised them their assistance, and offered them a carriage and horses to continue their journey. They took part in hunting expeditions, loafed about the streets, made purchases in the bazaars, visited the mosques, and went to the Turkish baths, where, overcome by the suffocating steam, they thought they were about to be embalmed.

In Cairo, Flaubert and Du Camp adopted the local costume. "As for my lordship, I am wearing a big Nubian shirt of white cotton, trimmed with pom-poms and of a cut it would take too long to describe," Flaubert wrote Louis Bouilhet. "My head is completely shaved except for one lock at the back (by which Mahomet is to lift me up on Judgment Day) and covered with a tarboosh which is of a screaming red and made me scream with the heat the first days I wore it. We look quite the pair of Orientals—Max especially is marvelous when he smokes his hookah and fingers his beads."[6]

At last they reached the pyramids: "That is where the desert begins," Flaubert reported. "I couldn't resist, I put my horse into a gallop, Maxime did the same, and I arrived at the foot of the Sphinx. When we saw that . . . my head spun for a moment and my companion went as white as the paper I'm writing on. At sunset, the Sphinx and the three Pyramids, all rosy, seemed drowned in light; the old monster fixed us with a terrifying stare."[7] They set up the tent for the first time and had dinner. The next morning they climbed the pyramid of Cheops, visited the interior of the fabulous monument, haunted by bats, saw the king's chamber, the queen's chamber. . . . Flaubert was suffocated by this breath of the past. How could one think of a modern novel in the presence of such venerable and mysterious remains? In any case, he was delighted to have acquired the look of an authentic explorer: "The sun has at last decided to darken up my skin, I'm turning antique bronze (which satisfies me), I'm putting on weight (which distresses me), and my beard is growing like a savanna in America."[8] He observed the natives as keenly as the monuments. To his brother Achille he confided his astonishment at all these women who didn't hesitate to expose their breasts so as to mask their faces: "In the countryside, for example, when they see you coming, they take their garment, pull it up over their faces to hide their features, and in so doing uncover what is conventionally called the bust, that is to say, the space between the chin and the navel. Ah, have I seen me some tits! have I seen some! have I seen some! Note: The Egyptian tit is very pointed, shaped like an udder and not at all exciting. But what *is* exciting, mark you, is the camels crossing the bazaars, the mosques with their fountains, the streets full of costumes from every land, the cafés choked with tobacco smoke, and the public squares resounding with the cries of jugglers and clowns. Over all that there floats—or rather, out of all that there emerges—a blazing color that takes hold of you, a singular charm that keeps you staring open-mouthed."[9]

At every opportunity he took notes: "It may be very useful to me somewhere." Curiosity led him to request an interview with the bishop of the orthodox Copts, who received him "with many courtesies." "Coffee was brought and I soon began to ask him questions concerning the Trinity, the Virgin, the Gospels, the Eucharist—all my old erudition of *Saint Antoine* came flooding back to me. It was superb, the blue sky over our heads, the trees, the books spread out, the old fellow ruminating in his beard before answering me, myself sitting cross-legged beside him, gesticulating with my pencil and taking notes, while Hassan stood motionless, translating aloud. . . .* I took profound pleasure in it all. This was truly the old Orient, land of religions and of flowing robes."[10] In the same letter he confessed to his mother that in spite of the thousand fleeting impressions of the journey, he was preoccupied with his future as a writer: "When I ask myself 'What shall I do when I return? What shall I write? What will I be worth then? Where should I live? What path should I follow?' etc., etc., I am full of doubts and indecisions. . . . I shall die at the age of eighty without having formed an opinion about myself, or perhaps without having written anything that showed me what I was capable of. Is *Saint Antoine* good or bad? That, for example, is something I often ask myself. Was it I who was mistaken, or the others?"

After two months in Cairo, Flaubert and his companion decided to sail up the Nile: their vessel was a light cangia painted blue, with two crossed sails. "The Nile is absolutely flat, like a river of oil," Flaubert wrote his mother. "On our left we have the whole Arabian mountain range, which when night falls is violet and azure. On the right, plains, then the desert."[11] But the grandiose landscape didn't prevent his thoughts from turning to France. At times, satiated with picturesque sights, he yearned for the peaceful retreat in Croisset. "Far away, on a river gentler, less ancient than this, I know a white

---

* Hassan was one of the two interpreters hired by the travelers.

house whose shutters are closed now that I am not there. The leafless poplars are shivering in the cold mist and the chunks of ice drifting in the river are being thrown up against the frozen banks. The cows are in the shed, the espaliers are covered with matting, and from the farmhouse chimney smoke rises slowly into the gray sky. I have left behind the long, Louis XIV terrace bordered with lindens, where in summer I stroll in my white dressing gown. In only six weeks now the trees will burgeon out, and every branch will have red buds. Then will come the primroses—yellow, green, pink, rainbow-colored . . . Oh primroses, my pretty ones, drop your seeds carefully, that I may see you when spring comes again!"[12]

At Esna the two friends went to visit the famous courtesan Kuchuk Hanem, who had just come from her bath. She was wearing a tarboosh on her black hair plaited in thin braids, wide pink trousers, and a transparent gauze veil around her torso. "She is a regal-looking creature, large-breasted, fleshy, with slit nostrils, enormous eyes, and magnificent knees; when she danced there were formidable folds of flesh on her stomach," noted Flaubert. She smelled of sweetened turpentine. She perfumed her guests' hands with rose water and drew them into her private apartments. There she performed for them the "Dance of the Bee," which Flaubert found very erotic. (The musicians had been blindfolded to prevent their being aroused by the sight.) Later, Flaubert and Du Camp returned to the courtesan's house and passed the night with her. The party lasted from six o'clock to half past ten, "with fucking during the intermissions." Finally, Flaubert made love with Kuchuk Hanem on a bed of "palm branches." "I sucked her furiously," he wrote. "Her body was covered with sweat, she was tired after dancing, she was cold. I covered her with my fur pelisse and she fell asleep, her fingers in mine. As for me, I scarcely shut my eyes. My night was one long, infinitely intense reverie. . . . Watching that beautiful creature asleep, snoring with her head against my arm, I thought of my nights in Paris brothels—a whole series of old memories came back. . . . At three o'clock I got up to piss in the street—the stars were shining. The sky was clear and immensely distant."[13]

At dawn the two friends bade farewell to the courtesan. Flaubert was very proud of having "fired five shots and sucked three times." And he noted with melancholy: "How flattering it would be to one's pride if on departing one could be sure of leaving a memory behind, sure that she would think of you more than of the others, that you would remain in her heart."[14]

Flaubert and Du Camp spent several months going up the Nile, amusing themselves shooting at pelicans, cranes, and crocodiles. "Lying on our divans and smoking our hookahs, we lived in silence, watching the banks slide by, and when a ruin appeared our *raïs* [captain] would stop the cangia," wrote Flaubert. Du Camp assiduously photographed everything he saw that was of interest. Flaubert, who helped him as best he could, had fingers blackened by silver nitrate from handling the sensitive plates. Both of them were now swarthy and bearded. Gustave had grown stout. On March 11 they reached the first cataract; on March 22, the second. Beyond that point the river was no longer navigable, and they turned back. Flaubert wrote his mother: "From now on we are only going to come closer to you by imperceptible degrees. . . . Sometimes I have a craving to see you that grips me all of a sudden like cramps of tenderness. At night before falling asleep I think of you fondly, and every morning when I wake up, you are the first thing that comes into my mind. . . . I can still see you leaning on your elbow with your chin in your hand, dreaming with your kind, sad air."[15] And also: "You may be weeping at this moment, turning your poor beloved eyes to the map, which means nothing to you but an empty space in which your son is lost. Ah no, come now, I shall return! You cannot be sick, because a strong desire keeps one alive. It will soon be six months since I left; in six months more it won't be long until my return—probably around next January or February."[16]

Back in Cairo on June 27, after visiting the caves of Solomon, the travelers decided to cross the desert on camelback. In the course of the journey a quarrel broke out. The two bottles of drinking water they had brought with them were accidentally broken. While they were perishing of thirst, Flaubert ironically recalled the lemon ices served at the Café Tortoni in Paris. Du Camp, exasperated beyond measure, shut him up. They didn't speak to each other for forty-eight hours. Fortunately, the next day they reached the Nile. The river water seemed the most delicious of drinks, and when their thirst was quenched they were reconciled.

At the beginning of July the two men were back in Alexandria, and at the end of the month in Beirut. Then they traveled to Jerusalem, on horseback, in short stages. "Jerusalem is a charnel house surrounded by ramparts," Flaubert wrote Louis Bouilhet. "Everything in it is rotting, the dead dogs in the streets, the religions in the churches (main theme). There are masses of dung and ruins. The Polish Jew with his foxskin cap glides silently along the dilapidated walls, in the shade of which the drowsy Turkish soldier tells his Mohammedan beads and smokes his cigarettes. The Armenians curse the Greeks, who detest the Latins, who excommunicate the Copts. It's even sadder than it is grotesque."[17] Nevertheless, he thought of Christ and imagined him climbing the Mount of Olives, wearing a blue robe and with beads of sweat on his temples. When he visited the Holy Sepulcher, he was revolted by the commercial exploitation of religion. "Everything possible has been done to make the holy places ridiculous. It's all whorish to the last degree: hypocrisy, cupidity, falsification, impudence, yes: but as for holiness, you can go fuck yourself."[18] He burst out laughing when he saw a big portrait of Louis-Philippe hanging on the wall of the Holy Sepulcher but was touched when a Greek priest blessed a rose and gave it to him: "I thought of the pious souls who would have been enchanted by such a present in such a place, and how wasted it was on me."[19] They also visited Bethlehem, Nazareth, Damascus, Tripoli. . . .

Back in Beirut, Flaubert recognized from unmistakable symptoms that he had contracted syphilis: "I want you to know, dear Sir, that in Beirut I picked up . . . seven chancres, which eventually merged into two, then one," he wrote Louis Bouilhet. "I'm being desperately careful about it. I suspect a Maronite woman of making me this gift, or perhaps it was a little Turkish lady. The Turk or the Christian? Which? Problem! Food for thought! That's an aspect of the 'Eastern Question' *La Revue des deux mondes* doesn't dream of. . . . Last night Maxime discovered, even though it's six weeks since he did any fucking, a double abrasion that looks to me very much like a two-headed chancre. If it is, that makes the third time he's caught the pox since we set out. There's nothing like travel for the health."[20]

He was worried and considered cutting the journey short. Originally he had planned to cross the Syrian desert and push on to the Caspian Sea by way of Baghdad. Suddenly this plan struck him as absurd. Besides, the routes were impassable, infested with bandits, and he was beginning to run out of money. To cap it all, Mme. Flaubert was begging her son to return as soon as possible. She was pining away; she was worn out with waiting. And he himself, confronted with so much splendor and squalor, felt a resurgence of nostalgia and remorse: "If you knew how well I can imagine you waiting for my letters. I see the garden . . . the house . . . you leaning out the window. . . . I hear the sound of the gate latch when the postman comes, and when there is nothing for you, what a sad day you spend!"[21]

In Beirut the two friends took ship for Rhodes. As soon as they arrived they were placed in quarantine, a cholera epidemic having broken out on the island. Once released, they left for Smyrna, then for Constantinople. On November 12 they reached Constantinople, which Flaubert found "as vast as humanity." There he learned of the death of Balzac. "One is always saddened by the death of a man one admires," he wrote Louis Bouilhet. "I had hoped to know him later, hoped he would like me. Yes, he was a talented man, one who had a fantastic understanding of his times. He, who had studied women so well, died as soon as he was married."[22]

A dinner was organized in honor of the travelers by the mother of Baudelaire and his stepfather, General Aupick, the French ambassador to the Sultan's court. During the conversation, Du Camp alluded to the growing reputation in Paris of one Charles Baudelaire. This remark cast a chill over the gathering.* But when dinner was

* Du Camp explains in his *Souvenirs littéraires* that he had been unaware of the family relationship and of the general's aversion to his stepson. —Trans. (FS)

over, Mme. Aupick drew Du Camp aside and asked him in an undertone, "You really think he has talent, the young poet you were speaking of?"

In the meantime, Mme. Flaubert had made a great decision: consumed with impatience, she would go to meet her son in Italy. She announced her intention to Gustave at the same time that she informed him of the marriage of his friend Ernest Chevalier. She would like him too to settle down and take a wife. He had just turned twenty-nine. Wasn't that a reasonable age to start a family? Flaubert answered her with a bitter sneer:

When is the wedding to be, you ask me, apropos of the news of Ernest Chevalier's marriage. When? Never, I hope. As far as a man can answer for what he will do, I reply in the negative. Contact with the world—and I've been rubbing shoulders with it now for fourteen months—makes me feel more and more like returning to my shell. . . . Besides, if I had to say how I feel deep down, and if it didn't sound too presumptuous, I would say: 'Too late, now. I'm too old to change.' When one has lived, as I have, a completely inner life, full of turbulent analyses and repressed enthusiasms, when one has so frequently excited and calmed oneself by turns, and employed all one's youth in learning to manage one's soul, as a horseman manages his horse . . . well, what I mean is, if one hasn't broken one's neck at the outset, chances are one won't break it later. I, too, am 'established,' in that I have found my seat, my center of gravity. . . . For me, marriage would be an apostasy: the very thought terrifies me. . . . Good old Ernest! There he is, married, established—and a magistrate to boot. What a perfect bourgeois and gentleman! How much more than ever he'll be the defender of order, family, property! But then he has followed the normal course. He too was an artist. . . . Now I'm sure that down where he is [in Grenoble] he's thundering against Socialist doctrines. . . . As a magistrate, he is reactionary; married, he'll be a cuckold; and so, spending his life between his female and his children on the one hand, and the turpi-tudes of his profession on the other, there he will be, the perfect example of the man who has managed to attain every-thing life has to offer. Phew! Let's talk about something else.[23]

When he reached Athens, he returned to this subject that was so important to him, this time in a letter to Louis Bouilhet: "Let us hope that in spite of your predictions, the trip to Italy will not inspire me to wed. Can you see the family, the warm atmosphere, in which the young person is growing up who is to be my spouse? Mme. Gustave Flaubert! Is it possible? No, I am not yet such a scoundrel as that."[24] As was his habit, he visited the brothels and made love with prostitutes. However, he gave up the idea of sleeping with a very pretty creature of sixteen, who asked to examine his penis first to make sure he wasn't sick. "Well! Since I still have an induration at the base of my prick and was afraid she would notice it, I played the respectable gentleman and jumped down from the bed crying out that she was insulting me. . . ."[25] In another letter, to his mother, he said he was "in an Olympian state": "What men those Greeks were! What artists! The sight of the Parthenon is one of the things that have moved me most deeply in my life. People can say what they please, Art is not a lie. Let the bourgeois be happy, I don't envy them their stodgy felicity."[26]

At the beginning of 1851, when he was leaving for the Pelo-ponnese, he wrote his mother that they would soon be reunited and warned her that she would find him considerably changed. His illness had made him lose much of his hair; he had gained weight; he wore a beard. But he promised to shave it off as soon as he reached Naples: "Two years from now, I shall be completely bald. . . . You will find me if not taller, at least fatter. When I look at myself in the mirror, it seems to me that I should have trouble turning around."[27]

At last the two friends left Greece for the south of Italy. In Naples, Flaubert kept his word and sacrificed his beard: "My poor beard, bathed in the Nile, blown by desert winds, long perfumed by the smoke of *tombac* [tobacco]! Underneath it I discovered a face enormously fatter than before. I am disgusting. I have a double chin and jowls."[28] As soon as they had landed, he visited the museums and went into ecstasies before the canvases of the masters. In Rome too they were enchanted. Indefatigable tourists, Gustave and Maxime could hardly contain their enthusiasm amid the ruins, paintings, statues. At the Corsini Palace, before a Virgin by Murillo, Flaubert had the impression that it was Elisa Schlésinger who had served as the model. "I have seen a *Virgin* by Murillo that haunts me like a perpetual hallucination," he wrote Louis Bouilhet.[29] And a few weeks later, again to Bouilhet: "I am in love with Murillo's *Virgin* in the Corsini Gallery. Her face follows me everywhere and her eyes pass before me again and again like two dancing lanterns."[30]

Still obsessed by the memory of Elisa Schlésinger, he experienced a violent emotion one day as he was leaving the Church of Saint-Paul-Outside-the-Walls. Suddenly he saw coming toward him a woman in a red bodice who was leaning on the arm of an older maidservant. The stranger was very beautiful, very pale, with black eyebrows: "A sudden frenzy struck me like a lightning bolt in the belly. I wanted to bound upon her like a tiger, I was stunned." He noted further: "The whites of her eyes were very particular. It was as if she had just awakened, as if she had come from another world, and yet her look was calm, calm! Her pupils of a brilliant black, so sharply defined that they seemed almost to be in relief, looked at you serenely. . . . A rounded chin, the corners of the mouth slightly downturned, with a bit of bluish mustache, the face as a whole round. . . . I shall never see her again!"[31]

This anonymous passerby was a revelation of his feminine ideal. A fiery brunette with black eyes and a light shadow above her lips. A mixture of Elisa Schlésinger and Eulalie Foucaud! And suddenly the enthusiastic patron of whorehouses was overwhelmed by a celestial vision. Always this contradiction between the crude appetites of the flesh and the seraphic aspirations of the soul. Always this shuttling between the low and the high, between the gutter and the radiant heavens, between the reality and the dream. What a pity that this woman was not destined for him! He would never even know her name. Already their paths, which had crossed for a moment, were separating forever. And Flaubert sighed: "I immediately wanted to ask her father for her hand in marriage."

One compensation: a few days later he was reunited with his mother, who had come to meet him in Rome as agreed. She had aged, grown thinner, and was suffering from furunculosis—doubtless the consequence of anxiety during the absence of her son. But now she was relieved. He stood there before her, tanned, laughing, vigorous. True, he had grown stout, he had lost a lot of hair, his eyes seemed smaller in his puffy face. No matter. She had him back. She would not let go of him again. Together they visited Florence and Venice—the journey of filial affection after the journey of friendship. Maxime Du Camp left them alone and returned to Paris. In any event, relations between the two men had cooled during the last weeks of their Eastern expedition. Living side by side, they had come to know each other better. Du Camp now saw Flaubert as merely an impetuous, undisciplined amateur, while Flaubert had discovered in Du Camp a careerist for whom literature was only a means of advancing himself in the world. A fraternal partnership was on the point of breaking up. Luckily, Mme. Flaubert was there beside Gustave to replace the faltering friend.

In June 1851 mother and son were back in Croisset. After twenty-one months away, Gustave was happy to return to the verdant countryside, the calm river under his windows, his study and his books. Having left with the idea of plunging into a romantic Orient, in the manner of Byron or Victor Hugo, he came back fascinated by a reality that was ragged and barbarous. He could not forget the mixture of filth and splendor, of squalor and insolent luxury. Basically, what had interested him during all his adventurous wanderings was not so much the landscapes as the faces, not so much the monuments as the crowds. He was increasingly drawn to his fellow creatures; his heart swelled with a despairing compassion for the pitiful fate of mankind.

He expressed his feelings in a letter to Louise Colet. He had hardly thought of her during the journey. But back in France, he found it natural to resume his old habit of writing to her. After holding out in resentment for a time, she answered him. She even

dared to come to Croisset to see him. The nerve of it! He refused
to receive her and had a servant ask her where she was staying in
Rouen. Then he appeared himself before the garden gate. Louise
hardly recognized him: "As for his person, it seemed very strange
to me under its Chinese get-up," she wrote. "Wide trousers, loose
cotton shirt, yellow silk necktie shot with gold and silver threads,
long, drooping mustache. His hair has grown thin and his forehead
slightly wrinkled, although he is only thirty. His eyes no longer
have that nervous movement of the old days."

He straightaway addressed the young woman, in a haughty tone
that made her heart sink, "What do you want with me, madame?"

"I want to speak with you," she answered.

"That is really impossible, here."

"Are you sending me away? So you think a visit from me would
dishonor your mother?"

"That's not it at all, but it is impossible here."

Finally she told him that she was staying at the Hôtel d'An-
gleterre in Rouen, and he promised to come to her there. He kept
his word. As soon as he was in her room, she reproached him bitterly
for his heartlessness, and he replied lightly that one must not "disturb ashes, the dust of relics." Then, as she confessed to him that
in desperation she was thinking of marrying Victor Cousin (she had
recently been widowed), he burst out laughing and said, "Marry
the Philosopher, and you and I will see each other!"

Seeing that he was getting ready to leave, she broke into sobs
and cried, "So I shall never, never, be in your arms again?"

"Why not?" he replied. "I told you I would come to see you,
that's certain."

"I kissed him passionately," Louise recounts; "he kissed me
too, but without losing his self-control."[32] She went out to the street
with him. They exchanged furtive kisses. Each time they stopped,
he murmured, "We must part." And she begged, "Just to the next
streetlight." Finally a longer embrace and they promised to meet
again.

A month later Flaubert wrote to her: "You must have found
me very cold the other day in Rouen. But I was as warm as it was

possible for me to be. I made every effort to be kind. Tender, no: that would have been disgracefully hypocritical, an insult to your honesty. . . . I love your company when it is not stormy. The tempests one enjoys in one's youth are tiresome in maturity. . . . I will see you soon in Paris, if you are there."[33]

So Louise knew where she stood. If she wanted to keep Gustave, she had to agree to resuming the old modus vivendi. Visits to Croisset prohibited. Brief encounters in Paris. And extensive exchanges of correspondence. Once again Mme. Flaubert triumphed. Her son preferred her to his mistress. He had returned to his pipe and slippers. He would never permit a female intruder to disturb the peace of Croisset. The truth was that he needed two women in his life. One to pamper him, fuss over him, adore him; the other to amuse him, at long intervals, with a trifling love affair.

It seemed to him at this point that he had turned an important corner in his career. He was nearing thirty. In spite of that wretched syphilis and the mercury treatment that was making his hair fall out, he was in full possession of his powers. To be sure, he had not yet published anything, with the exception of two little pieces in *Le Colibri* when he was fifteen. And yet—whether it was overweening pride or a mysterious prescience—he felt more worthy to be called a writer than most of the men who could lean on a pile of books with their names printed in big letters on the cover.

Chapter 11

MADAME BOVARY

By September Flaubert had made his decision: it would be the story of the adulterous woman. He wrote to Louise Colet: "Last night I began my novel. Now I foresee terrifying difficulties of style. It's no easy business to be simple. I'm afraid of lapsing into the sort of thing that Paul de Kock does or of producing a kind of Chateaubriandized Balzac."[1]* And he noted on his manuscript that he had started work on his name-day, St. Gustave's Day, September 19, 1851. He had hardly written a few lines when he had to stop to go to London with his mother and niece: they wanted to engage an English governess for Caroline, who was now five and a half. They took advantage of the trip to visit the Great Exhibition at the Crystal Palace—the first world's fair—and to call on Harriet Collier.

When they returned to Croisset, Flaubert went back to work with the feeling that he was laboring over a tedious school assignment. Now that he was struggling with a modern, realistic, everyday subject, he looked back with regret on the sumptuous extravagances of his *Saint Antoine*—especially because Maxime Du Camp wanted to publish excerpts from that work in *La Revue de Paris,* which he

* Paul de Kock (1793–1871) was a prolific and enormously popular author of racy novels and plays dealing with bourgeois life. According to *The Oxford Companion to French Literature,* these works were "written with an untiring comic vigour which made up for their complete lack of style." —Trans.

111

had founded with Louis de Cormenin, Arsène Houssaye, and Théophile Gautier. Before coming to a decision, Flaubert consulted his beloved Louis Bouilhet. Together they reread the most important pages of *Saint Antoine*. Bouilhet remained skeptical, declaring that the author had put into the text "all his defects and only a few of his good qualities."

"As for me," Flaubert wrote Du Camp, "I don't know what to think. My position is exactly in the middle. . . . If I do publish, it will be for the stupidest reason in the world—because I am told to, because I am emulating or obeying others, not from any initiative of my own. I feel neither the need nor the desire to publish. . . . The idiot who goes to a duel because his friends urge him to and tell him that he must, even though he himself has no desire to go and thinks it stupid, etc., is, at bottom, much more contemptible than the self-confessed coward who swallows the insult without even noticing it and stays calmly at home." He was disgusted with the world and analyzed his feelings as follows:

My youth (you knew only its latter phase) steeped me in an opiate of boredom, sufficient for the remainder of my days. I hate life. There: I have said it; I'll not take it back. Yes, life; and everything that reminds me that life must be borne. It bores me to eat, to dress, to stand on my feet, etc. . . . Do you think it has been out of mere perversity, without long deliberation, that I have lived to the age of thirty in this way you scold me for? Why have I not had a mistress? Why have I preached chastity? Why have I stayed in this provincial backwater? Do you think I don't have erections like other men, and that I wouldn't enjoy cutting a fine figure in Paris? . . . I am no more cut out for that sort of thing than to be a fine waltzer. Few men have had fewer women than I . . . and if I remain unpublished, that will be the punishment for all my youthful dreams of glory. Must one not follow one's own path? If I find it repugnant to move about, maybe I am right not to. Sometimes I even think it wrong of me to want to write a rational book, instead of letting myself indulge in all the lyricism, all the bombast, all the fantastic philosophical extravagance that might enter my head.[2]

Notwithstanding his aversion to composing this "rational book," he kept to a strict schedule in which writing occupied an important place. His study became a refuge from the assaults of life and at the same time a torture chamber from which he had no wish to escape. There he passed hours of excitement, of suffering, and of tenacious, obsessive labor. He loved the spacious room with its five windows, three giving on the garden and two on the river. Bookcases with spiral mahogany columns and shelves crammed with books. Here and there, portraits of friends. A high-backed armchair, a divan for naps or reveries, and a large oak table on which lay scattered sheets of paper, an inkstand in the shape of a toad, and an assortment of goose quills, for the master of these premises despised steel pens and blotters, which were good only for bank clerks. For art objects, the marble bust of his sister Caroline that had been executed by Pradier after the death mask, and a bronze Buddha. On the floor, a white bearskin. And beyond the walls, silence. In Croisset, all life was organized around the big spoiled child whom Mme. Flaubert refused to see as a grown-up.

Everything had to be quiet in the house until ten o'clock in the morning, for Flaubert, who wrote late into the night, never rose before then. People spoke in hushed voices, they walked on tiptoe, and little Caroline was asked to refrain from noisy games and loud laughter out of respect for her uncle's sleep. Finally he would ring energetically for his servant, who would bring him the mail and the newspapers, place a glass of cold water on his table, give him a pipe filled with tobacco, and open the shutters. After having smoked his first pipe and read a few letters, he would tap on the partition to call his mother. For a long time she would have been waiting for the signal. She would hasten to him, full of love and admiration, and sit down at his bedside for an intimate morning chat. Having lost her husband and daughter, and with her elder son married, she now lived only for her beloved Gustave. At eleven o'clock he would get up, dress, and consume a copious lunch. Seated with him around the table would be his mother, his uncle Parain, Caroline, and her teacher, Juliet Herbert. The food was heavy. Flaubert would eat heartily. After the meal, he would walk up and down on the terrace, under the linden trees, to aid digestion. During this stroll he would think about his novel and watch the boats pass on the Seine. Then he would give his niece a lesson. The governess had orders to teach the child only English. He kept history and geography for himself and took his role very seriously. Having completed this task, he would read until seven in the evening. The second meal at which the family gathered was as rich as the first. After dinner mother and son would again withdraw to converse about one thing and another, until nine or ten o'clock, when Mme. Flaubert would finally retire. It was then that he could devote himself to his painful passion for writing. Everything around him was asleep. The night protected him. Time was abolished. He was alone in the world with his characters in *Madame Bovary*. Riveted to his table, he would sometimes work seven hours at a stretch. The bargemen floating down the Seine would take the light shining in his window as a landmark on the black shore. In the vast silence of the countryside, Flaubert would be struggling with words. "I am finding it very hard to get my novel started," he wrote Louise. "I suffer from stylistic abscesses; sentences keep itching without coming to a head. I am fretting, scratching. What a heavy oar the pen is. . . ."[3] And again: "I spoil a considerable quantity of paper. So many deletions! Sentences are very slow in coming. What a devilish style I have adopted! A curse on simple subjects! If you knew how I was torturing myself you'd be sorry for me."[4]

Convinced that he had long months of work ahead of him, he did not even rejoice when he received the copies of *La Revue de Paris*, in which Maxime Du Camp had published Louis Bouilhet's long poem *Melaenis*. "The arrival of the copies of *Melaenis* made me sad," he confessed to Louise. "We (Louis Bouilhet and I) spent all of yesterday afternoon in a mood as dark as the back of the fireplace. We felt as if its publication were an act of prostitution, of abandonment, of farewell. . . . I wonder what's the use of my swelling the chorus of mediocrities (or of men of talent, which is synonymous) and fretting about a lot of petty matters which, even before I become involved in them, make me shrug my shoulders with pity. It is splendid to be a great writer, to put men into the frying pan of your words and make them pop like chestnuts. . . . But for that you must have something to say. Now, I will confess to you it seems to me I have nothing to say that everyone else doesn't have, or that hasn't been said equally well, or that can't be said better."[5]

But *Melaenis* was well received by both readers and critics, and Flaubert, while in principle he condemned immediate publication, was happy at his friend's success. There was no jealousy between them, but a warm openness, a manly partnership. "The *sieur* Bouilhet has caught on well," Flaubert noted without irony. "So now there he is, firmly ensconced among the literary tribe."[6]

He was sorry that Bouilhet had decided to leave Rouen and settle in Paris: "He's going to desert me, a decision of which I approve but which doesn't make me too cheerful when I think about it."[7]* He himself went to the capital from time to time to clear his head, to keep in touch with a few friends, and to meet the impetuous Louise. She submitted her manuscripts to him and he dutifully read and edited them for her. He was in Paris at the time of the coup d'état of December 2, 1851, and the repression of the republicans. "Several times I came close to having my head bashed in, without prejudice to the other times when I was almost killed by a saber, a rifle, or a cannon, for there were enough ways it could be arranged to accommodate all tastes. But I also saw perfectly. . . . Providence, which knows my fondness for the picturesque, is always careful to send me to the opening nights, when they're worth attending. This time I got my money's worth. It was a pretty sight."[8]

The political upheavals strengthened his proud determination to remain aloof from the world. It made little difference to him that henceforth France would be governed by a prince-president who would soon transform himself into an emperor. He was too busy

---

* Louis Bouilhet moved to Paris in the fall of 1853.

with his *Bovary* to concern himself with Louis Napoleon. In January 1852, when Maxime Du Camp was promoted to the rank of officer in the Legion of Honor, he burst out laughing and wrote Louise: "Here's news: young Du Camp has been made an officer in the Legion of Honor! How pleased he must be! When he compares himself with me and surveys the distance he has traveled since he left me, he must certainly think that I am far behind and that he has done very well for himself (outwardly). One day you'll see him land a position and leave good old literature flat. Everything is mixed up in his head: women, decorations, art, boots—they all swirl around at the same level, and so long as something advances his career, it's important."[9] Chained to his *Bovary* like a convict to a millstone, he sometimes wondered if he wasn't wrong to attach so much importance to the construction of a chapter, the rhythm of a sentence. "When all is said and done, Art is perhaps no more serious than a game of ninepins," he told himself. "Perhaps it's all nothing but a huge joke."[10] But he soon pulled himself together and exclaimed:

I have made progress in esthetics, or at least I have settled more firmly into the position I adopted early on. *I know how it must be done.* Oh Lord! if I wrote in the style I have in mind, what a writer I would be! . . . There are in me, literarily speaking, two distinct persons: one who is infatuated with bombast, lyricism, eagle flights, sonorities of phrase, and lofty ideas; and another who digs and burrows into the truth as deeply as he can, who likes to evoke a small fact as powerfully as a big one, who would like to make you feel almost *physically* the things he reproduces. . . . What seems beautiful to me, what I should like to write, is a book about nothing, a book dependent on nothing external, which would be held together by the internal strength of its style. . . . The finest works are those that contain the least matter; the closer expression comes to thought, the closer language comes to coinciding and merging with it, the finer the result. . . . That is why there are neither beautiful subjects nor ugly subjects. . . .[11]

His search for formal perfection set his nerves on edge. In letter after letter he complained to Louise: "Bad week. Work didn't go well; I had reached a point where I hardly knew what to say. . . . I made outlines, spoiled a lot of paper, floundered and fumbled. . . . Oh, what a rascally thing style is! I think you have no idea of the sort of book this is. I'm trying to be as buttoned up in this one as I was slovenly in the others and to follow a geometrically straight line. No lyricism, no commentaries, author's personality absent. It will make depressing reading. There will be atrocious things in it —wretched, sordid things."[12]

When she expressed admiration for his *Saint Antoine,* which she had just read in manuscript, he answered: "I am in an entirely different world now, the world of attentive observation of the most trivial details. My gaze is fixed on the mossy mold that grows in the soul."[13] Or else: "My nerves are as taut as brass wires. . . . Perhaps it's because of my novel. It's not going well. It's not working. I am wearier than if I were pushing mountains ahead of me. There are times when I could weep. It takes a superhuman will to write, and I'm only a man. . . . Ah, with what despair I look up at the mountaintops where I long to stand! Do you know how many pages I have done since I got back? Twenty. Twenty pages in a month, and working at least seven hours a day! And the end of all that? The result? Bitterness, inner humiliation."[14] And again: "Sometimes I don't understand why my arms don't drop from my body with fatigue, why my brain doesn't melt away. I am leading an austere life, stripped of all external pleasure, and am sustained only by a kind of permanent frenzy, which sometimes makes me weep tears of impotence but never abates. I love my work with a love that is frantic and perverted, as an ascetic loves the hair shirt that scratches his belly. Sometimes, when I am empty, when words don't come, when I find I haven't written a single sentence after scribbling whole pages, I collapse on my couch and lie there dazed, bogged down in a swamp of despair, hating myself and blaming myself for this demented pride that makes me pant after a chimera. A quarter of an hour later, everything has changed; my heart is pounding with joy."

He lived so intensely with his characters that when he found the right words to express their feelings, tears came to his eyes: "Last Wednesday I had to get up and fetch my handkerchief; tears were streaming down my face. I had been moved by my own writing: the emotion I had conceived, the phrase that rendered it, and the satisfaction of having found the phrase—all were causing me the most exquisite pleasure." After he had written that phrase, he would read it aloud to himself. He would shout it at the top of his voice to test its music and make sure it contained no awkward combination of sounds. If he encountered the least snag, he would go back to work, scratch out, write between the lines, polish until the words flowed naturally and harmoniously. Then he felt the rare thrill of having his words coincide with his thought. But this pleasure would only last for a few moments. Immediately afterward, he would be seized again by the certainty that he was incapable. "At times I have feelings of great despair and emptiness—doubts that taunt me in the midst of my simplest satisfactions. And yet I would not exchange all this for anything, because my conscience tells me that I am fulfilling my duty, obeying a decree of fate—that I am doing what is Good, that I am in the Right."[15]

Fortunately, Louis Bouilhet, who had not yet left Rouen for Paris, came to see him every Sunday in Croisset and encouraged the convict in his labors. Flaubert would read aloud what he had written during the week, and together they would pick the text apart, line by line. Bouilhet's reaction was generally favorable, and his visits had a tonic effect on Flaubert. Flaubert also drew sustenance from Louise. With the passage of time, she seemed to have settled down. He, for his part, had not changed his conception of the love he bore her. Writing to her on New Year's Eve, he closed with: "Yours, you who love me as a tree loves the wind; yours, you for whom I have in my heart something lasting and sweet, a feeling of tenderness and gratitude which will never perish; yours, poor woman whom I so often cause to weep and whom I would so like to cause to smile."[16] And also: "Yes, I love you, my poor Louise; in any case, I would like your life to be sweet, bordered with sandy paths, flowers, and joys. I love your beautiful face, so kind and open, the pressure of your hand, the touch of your skin under my lips. If I am hard on you, remember that it is only because of the feelings of sadness, of sharp irritability, and of deathly depression that plague and overwhelm me."[17]

When he was tired of living like a hermit, he would go to see her in Paris, stay at the hotel, make love, and leave again in a calmer frame of mind. Now that she was a widow, she was even freer with her expressions of passion. For that matter, she had other lovers besides Flaubert and made no secret of it. He was not in the least jealous. This solution, he thought, protected him from the danger of being monopolized. It was to his convenience to be at a distance from her and to share her. Sometimes, contemptuous as he was of bourgeois customs, he even sent his mistress little gifts: a paperweight, a bottle of sandalwood oil, an Egyptian ring. Back in his lair, he would recall the happy moments he had spent with her, but he was never in a hurry to repeat the experience. The memory of it was enough to sustain him for a few weeks: "A week ago today at this time, I was leaving you, *dripping* with love. How time passes! Yes, we were happy together, poor dear woman, and I love you in every possible way."[18]

While assuring her of his attachment, he repeated over and over that no woman would ever divert him from his work. "Every time the thought of you comes to my mind, it brings sweetness with it," he wrote her. "My trips to Paris, where you are now the only attraction, are like oases in my life, where I go to drink and to shake off the dust of my labor in your lap. . . . If I don't make them more often, it is the part of wisdom, because they disturb me too much. But be patient, later you will have me at greater length. In a year or eighteen months I shall take lodgings in Paris. I shall go more often and spend several months at a time there every year."[19]

From time to time, as in the past, he was afraid she might be pregnant. Would those cursed Redcoats ever make up their minds to land? At the mere idea of unwanted progeny he was seized with horror again: "I am worried about your Redcoats, although I have nothing to reproach myself for (which is something you always reproach me for). That I should have a son! Oh no, no, better to die in a gutter run over by an omnibus! The notion that I might transmit life to another creature makes me roar with infernal rage in the depths of my heart."[20] But luckily, each time it was only a false alarm. And each time, on hearing "the good news," he exploded with joy: "May the god of coitus grant that I never go through such agony again. . . . I was sweating blood while I waited for yours."[21] Once he was reassured, his tenderness for Louise redoubled. He even went so far as to congratulate her—he, the enemy of all literary honors—on having received another prize from the Académie Française. And, as he happened to be in Paris at the time, he was nice enough to attend the solemn meeting of the Académie at which the awards were distributed. Drumrolls, green uniforms, polite congratulations. This official performance delighted him for the sake of his mistress, who seemed thrilled with it, but convinced him even more that he must shun such things if he wanted to preserve his greatness.

Maxime Du Camp made the mistake of insisting that he should at last enter the arena of men of letters. Flaubert was furious and replied with a haughty clarification of his position:

> It seems to me that where I am concerned you suffer from a tic, or an incurable lack of comprehension that vitiates your judgment. . . . I have long since made up my mind on the matters you mention. I shall merely tell you that all the words you use—"hurry," "this is the moment," "it is high time," "your place will be taken," "become established," "inadmissible"—are for me a vocabulary devoid of sense. It's as if you were talking to an Algonquin. No understand. "Get somewhere"—where? To the position of MM. Murger, Feuillet, Monselet, etc., etc., etc., Arsène Houssaye, Taxile Delord, Hippolyte Ducas, and six dozen others?* No thanks. "To be known" is not my chief concern: that can give com-

---

* With the possible exception of Henri Murger, who is chiefly remembered for his charming *Scènes de la vie de bohème*, on which the libretto of Puccini's opera is based, the writers mentioned have sunk into obscurity. —Trans.

plete gratification only to very mediocre vanities. Besides, is there ever any certainty about this? Even the greatest fame leaves one longing for more, and seldom does anyone but a fool die sure of his reputation. Fame, therefore, can no more serve you as a gauge of your own worth than obscurity. I am aiming at something better—to please myself. Success seems to me a result, not the goal. . . . May I die like a dog rather than hurry by a single second a sentence that isn't ripe! I have conceived a manner of writing and a nobility of language that I want to attain. When I think that I have harvested my fruit I shan't refuse to sell it, nor shall I forbid hand-clapping if it is good. In the meantime I do not wish to fleece the public. That's all there is to it. . . . You tell me that it is only in Paris that one breathes "the breath of life." In my opinion your Parisian "breath of life" often has the odor of rotten teeth. In that Parnassus to which you invite me, one is visited more often by a miasma than by divine madness, and you will agree that the laurels gathered there are apt to be somewhat spattered with shit. . . . And there is unquestionably one thing that you do acquire in Paris—and that is impertinence; but at the cost of losing a bit of your lion's mane. . . . I told you I shall move to Paris when my book is done and that I shall publish it if I am satisfied with it. My resolution has not changed in the slightest. That is all I can say, and nothing more. And believe me, my friend, you would do well not to fret about me. As for the waxing and waning of literary quarrels, I don't give a damn.[22]

On receiving this letter, Du Camp climbed on his high horse and retorted that he did not understand these remonstrances and was hurt by them. Flaubert sensed that relations between them would never again be as affectionate and sincere as in the past. Nevertheless, he stuck to his guns. "It pains me to see you so sensitive," he wrote his friend.

But why begin the same old story all over again? Are you forever going to preach diet to a man who insists he is in good health? . . . Do I reproach you for living in Paris, for having published, etc.? . . . Have I ever advised you to lead a life like mine? . . . As for *my post* as a man of letters, I gladly relinquish it to you. . . . I am simply a bourgeois living retired in the country, occupying myself with literature and asking nothing of others, neither consideration nor honor nor even esteem. . . . You and I are no longer following the same road; we are no longer sailing in the same skiff. May God lead each of us to where he wants to go! As for me, I am not seeking port but the high seas. If I am shipwrecked, I absolve you from mourning.[23]

Having sent his friend these angry pages, he justified himself to Louise: "I am a very peaceable fellow up to a certain point—up to a certain frontier (that of my freedom), which no one is to pass. So, since he chose to trespass on my most personal territory, I knocked him back into his corner. . . . I am a Barbarian: I have the apathetic muscles of a Barbarian, the moodiness, the green eyes, and the tall stature; but I also have the élan, the stubbornness, the irascibility. All of us Normans have a little cider in our veins: it's a bitter, fermented drink that sometimes bursts the bung." And once launched on this self-analysis, he continued with evident satisfaction:

If, so far as sexual matters are concerned, I am so restrained, it is because early on I went through a period of debauchery that was beyond my age—deliberately, in order to find out. There are few women whom, mentally at least, I have not undressed from head to toe. I have worked flesh like an artist and I know what it is. I assure you I can write books capable of bringing the coldest readers into rut. As for love, all my life it has been my great subject for reflection. Whatever thought I didn't give to pure art, to the craft itself, I have put into that; and the heart I studied was my own. How many times, in my best moments, have I felt the cold steel of the scalpel entering my flesh! From this point of view, *Bovary*

will represent—to a certain extent, to the bourgeois extent,
to the extent that I have been able to make it so (in order for
it to be more universal, more human)—the sum total of my
knowledge of psychology, and that will be its only originality.[24]

At the time Flaubert wrote her this letter, Louise was carrying
on a heavy flirtation with Alfred de Musset. But one evening the
poet, drunk as usual, tried to take advantage of her in a carriage.
She repulsed him, opened the door, jumped out of the moving cab
onto the road, and hurt her knee. The scene took place on the Place
de la Concorde. Revolted and humiliated, Louise limped home and
wrote to Flaubert recounting her misadventure. For some time already, he had been warning her about her infatuation with "the
sieur de Musset." This time, in spite of his usual broad-mindedness,
he discovered that he was jealous: "I feel the need to bash him over
the head. . . . I could cudgel him with pleasure. . . . Oh, how I
wish he would come back and you would throw him the hell out in
front of thirty people. . . . If he writes you again, answer him with
a colossal letter of five lines: 'Why do I want none of you? Because
you disgust me and because you are a coward.' Farewell. I embrace
you, I press you in my arms, I kiss you all over. Yours, yours, my
poor outraged love."[25]
The Musset affair was soon forgotten in the midst of the torments of writing. Flaubert's true mistress was not Louise Colet but
Emma Bovary. For purposes of his novel, on July 18 he went to
the agricultural show in Grand-Couronne. He came back sick with
fatigue, boredom, and disgust over the "idiotic rustic ceremony."
But he had caught on the wing a thousand details that would be
useful to him when he composed his chapter. The drafting advanced
slowly. "A good prose sentence should be like a good line of
poetry—*unchangeable*, just as rhythmic, just as sonorous," he wrote
Louise.[26] And again: "The books that I most aspire to write are
precisely those for which I am least equipped. In this sense, *Bovary*
will have been an unprecedented tour de force (a fact that only I
will ever be aware of). The subject, character, effects, etc., are all

alien to me. . . . Writing this book, I am like a man playing the piano with lead balls attached to his knuckles."[27] Or again: "If my book is good, it will gently caress many a feminine wound. More than one woman will smile as she recognizes herself in it. Yes, I will have known your sorrow, poor unsung souls, and the secret melancholy you exude, like the dampness on the moss-covered walls of your provincial backyards."[28] And also: "What trouble my *Bovary* is giving me! Still, I am beginning to see my way a little. Never in my life have I written anything more difficult than what I am doing now—trivial dialogue. This inn scene may take me three months, I can't tell. . . . But I'll die rather than botch it."[29]

Guessing how his work was weighing on him, Louise urged him to come to Paris or to Mantes, but he resisted with obstinacy and irritation: "Don't keep repeating that you desire me, don't tell me all these things that distress me. What's the use? . . . since I can't work any other way. . . . Don't you think that I want you too, that I often grow weary too of such a long separation? But I assure you that a physical disruption of three days makes me lose two weeks, that I have all the trouble in the world to collect my thoughts afterward, and that if I have made this decision that vexes you, it is on the basis of unfailing and repeated experience."[30] Nevertheless, at the beginning of November 1852, he couldn't wait any longer and invited Louise to join him in Mantes. Their meeting was not so passionate as anticipated: "Your poor 'force of nature' was not gay yesterday. . . . Life is spent this way, in tying and untying strings, in separations, farewells, moments of suffocation and of desire. Yes, it was good, very good and very sweet. It is age that does that. As one grows older one becomes more serious in moments of joy, which makes them all the sweeter."[31]

It was with the feeling that he had lost six long days that Flaubert came back to his retreat, where Emma Bovary was waiting for him. And the work seized him again, like a malady that consumed him but also brought him ineffable delights. When he compared his concern for the perfection of psychology and style with the kind of false facility of a Maxime Du Camp, he said to himself that, decidedly, they did not have the same conception of literature, they were not plying the same trade. He was disgusted with his friend's latest novel, *Le Livre posthume*, which he found utterly insipid. "Pitiful, isn't it?" he wrote Louise. "It seems to me that our friend is ruining himself. Reading the book one feels he is completely played out. He is wagering all he has left and blowing his last note."[32] He himself lived in fear that he might not have the physical strength necessary to create the exceptional work he envisaged. He was again seized with nervous attacks. On December 1, 1852, he confided his terrible anxiety to Louise: "Every time I moved (literally), my brain throbbed in my skull, and I had to go to bed at eleven o'clock. I was feverish and completely despondent. . . . I also had a superstitious thought: tomorrow I shall be thirty-one. I have just passed that fatal thirtieth year which classifies a man. That is the age at which he assumes his future shape, takes his place in society, gets married, embraces a profession." In spite of his apprehensions, he was proud that he had remained free: "My style and my muscles are still supple; and if the hair is gone from my brow, I think there is still many a plume in my mane. . . . My flesh loves your flesh, and when I see myself naked it seems to me that every pore of my skin is yearning for you . . ."[33] While he was working, he was so tense that when his mother entered his study unexpectedly he uttered a cry of terror: "My heart pounded for a long time, and it took me a quarter of an hour to get over it. That's how absorbed I am when I am working. When I was surprised like that I felt a sharp sensation as if a dagger had been struck into my soul. What a poor machine is ours!"[34]

Alternating between highs and lows, sometimes he compared his novel to a "ratatouille"; sometimes he said he thought it was "going to work." He immediately added, however: "But I am bothered by my tendency to metaphor, decidedly excessive. I am devoured by comparisons as one is by lice, and I spend all my time squashing them. My sentences are crawling with them."[35] The further he advanced in the story, the harder he found it to respect both the psychology of the characters and the harmony of the language. At every moment he discovered an unbridgeable chasm between what he felt and what he expressed, between the thought and the word, between the fluctuating content of the dream and the text that took fixed shape on the paper. In the last days of January 1853 he observed that his book, which would have about "four hundred and fifty pages," was still only half done. But he didn't want to hurry. No one was waiting for it to be published. Not even himself. Suddenly he had a disagreeable surprise: on reading Balzac's *Médecin de campagne,* he discovered that the novel contained scenes identical to the ones described in *Bovary:* a visit to a wet nurse, a first day at school at the beginning of the story, "one sentence the same as one of mine." He panicked: "One would think I had copied it, if it weren't that my page is infinitely better written, no boasting intended."[36] He wondered if it was still possible to say anything new in literature.

In February he noted that his *Bovary* was "jogging along and beginning to take shape." On March 21 he said he was "exhausted from having bellowed all evening while I was writing." Six days later it was a different story: "*Bovary* is not exactly racing along: two pages in a week! Sometimes I'm so discouraged I could jump out a window. . . . Ah, I'll get there, I'll get there, but it will be hard! How the book will turn out I have no idea, but I warrant you it will be written. . . . Trying to say vulgar things simply but not coarsely! It's excruciating!"[37]

In the meantime, Louise had persuaded him to secretly receive letters from Victor Hugo, who was in exile on the isle of Jersey, and forward them to their addressees.* Fearing that the police might discover the subterfuge, he suggested that Hugo send his letters to Harriet Collier in London, who would send them on to France in other envelopes bearing a London postmark. He had retained a particularly tender feeling for this young person, who reminded him of the innocent excitement that had stirred him in Trouville. At long intervals they exchanged letters filled with a sweet nostalgia.

---

* Hugo had gone into exile in 1851 (at first voluntarily but later by imperial decree) to protest the rise to power of Napoleon III and the establishment of the Second Empire. He lived in the Channel Islands until 1870, when he returned to France. —Trans.

But Flaubert was also attracted by his niece's English governess. The rustle of skirts, near his mother, around the house, sent the blood pulsing through his veins. He made no move in that direction, but he had fantasies.

In any case, he felt that from the physical point of view he had frightfully deteriorated. He suffered from toothaches. "I am aging," he wrote Louise on March 31, 1853. "There go the teeth, and the hair will soon be gone too. Well, so long as one keeps one's brain: that's the main thing. How the process of annihilation takes over in us! Scarcely are we born when decay sets in, so that life is nothing but a long battle it wages against us, ever more triumphantly until the end—death. . . . There are mornings when I frighten myself, I look so wrinkled and worn." He lost a molar and another was threatened by an abscess. He had it pulled. The glands in his neck swelled. He had agonizing pains in the cerebellum. He could feel the blood throbbing in his head. In spite of his sufferings, he forced himself to go on with his novel according to the same strict schedule. When he had a sufficient pile of pages under his elbow, he would read a few chapters aloud—or, rather, spew them out, as he put it—for Louis Bouilhet of a Sunday. On June 28, 1853, at one o'clock in the morning, he wrote Louise: "I'm exhausted. My brain is dancing in my skull. I have just spent from ten o'clock last night until now recopying 77 consecutive pages, which now make only 53. It's stupefying. I've kept my head bent for so long that the vertebrae in my neck are broken. How many repetitions of words I have caught! How many *all*'s, *but*'s, *for*'s, *however*'s! . . . But there are some good pages, and I think the whole thing moves along." Soon he began to worry that by editing his manuscript so heavily he had drained all the force out of his style. "This afternoon I finally gave up on corrections, because I could no longer make any sense out of what I was doing. If you concentrate too long on a piece of writing you end up in a daze. . . . You reach a point where your mind's not functioning and then it's more sensible to stop." Still, he was pleased to have removed the "cement" that was "oozing out from between the stones." Now he could turn his attention to the next scene: "I have a fornication coming up that worries me considerably and that I mustn't evade, although I want to make it chaste—that is, literary, without spicy details or lascivious images. . . ."[38]

To thank him for forwarding his correspondence, Victor Hugo sent him his photograph. Flaubert replied effusively: "Since you extend your hand to me across the ocean, I take and grasp it. I grasp it proudly, the hand that wrote *Notre-Dame* and *Napoléon le petit*, the hand that has hewn colossi and fashioned bitter cups for traitors. . . ."[39] And he wrote Louise: "What a beautiful thing *Notre-Dame* is. I reread three chapters of it recently, including the sack of the church by the beggars. That's the sort of thing that's *strong*! I think the greatest characteristic of genius is, above all, *power*."[40] It was that power that he wanted to manifest itself on every page of *Madame Bovary*, but without the least touch of lyricism. He thought that extreme sobriety could be as striking, as evocative for the reader as the outpouring of feelings and the deluge of colors dear to the romantic authors. Convinced that he had chosen the best method of bringing his heroine's story to life, he finally allowed himself a respite from work. After a long visit with Louise, he went to join his mother in Trouville.

He arrived at sunset and was sad to note that the region was now crowded with cottages "in the style of the ones at Enghien," that in the garden of the house where he had used to live with his parents the new proprietor had planted artificial rocks, that everything had changed except the blue-green sea and the smell of salt water and kelp. He thought back to his youth, to Elisa Schlésinger, to Harriet Collier, and wrote Louise: "The memories I encounter here at every step are like pebbles that roll down a gentle slope to a great pit of bitterness I have within me. The mud is stirred up; all sorts of melancholy thoughts, like toads aroused from sleep, stick their heads up out of the water and make a strange music; I listen. Ah, how old I am, how old I am, poor dear Louise! . . . As for *Bovary*, it's impossible even to think about it. I have to be *at home* to write. The freedom of my mind depends on a thousand incidental circumstances that are very trivial but very important."[41]

For diversion, he went to see the ladies who plunged shivering into the sea, under the guidance of swimming instructors with hairy arms. They were separated from the men by signposts and wire netting. Each sex had its own enclosure in which to take the air and splash about in the cold water. "Nothing is more pitiful than these bags in which women encase their bodies, and these oilcloth caps," Flaubert wrote. "What faces! And how they walk! Such feet! Red, scrawny, covered with corns and bunions, deformed by shoes, long as shuttles or wide as washerwomen's paddles. And in the midst of it all, scrofulous brats screaming and crying. Farther off, grandmas knitting and respectable old gentlemen with gold-rimmed spectacles reading newspapers, looking up from time to time between the lines to survey the vastness of the horizon with an air of approval." He was overwhelmed by the ugliness and mediocrity of the human condition. His thoughts turned back to his novel and he shared his conclusions with Louise: "Everything one invents is true, you may be sure. . . . My poor Bovary, without a doubt, is suffering and weeping at this very hour in twenty villages of France."[42]

The hard rain that began to fall made him even more melancholy. Everything was gray—on earth, on the sea, in his soul. Flaubert was lodging with a pharmacist who, like Homais in his novel, "speechified at length and manufactured Seltzer water." "At eight o'clock in the morning, I am often awakened by the noise of the corks going off unexpectedly. Bang! Bang!" he wrote Louis Bouilhet.[43] So it was futile to run away from his *Bovary*: everything brought him back to it. He was convinced that his only salvation lay in writing: "Let us ask of life only an armchair and not a throne, only satisfaction and not intoxication. Passion is not compatible with the long patience demanded by our Craft. Art is vast enough to take complete possession of a man. To divert anything from it is almost a crime. It is stealing something from the Idea, failing to do one's Duty."[44] He was already looking forward joyfully to starting work again: "What an orgy of work I'm going to have when I get back! This vacation will not have been a waste of time. I feel refreshed. . . . I've done a lot of *summing up* here, and this is the conclusion I have come to after these four weeks of idleness: farewell—that is, farewell and forever to everything *personal*, intimate, relative. . . .

Nothing pertaining to myself tempts me as a subject. Youthful attachments . . . no longer seem beautiful to me. Let all those things be dead and never be resuscitated. . . . *Bovary*, which will have been an excellent exercise for me, may prove disastrous for me later because of the reaction it produces, because (this is weak and idiotic) it will have given me a revulsion for subjects laid in an ordinary setting. That's why I'm having so much trouble writing this book."[45]

On Friday, September 2, he was back in Croisset. On taking possession of his study again, he felt as if the familiar objects were welcoming him like so many friends who had missed him during the long separation. "During my absence everything had been brushed, waxed, polished . . . and I confess that I was charmed to return to my rug, my big armchair, and my divan," he immediately wrote Louise. "My lamp is burning. My pens await. So now begins another series of days, days like the others. And now begin the same feelings of melancholy and the same isolated moments of enthusiasm."[46]

Once more he was consumed by his work on *Bovary*. "At last I'm back at it again! It's going forward. The machine is turning again. . . . Nothing is obtained without effort. . . . The pearl is a sickness of the oyster, and style, perhaps, the secretion that flows from a deeper pain."[47] Louis Bouilhet proved a formidable critic. Under pressure from him, Flaubert rewrote three times certain paragraphs that were judged too limp. And his worries piled up. Uncle Parain died: "Another one gone. I can see him now in his winding-sheet as if the coffin in which he is rotting stood on my table before my eyes. I cannot stop thinking about the maggots that are eating his cheeks."[48]

Another piece of news that was hardly cheering: Harriet Collier had just married Baron Thomas Campbell: "One more sylph less. My feminine empyrean is emptying out completely. The angels of my youth are becoming housewives. All my old stars are turning into candles and the beautiful breasts on which my soul was rocked will soon come to look like pumpkins." As for Louise, the inevitable confidante, she kept obstinately returning to the idea of meeting Gustave's mother. To calm her down and gain time, he made a rather cowardly pretense of agreeing with her completely: "I repeat my promise to you: *I will do everything I can* to have you meet and know each other. After that, you will arrange matters as you see fit. I am racking my brains to understand why you feel it's so important. But *it's settled*, let's say no more about it."[49] Although he indeed said no more about this meeting, which was an idée fixe with Louise, he wrote her at great length about the progress and delays of his *Bovary*. "My head is on fire, as I recall it used to be after a long day on horseback. Because I've ridden my pen hard today. I have been writing since half past noon without stopping, except for five minutes now and then to smoke my pipe, and just now an hour for dinner. . . . It's taking too long. I think it will be the death of me, and besides I want to come and see you."[50]

In spite of this exhausting labor, he continued to correct Louise's poetic lucubrations line by line and even to write in her name articles on fashion for a women's magazine she edited. On October 17, 1853, Louis Bouilhet left Rouen and moved to Paris. For Flaubert, it was as great a shock as if his friend had died: "For me, he has already left. He will come back on Saturday; I shall see him again perhaps twice more. But it is over, the old Sundays have been broken off. I am going to be alone now, alone, alone. I am heartbroken with regret and humiliated by my powerlessness. . . . I am disgusted with everything. I think I would have been delighted to hang myself today if pride hadn't prevented me. It is certain that I am sometimes tempted to say the hell with everything, starting with *Bovary*. What a miserable damned idea it was to take a subject like that! Ah, I will have known them all right, the agonies of Art!"[51]

Although he swore he was ready to abandon his novel, he was working on it more intensively than ever. When Louise pressed him to take lodgings in Paris, he was evasive: "As for this question of my moving to Paris immediately, it must be postponed, or rather, it must be settled at once. It is *impossible for me at this time*. . . . I know myself; it would mean losing the whole winter, and maybe the whole book. . . . I am like a pan of milk: if the cream is to form, it must not be moved. . . . I have talked it all over with my mother. Do not accuse her (even in your heart), for she is rather *on your side.* We have agreed about the money, and this year she is going to make her arrangements concerning my furniture, linens, etc. I have already picked out a servant whom I shall take with me to Paris. So you see that it is an *unshakable determination. . . .* I'm not going to move anything in my study, because it will always be here that I write best, and here that I shall spend the most time in the end, because of my mother who is growing old."[52]

Thus he had finally dared to reveal to his mother that he had a mistress. She had suspected as much, of course, and had made no comment. Now he was as relieved as a child who has confessed his misbehavior. Once forgiven, he could go back to his toys. On November 10 he left for Paris with the intention of spending several days there. He stayed at the Hôtel du Helder. When Louise saw him again, she noticed that his feelings toward her had cooled. She was irritated by Louis Bouilhet, who was always at their heels. Their rare moments alone were stormy. When she repeated to Gustave that she absolutely insisted on meeting his mother, he jumped down her throat. And when she spoke to him of her financial worries, he declared he had no money. He had already lent her five hundred francs in 1852, then another hundred this year. Their last meeting was full of weariness and bitterness. He was sorry he had come. Twelve days away from his mother and from *Bovary*—it was too much! In any case, when he left Louise he promised to see her again soon. Back in Croisset, he wrote to her: "What a bad parting we had yesterday! Why? why? Next time will be better! Come, have courage! Be of good hope! I kiss your beautiful eyes, which I have so often caused to weep."[53] And three days later: "Yes, you are right, we were not alone enough during this trip. Perhaps our misunderstandings stem from that, for although our bodies touched, our hearts hardly had time to embrace. . . . Next year, even if *Bovary* isn't finished, I will come. I'll take lodgings. I'll stay at least four consecutive months each year."[54] Did he really believe it? He confided to Louis Bouilhet: "She makes me very sad, our poor Muse. I don't know what to do about her. . . . How do you think it will end? I suspect she is thoroughly tired of me. And for her own peace of mind it would be best if she broke with me. She is twenty years old, as far as feelings are concerned, and I am sixty."[55]

The truth was that he was tired of this old affair, exasperated by Louise's tears and recriminations, but he found it convenient to have a woman readily available when he came to Paris. He had only to be with her for twenty-four hours to want to escape, and yet when they were apart he took a secret pleasure in recounting to her how he had spent his day. Both of them were excessive by nature; they made love, quarreled, were reconciled in letters. Wasn't that more delicious, thought Flaubert, than face-to-face, in a bedroom? He wrote her: "I go to bed very late and get up very late too. Night falls early; I live by candlelight, or rather by the light of my lamp. I hear no step, no human voice. I don't know what the servants are up to, they wait on me like shadows. I dine with my dog. I smoke a great deal, keep a big fire going, work hard. It's wonderful!"[56] And also:

> I feel as if my skull were encased in an iron helmet. . . . I have been writing *Bovary*. I am up to their fornication, right in the midst of it: my lovers are sweating and gasping. . . . A little while ago, at six o'clock, as I was writing the word "hysterics," I was so swept away, was bellowing so loudly and feeling so deeply what my little woman was going through, that I was afraid of having hysterics myself. I got up from my table and opened the window to calm myself. My head was spinning. Now I have great pains in my knees, in my back, in my head. I feel like a man who has been fucking too much (forgive the expression)—I'm in a kind of rapturous lassitude. . . . It is a delicious thing to write, to be no longer *yourself* but to move in an entire universe of your own creating. Today, for instance, as both man and woman, lover and mistress at the same time, I rode in a forest on an autumn afternoon, under the yellow leaves, and I was also the horses, the leaves, the wind, the words the couple spoke and the red sun that made them half-close their love-drowned eyes.[57]

But Louise steadfastly refused to comprehend the attitude of a writer who was eager for solitude and closer to his characters than to the living creatures around him. Although she had been sternly ordered back to her kennel ten times over, she was still convinced that if Mme. Flaubert only saw her, that lady could not resist her charm. She said so again to Flaubert, and again he protested: "It is because I am *persuaded* that if she were to see you she would be cold to you, less than polite, as you put it, that I don't want you to see one another. Besides, I dislike this confusion, this mixing together of two different kinds of affection. . . . Once again I beg you to stay out of this. When the time is ripe and an occasion presents itself, I will know what to do."[58] When he tried to define his true feelings at this juncture, it seemed to him that it would be an insult to his mother's dignity to introduce to her a woman with whom he had slept. They belonged to two different worlds: the mother to the world of tenderness, care, and family memories, the mistress to the world of debauchery and fantasy. If he was to go on respecting his mother and desiring his mistress, they must remain unknown to each other.

In spite of his annoyance with Louise's pestering, he went to Paris in February 1854, spent several days at her fireside, presided over her supper parties, chatted with the poet Leconte de Lisle, who had become a regular visitor, and left again without any change having taken place in his relations with his burdensome "Muse." The following months, he wrote her less frequently, partly because he was tired of her, no doubt, but also because he was ill. "Terrible mercurial salivation, my dear sir," he wrote Louis Bouilhet. "I could neither speak nor eat. Dreadful fever, etc. Finally, *thanks to purges,* leeches, enemas, and also my *strong constitution,* I'm over it. I shouldn't even be surprised if my tubercle disappeared following this inflammation, for it has already diminished by half."[59] Bouilhet, who often saw Louise in Paris, kept him informed of the irrepressible woman's escapades. After her quarrel with Alfred de Musset, she had written a vengeful poem, "*La Servante,*" in which she presented him, in the guise of the poet Lionel, as a drunken has-been. Flaubert, to whom she sent the manuscript, advised her not to publish it: "Why insult Musset? . . . What business is it of yours? The poor fellow never tried to harm you. Why do you want to do him a greater wrong than he did you?"[60] But now a new rival appeared on the scene: Alfred de Vigny, fifty-five years old and a member of the Académie Française. Might he not help the "Muse" obtain another prize from the Académie? She slept with him, but she never lost sight of her prime objective: to get a permanent hold on the reluctant Flaubert. Bouilhet wrote to enlighten his friend: "Do you want me to tell you what I feel? Do you want me to say straight out what she is after, with her visits to your mother, with the comedy in verse, her cries, her tears, her invitations, and her dinners? She wants, she expects to become your wife! . . . I was thinking so without daring to formulate the idea to myself, but the word was boldly uttered to me, not by her, but as positively coming from her. That is why she refused the Philosopher."* And he added: "No one here takes her seriously. She makes herself wantonly ridiculous. I am distressed by it all, because at heart I am fond of her. . . ."[61]

Thus warned, Flaubert became even more mistrustful. When in letter after letter Louise renewed her complaints, he replied: "I think we are growing old, rancid, sour, and that each is adding his vinegar to the other's. As for me, when I look deep into my heart, this is what I feel for you: a great physical attraction first; then an attachment of the mind; a calm, manly affection; and a tender esteem. . . . You ask for love, you complain because I don't send you flowers? Flowers, indeed! Go find some nice fresh-faced young boy with perfect manners and all the right ideas. I am like the tiger, who has bristles of hair at the tip of his cock, which lacerate the female. . . . I feel that I would love you more ardently if no one knew I loved you. . . . That's the way I am, and I have enough work cut out for me without taking on the task of reforming myself emotionally."[62]

---

* A reference to Victor Cousin, who, Louise said, had recently proposed to her. The "comedy in verse" mentioned earlier was a play she had written in which two of the characters were thinly disguised portraits—one damaging, the other flattering—of Cousin and Flaubert, respectively. —Trans. (FS)

Although the correspondence dragged on for a few more months, the ties between them were now so tenuous that on October 16, 1854, Flaubert could write Bouilhet: "As for her, the Muse, it's all over. We can forget about it." When he went to Paris for a few weeks early in the following year, he preferred not to inform Louise of the visit. But she was alerted by mutual friends and hastened to come after him in his hotel on the Rue du Helder. He was not there. She came back several times and finally left a message saying that she was getting ready to leave for a trip abroad and absolutely must see him. "It would be childish to consult anyone and rude to refuse me," she wrote. "I shall therefore wait confidently at home this evening from eight o'clock until midnight." Furious at this intrusion into his private life, he answered her with a letter breaking off relations: "Madame: I am told that you took the trouble to call on me three times last evening. I was not in. And, fearing that if you persist in this way I shall be obliged to offer you repeated affronts, I am bound by the rules of courtesy to warn you that *I shall never be in*. Sincerely yours, G.F."[63] On this note Louise, with tears of rage and humiliation, wrote: "Poltroon, coward, and *scoundrel*," heavily underlining the last word. Was she going to attack him with a knife, as she had Alphonse Karr? No, but she was to pursue him for years with vengeful bitterness. As early as 1856 she painted a ridiculous portrait of him in a story, *Histoire de soldat*, that was published in *Le Moniteur*.

Having thus brutally rid himself of Louise, Flaubert had a feeling of emptiness, of course, but also of balance and serenity. Now that he no longer had to fear the reproaches, tears, rages, and swoons of his mistress, he saw his forthcoming move to Paris in a more favorable light. And it so happened that Louis Bouilhet had need of his presence. His play *Madame de Montarcy* had just been refused by the reading committee of the Comédie Française. Flaubert wrote to buck him up: "I am calling you to order, that is, I demand that you be convinced of your own worth. Come, old chap, my poor old fellow, my only confidant, my only friend, my only outlet, pluck up courage, think better of us than that! Try to deal with men and life with the same masterly ease (Parisian style) you have in dealing with ideas and sentences."[64] And again: "You have a talent that I see in no one else. But you lack what all the others have, to wit: self-assurance, the little worldly maneuvers, the art of shaking hands, of saying 'my dear friend' to a person one wouldn't want to have for a servant."[65] Incidentally, he informed his correspondent: "My wretched novel won't be finished before February. This is becoming ridiculous. I don't dare mention it anymore. . . . The leaves are falling. When you walk on the paths they are full of Lamartinian sounds that I greatly love.* Dackno [Flaubert's dog] lies by my fire all day long, and from time to time I hear the tugs on the river. That's the news."[66]

To get all the details right in the last pages of his novel, he consulted his brother Achille and Louis Bouilhet on medical matters and the Rouen lawyers on legal points. He also went to Paris, and there he came into contact with several easy women: an actress, Beatrix Person, who was a friend of Bouilhet's; another actress, Suzanne Lagier; and Louise Pradier. They were a refreshing change from the explosive Louise, who had definitively disappeared from his horizon. Now he had his own place, a little flat on the fifth floor at 42 Boulevard du Temple. A servant, Narcisse Barette, kept house for him. At the beginning of 1856 his mother came to stay with him. Two years later she was to rent an apartment on the floor above. In the meantime, Flaubert had renewed his friendship with Maxime Du Camp. Maxime insisted that he entrust the publication of *Madame Bovary* to *La Revue de Paris*. He offered two thousand francs, a decent amount. Flaubert was torn between the temptation to launch his novel in society and the terror of the stir it would inevitably create around himself. Would not this work, on which he had labored in secret for four and a half years, be deflowered, debased if he delivered it up to the stupid curiosity of the crowd? And if he threw himself into the literary free-for-all, would he not

---

* A reference to the great lyric poet Alphonse de Lamartine, whose *Méditations poétiques* (1820) marks the beginning of the romantic movement in French poetry. Lamartine often interprets the sights and sounds of nature as a reflection of his own intimate emotions, the mood evoked being typically one of brooding, elegiac melancholy. —Trans.

become one of those puppets he had despised all his life? Everything had been so peaceful as long as *Bovary*'s only readers were himself and Bouilhet. But it was precisely Bouilhet who was pestering him to make up his mind. He agreed and wrote his cousin, Olympe Bonenfant: "Know, oh cousin, that yesterday I sold a book (ambitious term!) for the sum of two thousand francs, and I'm going to continue! I have others that will follow. . . . The bargain is made, I shall appear in *La Revue de Paris* for six consecutive issues, starting in July. After which, I shall sell the thing again to a publisher who will put it out as a book."[67]

He returned to Croisset at the end of April, polished his text once more, and on June 1, 1856, announced to Bouilhet: "Yesterday I sent Du Camp the manuscript of *Bovary*, lightened by about thirty pages, not counting many lines cut here and there. I have deleted three long speeches of Homais's, an entire landscape, the conversations of the bourgeois at the ball . . . etc. You see, old chap, how heroic I've been. Has the book been improved by it? What is certain is that the thing as a whole has more movement now. If you go back to Du Camp's, I'd be curious to know what he thinks of it. If only *(inter nos)* those fellows don't postpone me! For I don't conceal from you, old friend, that *now* I want to see myself in print and as soon as possible."

He himself was surprised by his impatience. How did it happen that he had let himself be convinced so easily? Was it the pernicious atmosphere of the capital that had so contaminated him that he had been transformed into a man of letters like the others? Or was it because he was aware of the good qualities of his work that he now longed to have it disseminated? He felt that he was both a professional writer sure of his pen and at the same time a novice who had never yet faced the world's judgment. The winds of adventure were blowing all around him. With his heart pounding like a beginner's, he waited to see how Paris would react.

Chapter 12

THE BOOK, PUBLICATION, THE TRIAL

No sooner had Flaubert parted with the manuscript of *Madame Bovary* than he began to wonder if he had been wise to let the book be published—and even if he had been wise to write it. Who would be interested in the story of an adulterous woman of the petty bourgeoisie whose successive disappointments ended in suicide? From the beginning, he had been put off by this realistic subject as one alien to his stormy, lyrical temperament. Then, working against the grain, he had tried to bring it to life, looking upon the project as an excellent exercise in style. And little by little Emma had taken possession of him so completely that he was able to say: "Mme. Bovary is myself." But although he was captivated by her and identified with her, he kept a constant watch over his pen. And it was this mixture of hallucinatory obsession and cold control of expression that gave the work its unique color. From beginning to end of the novel, in spite of his tremendous inner excitement, Flaubert kept a rein on his imagination, mastered his impulses, and spoke in measured language. "One must write coldly," he said. Or again: "It is not with the heart that one writes but with the head." He was wary now of his youthful tendency to throw himself into a story. He no longer wanted the work to be an outlet for his own emotions. It was by effacing himself behind his characters, he thought, that he would bring them to life, not by intervening to approve or condemn their behavior. It was by remaining impartial and impassive that he would most effectively con-

139

vey their inner torment. It was by his own absence that he would ensure their presence.

Flaubert's scientific method of observing people and things was matched by a style as hard-edged as flint. Unrestrained and impulsive as he was in his letters, in *Madame Bovary* he was sparing of adjectives and metaphors. Everything was said in a few words, with incisive simplicity. The writer proceeds by scenes, as in a play. As each one unfolds, the reader learns more about the places that are the settings for the action and becomes more familiar with the protagonists. Not one unnecessary description. Long or short, they all have only one purpose: to illuminate the action. It has been said that the imaginary village of Yonville-l'Abbaye, where most of the story takes place, corresponds exactly to the real village of Ry, where Delphine Delamare lived. But it could just as well be Forges-les-Eaux, where Flaubert, his mother, and Caroline took refuge for a few weeks to escape the visits of Émile Hamard when he had lost his mind and wanted to take his daughter back.

As for Emma Bovary, it is very hard to discover the real origins of the fictional character. To be sure, the sad story of Delphine Delamare—deceiving a mediocre husband, contracting debts, and dying in despair—served as the point of departure for the first outline of the book. But Emma is also Louise Pradier, the faithless wife of the sculptor, who went from one man's arms to another's, borrowed money, was threatened with seizure of her property for debt, and thought about throwing herself into the Seine. She had confided in Flaubert, and he had read an anonymous manuscript, *Mémoires de Madame Ludovica*, relating her reckless adventures. Perhaps also he had been inspired by the famous Mme. Lafarge, who had just poisoned her husband, a clod who was incapable of understanding her romantic inclinations. And how can one help thinking of Elisa Schlésinger, Eulalie Foucaud, and Louise Colet as well? When he wrote his novel, memories of all the women he had loved crowded in upon him. He stole from each a little of her substance. From one he borrowed her hair, from another the color of her skin, from a third her love of finery, from a fourth her dresses, from a fifth the dreams of a frustrated wife. It all came together in his mind to form a unique character who did not resemble any of her models but who had the nerves, the blood, and the fierce longings of her creator. Yes, Flaubert was right when he said, "Mme. Bovary is myself." His heroine's nervous condition, with her excitements, her sudden flashes of fiery lights, her relapses, dizzy spells, and malaises—he knew all about that because he had suffered it himself during his work. He could swear all he wanted that "everything was invented" in his book; he had nevertheless represented himself in the guise of an unsatisfied woman, torn between her longings for an ethereal love and commonplace, everyday reality. Emma Bovary is the tragic struggle of a soul thirsting for the ideal and colliding with the ordinary demands of provincial life. Flaubert had felt this contradiction too often not to have expressed it forcefully, albeit changing sex. He too lived like a bourgeois and dreamed like a poet. But unlike Emma, to ensure his stability he had the outlet of literary creation.

Where did the name Bovary come from? Some people have seen it as a variation on the name of Esther Bovery, the plaintiff in a Rouen lawsuit in 1845; others think it was suggested by the name of Bouvaret, the proprietor of the hotel in Cairo where Flaubert had stayed in 1849 during his trip to the Middle East. If we accept this latter version, it is entirely possible that, as reported by Maxime Du Camp, Flaubert really did exclaim before the second cataract of the Nile: "I've got it! Eureka! Eureka! I'll call her Mme. Bovary." Countless scholars have likewise tried to discover the models for the other characters in the novel. Thus Rodolphe Boulanger, the elegant landowner whose mistress Emma becomes, is supposed to be Louis Campion, a village Don Juan who after many adventures committed suicide in 1852. He had been Delphine Delamare's lover and, as in the novel, it was a notary's clerk who had replaced him in that capacity. Father Bournisien is supposed to have many points in common with a certain Father Lafortune, and the pharmacist Homais, magnificent in his self-confidence and idiocy, is said to be the physical and moral portrait, hardly retouched, of the apothecary Jouanne who kept a shop in Ry. Investigators even claim to have identified the real-life originals of Mayor Tuvache and the merchant

Lheureux. And to be sure, Flaubert filled his work with a thousand direct observations. But these grains of truth were of infinitesimal importance in the task he had set himself. Starting from a minimum of facts, he breathed life into his characters, each of whom—an exceedingly rare achievement—became a human type. Thus *Madame Bovary* is not only Emma, her husband, Charles, and her lovers, Rodolphe and Léon, but the whole little society of the town of Yonville. The depiction of this provincial environment is necessary to our understanding of Emma's psychology. It is through the contrast between her and the others that the drama takes on its true magnitude. Those "others," incidentally, are all sorry specimens of humanity. In spite of his blind love for Emma, throughout the book Charles Bovary never rises above mediocrity. Homais parades a self-importance and a solemn stupidity that soon make him insufferable. Father Bournisien is a priest utterly without spirituality, Rodolphe is a cheap seducer, Léon is weak and spineless, Lheureux a slimy scoundrel. . . .

To organize the progress of his narrative, Flaubert adopted a work method based on meticulous preparation. Before beginning to write, he sketched out on paper, in telegraphic phrases, the general plan of the book. Then he developed the different parts in more detailed outlines. These outlines were followed by drafts written very freely, as inspiration dictated. Then began the arduous task of revision. He would go over his drafts word by word, tightening, chiseling indefatigably, rejoicing if at the end of the day he had saved a few sentences from the wholesale destruction. These sentences he would shout out loud in the silence of his study. If they passed that test, he would consider them definitive. If not, he would set to work furiously on them again until they sounded the way he wanted them to. And at the end of these exhausting verbal acrobatics he obtained the miracle of a prose that gave the illusion of naturalness and ease.

He had hardly sent his manuscript off to *La Revue de Paris* when he began to write again. This time he was trying to rework his *Tentation de Saint Antoine:* "I hope to make it readable and not too boring."[1] At the same time he was gathering documentation for a medieval legend. These projects were a pleasant change from the stifling atmosphere of *Bovary*. But he thought of the book constantly. He was worried by Maxime Du Camp's silence. "I acted like a fool in doing *as others do,* going to live in Paris, wanting to be published. So long as I wrote for myself alone, I lived in the perfect serenity of art. Now I am full of doubts and uneasiness. And for the first time I am finding that I don't want to write. I feel for literature the hatred that springs from impotence."[2]

Actually, he was not wrong to be alarmed. In Paris when Maxime Du Camp's codirectors at *La Revue de Paris,* Louis Ulbach and Léon Laurent-Pichat, read the manuscript, they were afraid that publishing it would create a scandal. Censorship was severe under the Second Empire. The authorities already thought *La Revue* was too liberal. They might well take the immorality of the work as a pretext for suppressing the magazine permanently. "We were about to publish," Ulbach wrote, "a strange and daring work, cynical in its negation of everything, unreasonable by virtue of an excess of reason, false because of too many true details, badly observed on account of the fragmentation, so to speak, of the observation; a work devoid of noble sadness . . . of élan . . . of love." On July 14, on the advice of Laurent-Pichat, Du Camp sent Flaubert a letter informing him that his novel was too much in need of tightening to be published as it stood: "We will make the cuts we think indispensable; and later you will publish it in a volume in whatever form you choose: that is your affair. . . . You have buried your novel under a heap of details which are well done but superfluous: it is not seen clearly enough, and must be disencumbered—an easy task. We shall have it done under our supervision by someone who is experienced and clever; not a word will be added to your manuscript, it will merely be pruned; the job will cost you about a hundred francs, which will be deducted from your payment, and you will have published something really good instead of something imperfect and padded."

Dumbfounded at this cavalier treatment of a text that had cost him so much toil, Flaubert scrawled on the back of the letter: "Unbelievable!" And he rushed to Paris to plead the cause of his book. After a heated discussion with Laurent-Pichat, he made a few concessions on details and left reassured. In its issue of August 1, 1856, *La Revue de Paris* announced the forthcoming publication of *Madame Bovary (Moeurs de province)*, but because of a printer's error, the author's name was given as Faubert, without the *l*. (Faubert was the name of a grocer on the Rue de Richelieu, opposite the Comédie Française.) "This strikes me as an inauspicious beginning," noted Flaubert. "I haven't even appeared yet and they're already cutting me to pieces."[3] In Croisset the summer was scorching, the mosquitoes voracious; Flaubert worked fitfully on his *Saint Antoine* and waited impatiently for news of *Bovary*. He was convinced that Laurent-Pichat was delaying publication of the novel so as to wear him down and prepare him for further cuts: "But I have his word, and I shall give it back to him, thanking him prettily, if they go on like this much longer. . . . *I am heartily sick of Bovary. And I can't wait to be rid of her*."[4] At last, on September 21, 1856, he was reassured: a letter from Du Camp informed him that his novel—all of it—would begin appearing on October 1. When he received the first copies of the magazine and saw his prose in print, he felt a mixture of pride and embarrassment. Now the die was cast. Even if he wanted to, he couldn't change a comma. He had put his dreams up for sale. His Emma, the companion of so many feverish nights, had become everybody's Emma. And then, there were the typographical errors! "I have only noted the printing errors, three or four repetitions of words that shocked me and a page that was full of *which*'s and *who*'s."[5] One thing was certain: nothing in his text had been changed. He thanked Laurent-Pichat for that and justified his obstinate refusal to let the story be watered down: "Do you think that this ignoble reality, so distasteful to you in reproduction, does not turn my stomach as it does yours? If you knew me better you would know that I abhor ordinary existence. Personally, I have always held myself as aloof from it as I could. But esthetically, I wanted this once—and only this once—to plumb its depths. Therefore I plunged into it heroically, into all its minutiae, accepting everything, telling everything, depicting everything, pretentious as that may sound. I am expressing myself badly, but well enough for you to understand the general trend of my resistance to your criticisms, judicious as they may be. You were rewriting my book. . . . Art requires neither complaisance nor politeness: nothing but faith—faith always, and freedom."[6]

But in November 1856, Du Camp learned from someone close to official circles that *La Revue de Paris* was in danger of incurring a lawsuit if it continued to publish *Madame Bovary* in its present form. Once again he tried to obtain Flaubert's permission to delete the dangerous passages. Flaubert protested and refused. Du Camp insisted: "This is no laughing matter," he wrote on November 18, 1856. "Your scene in the cab is *impossible*—not for us (we couldn't care less), not for me (I will be signing the issue), but for the criminal court, which would condemn us out of hand. . . . We have had two warnings; they are lying in wait for us, and if they get another shot at us they won't miss." Ulbach for his part, and for the same reasons, was asking Flaubert to cut from the end of the novel the scene in which Emma is given extreme unction and the one where the priest and the pharmacist keep vigil over the body. Flaubert fumed and finally agreed to a few minor changes. But when he read the issue of December 1, 1856, he found that many cuts had been made without his consent. He promptly exploded and turned on Laurent-Pichat, who had deceived him by promising to respect his work: "*I will do nothing:* I will not make a correction, not a cut; I will not suppress a comma; nothing, nothing! But if *La Revue de Paris* thinks that I am compromising it, if it is afraid, there is something very simple it can do, and that is to stop publication of *Madame Bovary* at once. I am utterly indifferent." And he added: "By eliminating the passage about the cab you have not made the story a whit less shocking; and you will accomplish no more by the cuts you ask for in the sixth installment. You are objecting to details, whereas actually you should object to the whole. The brutal element is basic, not superficial. Negroes cannot be made white, and you cannot change the *blood* of a book. All you can do is to weaken it."[7]

Du Camp went to see Flaubert to try to bring him to reason, but he ran into a stone wall: "I don't care; if the bourgeois are exasperated by my novel, I don't care; if we are taken to criminal court, I don't care; if *La Revue de Paris* is suppressed, I don't care! You had only to refuse *Bovary*; you took it, so much the worse for you: you will publish it as it stands."[8] Then Du Camp tried to win over Mme. Flaubert to his cause. But she refused to get involved in an affair she didn't understand a word of. In the end, the editors of the magazine stuck to their guns and Flaubert demanded that they insert at the head of the last installment the following disclaimer from the author:

> Considerations which it is not in my province to judge led *La Revue de Paris* to omit a passage from the issue of December 1; its scruples having been again aroused on the occasion of the present issue, it has thought proper to omit several more. Consequently, I hereby decline responsibility for the lines which follow. The reader is asked to consider them as a series of fragments, not as a whole.

On Christmas Eve Flaubert signed a contract with Michel Lévy for the publication of *Madame Bovary* in book form, giving the publisher the rights to the novel for five years, in return for the sum of eight hundred francs. In the meantime, *Le Nouvelliste de Rouen* had also undertaken to publish the novel in serial form. But like *La Revue de Paris*, the local newspaper had its scruples and on December 14 advised its readers that "we have decided to cease publication of *Madame Bovary* after this issue, because we could not continue without making a number of cuts in the text." At that moment Flaubert was in Paris. He was busy as the self-appointed publicity agent for Louis Bouilhet's play *Madame de Montarcy*, which was having a highly successful run at the Théâtre de l'Odéon. As for *Madame Bovary*, most of the reactions he heard seemed favorable. "Bovary is getting on better than I had expected," he wrote Louis Bonenfant. "It's only the women who think I am 'a dreadful man.' They find that what I write is too true. That's really what they're indignant about. . . . I will confess to you, in any case, that I am utterly indifferent to it all. The morality of Art consists in its very beauty, and the things I prize above all else are first style, and then truth. I think I have put into the portrayal of bourgeois life, and of a woman whose character is naturally corrupt, as much literature and propriety as possible—given the subject, of course. I am not about to begin another such labor. It goes against the grain for me to depict a commonplace milieu, and it is because it went against the grain that I chose that one, which is ultra-commonplace and 'inartistic.' Working on it will have served to limber up my hand; on to other exercises now."[9]

Nevertheless, the government was becoming disturbed over the rumors about this daring book. The public prosecutor made an inquiry into the matter. The text of the novel was examined under a microscope and was found to contain many passages that were "an outrage to public morals." The author, the editors, and the printer of *La Revue de Paris* were obviously responsible. Flaubert sensed the gathering storm and, far from caving in, rose up in indignation. He had withdrawn from society, but when the occasion demanded, he was ready to enter the fray. Leaving his cozy nest, he confronted his accusers with all the fury of outraged innocence. "My case is a *political affair*, because the government wants at all costs to exterminate *La Revue de Paris*, which is a thorn in its side," he wrote on January 1, 1857, to his brother Achille. "It has already had two warnings, and it would be very shrewd to close it down on a third offense for an attack on religion. Because the chief thing that is held against me is a description of extreme unction that I *copied* from the missal. But these worthy magistrates are such asses that they are totally ignorant of the religion they are supposed to defend. My examining magistrate, M. Treilhard, is a Jew, and it's he who is prosecuting me! It's all sublimely grotesque. . . . I'm going to become the lion of the week; all the high society whores are fighting over copies of *Bovary* in hopes of finding obscenities that aren't there."

Forgetting his principles of proud withdrawal from the world and contempt for the representatives of power, he went to see the Minister of Education and the director-general of police. "They thought they were attacking some poor penniless devil, and when they found out first that I had private means, that woke them up a bit," he wrote again to his brother, two days later. "They must be made to understand at the Ministry of the Interior that in Rouen we are what is called *a family*, that is, that we have deep roots in that part of the country and that by attacking me, especially for immorality, they will offend many people. I expect that the letter from the Prefect [of Rouen] to the Minister of the Interior will have a great effect." He was so convinced that the judges, once duly enlightened, were going to give up the proceedings that he almost rejoiced over the scandal created by his novel. While not long since he had been hesitating to have it published, now he puffed out his chest at the thought that so many people were talking about it. Riding the wave of success, he confided to Achille: "You can be sure, dear brother, that in any event, I am now considered a *Somebody*. If I get out of this (which I think very probable), my book will sell really well. . . . Never mind! Keep working on the Prefect and don't stop until I tell you to."[10] He even went so far as to propose to his brother a strictly political maneuver: "Try to have someone suggest *adroitly* that it would be dangerous to attack me, to attack *us*, because of the approaching elections."[11] And he explained: "The only thing that will really have an influence will be the name of father Flaubert and the fear that if I am convicted it might antagonize the people of Rouen in the forthcoming elections. At the Ministry of the Interior they are beginning to regret having rashly attacked me. What will stop them is to make them see the *political disadvantages* of the thing."[12] It was not only in Rouen that he sought support. In Paris too, where he had been living since mid-October, he was rallying his influential friends. The Princess of Beauvau, who was "an ardent Bovaryste," went twice to see the Empress Eugénie to defend the writer. Everything seemed to indicate that the case had been dropped. Its only effect would have been to win partisans for the courageous author.

During this time parts of *Saint Antoine* were appearing in the magazine *L'Artiste* and giving the public a new view of Flaubert's talent. His colleagues applauded him, Lamartine sang his praises "very loudly," which surprised him, *La Presse* and *Le Moniteur* made him "very decent" proposals, he was asked to write a comic opera, and various papers, "large and small," spoke respectfully of *Madame Bovary*. Flaubert explained it to his beloved Elisa Schlésinger, who had just written him a letter of tender friendship: "That, dear madame, without any modesty, is the balance sheet of my fame." And he added: "So I am going back to my poor life that is so quiet and tame, in which sentences are adventures and the only flowers I gather are metaphors. I shall write as in the past, solely for the pleasure of writing, for myself alone, without any lurking thoughts of money or publicity."[13]

But on January 15, when Flaubert thought he was safe from the thunderbolts of justice, his lawyer from Rouen, Maître Sénard, informed him that the case had been referred to criminal court. Stunned by this sudden reversal, Flaubert wrote Achille: "I thought the affair was all over. Prince Napoleon had said as much three times to three different persons. . . . I am lost in a whirlwind of lies and slanders. There is *something* behind it all, someone invisible and relentless. . . . I expect no justice, I will do my time in prison; of course I will not ask for clemency—that is what would really dishonor me. . . . And they won't shut me up in the least! I will go on working as in the past, that is to say, jut as conscientiously and independently. Ah, I'll give them novels, all right! And real ones! . . . Meantime, *Bovary* continues to be successful; it's really causing a stir—everyone has read it, is reading it, or wants to read it. My persecution has won me widespread sympathy. If my book is bad, the persecution will make it seem better; if, on the contrary, the book is to endure, it will be a pedestal for it. . . . At any moment now I expect the summons that will name the day when—for the crime of writing in French—I am to take my place on the bench reserved for pickpockets and pederasts."[14]

With every day that passed he was more convinced that by attacking him, the public prosecutor had transformed him into a literary martyr. He had emerged from the shadows and become, in spite of himself, the shining symbol of talent insulted. "The various steps I have taken have been very beneficial, in that *opinion* is now on my side," he wrote Achille. "There isn't a literary man in Paris who hasn't read me and doesn't defend me; they are all sheltering behind me—they feel that my cause is theirs. The police have blundered. They thought they were attacking a run-of-the-mill novel and some ordinary little scribbler; whereas now (thanks in part to the persecution), my novel is looked on as a masterpiece; as for the author, he has for defenders a number of what used to be called *grandes dames;* the Empress, among others, has twice spoken in my favor."[15] Lamartine received him, paid him "extravagant" compliments, and promised to support him at the trial. And Flaubert commented: "That surprises me greatly. I would never have thought the bard of Elvire would conceive a passion for Homais."* In any case, now he was sure that his "stock was going up." *Le Moniteur* offered to pay him ten sous a line, "which for a novel like *Bovary* would amount to about ten thousand francs." Conclusion: "Whether I am convicted or not, I've made a place for myself."[16]

Nevertheless, he was in a great state of excitement when, at 10:00 A.M. on January 29, 1857, he appeared before the Court of Summary Jurisdiction of Paris (6th Division) at the Palais de Justice. His codefendants were Auguste Pillet, the printer, and Laurent-Pichat, editor of *La Revue de Paris.* The public prosecutor, Ernest Pinard, began his indictment in a caustic mode. Having summarized the plot of the novel, he identified the passages that he judged obscene or blasphemous, supporting his argument with numerous quotations. In his opinion, while the printer was only half guilty, and while the editor of the magazine could invoke in his favor his refusal to publish certain scabrous episodes, the author had no excuse. "Art without rules is no longer art!" he cried. "It is like a woman who removes all her clothes. To impose on art the single rule that it must respect public decency is not to enslave it but to honor it. One cannot grow without rules."

When Maître Sénard rose for the defense, the audience held its breath. In the courtroom were many pretty women, a few famous faces. It was a very Parisian trial. Flaubert felt ready to faint with so many eyes fixed on him. What would he not have given to bury

---

* In *Méditations poétiques* "Elvire" appears frequently as the poet's beloved. —Trans.

himself in his provincial retreat again! The lawyer's voice rang out with superb confidence. He spoke for four hours without interruption. Flaubert gratefully drank in his words. "Maître Sénard's speech was splendid," he wrote his brother the next day. "He crushed the public prosecutor, who writhed in his seat and made no rebuttal. We flattened him with quotations from Bossuet and Massillon, smutty passages from Montesquieu, etc. The courtroom was packed. It was marvelous, and I was in fine form. At one point I allowed myself personally to contradict the prosecuting attorney, who was immediately shown to be acting in bad faith, and retracted. In any case, you will see all the proceedings word for word: I had a stenographer (at sixty francs an hour) taking it all down."[17] Maître Sénard first spoke of the noble character of the father of the accused, then about the talents of his two sons, one of whom was a doctor, as he himself had been, at the Hôtel-Dieu in Rouen, while the other was an outstanding writer. Analyzing the novel chapter by chapter, he showed that it was profoundly moral, since the heroine was punished for her sins. He quoted a letter from Lamartine stating that *Madame Bovary* was the finest work he had encountered in twenty years. He read aloud the entire scene in the cab to prove that it contained no lascivious details. Finally, coming to the description of the rite of extreme unction, he revealed that in writing it the author had only transposed into French the Latin text that appeared in the Roman Catholic missal. Every blow struck home, and Flaubert's courage surged back. "Throughout his speech, old Sénard spoke of me as a great man and called my book a masterpiece," he wrote in the same letter.

The verdict was pronounced on February 7, 1857. While reprimanding the accused for their irresponsibility in publishing a work that was offensive to public decency, the court acquitted them and dismissed them without costs. For the first time in months, Flaubert breathed freely. But he was exhausted and demoralized. "My trial has left me aching all over, physically and mentally, so that I can't take a step or lift a pen," he wrote Louise Pradier. "This uproar over my first book seems so alien to art that I am disgusted and bewildered by it. How I miss the old days before all this, when I remained as mute as a fish! And then, I am worried about the future: what can I write that would be more inoffensive than my poor *Bovary*, who has been dragged into criminal court by the hair, like a whore? . . . However that may be, and in spite of the acquittal, my position is still that of a suspect author. A poor sort of fame! . . . I am going to return without delay to my house in the country, far from humankind, as they say in tragedies, and there I shall try to fit new strings to my poor guitar that they spattered with mud even before its first tune was played."[18] In a letter to another friend he declared: "I have lost a great deal this winter. I was worth more a year ago. I remind myself of a prostitute. . . . I am disgusted with myself."[19] And to another: "I long to return, and forever, to the solitude and silence I emerged from; to publish nothing, so as never to be talked of again. Because it seems to me that it's impossible to say anything these days. Social hypocrisy is so ferocious!"[20] At present he was repelled by the idea of seeing his novel appear in book form. But his friends and his mother insisted that he should not give up the project. In any case, he had signed a contract with Michel Lévy. He could not back out of it. But if he reinstated in the book the passages that had been deleted in *La Revue de Paris*, would he not expose himself to another lawsuit? Well, that couldn't be helped. The public had a right to the complete text. *Madame Bovary* deserved one last fight.

In April 1857 the novel was in the bookstores. Two volumes. A press run of 6,600 copies. The groundwork having been laid by the scandal of the trial, the book was immediately successful. The edition was soon sold out and a second printing of 15,000 copies was issued, but since the author had already signed the contract, Michel Lévy merely gave him a bonus of five hundred francs. However, although publication of the book didn't bring Flaubert much financial benefit, it greatly enhanced his reputation. He received enthusiastic letters from Victor Hugo, from Champfleury, the leader of the realist school, and even from the influential critic Sainte-Beuve, who, however, deplored the absence of gentle, pure, deep feelings in a work of this importance: "That would have been a relief. It would have reminded the reader that there is some good even in the midst of evil and stupidity." Sainte-Beuve also wrote an article on *Madame Bovary* in *Le Moniteur*. After a few mild criticisms, he acknowledged that the work was "entirely impersonal," which was "a great proof of strength." And he noted that as the "son and brother of eminent doctors, M. Flaubert wields the pen as others wield the scalpel." This admiration expressed in an official government newspaper was not, however, shared by the other critics. Far from it. "It is the morbid excitement of the senses and the imagination in a discontented democracy," declared M. de Pontmartin. "Second-rate art . . . we deserve better," wrote Paulin Limayrac in *Le Constitutionnel*. "A labored, vulgar and reprehensible work," was the judgment of Veuillot in *L'Univers*. In *Le Journal des débats*, Cuvillier-Fleury delivered himself of the following prophesy: "*Madame Bovary*, if she manages to grow old, has all the future of a secondhand clothes dealer." Charles de Mazade, of *La Revue des deux mondes*, acknowledged that Flaubert had a bit of talent: "Only, up until now that talent has consisted more of imitation and affectation than of originality. The author has a certain gift for close, bitter observation, but he grasps objects, so to speak, from the outside, without penetrating to the depths of moral life." Duranty, in his review *Le Réalisme*, wrote: "There is neither emotion nor feeling nor life in this novel, but a strong force of arithmetical calculation. . . . The style is uneven, as it always is when a man writes artistically without feeling; one finds a pastiche here, a lyrical passage there, nothing personal. . . . Before this novel appeared, one thought it would be better. Excessive study is no substitute for the spontaneity that comes from feeling." And Granier de Cassagnac, after a few all-purpose compliments, compared *Madame Bovary* to "a big pile of manure." In the midst of this chorus of censure, one flattering assessment appeared in *L'Artiste*, a journal with a limited circulation, to be sure. There the reviewer said that, working on "a banal canvas," the author had painted in "a style that was vigorous, picturesque, subtle, and exact," that he had put "the most burning and passionate feelings into the most commonplace adventure," and that the result was "a marvel." The article was signed Baudelaire.

Flaubert

The publication of *Madame Bovary* brought Flaubert many letters from women who were moved by the heroine's fate and recognized themselves in her. The one who wrote him most regularly was an exuberant novelist, Mlle. Leroyer de Chantepie, twenty-one years older than he, who lived in the provinces and sent him, as tokens of her esteem, her portrait and two of her books. Worn out by the ordeal of the lawsuit, he felt the need to confide in a woman, especially one who admired him. Since Louise Colet was no longer available for correspondence, he fell back on Mlle. Leroyer de Chantepie. When she questioned him about the genesis of *Madame Bovary*, he replied: "*Madame Bovary* has nothing true in it. It is a *totally invented* story; I put into it none of my own feelings and nothing from my own life. The illusion (if there is one) comes, on the contrary, from the *impersonality* of the work. It is a principle of mine that one must not write about himself. The artist in his work should be like God in his creation—invisible and all-powerful: his presence should be felt everywhere, but he should never be seen." And he went on, unbosoming himself to the stranger: "For a long time, madame, I lived a life like yours. I too have spent several years completely *alone,* in the country, hearing no other sound in winter but the sighing of the wind in the trees and the cracking of the ice as it drifted down the Seine under my windows. If I have come to have some understanding of life, it is because I have not lived much in the ordinary sense of the word, for while I have eaten little I have ruminated a great deal. I have associated with different kinds of people and seen different countries. I have traveled on foot and on the backs of dromedaries. I know the stockbrokers of Paris and the Jews of Damascus, the pimps of Italy and the Negro jugglers. . . . Add to this—to have my portrait and my complete biography—that I am thirty-five years old and five feet eight inches tall, with the shoulders of a stevedore and the nervous irritability of a kept woman.* I am a bachelor and a recluse."[21]

---

* At other times Flaubert described himself as measuring 1.83 meters, or exactly six feet.

The Book, Publication, the Trial

A few days later he confided further in Mlle. Leroyer de Chantepie:

> I loved a great deal, in silence. And then, at twenty-one I
> almost died of a nervous disease brought on by a series of
> irritations and sorrows, by sleepless nights and fits of anger.
> This malady lasted ten years. . . . I was born in a hospital
> (the hospital of Rouen, where my father was chief surgeon;
> he left a name illustrious in the art of medicine) and grew up
> in the midst of all the afflictions of mankind, separated from
> them only by a wall. As a small child I played in a surgical
> amphitheater. Perhaps that is why I have a manner that is at
> once funereal and cynical. I have no love of life and no fear
> of death. I find nothing terrifying, even, in the possibility of
> absolute nothingness. I am ready to throw myself into the
> great black hole with serenity. And yet, what appeals to me
> more than anything else is religion. I mean all religions, not
> one more than another. I find each dogma in particular re-
> pellent, but I consider the feeling that invented them as the
> most natural and poetic feeling of humanity. . . . I have no
> sympathy for any political party, or rather, I detest them all.
> . . . I hate all despotism. I am a rabid liberal. That is why
> socialism strikes me as a pedantic horror that will be the death
> of all art and all morality. I have been present, as a spectator,
> at almost all the popular uprisings of my time.[22]

Clearly, it tickled his vanity to explain himself, to tell his story,
to arouse admiration and pity. While claiming to hate himself, he
discoursed upon the peculiarities of his character and his life with
entire complacency. He considered himself—and wanted to be
considered—astonishing. His pride shone through a superficial
modesty. Had he become another man since the publication of *Madame Bovary*? He hoped not, and yet his contact with the bustling,
frivolous world of men of letters had aroused in him the still unconscious desire to assert himself as a great writer, to win a large

audience, to be esteemed by his peers, by the public, and by the press. Even as he rejoiced that he would soon be escaping from the capital and all its foolish gossip, he was sure that before long an irresistible attraction would bring him back. There were two opposite poles to his life now, one in the city and one in the country. In Paris he threw out his chest and strutted; in Croisset he reflected and wrote. Lately a fabulous subject had been uppermost in his mind: the revolt of the mercenaries in Carthage. In the greatest excitement, he confided in Mlle. Leroyer de Chantepie: "Before returning to the country, I am busy with some archaeological work dealing with one of the least-known periods of antiquity—a task that is preparation for another. I am going to write a novel in which the action takes place three centuries before Christ, for I feel the need to leave the modern world behind. My pen has been dipped in it too long, and besides, I am as weary of portraying it as I am disgusted by the sight of it."[23]

Henceforth he was sure that the way to escape from all the baseness of *Madame Bovary* was to plunge into a past of splendor and violence. "I'm having a lot of trouble with Carthage!" he confessed to a new friend, the writer Ernest Feydeau. "What worries me most is the foundation, I mean the psychological part; I need to meditate profoundly in 'the silence of the study,' amid 'the solitude of the fields.' There, perhaps, by masturbating my poor mind, I may manage to squeeze something out of it."[24] But the die was cast: even before he had written the first line of this new book, he knew that if he was at all satisfied with it, he would have it published. Like *Madame Bovary*. The days when he had kept his work a secret were gone forever.

Chapter 13

SALAMMBÔ

Croisset again, with its comfort, its silence, its trees leafing out, its calmly flowing river. Back with his mother, who pampered him, and his niece, who was now eleven and a half and who delighted him with her affectionate and mischievous ways, Flaubert resumed his habits of work and meditation. The company of these two women, one withered and tired, the other in all the freshness of childhood, was a relief after the tumult and intrigues of Paris. With a voracious appetite he devoured pell-mell the most difficult books about ancient Carthage. He wanted to know everything about the time and place that would be the setting for his new novel. "As for me, I have indigestion from a surfeit of books," he wrote Jules Duplan. "I belch in folios. Since March I have taken notes on fifty-three different works. Now I am studying the art of warfare, indulging in the delights of counterscarp and horseman and boning up on ballistae and catapults. I think at last I'm going to be able to extract new effects from the foot soldier of antiquity. As for the landscape, it's still very vague. I don't yet *feel* the religious side. The psychology is cooking slowly. But it's a heavy thing to mount, old chap. I've plunged into a damn hard task. I don't know when I shall finish it, or even when I shall begin."[1] And again, to Frédéric Baudry: "I'm afraid I've embarked on a brute of a task. Sometimes I think it's superb. But there are days when I feel as if I were navigating through shit."[2] The pile of trimmed quill pens on his table struck him as "a bush of terrible thorns," his inkstand as "an ocean" in which he was drowning; the sight of the blank paper gave him "vertigo."[3] On his reading list were Polybius, Appian, Diodorus Siculus, Isidorus, Cornelius Nepos, Pliny, Plutarch, Xenophon, Livy, and the eighteen volumes of Cahen's annotated French translation of the Old Testament. "Let us don the mask of tragedy, and let the great tirades commence!" he exclaimed. "It's good for the health."[4] And to explain his rage for documentation, he said: "In order for a book to *sweat* truth, you have to be stuffed to the ears with your subject. Then the color comes naturally, as an inevitable result and like a flowering of the idea itself."[5]

Absorbed by the preparation of his new book, he lost interest in the fate of *Madame Bovary*. When he read the violent criticism of his "immoral" novel, he shrugged his shoulders and called the reviewers imbeciles. These hacks were all jealous men who hadn't understood the first thing about the great battle he was waging. When he learned that Baudelaire's *Fleurs du mal* was also the object of a lawsuit, he wrote the author: "Why? Against what have you committed an 'offense'? . . . This is something new, to prosecute a book of verse. Up to now the bench has left poetry strictly alone. I am highly indignant."[6] But now the priest of the parish to which Croisset belonged attacked Flaubert in his Sunday sermon. "The curé of Canteleu is *thundering* against *Bovary* and *forbids* his female parishioners to read me," he wrote Jules Duplan. "You will think me silly, but I assure you that this tickles my vanity enormously. I am more flattered by this success than by any possible praise."[7] And a few days later, to Louis Bouilhet: "So now I have had it all: attack by the government, abuse from the press, and hatred from the priests."[8]

At the beginning of October Flaubert finally began a first draft of his novel, which for the time being he titled *Carthage*. "In my first chapter I've gotten up to my little woman. I'm polishing her costume, which is great fun: it has quite put me back in form. I'm wallowing like a pig in the jewels I'm surrounding her with. I think there's a 'purple' or a 'diamond' in every sentence in the book. Overdone! But I'll take some of them out."[9] In November he changed his title and informed Charles-Edmond, editor of *La Presse:*

Salammbô

"The title of my thing (I think) will be *Salammbô, roman carthaginois*. That's the name of Hamilcar's daughter, a daughter invented by your humble servant. But . . . it's not going well at all. I am sick, morally in particular, and if you want to do me a great favor, you won't talk about this novel any more than if it didn't exist."[10]

And now he went through his usual succession of moods: crises of discouragement followed by bursts of enthusiasm: "I have undertaken something bold, my boy, something very bold, and there are plenty of hurdles to break my neck over before I reach the end. Don't worry, I'm not going to give up. Gloomy, grim, desperate, but not chickenhearted. Still, just think what I've let myself in for: trying to resuscitate an entire civilization about which we know nothing."[11] Or again: "The problem is to find the right tone. It can be achieved by extreme *condensation* of the idea, either naturally or through an effort of will, but it is not easy to constantly imagine things that might be true—that is, a series of striking, probable details—in a setting that is two thousand years old."[12] When he was writing *Madame Bovary* he had complained about being plunged in a modern world that was repugnant to him; now that he was writing *Salammbô* he suffered because his model was so remote in time and space. This time he had to invent everything and somehow manage to give his lies the force of truth. The hardest thing was to make characters who had lived twenty centuries earlier think and talk. "I feel that what I am writing is false, do you understand?" he wrote Mlle. Leroyer de Chantepie. And to Ernest Feydeau: "The descriptions I can get away with, but the dialogue, what a disaster!" The two letters were written on December 12, his birthday. "This evening I shall turn thirty-six," he told Mlle. Leroyer de Chantepie. "I remember several of my birthdays. Eight years ago today I was coming back from Memphis to Cairo, after having slept at the Pyramids. I can still hear the jackals howling and the gusts of wind that shook my tent. I have a notion that sooner or later I will go back to the Orient, that I will stay there and die there."

In the meantime, he was getting ready to leave Croisset for Paris and to abandon the ancient mysteries of *Salammbô* in favor of the "monstrous debauches" of the capital. A well-deserved bit of relaxation, he thought. In Paris he saw Sainte-Beuve, Gautier, Renan, Baudelaire, Feydeau, the Goncourt brothers, and a few women who were much in fashion: Jeanne de Tourbey, Aglaé Sabatier, nicknamed *"la Présidente,"* the actress Arnould-Plessy. In this little group the talk was mostly about literature. Romanticism was passé. Alfred de Musset had just died, Marceline Desbordes-Valmore was very old, very much forgotten. Who read Chateaubriand, Vigny, Stendhal, or Lamartine nowadays? Of the great figures of the preceding era, the only ones still in favor were Balzac, George Sand, Alexandre Dumas, and the exiled Hugo, who fulminated against the empire from afar. Already other voices were making themselves heard. As a reaction against the intellectual movement of their predecessors, who had preached the supremacy of emotion, imagination, and dreams, young men like Champfleury and Duranty were trying to introduce a timid realism. But the most popular writers of the day were still men like Paul Féval, whose sensational adventure novels were appearing in serial form, or Edmond About, the author of fanciful tales and harmless, amusing social satire. Flaubert disdained the literary rat race, but he was happily excited to talk with fellow writers who, like himself, were busy juggling with words. After one of these discussions, the Goncourt brothers noted with irritation in the diary they kept: "Flaubert and Feydeau debating a thousand recipes for style and form; little mechanical tricks expounded earnestly and pompously; a discussion that was childish and grave, ridiculous and solemn, about ways of writing and rules for good prose. . . . We thought we had stumbled upon an argument between two Byzantine grammarians."[13] For Flaubert, however, these questions of writing were far from insignificant. He declared that there was no such thing as a work without style. And he wanted to prove it with *Salammbô* even more clearly than with *Madame Bovary.* When Mlle. Leroyer de Chantepie wrote him that since he had become a Parisian he was now "a boulevardier," "a man in vogue in society," adulated and sought after, he protested vigorously: "I swear to you that I am nothing of the sort. . . . On the contrary, I am what is called a bear. . . . Sometimes, even in Paris, I don't go out for a week. I have good relations with many artists, but I frequent only a few of them. . . . As for what is called *society*, I never go into it. I don't know how to dance, or waltz, or play a single card game, or even how to make conversation in a salon, for everything that people say there strikes me as idiotic."[14] For a few days he was in a great state of anxiety over a new sort of problem. The Théâtre de la Porte-Saint-Martin had proposed to put on a play drawn from *Madame Bovary*. He hesitated, consulted Louis Bouilhet, and finally refused what he considered to be a compromise unworthy of him and of his book. "All I was supposed to give them was my title, and I would have had half the royalties. They would have had the thing knocked together by some celebrated hack. . . . But this fiddling around with art and money struck me as unseemly. I refused the whole thing straight out and retreated to my lair. When I do a play, I'll enter the theater by the front door or not at all."[15] And he explained to Alfred Baudry: "It's about thirty thousand francs' worth of earnings that I'm giving up. Shit, that's the way I am, poor but honest. I was about to enter the ranks of hacks, but my pride rebelled. That's the story."[16]

Having taken this heroic decision, he felt more determined than ever to carry on with *Salammbô*. But he was convinced that to give his work more verisimilitude he must go to the places where the action was to unfold, breathe in the smells of the country, bathe in its light. It would be a very short trip, since he would only have to visit the region around Carthage. On March 23 he announced to Baudry: "Two weeks from today, on Wednesday, April 7, I'm lighting out for 'the shores of the Moor,' where I hope not to remain a captive.* I have had a pair of riding boots built that gives me voluptuous pleasure. In short, your friend is looking forward to seeing waves and palm trees again." For a while he had thought he would be unable to leave, because his mother had fallen ill: pleurisy. But

* A reference to *Les Hirondelles* [The Swallows] by the enormously popular songwriter Pierre-Jean Béranger, who had died the preceding year. The verses tell of a French soldier who is held captive "on the shores of the Moor." —Trans.

under the care of Achille she had recovered and was now quite well again. She was nonetheless worried to death to see her son launching forth on another exotic adventure. "How our affections make us suffer!" Flaubert wrote Mlle. Leroyer de Chantepie. "There is no love which is not sometimes as heavy to bear as hatred! One feels this especially when one is going on a journey! . . . In a week I shall be in Marseilles, in two weeks in Constantine, and three days later in Tunis. . . . It will be the fourth time I have been to Marseilles, and this time I shall be alone, absolutely alone. The circle has shrunk. The same thoughts I had in 1849, when I sailed for Egypt, I am going to turn over in my mind again in a few days, while walking the same pavements. Thus in life one constantly goes around the same series of troubles, like a squirrel in a cage, panting at every step."[17]

On Monday, April 12, 1858, he left his flat in Paris and took a cab to the station. In his pocket, a notebook in which to record his impressions: "I smoke one pipe after another, mulling over all my old memories." In Valence he stuffed himself "speedily and with delight"; in Avignon he sampled sherbets; in Marseilles he "crammed" himself with bouillabaisse. Then the obligatory pilgrimage to the hotel on the Rue de la Darse. The ground floor was now occupied by a cheap shop. On the second floor a barber and wig maker plied his trade. With tender thoughts of Eulalie Foucaud's caresses, Flaubert had himself shaved. The wallpaper was still the same. Two days later he embarked on the steamer *Hermus,* among emigrants and soldiers. As a remedy for seasickness, he chewed bread rubbed with garlic. Then the swells abated. "It's a beautiful night," he wrote Louis Bouilhet, "the sea flat as a lake of oil; old Tanit is shining, the ship's engine is chugging away, the captain is smoking on a couch beside me, and the deck is packed with Arabs bound for Mecca.* Lying in their white burnooses, with their faces veiled and their feet bare, they look like corpses in their shrouds. We also have some women and children on board. The whole lot, all jumbled together, are sleeping or dismally vomiting;

---

* Tanit was the Carthaginian moon goddess.

the Tunisian coastline, which we are following, is visible through the mist. . . . The only important thing I have seen so far is Constantine, Jugurtha's city. It is surrounded by an immense ravine, tremendous, vertiginous. I walked along the top and explored the interior on horseback. . . . Vultures wheeled in the sky. So far as vile things are concerned, I have never seen anything finer in that line than three Maltese and an Italian (on the outside seat of the coach to Constantine) who were drunk as Poles, stank like carrion, and roared like tigers. These gentlemen were making obscene jokes and gestures, accompanying it all with farts, belches, and much chewing of garlic, in the dark by the glow of their pipes. What a journey! And what company! It was Plautus raised to the twelfth power."[18]

He visited cool, silent mosques, admired a man who was writing crouched over a little stand beside the tomb of a holy man, met on the road three fellows as thin as skeletons who were eaters of hashish and hunters of porcupines, which they considered a great delicacy. During a dinner with the director of the postal service and three other guests, he was astonished to learn that "they knew *Bovary!*" Back to Philippeville; then they headed for Tunis over an arid plain. Flaubert spent the night in a mud hut with a roof of reeds. "The camp dogs were barking. They are in the habit of barking all night to keep the jackals away." On Sunday, May 2, he visited the ruins of Utica. A pile of shapeless blocks "as if they had been knocked down by an earthquake." Farther on, at last he discovered the landscape of *Salammbô*. "All of Carthage is much lower than I am, white houses, green public squares: wheat. . . . A dromedary on a terrace, turning a well: *it must have been just so in Carthage.*" Nevertheless, he told Louis Bouilhet: "I am not thinking at all about my novel. I am looking at the country, that's all, and having a great time. . . . I know Carthage thoroughly and at all hours of the day and night."[19] To Ernest Feydeau he recounted that he spent most of his time on horseback, that he went to Moorish cabarets to hear Jewish singers, that he had taken part in a scorpion hunt, and that he had killed with his whip a snake "about a meter long" that was coiling around the legs of his mount. He roamed the region with a renewed sense of wonder, going from one landscape to another, from one adventure to another, visited Bizerte, "a charming city, a half-abandoned oriental Venice," and attended the ceremony of kissing the hand of the bey, a graying personage "with heavy lids and a drunken look in his eye." The procession began. Each one applied his lips twice to the bey's palm: "First the ministers, then the men with green or pumpkin-colored turbans. The soldiers in uniform were pitiful: fat asses in shapeless pants, down-at-heel shoes, epaulettes attached with pieces of string, an immense quantity of crosses and gilt; the priests, white, thin, sinister, or stupid: the sanctimonious look is the same everywhere, the intolerance of Ramadan reminded me of the intolerance of the Catholics' Lent."[20]

Having returned to Tunis, he attended an exhibition of horsemanship that took place in a cloud of dust. Then he pushed on to the plain of Bardo, the gorges of Djarkoub-el-Djedavi, covered with wild jujube trees, and the plain of Mez-el-Bab. There he inspected the ruins and noted: "Is this not the place where Hamilcar's bridge stood?" Through a great effort of imagination he tried to raise the ruins again, to reconstruct cities and introduce into this artificially rebuilt setting the phantoms of his characters. But the present resisted the past. And he continued his tour, on horseback, to Testour, Tugga, El Kef. . . . Already he foresaw the end of his expedition: "I am leaving here the day after tomorow and returning to Algeria *overland*, which is a journey few Europeans have made," he wrote Jules Duplan on May 20, 1858. "In this way I shall see everything I need for *Salammbô*. Now I have a thorough knowledge of Carthage and its surroundings. . . . I have been very chaste on this trip. But very gay, and glowing with health as strong as marble."

On May 24, in Rieff, he saw a Roman tomb, took "an excellent Turkish bath," and slept in a tent with the Bedouins. In Guelma, at night, he had to fight off an invasion of fleas. In Constantine he stayed at a hotel and went to a bathhouse, where he put himself into the hands of a Negro masseur. "The one in Rieff massaged my knees with his head," he reported. At last he took ship for Marseilles. The deck was crowded with "officers of the African army returning home."

The rest of the journey was sadly lacking in picturesque elements. "Arrival in Marseilles at two o'clock. Customs intolerable. Omnibus. Hôtel Parrocel. Bath. Running short of money. . . . I leave alone in an open carriage. . . ." On the train the other travelers in his compartment were of no interest. "Solid lunch in Dijon. Boredom in the afternoon, heat. What a stupid country France is!" And then Paris again: "The boulevard in summer. My house empty. Rush to get to Feydeau's; I am served dinner. . . . Supper at the Café Anglais. I sleep on my couch. Lunch at the Café Turc. Visits to La Tourbey, Sabatier, Mme. Maynier." On June 7 and 8 he saw among others Louise Pradier, Alexandre Dumas *fils*, and the actress Mme. Person, dressed (Lord knew why) in a sailor costume topped by a red wig.

Back in Croisset he recopied his notes during the night of June 12–13 and concluded: "To a considerable extent my journey has already receded into the past and been forgotten; everything is confused in my head, I feel as if I had just come from a masked ball that had gone on for two months. Will I get to work now? Will I be bored? Oh, may I be suffused with all the energies of nature I have inhaled, and may they breathe forth in my book! Powers of artistic emotion, come to my aid! Help me to resurrect the past! Beauty must guide my pen, but all must be living and true! Have pity on my purpose, oh God of all souls! Give me strength—and hope!"

When he went back to his manuscript he was bitterly disappointed. Not one page that stood up. His journey had opened his eyes to antiquity as it really was. "I must inform you that *Carthage* has to be entirely done over, or rather done from scratch," he wrote Ernest Feydeau. "I am *demolishing everything*. It's absurd! impossible! false! I think I'm going to find the right tone. I'm beginning to understand my characters and to take an interest in them. That's already a great deal. I don't know when I shall finish this colossal piece of work. Maybe not for two or three years. In the meantime, I beg everyone who comes near me not to speak a word about it. I even feel like sending out cards announcing my death. My mind is made up. The public, the printer, and time no longer exist: to work!"[21]

Flaubert's indifference to the details of publishing was reinforced, of course, by the conviction that to him, literature would never be a way of making a living. Thanks to his mother's income, he was shielded from want. He could be supercilious toward people who had to live by their pens. The year before, he had confided to Mlle. Leroyer de Chantepie: "I live with my mother and a niece (the daughter of a sister who died at the age of twenty), whom I am educating. As for money, I have *pretty nearly* enough to live on, for it is said I have expensive tastes, although I lead a very regular life. Many people think me rich, but I find myself continually short of money, having in my heart of hearts the most extravagant desires, which I do not satisfy, of course. And then, I haven't the least notion how to count; I don't understand a thing about business matters."[22]

Free from pecuniary considerations, he eagerly went back to work. Since the weather was hot, he went swimming every day in the Seine and declared proudly to Ernest Feydeau: "I swim like a salamander. I have never felt better. I am in a good and hopeful mood. When one is feeling fit one must store up courage for the times when one's health will be failing. They will come, alas!"[23] And again to Feydeau: "I have retreated into my cave (and mentally even more than physically). For the next two or three years, perhaps, nothing in this world that goes on in literature is going to touch me. As in the past, I am going to write for myself, for myself alone. As for *La Presse* and Charles-Edmond, shit, double shit, and shit again! . . .* I am sure that what I am writing will not be a success, and so much the better! I don't give a bloody damn. . . . I don't want to make a single concession anymore; I'm going to write horrors, I'll put in male brothels and snake stews, etc. Because, darn it all! you have to have a little fun before you croak."[24]

He worked "like fifteen oxen," wondered if he would find a reader capable of swallowing four hundred pages "of such a piece

---

* Flaubert had rashly promised Charles-Edmond, editor of *La Presse*, the publication rights to his next novel.

of architecture," and shouted out his sentences from morning to night till his "chest was ready to burst." "The next day, when I reread what I've done, I often cross everything out and start over again. And so on. The future offers me nothing but an infinite series of words crossed out—not a very amusing prospect."[25] And he explained further: "No one since the beginning of literature has ever undertaken such an insane project. It's bristling with difficulties. To make people speak a language *that they didn't think in!* Nothing is known about Carthage. . . . I have to find a middle way between the overblown and the real. . . . I am convinced that good books are not written this way. This one will not be a good book. No matter, so long as it makes me dream of great things! Our worth is to be measured more by our aspirations than by our achievements."[26] At the end of October his anxiety over the novel was causing him "atrocious stomachaches." "No one, since pens have been in existence, has suffered as much as I because of them. What daggers! And how one lacerates one's heart with those little tools!"[27]

As soon as he was better, he left for Paris again. To the friends he met there he extolled the sulfurous talent of the marquis de Sade, whom he had just reread and whom he rated very highly. In November he dined at the Goncourts' with Gavarni, Charles-Edmond, Saint-Victor, and Mario Uchard. His hosts noted in their *Journal*: "Flaubert, a mind haunted by M. de Sade, to whom he constantly returns, as to an enticing mystery. Basically, a glutton for depravity, seeking it out, happy to see a cleaner of cesspools eat shit and exclaiming, still with reference to Sade: 'It's the most amusing nonsense I've ever run across!' . . . For the setting of his novel he has chosen Carthage, as the home of the rottenest civilization on earth."

At the end of November Flaubert packed his bags and went "back to Carthage," as he put it—that is, to Croisset. It was very cold. Logs were blazing in the fireplace. Flaubert worked "at a great rate," every night until four in the morning. Solitude intoxicated him "like alcohol." He hardly noticed the dawn coming up, he said. Not an event, not a sound. "It is complete, objective nothingness." "At every line, at every word my vocabulary fails me." Still, the book advanced somehow. "I've finally achieved the erection, Monsieur, by dint of self-flagellation and masturbation. Let's hope that joy will follow."[28] At the end of the year, according to his calculations he was still only a quarter of the way through the book. But there was no hurry. The longer one took to write a manuscript, the more likely it was to escape the mediocrity of the common run of books. "A polar bear is not more solitary and a god is not more calm," Flaubert told Mlle. Leroyer de Chantepie. "I no longer think of anything but *Carthage,* and that is what is necessary. A book has never been anything for me but a *way of living* in a particular milieu."[29] With Ernest Feydeau he used cruder language: "Oh, what a real pain in the ass Carthage is sometimes! . . . You tell me that you need money, you wretch! And me! . . . Never mind! . . . You will see me driving a hackney carriage before you see me *writing for money.*" And in conclusion, he offered this piece of advice from a man leading a life without women to a fellow writer who was of too amorous a disposition: "Be careful not to ruin your intelligence in commerce with the ladies. You will lose your genius in the depths of a womb. . . . Keep your priapism for style, fuck your inkstand, calm yourself down with meat, and be very sure, as Tissot of Geneva says (*Traité de l'Onanisme,* page 72, see the engraving), that losing one ounce of sperm is more fatiguing than losing three liters of blood."[30]

On February 19 he returned to Paris but only visited a few friends in literary circles and a few actresses. One day the Goncourt brothers received an unexpected visit from him: "A ring at the door. It was Flaubert, who had been told by Saint-Victor that we had seen a battle mace somewhere that was more or less Carthaginian, and who had come to ask us for the address. Difficulty with his Carthaginian novel. Nothing to go on. To reconstruct the scene he had to invent something probable. . . . He has an extraordinary resemblance to portraits of Frédérick Lemaître as a young man: very tall, very well built, with large protuberant eyes under heavy lids, full cheeks, rough, drooping mustaches, and a blotchy, uneven complexion."[31]★

★ Frédérick Lemaître was a celebrated actor of the time. —Trans.

When he had returned to Croisset, Flaubert received a letter from Ernest Feydeau: "You are very fortunate that thanks to your private income, you can take your time over your work." Flaubert was nettled and shot back a reply: "My fellow writers are always throwing in my face the three sous of income that keep me, precisely, from starving. It's easier to do that than to imitate me. I mean, than to live as I do: first, in the country for three quarters of the year; second, *without a wife* (a small point that is rather delicate but of considerable importance), without a friend, a horse, a dog, in short without any of the attributes of human life; third, for me everything outside the work itself counts for nothing. . . . The impatience of men of letters to have their works printed, acted, known, praised is an astonishment to me, like a form of madness. All of that seems to me to have as much to do with their task as it does with dominoes or politics. . . . I could have been rich; I said fuck everything, and I continue to live like a Bedouin in my desert and my pride. Shit, shit, and supershit—that's my motto."[32]

When the heat of summer returned, he felt revivified. "I revel in this temperature," he wrote Mme. Jules Sandeau. "The sun brings me to life and intoxicates me like wine. I spend my afternoons in a slovenly costume that is scarcely decent, with the windows closed and the Venetian blinds drawn. In the evening I plunge into the Seine, which flows at the bottom of my garden. The nights are exquisite and I go to bed at daybreak. There you have it. Besides, I passionately love the night. It fills me with a great calm. . . . You ask if my novel will soon be finished. Alas, no! I am a third of the way through. . . . I write the way one plays the violin, with no other purpose than to amuse myself, and it sometimes happens that I do *pieces* which are to serve no purpose in the work as a whole and which I afterward destroy. With such a method, and a difficult subject, a volume of one hundred pages can take ten years."[33]

On August 15 Achille Flaubert and Louis Bouilhet were decorated with the Legion of Honor. Flaubert's first thought was that this cross Bouilhet had been awarded was likely to excite the jealousy of certain persons "who would take revenge" when his next play appeared. His deep feelings of friendship made him rejoice on behalf of those he loved when they received a distinction for which he himself had no desire. At the end of September he received a copy of Victor Hugo's latest collection of poems, *La Légende des siècles,* and plunged enthusiastically into the forest of rhymes. "What a man old Hugo is!" he exclaimed to Ernest Feydeau. "God almighty, what a poet! I have just swallowed the two volumes at one gulp. . . . I'm beside myself! Tie me up! Ah, I feel better! . . . Old man Hugo has made me lose my mind!"[34] And he added: "My work is going a little better. I'm in the midst of a battle of elephants, and I can assure you that I am killing men like flies. I am spilling oceans of blood." But at this time Ernest Feydeau was too worried about his wife's health to take an interest in literature. The doctors, he said, had given her up for lost. To bolster his courage a little, Flaubert, with a ferocious egotism, found nothing better to tell him than that for an artist devoted to truth, the observation of suffering was necessary and valuable. In his view, a writer should consider every event in his life, no matter how cruel, as an excuse to enrich his work. A book that was not nourished by the blood of its author was a mere pile of paper. Anyone who claimed to know how to use a pen must come to look upon pain as an indispensable element of creation. There could be no genius without this professional approach to life. "Poor little woman!" he wrote Feydeau. "It is frightful! You are having, and are going to have, *good* scenes, which you will be able to turn into *good* studies! It's a high price to pay for them. The bourgeois little suspect that we are serving them up our hearts. The race of gladiators is not dead; every artist is one. He entertains the public with his agonies. . . . The only way not to suffer too much in such crises is to study oneself with the greatest intensity."[35]

Feydeau's wife died on October 18, 1859. He informed his friend in a despairing letter. Flaubert, much moved, replied: "In the name of the only thing in this world that is worthy of respect, in the name of the Beautiful, hang on tight with both hands, make a furious leap with both heels, and leave it all behind! Of course I know that sorrow is a pleasure and that one enjoys weeping. But the soul dissolves, the mind melts in tears, suffering becomes a habit and a way of looking at life that makes it intolerable. . . . You are still young. I think you have in you great works to be brought forth. Remember that you must write them."[36]

His wish was fulfilled. After a few days of prostration, Feydeau confessed to him that he had gone back to work. Flaubert congratulated him at once, as on a victory over the wretched condition of the married man: "Carry on, my poor friend! Fasten onto an idea! Ideas are women who at least don't die and don't deceive you." And to take his mind off his troubles he recommended that Feydeau read the novel *Lui*, which had just been published over the signature of Louise Colet: "You will recognize your friend in it, served up in fine fashion. . . . As for me, I come out of it as pure as the driven snow, but as a man who is insensitive, miserly, in short a gloomy imbecile. That's what it is to have copulated with a Muse. I laughed so hard I nearly split my sides."[37]

While he went on fussing over *Salammbô*, which was progressing slowly, he dreamed of joining a French expedition to China, "country of painted screens and nankeen." What held him back was his mother, who, he said, was "beginning to grow old and for whom this departure would be the last straw." However, he agreed with her that a stay in Paris would do them both good. She went first. Before going to join her, he wrote Maurice Schlésinger: "I shall probably find Paris as stupid as I left it, or more so. The mediocrity increases with the widening of the streets. The idiocy rises to the height of the beautifications. . . . It won't be this year that I finish my book on Carthage. I write very slowly, because for me a book is a special way of living. In connection with a word or an idea, I do research, I let my mind wander, I go off into endless reveries."[38]

On December 20 he finally arrived in the city which he claimed to detest but which he could not do without for long. No doubt there was an element of playacting in his posture as a man of letters living like a hermit and put off by the turpitude of the capital. He billed himself as a caveman, but he took pleasure in receiving friends at his home on Sundays and in dining often at the house of Mme. Sabatier, who was the official mistress of the banker Mosselmann, the friend of Baudelaire, and the celebrated model for Clésinger's marble *Femme piquée par un serpent*. In the midst of this social hubbub, he missed Louis Bouilhet, who now lived in Mantes. However, his friend's career was shaping up well. He was preparing a collection of poems, and the administration of the Comédie Française had commissioned him to write a work to celebrate the forthcoming annexation of Savoy by France. Flaubert exploded with indignation over the latter proposal: "Never! Never! Never! They're setting you up to take a licking, and a good one! *I beg of you,* do not do it!" And also: "By accepting, you lower yourself and, to speak plainly, you degrade yourself. You will lose your status as a pure poet, an independent man. You will be categorized, enrolled in the regiment, captured. Never any politics, for God's sake! It brings bad luck and it's unclean."[39]

At the beginning of the new year Flaubert was associating regularly with the popular writers of the day. He met Octave Feuillet at Jules Janin's, became friends with Paul de Saint-Victor and the Goncourt brothers, dined with Maury and Renan. On January 12 he was part of a merry gathering around the Goncourts' table. The talk was about Louise Colet's novel *Lui*, in which he was portrayed in the guise of Léonce, about the latest plays, about actresses and the strange ways of females. "I have found a very simple way to do without them," Flaubert declared. "I lie facedown, and during the night . . . it's infallible." One by one the guests departed. Flaubert stayed on after the others. "We were alone with him in the drawing room filled with cigar smoke," noted the Goncourts. "He, pacing up and down on the carpet, bumping his head on the chandelier, pouring himself out, opening up to us as to kindred spirits. He told us about the retired, unsociable life he leads, shut in and closed off even in Paris. Detesting the theater, enjoying no other diversion than the Sunday dinners given by Mme. Sabatier, *la Présidente,* as she is called in society. He loathes the country, works ten hours a day but wastes a great deal of time, losing himself in reading and always ready to play truant from his work and go off on side excursions. . . ." The discussion turned to style in the novel, and Flaubert exclaimed: "Do you understand how idiotic it is to struggle to eliminate the assonances from a sentence or the repetitions from a page? For whom? . . . Yes, form: how many readers take satisfaction and delight in form?" Whereupon he cited the three authors who, in his opinion, wrote the best: La Bruyère, Montesquieu, and Chateaubriand in certain passages. "And there he was," wrote the Goncourts, "his eyes starting from his head, his face flushed, his arms stretched wide as for a stage embrace, with the span of an Antaeus, drawing from his chest and throat fragments of [Montesquieu's] *Dialogue de Sylla et d'Eucrate,* and flinging their brazen sound at us like the snarl of a lion." Then Flaubert came back to his anxieties over the struggle for perfection in *Salammbô* and said with a sigh: "Do you know the sum total of my ambition? It's to have an intelligent, well-read man shut himself up with my book for four hours and to give him an orgy of historical hashish. That's all I want. . . . After all, work is still the best way of escaping from life!"

On January 25 it was the Goncourt brothers' turn to visit him. "There we were on the Boulevard du Temple, in Flaubert's study, with windows giving on the boulevard and a gilded Indian idol in the middle of the mantelpiece. On his writing table lay pages of his novel, which were almost nothing but lines crossed out. Great compliments on our book, warm and sincere, which did our hearts good. A friendship of which we are proud and which he demonstrates frankly, openly, with a sort of robust familiarity and generous lack of reserve." Five days later the Goncourts spent the evening at Flaubert's with Louis Bouilhet, who, they said, had "the physique of a handsome workingman." "Talk about de Sade, to whom Flaubert's mind always returns, as if fascinated." He defined de Sade as follows: "He is the spirit of the Inquisition, the spirit of torture, the spirit of the medieval Church, the hatred of nature. There is not one tree in de Sade, not one animal." Sitting by the fire, he told the Goncourts about his first love for Eulalie Foucaud: "Ecstatic fucking, then tears, then letters, then nothing." However, in the course of repeated meetings, the two brothers came to lose certain illusions about their new friend. After having showered him with praise, they discovered all his faults. They were too refined, too

sophisticated not to be offended by his rustic manners. "We recognize now that there is a barrier between us and Flaubert," they
wrote in their *Journal* on March 16, 1860. "At bottom, he is a
provincial and a poseur. One has the vague sense that he undertook
all his great travels partly to astonish the people of Rouen. His mind
is as coarse and heavy as his body. Delicate things don't seem to
touch him. He is chiefly sensitive to the big bass drum of sentences.
There are very few ideas in his conversation, and they are presented
loudly and solemnly. His mind, like his voice, is declamatory. The
stories, the figures he sketches have about them a smell of old fossils
in some sub-prefecture. He wears white waistcoats of ten years back,
the kind Macaire wore to court Eloa.* With regard to the Académie
and the Pope, he still goes into fits of rage and indignation of which
one might say, as de Maistre did of unbelief, 'It's vulgar!' . . . He
is clumsy, excessive, and without lightness in anything—in jests,
exaggeration, imitation. . . . His loutish jokes lack charm."

In spite of this uncharitable assessment, the Goncourts continued to see Flaubert and to treat him with the greatest affability. He
would gladly have remained in Paris another few weeks, but he had
to return to the provinces to attend the wedding of Achille's daughter, Juliette, and one Adolphe Roquigny: "He is a strong man who
seems as gentle as a lamb. The young people appear to be in love.
That's all very good. Everyone is delighted. Happy are those who
live in the good, simple, natural way! . . . Therein lies all the
happiness of life, no doubt. And yet, if it were offered to me, would
I accept?"[40] The religious ceremony took place in Rouen on April
17, 1860. To Flaubert, the family celebrations, with the flowers,
embraces, speeches, and banquets, were an almost unendurable
torment. "I got indigestion from a surfeit of bourgeois," he wrote
Ernest Feydeau. "Three dinners and a lunch! And forty-eight hours

* The reference is to two of the leads in *Robert Macaire*, a satirical comedy
written by Frédérick Lemaître, who also created the title role, that was a smash
hit in 1834. The reader may have seen Macaire, white waistcoat and all, in
some of the cartoons of Daumier, who seized upon the character of the re-
sourceful swindler and made him into a symbol of the greed and hypocrisy of
bourgeois society under Louis-Philippe. —Trans.

in Rouen. That's heavy! I'm still belching the streets of my native city and vomiting white ties."[41] When the Goncourts sent him their latest book, *Les Maîtresses de Louis XV*, he congratulated them on the quality of the work and, without suspecting their true feelings about him, closed his letter with the words, "You are very kind to have sent me the book, to have so much talent and to love me a little."[42] In another letter he spoke to them about his own work, which was progressing slowly: "With such a subject, realism is well nigh impossible. There remains the expedient of 'waxing poetical,' but then one lapses into the style of a lot of old chestnuts from *Télémaque* to *Les Martyrs*. . . . * In spite of it all, I push on, but consumed by doubts and anxieties."[43] To a new friend, Mlle. Amélie Bosquet,† he confirmed the difficulties of the task he had undertaken: "At the moment I am overwhelmed with fatigue. I am carrying two entire armies on my shoulders: thirty thousand men on one side, eleven thousand on the other, not counting the elephants with their elephant drivers, the servants, and the baggage. . . . When I think that I shall get no credit for all the pains I am taking, and that any Tom, Dick, or Harry—a journalist, an idiot, a bourgeois—will have no trouble pointing out (and perhaps correctly) any number of stupidities in the parts that seem best to me, I lapse into a bottomless melancholy, I have depressions as black as ebony, a mortal bitterness, and doubts that toss me as on an ocean of refuse."[44] He envied Feydeau, who had left his writing table and was now traveling in Tunisia, where, without doubt, he was intoxicating himself with vast horizons and sleeping with submissive, expert women. And he predicted to his friend that on his return he would have no more taste for the caresses of his female compatriots: "You will regret that silent lovemaking in which souls alone speak to each other, that tenderness without words, that animal passivity

---

* For *Télémaque*, see the footnote on page 11. As its name suggests, the story is an extension of the *Odyssey* and its style an imitation of the Homeric. Chateaubriand's epic poem in prose *Les Martyrs, ou le Triomphe de la religion chrétienne* (1809) is set in the third century and is likewise couched in elaborate pseudo-classical rhetoric. —Trans.

† Mlle. Bosquet was a journalist and novelist and a determined feminist.

which causes manly pride to swell."[45] But what he found even more surprising was the adventure of Maxime Du Camp, who on a sudden impulse had enlisted in Garibaldi's army and was taking part in the expedition of the thousand volunteers: "If you have five minutes ahead of you, my good Max, send me a word just so that I know what's become of you, for God's sake! If you are dead, alive, or wounded. . . . You beast! Will you never stay quiet?"[46]

In the last half of August he returned to Paris to do some further research and dined at the critic Aubryet's with the Goncourts, Saint-Victor, Charles-Edmond, Halévy, and Gautier. From the beginning of the conversation the sparks flew. Everyone had a definitive judgment to contribute about some book, play, or author. "Well," shouted Flaubert, "there is one man I detest even more than Ponsard, and that's that fellow Feuillet!"* And he launched into a panegyric on Voltaire, whom he held to be "a saint," which raised an outcry from the other guests.

After a short visit to Étretat, where he gazed at the sea dreaming of his youth, he returned to Paris to attend the opening of Louis Bouilhet's play *L'Oncle Million* at the Odéon. "Flaubert dropped in," wrote the Goncourts. "Still buried out there in his Carthage, leading the life of a wood louse and laboring like an ox. . . . In his novel he's come to the fornication scene, a Carthaginian fornication, and, he says, 'I really have to work my readers up into a state; I have to make a man who thinks he's laying the moon screw a woman who thinks she's being laid by the sun.' "[47]

The opening night of *L'Oncle Million,* on December 6, 1860, was a disaster. Flaubert was as dismayed as if the failure had been his own. "As you know (or do not know)," he wrote Jules Duplan, "Bouilhet's play was a flop. The critics were abominable and the director of the Odéon was worse. . . . Oh, it was lovely! lovely! lovely! The Emperor was supposed to come and didn't. . . . As for

---

* François Ponsard was a poet and playwright, Octave Feuillet a novelist and playwright. Although both were much admired at the time and elected to membership in the Académie Française, they are now virtually forgotten. —Trans.

Bouilhet, he is devastated and in a rotten position. He was going to go to see you, but I think he is so depressed that he has gone into hiding."[48]

Flaubert already felt that he had stayed in Paris too long. Leaving his mother and Caroline in the flat on the Boulevard du Temple, he returned alone to Croisset to work. "I am becoming highly ridiculous with my eternal book that is never published, and I have sworn to myself to finish it this year," he wrote Mlle. Leroyer de Chantepie. "I am here with an old servant, getting up at noon and going to bed at three in the morning, without seeing anyone or hearing anything about what is going on in the world."[49]

Holed up in this literary hothouse, he received a book from Michelet, *La Mer,* and at once sent the historian heartfelt thanks. "In school I devoured your *Histoire romaine,* the first volumes of the *Histoire de France,* the *Mémoires de Luther,* the *Introduction* [*à l'histoire universelle*], everything that came from your pen, with a pleasure so deep and intense that it was almost sensual. . . . Since I have become a man, my admiration has been consolidated."[50] Also in January, he learned that Ernest Feydeau, the recent widower, was marrying again. Decidedly, the man was deranged to insist on taking a wife when celibacy had so many advantages for an artist. Nonetheless, Flaubert congratulated his friend: "Blessings on her; accept all my good wishes; I don't have to tell you that they are sincere and profound." But he could not refrain from adding: "We are hardly taking the same paths. . . . You believe in life and love it, whereas I mistrust it. I am fed up with it and partake of it as little as possible. It's more cowardly, but more prudent." As for his *Salammbô,* he told his correspondent that it was going forward, "with good days and bad (more of the latter, of course)."[51]

Another three months of work and he rushed to Paris to read extracts of his novel to his friends. "The solemn ceremony will take place on Monday," he wrote the Goncourts. "Flu or no flu. Never mind. Shit! Here is the program: 1. I shall begin yelling at four o'clock sharp. So come around three. 2. At seven o'clock, oriental dinner. You will be served human flesh, bourgeois brains, and tigers' clitorises sautéed in rhinoceros butter. 3. After coffee, resumption of the Punic bellowing until the listeners expire from exhaustion. How does that sound?"[52] On Monday, May 6, 1861, the Goncourts came as agreed. "Flaubert," they wrote, "read aloud in his booming, sonorous voice that lulls you with a sound liked a bronze purr. At seven o'clock we dined. . . . Then after dinner and a pipe, the reading was resumed." The Goncourts dared not tell Flaubert what they thought of his book, the most important passages of which he had "bellowed" to them. But they confided their disappointment to their diary: "*Salammbô* is not up to what I expected of Flaubert. His personality, which was so well hidden, so completely absent from that very impersonal work *Madame Bovary*, comes through here, inflated, melodramatic, declamatory, wallowing in bombast and in crude, almost garish colors. Flaubert sees the Orient, and the ancient Orient, as if it were a cabinet full of Algerian bric-a-brac. Some of his effects are childish, others ridiculous. . . . The feelings of his characters . . . are the everyday, universal feelings of all humanity, and not of Carthaginian humanity; and his Mathô is basically nothing but an operatic tenor in a barbaric poem. . . . Almost every sentence has a *like* or *as* supporting a comparison the way a candlestick supports a candle." Flaubert was so exceedingly naive that he never suspected how disappointed his friends had been. He went back to Croisset bursting with enthusiasm. "I don't think I shall have finished before the end of this year," he wrote Feydeau. "But even if I am still at it ten years from now, I will not return to Paris until *Salammbô* is done. I have sworn it to myself."[53]

And the litany began again: he loathed this book, he had nervous complaints, he was exhausted, the description of the siege of Carthage had finished him: "The war machines are giving me fits! I am sweating blood, pissing boiling water, shitting catapults, and belching sling stones," he wrote the Goncourts. On January 2, 1862, he informed them that he had just emerged still panting from the battle of the Defile of the Axe: "I'm piling horror on horror. Twenty thousand of my fellows have just died of starvation after eating each other; the rest will end up trampled by elephants and devoured by lions." Already he was thinking about possible publication. But he preferred not to hurry. And indeed, there was talk in Paris about the forthcoming publication of Victor Hugo's *Misérables*. "I think it would be a bit imprudent and impudent to risk appearing alongside something so great," Flaubert wrote Mlle. Leroyer de Chantepie. "There are certain persons before whom one should bow and say: 'After you, Monsieur.' Victor Hugo is one of them."[54] He was surprised by another piece of news: Baudelaire wrote asking him to try to persuade the novelist Jules Sandeau to support Baudelaire's candidacy for the Académie Française. How could this morbid, blasphemous poet who had been convicted in criminal court of obscenity for *Les Fleurs du mal*** and who had just published *Les Paradis artificiels, opium et haschisch*, aspire to sit among the purest representatives of bourgeois literature? Flaubert laughed incredulously, approached Sandeau without great hope of success, and replied to Baudelaire: "Wretch, so you want the dome of the Institut to collapse? I can see you sitting between Villemain and Nisard."[55]†

In the days that followed, he recopied the last pages of his manuscript, took purgatives "to banish the peccant humors and arrive fresh in the capital,"[56] and prepared to leave again for Paris, where he planned to spend several weeks. On February 21 he dined with the Goncourt brothers at Charles-Edmond's and talked about his tumultuous relations with Louise Colet. "For that matter, there is no bitterness, no resentment on his part toward this woman who seems to have intoxicated him with her insane, dramatic love filled with thrills, sensations, and shocks," noted the Goncourts. "There is in Flaubert's nature a coarseness that responds to the sort of woman who is terrifying in her sensuality and the violence of her emotions, who exhausts a lover with her transports, her rages, her physical or spiritual frenzies." In a mood for confidences, Flaubert declared that at one time he had been so exasperated by Louise that he had almost killed her. "I could hear the bench in the Court of Assizes creaking under me," he said, rolling his eyes with a terrible

* The prosecutor in Baudelaire's case, which came to trial not long after Flaubert's, was again Ernest Pinard.

† The Académie Française is a part of the Institut de France. Abel Villemain had been a professor of literature at the Sorbonne and Minister of Education under Louis-Philippe; Désiré Nisard was a literary critic. —Trans.

look. While his friends admired his astonishing capacity for work, they criticized him behind his back. One day Théophile Gautier confided to the Goncourts that he thought the writing methods of the author of *Salammbô* were absurd. Years and years to put together four hundred pages—what madness! And then, what was the point in bawling out one's text to judge its harmony? "A book is not made to be read aloud," said Gautier. "We have pages, both of us . . . that are just as rhythmic as anything he's done and without our having gone to such pains. There is one thing for which he feels a remorse that poisons his life. It's that in *Madame Bovary* he put two genitives one on top of the other: *une couronne de fleurs d'oranger* [a crown of orange blossoms]. He is very upset over it; but there was nothing he could do, it was impossible to say it any other way."[57] On March 29 Flaubert received the Goncourts at his apartment, sitting cross-legged, Turkish fashion, on his divan. He was in high spirits and spoke of his desire to write a book on the modern Orient, "the Orient in Western dress," in which he would depict "all the European riffraff—Jews, Muscovites, Greeks. . . ." After dinner the three men went to Gautier's, in Neuilly. There, Flaubert was asked to perform the "Dance of the Drawing Room Idiot." He readily agreed, borrowed a tailcoat from Gautier, and turned up his detachable collar. "I don't know what he did with his hair, his face, his physiognomy," noted the Goncourts, "but he was suddenly transformed into a marvelous caricature of an imbecile. Gautier, seized with a spirit of emulation, took off his coat and, sweating, with beads of perspiration standing on his forehead, his big rump crushing his hams, did us the 'Dance of the Creditor.' And the evening ended with gypsy songs."

After the fun and games, back to solitude and work. On April 14, 1862, Flaubert could write Mlle. Amélie Bosquet: "I have five pages to go to be completely finished; they are not the easiest, and I am exhausted. It's exactly five years that I have been working on this interminable book." And ten days later to Mlle. Leroyer de Chantepie: "Last Sunday, at seven in the morning, I finally finished my novel *Salammbô*. It will take me another month for the corrections and copying, and then I shall return here [to Paris] in mid-September to have the book published at the end of October. But I'm utterly exhausted. I have a fever every night and can scarcely hold a pen. The end was heavy going and it came hard."[58]

Looking at his pile of manuscript, he felt a mixture of pride, anxiety, and fatigue. Rereading it, he discovered that one sentence out of two was lame. "It is impossible for me to go on correcting *Salammbô*. The sight of my handwriting turns my stomach," he wrote Caroline.[59] And again, also to Caroline: "My copyist is making me furious. I was supposed to have everything tomorrow and I still have only eighty pages. I'll be lucky if the whole manuscript is copied by the end of the week."[60] Already he was worrying about practical questions: With which publisher should he deal? At what price? And for what approximate date of publication? He was afraid of the competition. *Les Misérables* was enjoying a smashing success. Was it really the right time to cast *Salammbô* into the arena? Personally, he considered Hugo's novel detestable, and he said so to Mme. Roger des Genettes:* "Well, our god is on the decline! I find *Les Misérables* exasperating. But one is not allowed to say anything against it: one would sound like a police spy. The author's position is impregnable, unassailable. I, who have spent my life worshiping him, am now *indignant*! But I *must* speak my mind. I find neither truth nor greatness in this book. As for the style, it seems to me deliberately incorrect and low. It's a way of flattering the common people. . . . Characters that are all of a piece, as in tragedies! Where are there prostitutes like Fantine, convicts like Valjean? . . . They are puppets, figures made of sugar candy. . . . Endless explanations of things that have nothing to do with the subject and no explanation whatever of things that are indispensable. On the other hand, sermons telling us that universal suffrage is a very fine thing, that the masses need education—that is repeated ad nauseum. Decidedly,

---

* A new correspondent of Flaubert's. He had met her at Louise Colet's. Louis Bouilhet had fallen in love with the young woman, and Flaubert himself found her charming.

in spite of some fine passages—and they are rare—this book is puerile. . . . Posterity will not forgive that man for trying to be a thinker, which goes against his nature."[61]

Actually, the things he was objecting to in Hugo's book were the excesses in the writing, the lyrical flights, the romanticism that was now behind the times. And suddenly a terrible thought struck him: was not *Salammbô* open to the same criticism?

Anne-Caroline Fleuriot Flaubert,
Gustave Flaubert's mother.
Portrait by E.H. Langlois, 1830.
(Photo Jean Collas.)

Dr. Achille-Cléophas Flaubert,
Gustave Flaubert's father.
(Archives Tallandier, photo Jean Dubout.)

Gustave Flaubert as a child.
Portrait by E.H. Langlois.
(Photo Jean Collas.)

M. FLAUBERT.

Gustave Flaubert's birthplace, the Hôtel-Dieu of Rouen.
(Edimédia, photo Dominique Vieau.)

Gustave Flaubert, private collection.
(Photo Pascal Soalhat.)

Gustave Flaubert as an adolescent.
Pencil drawing by Delaunay.
(Archives Tallandier, photo Roger Viollet.)

Élisa Schlésinger and
her daughter.
Portrait by Devéria.
(Archives Tallandier.)

Louise Colet. Lithograph by
Grégoire and Deneux.
(Photo Harlingue-Viollet.)

Vieux Habou Roudou Rousssou

C'est tout bonnement superbe! ce
printemps. J'ai pâli dès la première
colonne et mouillé deux ou trois fois.
— Comme ça se voit! nom de Dieu!
et le plus étonnant, c'est que les deux
héros sont extra-amusants, et mêlement
nagés dans cette grande nature. Le §§ XXVIII
sur le pied est qq chose de délicieux —
enfin je ne sais comment vous exprimer
mon enthousiasme. — et dis merde.
voilà! C'est foutu! — & je m'y connais

donnez vous une crâne poignée demain
de ma part & croyez à l'attachement ble

Gus Flaubert
dit l'idiot des Salons
(Th. Gautier)

Holograph letter of Gustave Flaubert. (Archives Tallandier, photo Roger Viollet.)

Page from the manuscript of *L'Education sentimentale* (from the first part of Chapter V). (Archives Tallandier.)

JOURNÉE DU MERCREDI 23 FÉVRIER

Uprising in Paris, February 23, 1848: The dead are carried through the streets in tumbrels.
(Photo Bulloz.)

Cartoon by Cham. The figure on the left is labeled "The Cold," and the legend reads: "You've come awfully late, my good fellow!" " 'S not my fault, I fell asleep reading *Salammbô*."
(Photo Roger Viollet.)

— Vous arrivez joliment tard, mon bonhomme !
— C'est pas ma faute, je me suis endormi en lisant *Salammbô*

Caricature
of Flaubert,
lpel in hand,
dissecting
Ime. Bovary.
lorer Archives,
sat Collection.)

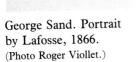

George Sand. Portrait
by Lafosse, 1866.
(Photo Roger Viollet.)

Louis Bouilhet.
(Photo Jean Collas.)

Guy de Maupassant.
(Photo Harlingue-Viollet.)

Maxime Du Camp.
Photograph by Félix Nadar.
(Photo Roger Viollet.)

Ivan Turgenev.
(Photo Roger Viollet.)

Victor Hugo.
(Photo Roger Viollet.)

(*below left*:)
Emile Zola.
Pastel by Henri Groux.
(Photo Jean Collas.)

Charles-Augustin
Sainte-Beuve.
(Photo Roger Viollet.)

(*opposite, at right*:)
Ernest Chevalier.
(Photo Pascal Soalhat.)

Théophile Gautier.
(Photo Roger Viollet.)

Gustave Flaubert's notebooks.
(Photo Raymond Landin.)

View of Rouen in 1847.
(Photo Jean Collas.)

Barbey d'Aurevilly.
Portrait by Lévy.
(Archives Tallandier,
photo Roger Viollet.)

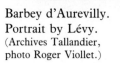

Caroline Hamard,
Gustave Flaubert's niece.
She married Ernest
Commanville and, when
he died, was remarried
to Dr. Franklin Grout.
(Explorer Archives.)

Gustave Flaubert.
Sketch by de Liphart, 1880.
(Archives Tallandier,
photo Roger Viollet.)

(*opposite, at right:*)
Gustave Flaubert.
(Edimédia, photo de Mulnier.)

Gustave Flaubert's study,
as it was reconstructed
in the pavilion at the
Croisset museum.
(Archives Tallandier,
photo Roger Viollet.)

Death mask of Gustave Flaubert
in the Carnavalet museum.
(Photo Bulloz.)

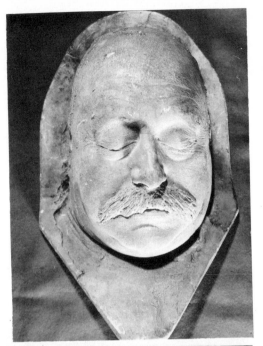

The pavilion housing the
Flaubert museum in Croisset.
(Photo Roger Viollet.)

Chapter 14

IN SOCIETY

Flaubert was unable to deal with money matters by himself and first consulted Jules Duplan about getting *Salammbô* published. He wanted Michel Lévy to sign a contract on faith, without having read the manuscript: "As soon as one has made a name in literature, it is customary to sell a pig in a poke. He has to buy my name and nothing else."[1] Besides, he explained in another letter, "Just to think of the look on Lévy's face when he lays his paws on *my pages* is more repugnant to me than any criticism could be."[2] In any case, he was dead set against the notion of an illustrated edition: "As for illustrations, if I were to be offered a hundred thousand francs, I swear to you that not one would appear. . . . The mere idea of it makes me frantic. Never, never! . . . Ah, show me the fellow who will paint the portrait of Hannibal and draw a Carthaginian armchair! He will do me a great service. It was hardly worth the trouble using so much art to leave everything vague if some clod is going to come along and destroy my dream with his stupid precision."[3] With a pang at parting, he sent the copy of the manuscript off to Paris. It was to remain until further notice in the keeping of Jules Duplan's brother Ernest. "I have at last resigned myself to considering an interminable piece of work as finished," he wrote the Goncourts. "Now the umbilical cord is cut. What a relief! I don't want to think about it anymore."[4]

At Flaubert's request, it was Ernest Duplan who negotiated with Michel Lévy. Flaubert, who had dreamed of selling the work for thirty thousand francs, declared himself ready to accept twenty thousand. But the discussions bogged down. In July he grew impatient. "In order for my book to appear at the beginning of November, the printing would have to start in mid-September," he wrote Ernest Duplan. "There are only three possible publishers: Lévy, Lacroix, and Hachette. See what can be done, feel them out! And try to get me a fairly substantial sum, without sacrificing principles."[5] He was so obsessed by these dealings that he couldn't work. He felt "as dry as a pebble and as empty as a jug with no wine."[6] Since his mother wanted to go to Vichy to take the waters, he went with her. Then, giving up the struggle, he lowered his demands and agreed to make a deal with Lévy for ten thousand francs, without the manuscript having been read and with the assurance that the volume would not be illustrated. (That same year Victor Hugo had received three hundred thousand francs for *Les Misérables*.) In addition, Lévy insisted that the agreement be signed for ten years, that *Madame Bovary* remain his property during that time, and that the author turn over to him at the same price his next novel, which had to be "modern." To impress the public, they would let it be rumored that the sum paid for *Salammbô* was indeed thirty thousand francs. Flaubert promised not to deny it.

On September 8 he was in Paris going over his manuscript one last time: "Right now I am busy removing the superfluous *and*'s and some mistakes in French," he wrote the Goncourts. "I go to bed with the *Grammaire des grammaires* and my worktable is loaded with the volumes of the Académie's dictionary. It will all be finished in a week."[7] More agonizing over the printer's proofs, which he read pen in hand: "I am making the last corrections on the proofs, which is very irritating. I could leap out of my chair with rage when I discover all the slips and foolish errors in my work. I have so much trouble when just one word has to be changed that it keeps me awake at night."[8]

At last, on November 20, 1862, *Salammbô* appeared in the bookstores: a handsome in-octavo volume with a yellow cover, in a first edition of two thousand. Flaubert distributed copies on fine laid paper to his friends and gave a reception on the Boulevard du

In Society

Temple. While declaring that he disdained financial success, he took great pains over the launching of the book. However, it soon became known in literary circles that *Salammbô* had been sold to Michel Lévy not for thirty thousand francs but for ten thousand. The Goncourts were offended by this commercial chicanery unworthy of a man of letters and noted in their *Journal* for November 21: "I am beginning to think there is something of the Norman—and of the craftiest, most dyed-in-the-wool Norman—deep down in this fellow who is so open in appearance, so exuberant on the surface, who has such a hearty handshake, who displays so ostentatiously so much scorn for success, reviews, and publicity, and whom, ever since the false story of his contract with Lévy and the big drum-thumping over it, I have seen surreptitiously accepting the rumor, forming useful social connections, working at his success harder than anyone else, and, for all his air of modesty, launching into direct competition with Hugo."* And indeed, after the years of seclusion and silence, Flaubert was bursting out in all directions: never mind his principles of reserve and haughtiness. Caught up in the workings of the Paris literary machine, he was ready to do anything to make *Salammbô* a success. But could one capture the interest of the public with the story of this Carthaginian heroine Salammbô, daughter of the general Hamilcar and priestess of Tanit, who goes to the tent of the chief of the mercenaries, Mathô, gives herself to him, and persuades him to return the sacred veil which he has seized and on which the fortunes of the republic depend? The bloody defeat of the barbarians, the execution of Mathô, the death of Salammbô—would all these violent scenes disappoint the female readers of *Madame Bovary*? And wouldn't the archaeologists be tempted to attack a novelist who claimed to be resuscitating the remote past?

Salammbô was the work of a visionary. Flaubert had not used the events he recounted to support a thesis, as Chateaubriand had done in *Les Martyrs*. He had not been content to reconstitute a vanished civilization in the manner of a Michelet or an Augustin

* The inhabitants of Normandy have long had a reputation for prudence, shrewdness, and duplicity. —Trans.

185

Thierry. Nor had he tried to write a psychological novel. Each of his characters was all of a piece, with a central passion and strong, simple instincts that made him or her act without deviation. Salammbô—who is said to have been inspired by Jeanne de Tourbey, a striking brunette who was a friend of Louise Pradier's and the official mistress of Marc Fournier, the director of the Théâtre de la Porte-Saint-Martin—was far from having the complexity of an Emma Bovary. The action was motivated more by politics than by sentiment. The story followed the rise and fall of ambitions, rivalries, and struggles for influence, not the rhythm of heartbeats. With its vivid descriptions, tense style, and fantastic subject, it was an epic which took possession of the reader like a hallucination and from which he emerged surfeited with barbaric color and violence. "A mirage," Flaubert said in his letters. He had attained his goal. The work was one of a kind. Situated at the opposite pole from *Madame Bovary*, it defied classification. It was successful with the public at first because of the curiosity it aroused. Before its appearance, readers and journalists had been wondering if the author could bring off something in a different vein. They got their answer! *Salammbô* burst on the scene like an operatic spectacle; it exploded like a bomb full of precious stones. People talked about a "horrifying rain of blood." Some went into ecstasies, others were outraged, still others shrugged their shoulders. The press, for the most part, was unmerciful. From *Le Monde* to *L'Union*, from *La Patrie* to *Le Figaro*, it was a hail of invectives against a writer who offended the sensibilities of his contemporaries. Charles-Augustin Sainte-Beuve, who had very cordial relations with Flaubert, said he was irritated and disappointed by *Salammbô*'s grandiloquence. In three long articles in *Le Constitutionnel*, the critic denounced the book's failings, but the very fact that he devoted so much space to it underlined the importance of the event. He began by declaring that one could not "reconstruct an ancient civilization," which, in his opinion, explained the author's failure. To be sure, he had done an enormous amount of work, but he had labored too hard over it, had not kept himself above his subject. The heroine, Salammbô, said Sainte-Beuve, was lifeless. Her behavior was incomprehensible in terms of human logic. In the description of atrocities, Flaubert revealed a "touch of sadistic imagination." The erudition he displayed would require a glossary. As for the style, it was pompous, bombastic, "paved with multicolored pebbles and precious stones." In conclusion, while the novelist had made a titanic effort, it was nonetheless certain that that effort had miscarried. But he had proved that he had power, and under these conditions, "the misfortune of having failed in his principal intent was not so great."

Flaubert took it hard and on December 23 replied to Sainte-Beuve with a long letter of justification. "Your third article on *Salammbô* has mollified me (I was never very angry). My closest friends were a little annoyed by the other two; but as for me, you had told me frankly what you thought of my big book, and I am grateful to you for having been so forbearing in your criticism." After this preamble he proceeded to the counterattack. Point by point, in detail, relentlessly and with humor, he defended his novel. According to him, everything in it was true. He had not invented any tortures. By accusing him of sadism, Sainte-Beuve was giving arguments to those who had already dragged him into court for *Madame Bovary*. As for the style, "I sacrificed less in that book than in the other to well-rounded sentences and balanced periods," wrote Flaubert. "The metaphors are few and the epithets correspond to reality." And he concluded as follows: "While you have given me some scratches, you have clasped my hands very affectionately, and even though you have laughed at me a little, you have nevertheless made me three deep bows: three long articles which are very detailed, very important, and which must have been more painful to you than they are to me. . . . You have not been dealing with either a fool or an ingrate." Like a good sport, Sainte-Beuve announced that when the *Salammbô* columns were reprinted in the next volume of the *Lundis*, he would include Flaubert's reply.*

At the same time that Sainte-Beuve was discreetly blasting him,

* *Les Causeries du lundi* [Monday Chats] were collections of weekly articles that Sainte-Beuve had written on various literary subjects for *Le Constitutionnel* and other periodicals. —Trans.

a favorable article appeared here and there. In *Le Moniteur universel* Théophile Gautier declared that reading such a work was "one of the most violent intellectual sensations one can experience." Flaubert thrilled with pride. Now he was revenged on Sainte-Beuve: "What a beautiful article, my dear Théo, and how can I thank you? If someone had told me twenty years ago that the Théophile Gautier with whose work I was filling my imagination would one day write such things about me, I should have gone mad with pride."[9]

But now the scholars joined in the fray. Writing in *La Revue contemporaine*, Guillaume Froehner, a young German archaeologist heavily armed with diplomas, criticized the author's documentation. Flaubert was furious. While he was willing to accept the literary objections of a Sainte-Beuve, he could not endure having some conceited pedant find fault with his historical research. In a long, scathing letter he demonstrated that he had put nothing into his novel which was not based on irrefutable texts, demolished his adversary's arguments one by one, ridiculed him with cheerful ferocity, and concluded: "Let me reassure you, Monsieur: although you seem frightened by your own strength and seriously think that you have torn my book to shreds, have no fear, set your mind at rest! For you have not been 'cruel'—only frivolous."[10]

If, on the whole, the critics were less than enthusiastic, Flaubert's self-esteem found compensation in the reaction of his peers. Victor Hugo, Baudelaire, Michelet, Fromentin, Berlioz, Manet, and Leconte de Lisle declared themselves captivated. On January 27, 1863, George Sand published a splendid article in *La Presse:* "I love *Salammbô*. Flaubert's form is as beautiful, as striking, as concise, as grandiose in its French prose as any fine poem known in any language." Flaubert had no great opinion of the novels of George Sand and hardly knew her. But he was overwhelmed by this generous assessment of his own work and thanked her profusely. She replied: "My dear brother, you must not be grateful to me for having fulfilled a duty. . . . We are but slightly acquainted. Do come to see me when you have time. It is not far and I am always at home, but I am old, so don't wait until I am in my second childhood."[11] Another letter from Flaubert: "I am not grateful to you for having fulfilled what you call a duty. I am touched by the goodness of your heart and proud of your friendly feeling for me. That is all." But in answer to her invitation to come to see her at Nohant, he said "neither yes nor no, like a true Norman."[12]* Maybe he would go one of these days, next summer. . . . In the meantime, he asked his illustrious correspondent for her portrait to hang in his study.[13] And he addressed her as "dear master."†

Notwithstanding the hostility of some of the press, *Salammbô* was making its way with the public. The Empress found it fascinating and stayed up reading until late at night. The Emperor was interested in the military aspect of the work and discussed ballistae, catapults, and other war machines with his entourage. At court, it was good form to admire the author. The craze of the imperial drawing rooms spread to the towns. Fashion seized upon Flaubert's heroine. At masked balls ladies often wore Punic costumes. Mme. Rimsky-Korsakov appeared at a reception at the Palais des Tuileries swathed in the transparent, gold-spangled veils of Hamilcar's daughter, with a belt in the form of a serpent around her waist. *Le Journal amusant* published a dialogue between "the two sisters," Emma Bovary and Salammbô, which attacked the author and his characters. The Théâtre du Palais-Royal announced a satiric review in four scenes titled *Folammbô, ou les Cocasseries carthaginoises* [Folammbô, or the Carthaginian Follies]. Musicians discovered in *Salammbô* a wonderful subject for an opera, and Flaubert, who had refused to allow *Madame Bovary* to be produced as a play, was greatly taken with the idea of a grand lyrical spectacle. He thought of Verdi, then of Berlioz, then of Berlioz's disciple Reyer for the score and of Gautier for the book. But the affair dragged. In any case, Flaubert's second published novel stirred up the same excitement among the public as the first, but this time there was no trial to arouse wide-

* Another reference to the alleged wiliness of the natives of Normandy. Since at least the seventeenth century in France, to "answer like a Norman" has meant to give an evasive or ambiguous reply. —Trans.

† Flaubert calls Sand *maître* (masculine gender) out of respect for her literary stature, but in deference to her sex, he uses the feminine form of the adjective (*chère*). —Trans.

spread curiosity. The book owed its success only to itself. And the author, who professed to despise all the external signs of celebrity, became a very Parisian personage much sought after in society. Intoxicated by his success, he accepted many invitations, but it was still with his fellow writers that he felt most at ease. With a few others he went to dinners at the Restaurant Magny, where Sainte-Beuve was a regular customer. At one of these dinners he met Ivan Turgenev, and a spark of mutual attraction flew between the two men at once. Indeed, the elegant, good-natured Russian captivated all those present, starting with the Goncourts. "He is a charming colossus, a gentle, white-haired giant," they wrote. "He is handsome, but with a kind of venerable beauty. . . . There is the blue of heaven in Turgenev's eyes. To the benevolence of his expression is added the caressing little singsong of the Russian accent, something like the cantilena of a child or a Negro."[14]

But the attractions of fame and friendship were not enough to keep Flaubert in Paris for long. Having had his fill of compliments, criticisms, social events, and belly laughs over off-color jokes at the Magny dinners, he left for Croisset again. And Sainte-Beuve could say of him, repeating the remark of the Academician Lebrun: "He comes out of this a more considerable person than before."

As if to confirm this judgment, on returning to the country Flaubert learned that he had been attacked from the pulpits of two Parisian churches, Saint Clotilda's and the Church of the Trinity, as a corrupter of morals. "There, the preacher is one Father Becel," wrote Flaubert. "I don't know the name of the other one. Both of them thundered against the indecency of the masquerades, against Salammbô's costume! The said Becel recalled La Bovary and claimed that this time I was trying to bring back paganism. Thus both the Académie and the clergy detest me. I find that flattering and exciting. . . . After *Salammbô* I should have started work immediately on *Saint Antoine*; I was in good form, and it would have been finished by now. I am dying of boredom. My idleness (which is not that, because I'm racking my brains like a poor wretch), my nonwriting, I should say, weighs heavily upon me. What a damnable state to be in!"[15]

In Society

None of the subjects that presented themselves really excited him. His mind was floating in space without ever fixing on anything definite. He hesitated between a new version of *Saint Antoine* and a modern novel that might be a recasting of his *Education sentimentale*. Undecided, dissatisfied, he accompanied his mother to Vichy again. Staying with her at the Hôtel Britannique, he felt his spirits sink ever lower as he morosely watched all the "disgusting bourgeois" gravely and punctually drinking their glasses of water. The town was lacking in "cocottes." "They are waiting for the Emperor to arrive before they come running," he wrote. "A very amiable bourgeois informed me that since last year a new house of prostitution had been established, and he was even so kind as to give me the address. But I didn't go; I am no longer gay enough or young enough to worship the Venus of the common people. The need for the ideal is a proof of decadence, say what you will!"[16]

Returning to Croisset at the end of August, he worked on a "fairy play," *Le Château des coeurs* [The Castle of Hearts], which even before it was finished was rejected "on the basis of the outline" by Marc Fournier, the manager of the Théâtre de la Porte-Saint-Martin. It was true that the play could be dismaying to a showman. In writing it Flaubert had hoped to introduce to the stage a new genre inspired by certain comedies of Shakespeare. To this end, he had started reading, with his usual patience, numerous modern "fairy plays" involving magic and spectacular stage effects. He had asked Louis Bouilhet and the comte Charles d'Osmoy to collaborate with him, and all three of them had set to work. The story of *Le Château des coeurs* concerned two innocent lovers who in order to be united had to evade, with the help of the fairies, a series of traps laid for them by various evil spirits, gnomes who detested all noble impulses of the human heart. The plot alternated between realism and fantasy, the dialogue between naive pomposity and heavy irony. Flaubert was quite disappointed in the result. "I am ashamed of it," he confessed. "I find it disgusting—that is, inconsequential, *tiny*. . . . I am secretly humiliated: I have produced something mediocre, inferior."[17] In spite of this harsh judgment, he did not despair of having his play produced. He had been bitten by the theater bug and now he too wanted to know the blaze of publicity, the excitement behind the scenes, the applause of a wildly enthusiastic house.

On October 29, 1863, the Goncourts came to visit him in Croisset. He went to pick them up at the Rouen station with his brother Achille, "a tall, Mephistophelian fellow with a great black beard." A cab took them to Croisset. "There we were, in that study which had been the scene of such dogged and unceasing work, which had witnessed so much labor and from which had issued *Madame Bovary* and *Salammbô*," wrote the Goncourts. "Oaken bookcases with twisted columns. . . . The white marble bust of his dead sister, by Pradier. . . . A divan bed made of a mattress covered with a Turkish fabric and piled with cushions . . . the worktable, a large round table covered with green baize, where the writer dips his pen in an inkstand in the form of a toad. . . . Here and there, on the mantelpiece, the tables, the bookshelves, Oriental bric-a-brac—amulets with the green patina of Egypt, arrows, weapons, musical instruments. . . . This room represents the man, his tastes and his talent: his true passion is for this crude Orient; in this artistic nature there is a deep strain of the Barbarian."[18]

The next day, October 30, Flaubert read the brothers *Le Château des coeurs*. They were appalled to find the play so worthless: "A work of which, in my esteem for him, I thought him incapable. To have read all the 'fairy plays' only to end up writing the most undistinguished one of all!" For the rest, they observed that their friend's household was "rather austere, very bourgeois, and a little pinched," that "the fires in the fireplaces were meager," and that even the fare at table savored of "Norman thrift." According to them, Flaubert's mother had "beneath the features of an old woman, the dignity of a great past beauty." As for his niece Caroline, "the poor girl, caught between her studious uncle and her aged grandmother, talks gaily, looks at you with lovely blue eyes, and makes a pretty pout of regret when, at about seven o'clock, after Flaubert's 'Good night, old dear' to his mother, Grandma takes her up to bed."

On November 1 the three friends stayed indoors the whole day;

In Society

Flaubert was reading aloud his early works. Before dinner he rummaged in a trunk and brought out Oriental costumes: "And soon he was getting all of us up in fancy dress, he himself splendid in his tarboosh, looking magnificently Turkish with his handsome thick features, ruddy complexion, and drooping mustache." He also read them his *Notes de voyage* and expounded his views on art and on women. "On all subjects he has theses that cannot be sincere, opinions adopted for show, for an elegant effect, paradoxes of modesty," noted the Goncourts maliciously.[19] They left worn out by Flaubert's booming voice, his torrent of words, his mordant judgments.

A month later he joined them again in Paris. As a signal honor, he had been invited to dinner, along with the brothers, by Princess Mathilde, daughter of Napoleon's brother Jerome Bonaparte and cousin of the Emperor. He immediately fell under the spell of this dumpy woman with the blotchy complexion, small eyes, and girlish smile. Proud of having been singled out by a person of such high rank, the recluse of Croisset, the man who scorned fashonable gatherings, held forth at table to show himself to advantage. The Goncourts were irritated: "Flaubert and Saint-Victor got unbearably on our nerves with their redoubled mania for things Greek. They finally reached the point of admiring even the wonderful shade of white of the Parthenon, which, Flaubert exclaimed enthusiastically, is 'as black as ebony'!"[20] Flaubert, who was now definitively launched in high society, also won the esteem of the princess's brother, Prince Jerome Napoleon, who called him "my dear friend." Although he proclaimed to all and sundry that this benevolence was due to the certainty that he, Flaubert, was too proud ever to ask for "either a cross [of the Legion of Honor] or a tobacconist's shop," he was nevertheless very honored to be on familiar terms with so brilliant a personage. At about this time the prince had become the protector of Jeanne de Tourbey, who had organized a salon almost as fashionable as Princess Mathilde's. At her house there gathered, among others, Sainte-Beuve, Gautier, the Goncourts, Renan, Turgenev, Dumas *fils*.

In the meantime *Le Château des coeurs*, in a reworked version,

had been presented to the director of the Châtelet, Hippolyte Ho-
stein, for a reading. Another rejection. A messenger brought the
manuscript back to Flaubert without even a letter of regrets.

But the fate of his play was no longer uppermost in Flaubert's
mind. Family affairs that were of far greater importance now claimed
his attention. The future of his niece Caroline was at stake. She had
just turned eighteen and had become infatuated with her drawing
master, Maisiat, a talented painter. She was in such a state of excitement that her grandmother thought it indispensable to intervene
by marrying her as quickly as possible to a suitable party. In 1860,
among the guests at the wedding of Juliette Flaubert and Adolphe
Roquigny had been one Ernest de Commanville, a man of about
thirty, a lumber merchant whose fortune seemed sufficient and who
had a fine presence. Mme. Flaubert liked him very much and was
pressing her granddaughter to accept the excellent match. Caroline
rebelled, wept, hesitated, confided in her uncle by letter. He was
as perplexed as she was. To him, she was still a child. It was not
so long since he had been listening to her recite her lessons. And
now they were going to shove her into a man's bed. By leaving the
house she would deprive him and his mother of a fresh, spontaneous
companion who brought them happiness. Selfishly, he deplored the
prospect. But reason told him that she should yield. "So, my poor
Caro, you're still in the same uncertainty, and perhaps now, after
a third meeting, you're no further advanced," he wrote her.

> It's such a serious decision to make that I'd be in exactly the
> same state of mind were I in your pretty skin. Look, think,
> explore yourself heart and soul; try to discover whether this
> gentleman can offer you any chance of happiness. . . . Your
> poor grandmother wants you to marry, fearing to leave you
> alone in the world, and I too, dear Caro, should like to see
> you united with a decent young man who would make you
> as happy as possible! The other night, when I saw you crying
> so bitterly, your distress nearly broke my heart. We love you
> dearly, my pet, and the day of your marriage will not be a
> merry one for your two old companions. Although I am hardly

of a jealous nature, in the beginning I shall have no liking for the fellow who becomes your husband, no matter who he is. But that's not the point. In time I'll forgive him, and I'll love and cherish him if he makes you happy. . . . Yes, my darling, I declare I'd rather see you marry a grocer who was a millionaire than a great man who was indigent. For the great man wouldn't just be poor; he would sometimes be brutal and tyrannical and cause you so much sorrow that he would drive you to madness or idiocy. . . . I am like you, you see; I don't know what to think; I keep saying white one moment and black the next. . . . It will be hard for you to find a husband who is your superior in mind and upbringing. . . . So you are faced with having to take a young man of good character who is nevertheless inferior. But will you be able to love a man whom you look down upon? . . . No doubt they will badger you for a quick answer. Don't do anything in a hurry.[21]

In spite of himself, he thought of the disappointment and dismay of the married woman that he had analyzed so lucidly in *Madame Bovary*. Would not Caroline, with a commonplace husband, meet a fate like Emma's? Mme. Flaubert held her ground against her granddaughter, who weakened and resigned herself. One last hitch: when it came to questions of civil status, it developed that the suitor had no right to the aristocratic *de* he had adopted and that he was an illegitimate child whose very name was open to doubt. Two court decrees, of January 6 and 10, 1864, were obtained in haste from Le Havre to regularize the situation. Commanville's material and social position, however, could not have been clearer: he owned a sawmill in Dieppe, importing timber from the north and reselling it as lumber in Rouen and Paris. That seemed perfectly sound.

With his peace of mind somewhat restored, Flaubert plunged back into the distractions of the capital, disparaging them, as was his wont, even as he sought them out. Wednesday dinners at Princess Mathilde's; soirees at Jeanne de Tourbey's; excursions with Prince

Napoleon; conversations with the Goncourts, Gautier, Ernest Feydeau, and Jules Michelet; dinners for men only at Magny's, where they would eat famously, drink hard, and argue nonstop about art, literature, and women. Caught up in the whirl of pleasures, Flaubert wrote his niece with childish pride: "Saturday I dined at Princess Mathilde's, and last night (the night of Saturday-Sunday) I was at a ball at the Opéra until five in the morning, with Prince Napoleon and the Ambassador from Turin, in the grand imperial box."[22]

At times he felt as if he were two different people: in Croisset an unsociable savage, and in Paris a gay reveller happy to be seen in good company. Sometimes he favored the shadowy silence of the depths, sometimes the vain excitement of public life. Where was the true Flaubert? Surely in his provincial retreat; here in Paris he was dispersed, amusing himself, playing a role. The Goncourts described him at a dinner at Magny's, on January 18, 1864: "Flaubert, with his face flushed and his eyes rolling, proclaimed in his booming voice that beauty was not erotic, that beautiful women were not meant to be laid, that the only useful purpose they served was to inspire statuary, and that love was born of that mysterious element which was produced by excitement and only very rarely by beauty. . . . Chaffed about it, he went on to say that he had never really laid a woman, that he was a virgin, and that he had used all the women he had had as the mattress for another woman, the woman of his dreams." He also declared weightily that "coitus was in no way necessary to the health of the organism and that it was a necessity created by our imagination." His companions burst out laughing, protested. And he became entangled in his own demonstration. There was a strange contrast between the crudeness of the opinions he expressed about love when he was with men and the delicacy he showed in dissecting the feminine sensibility in his novels. A few days later, at Princess Mathilde's, he was equally talkative, although more careful of his language, and the Goncourts noted with irritation his need to occupy center stage: "At the Princess's I studied Flaubert's curious efforts to attract the attention of the mistress of the house, to make people notice him, speak to him, which he tried to do through an obsessive preoccupation with glances, expressions, and poses. I sensed in everything about him a need—nay, a painful craving—to occupy people's attention, to possess it forcibly and keep it for himself alone. And I secretly laughed to see this man who so loudly scoffs at all human vanities display such a fierce hunger for little bourgeois triumphs."[23]

In February Flaubert was following with feverish excitement the rehearsals of Louis Bouilhet's new play, *Faustine*. It was an unequivocal success. "Their Majesties seemed very pleased the other day, which draws audiences," Flaubert wrote happily to his niece. And he added a postscript: "Regards to Monsieur my future nephew."[24] On February 29 he attended the opening of George Sand's *Marquis de Villemer* at the Théâtre de l'Odéon and, sitting in the third gallery next to the head of the claque, with his face flushed, his eyes starting from his head, his balding brow gleaming with sweat, he jumped up and down in his seat and clapped as if he were deaf. When would it be his turn to be applauded for *Le Château des coeurs*? For the time being, the "fairy play" was of no interest to anyone. He consoled himself with thoughts of his future novel, but he didn't feel ready to write it yet. Besides, it was time to go back to Croisset. "I am very happy to think that in a week we shall be living together again," he wrote Caroline. "The pains in your grandmother's knee will have dissipated, let us hope, and before your marriage we'll spend a little time together as in the old days."[25]

On April 6, 1864, in the town hall of Canteleu, Caroline Hamard became Caroline Commanville. In the church, looking at his niece, so young and fragile in her white veils beside her robust husband twelve years older than she, Flaubert had a foreboding of tragedy. But the grandmother, though she wiped away a tear, seemed delighted. Thirty persons sat down to the banquet. Shortly thereafter, the couple left on their honeymoon: the obligatory trip to Italy. She was hardly gone before Flaubert wrote her at the address she had given him: "So, my poor pet, my dear Caroline, how are you? Are you pleased with your journey, with your husband and the marriage? How I miss you! And how I long to see you again and have a talk with your sweet self! . . . Your grandmother is counting the days until your return: it seems to her that you have been gone for centuries."[26] And three days later: "It was about time your letter arrived, my dear Caro, for your grandma was beginning to go out of her mind. We explained to her that it took time for the mail to bring news of you, but it was of no use, and if we hadn't had some today, I don't know how things would have gone tomorrow. . . . I have gone back to work, but it's not going well at all! I'm afraid I have no more talent and have become a total idiot, a cretin of the Alps."[27]

Waiting for the mail together, the mother of seventy and the son of forty-two made a strange and apparently indissoluble couple. Now that she had married off her granddaughter, Mme. Flaubert, anxious, frail, and despotic, showed redoubled affection for Gustave. Even when they did not speak, they communed together as they revolved old memories. Alone with each other in Croisset, they had the sense of a sweet, melancholy connection with the family's entire past. Their conversations, their silences created an intimate atmosphere, the close, musty atmosphere of long-closed rooms. "As one grows older and the circle around the hearth shrinks, one turns back to the old days, to the time of one's youth," Flaubert wrote Ernest Chevalier.[28] From letter to letter he followed the itinerary of the newlyweds: Venice, Milan, Lake Como. . . . According to what Caroline said, she was very happy with Ernest Commanville. But could one believe what a young bride confided to her uncle and grandmother?

At last the travelers returned. Caroline proved eager for social life. The Commanvilles had many friends among the high society of Rouen. Everything was for the best. Relieved, Flaubert headed back to Paris. There he worked on the outline of his next book, which he described as "a Parisian novel." "The principal theme has emerged, and the course is now clear," he wrote Caroline. "I don't intend to begin writing before September."[29] In the interim he planned to spend a lot of time at the Imperial Library doing research and taking notes. He wanted this work, which was daily taking clearer shape in his mind, to be as perfect, impersonal, and despairing as *Madame Bovary*. But was it perhaps a mistake to try to bring readers back to the grayness of the contemporary world after the glittering Carthage of *Salammbô*, which had been so successful? No matter; for him literature was synonymous with risk. To write was to do battle. The more uncertain the outcome seemed, the more he felt the need to struggle until his strength was exhausted.

Chapter 15

A NEW FRIEND:
GEORGE SAND

More comings and goings between Croisset and Paris, then a holiday in Etretat with his mother, followed by a trip to Villeneuve-Saint-Georges to do research—"socialist readings" that gave him a hatred for the likes of Fourier and Saint-Simon ("What despots and what boors! Modern socialism reeks of pedantry!"[1])—and then on September 1, 1864, Flaubert began to write his novel. No hesitation as to the title: the book would be called *L'Education sentimentale*, like the one he had written nineteen years earlier. But the subjects would be so different that no one could possibly confuse the two. He explained it in a letter to Mlle. Leroyer de Chantepie: "For the past month I have been harnessed to a novel about modern life, which will be laid in Paris. I want to write the moral history of the men of my generation—or, more accurately, the history of their *feelings*. It's a book about love, about passion; but passion such as can exist nowadays—that is to say, inactive. The subject as I have conceived it is, I believe, profoundly true, but for that very reason probably not very entertaining. Facts, drama, are a bit lacking; and then the action is spread over too long a period. In short, I'm having a good deal of trouble and am full of anxieties."[2] And to Mme. Roger des Genettes: "Have you ever reflected upon the sadness of my existence and on all the strength of will it takes me to live? I spend my days absolutely alone, with no more company than if I were in the depths of Central Africa. Finally at night, after having cudgeled my brains to no avail, I manage to write a few lines, which next morning I find detestable. Have I grown old? Am I worn out? I think so. . . . In the last seven weeks I have written fifteen pages, and even those are not worth much."[3]

He was happy to abandon his thankless labor to run down to Paris and fulfill social obligations. In November for the first time he was invited by the Emperor to spend a few days at the Palais de Compiégne. To be sure, in his court outfit—knee breeches, stockings, and pumps—he felt rather as if he were going to a fancy-dress ball, but he bowed gratefully before Their Majesties. The Empress gave him a charming welcome, the magnificence of the salons dazzled him, the compliments he received from important personages went to his head. When he returned to the Boulevard du Temple he wrote Caroline: "It's four o'clock and I have only just woken up, for the Court ceremonies have left me totally exhausted . . . The bourgeois of Rouen would be even more flabbergasted than they are already if they knew of my successes at Compiégne. I am not exaggerating. In short, instead of being bored, I had a very good time. But the hard thing is all the changing of clothes and the precise timing of events."[4]

Even back in Croisset, he was mindful of the social amenities and wrote Jules Duplan: "On New Year's Day please put my name down in the visitors' book at the Prince and Princess's at the Palais-Royal. Ask Madame Cornu if the same thing is done at the Tuileries.* In that case, it would be a second commission for you." His liking for high society was now shared by Caroline, who was being courted assiduously by Baron Leroy, the prefect of Rouen. She received billets-doux from this amiable official and found Parma violets placed on her prie-dieu at the cathedral. Flaubert teased her about her frivolity. "Madame likes society," he wrote her from Paris. "Madame knows that she is pretty. Madame likes to be told so."[5] And a few days later: "Are you still the delight of the drawing rooms of Rouen in general and of Monsieur the Prefect's in particular?

* Hortense Cornu was the goddaughter of the Emperor's mother, Queen Hortense, and a confidante of the Empress Eugénie.

A New Friend: George Sand

The said Prefect appears to me to be enchanted with your person. I think you degrade yourself a little by spending so much time in the company of my unspeakable fellow townsmen." She scoffed at his warnings and gaily continued to carry on her flirtation with the prominent man. She was fascinated by everything that related to Parisian society. She envied her uncle for associating with famous people. When she insisted that he tell her about the latest ball given by Prince Jerome, he amiably obliged: "What surprised me most was the number of salons—twenty-three, each opening into the next, not counting the smaller side rooms. The Monsignor was astonished by the number of persons I knew.* I must have spoken with two hundred. In the midst of this 'brilliant society,' what should I see but a bunch of familiar faces from Rouen! . . . I retreated in horror from that group and went and sat on the steps of the throne beside Princess Primoli. . . . I gazed with admiration at the Regent (15 million) on the Empress's head; it's quite a pretty thing."† And a little further: "Princess Clotilde, seeing me with Mme. Sandeau on my arm, asked her cousin Mathilde if that was my wife—inspiring many pleasantries by both princesses at my expense. Such are the witty tidbits I have to report to you."[6]

With these grandes dames he felt a certain timidity that prevented him from courting them. He was closer to women like Louise Pradier, who had no doubt granted him her favors but who was no longer young, Esther Guimond, who was aging too and plain besides, Suzanne Lagier, an actress who had become a café singer, and the ones he called his "three angels": Marie-Angèle Pasca, Mme. Charles Lapierre, and Mme. Charles Brainne. He was attentive to all of them but made none his official mistress. The experience with Louise Colet had been enough for him. He preferred to amuse himself verbally with female friends and to go to a prostitute when nature demanded it. In that way, at least, he was not disturbed in

---

* "Monsignor" was a nickname for Louis Bouilhet.

† The Regent was an enormous diamond, so called after the duc d'Orléans, who had purchased it in 1717 when he was Regent of France. —Trans. (FS)

his work. Tenaciously, he exhausted himself scaling the chapters of his novel, which rose before him, he said, like "a mountain to climb." "And my knees are tired and I'm panting for breath."[7] He even complained to Princess Mathilde: "What exactly is wrong with me? That's the problem. What is certain is that I am becoming a hypochondriac, my poor brain is tired. I am told I should seek some diversion; but by doing what? . . . I am assailed by sad memories and I see everything as if it were wrapped in a black veil. In short, I am now a *pitiful man*. Is it the beginning of the end, or a temporary condition? I am trying various remedies; among others, I have given up smoking, or almost."[8]

Caroline came down from Rouen to cheer him up. He regained his health, attended a dinner at Théophile Gautier's, "a real caravansary," and another at Magny's in honor of Sainte-Beuve, who had been appointed a senator. As they were leaving the restaurant, he tried to impress the Goncourts with one of the shocking confidences he was so fond of making: "When I was young, my vanity was such that when I went to a brothel with my friends I would pick the ugliest girl and insist on fucking her in front of everyone without taking my cigar from my lips. It was no fun for me, but I did it for the gallery." Was it not again for the gallery that he was now boasting about his sexual prowess of former days? "Flaubert still has a little of that vanity," noted the Goncourts, "which means that although he is by nature frank, he is never perfectly sincere in what he says he feels or suffers or loves."[9]

And now he was restless again. He had hardly returned to Croisset when he left for London, then for Baden, where he found not only Maxime Du Camp but also his beloved Elisa Schlésinger, who had lived in that city for a long time. Was this meeting accidental, or had he sought it because he was working on *L'Education sentimentale* and felt the need to refresh his memories of love? Elisa had grown old and faded, and her mental health was unstable. She had even been confined for seventeen months in a sanatorium near Mannheim. On seeing her again, Flaubert must have had the dizzying sensation of the flight of time, the attrition of passions, the vanity of youthful illusions. When he returned to Croisset he found his mother ill: "Shingles complicated by general neuralgia, which makes her cry out so at night that I have been obliged to abandon my room."[10] To restore the patient's strength they made her drink a tonic of wine with cinchona and put her on a diet of red meat. But she missed her granddaughter, whom she now saw only rarely. Flaubert too regretted the good old days when Caroline's laughter had filled the house with life. He consoled himself by working even more intensely on his manuscript. "As for me," he wrote his niece, "I think I am back in working form. I went to bed last night at four o'clock and I'm beginning to bellow again to a sufficient extent in the silence of my study. That does me good."[11]

He hoped the first part of the novel would be finished by the end of the year. But in November he had to rush to Paris to support the Goncourt brothers with his applause at the opening of their play *Henriette Maréchal* at the Théâtre-Français. Notwithstanding this proof of friendship, the Goncourts noted in their *Journal:* "I think I have found the true definition of Flaubert, of the man and his talent: he is an academic savage."[12] During the rehearsals, there was anxiety lest the show be forbidden by the censor as too daring. Flaubert was furious: "Don't beat about the bush, my lads," he told the Goncourts. "Go directly to the Emperor." The opening night was tumultuous. Flaubert, Princess Mathilde, and a few other friends clapped to bring down the house, but the rest of the audience did not follow suit. When the curtain fell on the last scene, there was such an uproar that the actor Got could not even announce the names of the authors. *Henriette Maréchal* was closed, by order of the government, after the sixth performance. "It's all so unbelievable it's enough to drive you mad," wrote Flaubert. "I have the feeling there are priests mixed up in the cabal against you."[13] And he went back to Croisset, his "true domicile, the one where I live most often," as he put it to Princess Mathilde. She sent him as a remembrance a watercolor she had done, which reached him after a worrisome delay and which with great emotion he hung on the wall of his study between the bust of his sister and a mask of Henri IV. He couldn't get over being esteemed, perhaps even loved, by so many people close to the seat of power. Decidedly, the obscure, toiling masses were made to be enlightened and guided by an elite. In art as in politics, it was necessary to have leaders, masters, aristocrats of thought and feeling. "What is important in history," he told Mlle. Leroyer de Chantepie, "is a little band of men (three or four hundred in each century, perhaps) which has never varied from Plato's time to our own; they are the ones who have done everything and who are the conscience of the world. As for the lower orders of society, you will never lift them up."[14]

As soon as he had finished the first part of *L'Education sentimentale*, he packed his bags again. The railway had brought Paris so close to Rouen that for any trifle he could jump on the train and be back in the capital. Henceforth he had two home ports, and he sped from one to the other with his manuscript in his luggage. People thought he was holed up in Croisset, but he was on the Boulevard du Temple; they came to visit him at his flat in Paris, but he had already left for the country again. In Paris he went to see the porcelain workers in the Faubourg Saint-Antoine and the Barrière du Trône, read treatises on faience, and prepared for the next part of his novel. As he had anticipated, his mother wanted to come to stay with him. Unfortunately, he had no room for her and her maid Joséphine, because his own servant was already sleeping in the kitchen. What was to be done? Obstinate and hypersensitive as she was, she would surely imagine that he had invented this excuse not to receive her. He begged Caroline to make the old lady see reason: "So," he wrote his niece, "either (1) she must resign herself to doing without a maid; or (2) I must send my servant to the hotel every night; or (3) your grandmother must stay at the Helder, which frankly would be simpler and more convenient both for her and for me. But I would hang myself rather than tell her so myself."[15]

In the end, Flaubert, his mother, and the servants all squeezed into the apartment on the Boulevard du Temple. At his request she had brought him some Oriental garments that he had bought during his trip to Africa. He liked to put them on to impress his friends. On February 12 he brought George Sand to one of the dinners at the Restaurant Magny on the Rue Dauphine. The only woman admitted to this circle of men, she was disconcerted at first by the

A New Friend: George Sand

merry camaraderie of the guests and the boldness of their talk. They all treated her with deference, because of her reputation and her age. At sixty-two, she was the grandmother of the world of letters. "She sat beside me," wrote the Goncourts, "with her beautiful, charming face, in which every day, as she grows older, the characteristics of the mulatto become a little more pronounced.* She looked shyly around at the assembled company and whispered in Flaubert's ear: 'You are the only one here I feel comfortable with.' . . . She has wonderfully delicate little hands, almost entirely hidden in lace cuffs."

The following month, still toiling over his novel, Flaubert asked Sainte-Beuve for information on the neo-Catholic movement of around 1840: "My story goes from 1840 to the coup d'état [of December 2, 1851]. I need to know everything, of course, and before I start writing I have to enter into the atmosphere of the time. . . . I can't go to see you because I have a horrible boil that prevents me from getting dressed. It's impossible for me to go to libraries. I'm wasting my time and eating my heart out."[16] For two weeks he dragged around his apartment "harnessed up in bandages and covered with cataplasms." His only consolation was work. In April, still only partly recovered, he attended as a witness the very literary wedding of Judith Gautier, elder daughter of Théophile, and the poet Catulle Mendès. But he expected nothing good to come of the union of the ill-matched couple. In any case, he believed more firmly than ever that artists should remain celibate. Constantly turned inward, questioning himself, examining himself, and always ready to comment on his moods to his friends, he confided to the Goncourts: "There are two men in me. One you see, with a narrow chest and a lead bottom, the man made to sit bent over a table; the other, a traveling salesman with all the gaiety of a traveling salesman on a trip, and a taste for violent exercise."[17] Such as he was, George Sand was taken with him. She exerted her fading charm on him. On May 21 she appeared at the Magny dinner in a dress "the color

---

* This curious reference to George Sand's "mulatto" appearance reflects a subjective impression rather than her actual heredity. —Trans.

of peach blossoms." "The dress of a woman in love, which I suspect had been put on with the intention of raping Flaubert," noted the Goncourts. Flaubert was touched by this new friendship in which tenderness was mingled with flirtation. He knew that George Sand was too old for their affection to degenerate into intimate relations, and that reassured him. To love and esteem a woman with whom one was certain never to go to bed was, he felt, the ideal situation for a man of letters who had passed his prime.

Since he was supposed to be close to the throne, his niece questioned him about the alarming rumors circulating in Rouen on the subject of a possible armed conflict. He confidently reassured her:

> You ask me what I think of the political situation and what is being said about it. I have never thought there would be a war, and now people are saying that perhaps everything will be worked out. . . . These worthy bourgeois who appointed Isidore to defend order and property don't understand anything any more. . . .* Well, in my opinion, the Emperor is stronger than ever. . . . So our friends the Italians are going to have a set-to with Austria, but France will quickly put a stop to it. Venice will be taken from Austria and she will be given the provinces of the Danube as compensation. Our troops will be recalled from Mexico and it will all be over very soon. . . . In short, I think that if there is a war, we will take very little part in it and it will end quickly. France cannot allow her achievement—that is, the unity of Italy—to be destroyed, and she cannot herself destroy Austria, for that would mean delivering Europe up to Russia. Therefore, we will stand in the middle and keep the others from fighting too hard.[18]

These optimistic predictions proved wrong. On July 3, 1866, the Prussian army crushed the Austrians at Sadowa. The victory

---

* "Isidore" was a nickname for Napoleon III.

revealed the Prussians' tactical skill and the power of their weaponry, which included the rifle with firing pin.* Suddenly France herself felt threatened by her formidable neighbor. But Flaubert still did not believe a war was coming. That same month he went to London, where he saw Gertrude Tennant and her sister, Mrs. Campbell, then to Baden, where Maxime Du Camp was making his annual visit. He had hardly returned to Croisset, in mid-August, when he left again for Saint-Gratien, where Princess Mathilde had a summer residence. An important ceremony awaited him there: he was awarded the insignia of a knight of the Legion of Honor. After having derided his friends who had had the weakness to accept the decoration, he himself now swelled with pride with the red ribbon in his buttonhole. Obviously, it was Princess Mathilde who had intervened in his favor with the Minister of Education. "I do not doubt the good will of M. Duruy," Flaubert wrote the princess, "but I imagine that the idea was somewhat suggested to him by another. To me, therefore, the red ribbon is more than a favor, almost a keepsake. I did not need that to have Princess Mathilde often in my thoughts."[19] And he told Mlle. Amélie Bosquet: "What pleases me about the red ribbon is the joy it gives to those who love me. . . . Ah, if only one received it at the age of eighteen!"[20] Another mark of esteem: George Sand dedicated to him her novel *Le Dernier Amour*. But Flaubert was embarrassed to see his name coupled with so compromising a title. The dedication, he said, was the source of "the most amiable pleasantries." Could it be that he was the "last love" of the lady of Nohant? And now she informed him that she was going to visit Croisset, from August 28 to 30, 1866.

The household was immediately turned upside down. Caroline's old room was hastily prepared for the visitor. Flaubert met her on the station platform in Rouen and took her for a drive around the city, after which they went to Croisset. "Flaubert's mother is a charming old lady," George Sand wrote in her diary on August 28.

* A reference to the Dreyse needle-gun, the standard arm of the Prussian infantry and the first successful breech-loading firearm produced for military issue.

"The place is silent, the house comfortable, pretty, and well arranged. And good service, cleanliness, water, *needs anticipated,* everything one could wish. I am pampered like a princess." In the evening he read her his *Tentation de Saint Antoine* in the 1856 version, and she found the work "superb." They went to bed at two in the morning. Next day they took the boat for La Bouille in the rain, came back to the house for a cup of tea, played cards, and at the end of the two-day visit, Mme. Sand wrote in her notebook: "I am mad for Flaubert." As soon as she was back in Paris, she sent Flaubert a thank-you note: "I am truly touched by the kind welcome I received in your quiet, comfortable retreat where a stray animal of my species is an anomaly that might have been thought a nuisance. Instead of that, I was received like one of the family, and I could see that this great courtesy came from the heart. . . . And then you—you are a good, kind boy, for all that you are a grown man, and I love you with all my heart."[21] And she sent him the complete collection of her works: seventy-five volumes. He who had published so little was staggered by this prodigious output. Nevertheless, his friendship for the prolific author inclined him to indulgence. "I think you're very hard on *Le Dernier Amour,*" he wrote Princess Mathilde. "In my opinion there are some quite remarkable things in the book. . . . As for its faults, I have pointed them out to the author in person, for *She* dropped into my cabin unexpectedly. . . . She was, as always, very natural and not at all a bluestocking."[22] He was so happy about the meeting with her at Croisset that he invited her to come back as soon as possible, this time "for a week at least." "You shall have your room, with a little table and everything needed for writing. Is it agreed?" And in the same letter he told her: "I know few men less 'dissolute' than I. I have dreamed a great deal and done very little."[23] This confession was the first of a long series. He trusted George Sand, and corresponding with her afforded him the same sort of release and freedom from constraint he had enjoyed in the old days, writing to Louise Colet. He talked to her, from a distance, about himself, his thoughts, tastes, work, his fatigue, his art, and his conception of the world: "I do not have, as you do, the sense of a life that is beginning, the astonishment of an existence freshly unfolding. It seems to me, on the contrary, that I have always existed. And I possess memories that go back to the Pharaohs. I see myself at different periods of history very clearly, in different circumstances and plying different trades. My present self is the result of all my vanished selves. . . . Many things would be explained if we could know our *real* genealogy."[24]

True to her word, on November 3, 1866, George Sand was back in Croisset. And the first delightful experience was repeated point for point. They went for walks, Flaubert read his guest first his "fairy play," then *L'Education sentimentale* ("It's good, good," was her reaction), they chattered until two in the morning, went down to the kitchen to eat some cold chicken, out to the pump for a drink of cold water, then back up to the study, where they talked some more until dawn. After a week of this festival of friendship, they parted and Flaubert observed: "Though she's a bit too benevolent and benign, she has insights that evince very keen good sense, provided she doesn't get on to her socialist hobbyhorse."[25] These were only mild reproaches. On the whole he was captivated. He was almost ready, even, to pardon George Sand for her unfortunate tendency to preach an egalitarian, virtuous democracy. "I've been all at sixes and sevens since you left," he wrote her. "I feel as if I hadn't seen you for ten years. You are all we talk about, my mother and I; everyone here loves you. . . . I don't know what to call the feeling I have for you: it's a very particular kind of affection, such as I have never felt for anyone until now. . . . A Rouen newspaper, *Le Nouvelliste*, reported your visit to Rouen, with the result that on Saturday, after leaving you, I ran into several bourgeois who were indignant with me because I hadn't exhibited you."[26] Then he told her how the night before, a fire had broken out at his woodseller's and he had worked so hard at the pumps that when he got home he had had to take to his bed with pains in his back. Naturally, his novel was going badly and he didn't know if he could bring it off. He envied her (at least, so he said) her facility: "*You* don't know what it is to spend an entire day with your head in your hands, racking your poor brains in search of a word. With you, the flow of ideas is broad, continuous, like a river. With me, it's a tiny trickle.

211

I can achieve a cascade only by the most arduous artistic effort."[27] When she expressed surprise that he always talked to her about his "painful work" and suggested that perhaps this was only a pose on his part, he replied despondently: "I don't wonder that you fail to understand my spells of literary anguish. I don't understand them myself. They exist, however, and are violent. At such times I no longer know how to go about writing, and after infinite fumbling I succeed in expressing a hundredth part of my ideas. Nothing spontaneous about your friend! Far from it! . . . And then, I feel an unconquerable aversion to putting on paper anything that comes from my heart. I even think that a novelist *hasn't the right to express his opinion* on anything whatsoever. Has God ever expressed his opinion? That is why there are so many things that make me gag —things I long to spit out, and which I choke down instead. Indeed, what would be the use of uttering them? Any Tom, Dick, or Harry is more interesting than Monsieur G. Flaubert, because they are more *general* and consequently more typical."[28]

Now he had a bowl of goldfish: "They amuse me. They keep me company while I eat my dinner." But once again solitude began to weigh on him. He went back to Paris, saw a few friends, applauded Louis Bouilhet's play *La Conjuration d'Amboise,* which was a smash at the Odéon, and received a visit from Hippolyte Taine, who on seeing him close up was struck by "the brutal energy of his face and his heavy eyes, like a bull's," his bloodshot complexion, and the crudeness of his language. But in spite of Flaubert's violent appearance, the author of *L'Histoire de la littérature anglaise* thought him a "good fellow," who was very natural, neither pretentious nor a flatterer, and fond of ideological discussions.

When he returned to Rouen in December 1866, Flaubert was delighted to learn that Bouilhet's success in Paris had created a great stir in the provinces. "His fellow townsmen, who had totally ignored him until this moment, now that Paris applauds him are screaming with enthusiasm," he wrote George Sand. "He will return here next Saturday for a banquet being given in his honor: eighty guests at the least, etc."[29] His friend's success did not stimulate him to speed up his own work, however. He was in no hurry to publish a book with which he was increasingly dissatisfied: "To me, the depiction of modern French bourgeois gives off a peculiar stench," he declared to his "dear great heart," his "beloved old troubadour," as he called George Sand.[30] And he confided to Mme. Roger des Genettes: "I hear no other sound than the crackling of my fire and the ticking of my clock. I work by lamplight about ten hours out of the twenty-four. . . . Basically, what distresses me is the conviction that I am doing something useless, I mean something contrary to the goal of art, which is exaltation of some kind. But with the scientific demands that are made nowadays and a bourgeois subject, the thing seems absolutely impossible. Beauty is not compatible with modern life. So this is the last time I'm going to get involved with it; I've had enough."[31]

In spite of this declaration, he hastened to ask Ernest Feydeau for details of stock market transactions that he wanted his hero, Frédéric Moreau, to engage in. He himself was increasingly obsessed with money worries. "Right now I manage to pay for my paper but not for the excursions, trips, and books my work demands," he confessed to the novelist René de Maricourt. "And actually, I think that's a good thing (or I pretend to think so), for I don't see any connection between a five-franc coin and an idea. One must love art for its own sake; otherwise, the most insignificant occupation is better."[32] And during the night of January 12–13, 1867, he wrote of his distress to George Sand: "Life is not easy! What a complicated, expensive business! I know something about it. One needs money for *everything*, so that with a modest income and an unremunerative occupation, one must resign oneself to having little. And so I do! It has become a habit; but on days when the work goes badly, it's not much fun. . . . I go whole weeks without exchanging a word with a human being, and at the end of the week I cannot recall a single day or a single event. I see my mother and my niece on Sundays, and that's all. My only company consists of a band of rats who make an infernal racket in the attic over my head, when the water isn't roaring and the wind dies down. The nights are black as ink, and I am surrounded by a silence like that of the desert. One's sensitivity is inordinately heightened in such a setting."

By his own admission, he was becoming "unsociable." When invited to dinner at his niece's house in Rouen, he took a wicked pleasure in shocking the other guests by his outrageous remarks. When George Sand advised him to take some exercise, he went walking by moonlight for two and a half hours in the snow, pretending he was traveling in Russia or Norway. He complained that in undertaking the novel he had condemned himself to a thankless chore, and asked his correspondent for "a recipe for working faster." Formerly, he said, his heart had been relatively dry, but with increasing age, he had been "feminized": "I get emotional over the least thing. Everything disturbs and agitates me; to me, as to the reed, everything is the north wind."[33]★ Fortunately, in the meantime his mother had been able to sell her farm of Courtavant, in Champagne, for fifteen thousand five hundred francs. He himself had obtained a loan of five thousand francs from Michel Lévy. The vise was loosening. Turgenev came to spend a day in Croisset, charmed his hosts with his gentle gaze, patriarchal white beard, and elegant conversation, and went away having won their hearts.

Liberated from his financial constraints, Flaubert returned to Paris for three months. When the Goncourts saw him again, they were struck by his flourishing appearance and ready flow of talk, which they had somewhat forgotten in his absence: "Flaubert's healthy look, ruddy and corpulent, countrified by ten months of exile, made the man seem a little offensive to us and too exuberant for our nerves."[34] He too, incidentally, was disappointed by his friends. He found them excessively preoccupied with politics. After a dinner at Magny's, he wrote George Sand: "At the last Magny dinner the conversation was so like what one would expect at a gathering of concierges that I swore to myself I'd never set foot in the place again. The whole time they talked of nothing but M. de Bismarck and Luxembourg. I'm still fed to the teeth with it all! In any event, I'm becoming hard to live with."[35] Notwithstanding his

★ An allusion to La Fontaine's fable *Le Chêne et le roseau,* in which the oak tree says to the reed: "The slightest breeze . . . makes you bow your head. . . . To you everything is the north wind." —Trans.

irritable mood, he went to the opening of a play by Alexandre Dumas *fils* at the Gymnase and to various society receptions, where he tried to appear to advantage. Everywhere, he observed a latent anxiety, an embryonic fear of what the future held in store. "The political horizon is growing dark. No one can tell why, but it is growing dark, even black," he wrote ironically to Caroline. "The bourgeois are afraid of everything! Afraid of war, afraid of strikes, afraid of the (probable) death of the Imperial Prince; there is universal panic. To find such a degree of stupidity, one has to go back to 1848! Just now I am reading a lot about that period: the impression of folly I get from it comes on top of the one given me by the contemporary state of mind, so that I have on my shoulders mountains of idiocy."[36]

Not content with plunging into books and newspapers relating to the period of his novel, he went to Creil to see a pottery works he wanted to describe. But when George Sand invited him to Nohant, he again declined, on pretext that his mother, who had recently had a slight attack, was ill and needed him with her. Before going back to Croisset, he went with Princess Mathilde to visit the Universal Exposition, which he found "overwhelming." In the meantime, the rumors of war had quieted down. The bourgeois were raising their heads again. One could think about serious things once more—art, philosophy, literature: "Axiom: hatred of the Bourgeois is the beginning of virtue. Personally, I include in the word 'bourgeois' the bourgeois in overalls as well as the ones in frock coats. It is we, and we alone—that is, the educated—who are the People, or, to put it better, the tradition of Humanity."[37]

On May 2, 1867, Louis Bouilhet, who was now in the good graces of his fellow townsmen, was appointed director of the Municipal Library of Rouen with a salary of four thousand francs a year and official housing. On June 10 Flaubert was invited to a ball given at the Tuileries for the foreign sovereigns Alexander II of Russia, the King of Italy, and the King of Prussia, as well as the Prince of Wales, all of whom had come to Paris for the Exposition. "The sovereigns wishing to take a look at me, as one of the most splendid curiosities in France, I am invited to spend the evening with them next Monday," he had written Caroline.[38] By now he should have been blasé about associating with the high and mighty. He was not. He was dumbfounded by the splendor of the ball. In the salons filled with crinolines, dress coats, and uniforms, he felt like a trained bear bewildered by the sound of the tambourines. He made himself agreeable to the ladies, observed everything keenly, and told George Sand afterward: "No joking whatever: it was splendid." But he hadn't liked the Czar of Russia: "I thought him a boor." For purposes of research he went to the Jockey Club and the Café Anglais; then he returned to Croisset, then came back to Paris with his mother to show her the Exposition, then again shut himself up with his manuscript in Croisset. This time, he wrote Armand Barbès asking for information about certain historical events in which he had been personally involved. Barbès having obliged, he thanked him effusively: "The details you have sent me will be put (incidentally) into a book I am writing, in which the action takes place from 1840 to 1852. Although my subject is purely one of psychological analysis, I sometimes touch on the events of the period. My foregrounds are invented and my backgrounds real."[39] He continued working at the same pace. But his nerves were on edge. The least annoyance was intolerable to him: "I fear the squeaking of a door more than the betrayal of a friend," he confessed to Princess Mathilde. "It is true that I am a sick man, that my nerves are raw; my external resemblance to a stout gendarme is deceptive. You see that I am talking about myself like a silly woman."[40] At this point he hoped that if he worked "like thirty thousand slaves," he could finish his novel by the spring of 1869. Another two years of wrestling with characters he was fed up with. He had just turned forty-six. He would be forty-eight when the book was published. "Looking back, I don't see that I've wasted my life, and yet what have I accomplished, God help me? It's time to produce something worthwhile."[41]

As he grew older, his political opinions became increasingly categorical. He told Princess Mathilde: "As for the fear which the good people of France have of Prussia, I confess that I don't understand it in the least and that for my part, I find it humiliating."[42] He applauded the courage of Sainte-Beuve, who a few months before

A New Friend: George Sand

had made an eloquent plea in the Senate for complete freedom of the press. His *bête noire* was Louis-Adolphe Thiers. "Let us roar against M. Thiers!" he wrote George Sand. "Is it possible to find a more triumphant imbecile, a more abject ass, a more turdlike bourgeois? No! Nothing can give an idea of the vomiting inspired in me by this old diplomatic idiot, rounding out his stupidity like a melon ripening on a manure pile—the manure pile of the bourgeoisie! . . . To me he seems as eternal as mediocrity itself! It kills me just to think of him."[43]

His violent opinions were known to his fellow citizens of Rouen. They thought of him as a sort of anarchist, an enemy of morality, religion, and public order. They did not suspect that he was so chiefly in words and that his true ideal—a stay-at-home, peaceable, pipe-and-slippers ideal—was not so different from their own. When the weather was fine they would go for a walk in Croisset along the banks of the Seine and would sometimes see from a distance, in the Flauberts' garden, a tall figure wrapped in a scarlet dressing gown. The "red man" displaying his convictions! They would point him out to their children like a bogeyman. If they had known how alone, weary, and disoriented he was, they would have pitied him instead of fearing and reviling him.

Chapter 16

L'EDUCATION
SENTIMENTALE

The year 1868 began badly for Flaubert. The little daughter of his niece Juliette died of pneumonia following a case of measles: "You cannot imagine anything more pitiful than this young woman [the mother, who was ill herself], with her head on her pillow, repeating through her tears: 'my poor little girl,' " he wrote Jules Duplan. "The grandfather (my brother) is completely distraught. As for my mother, so far at least, she is bearing it better than I would have expected."[1] He could think of only one antidote for mourning: Paris. He hastened there, this time scorning the Magny dinners, "where the company is now interspersed with faces I can't abide,"[2] but going every Wednesday to Princess Mathilde's, where he would find the Goncourts and Gautier. These social events distracted him only briefly from his manuscript. He was starting on the historical part and was worried about it: "I'm having a great deal of difficulty fitting my characters into the political events of '48," he confessed to Duplan. "I'm afraid the backgrounds will devour the foregrounds; that's the trouble with a historical novel. The historical figures are more interesting than the fictional characters, especially when the latter have moderate passions; people will be less interested in Frédéric than in Lamartine. And then, which of the real events to choose? I am puzzled; *it's hard!*"[3] And he told Jules Michelet that in studying this period he had become convinced that the Catholic clergy had had a pernicious influence on the course of events. But he also needed firsthand experience.

He believed more than ever that for a novelist, nothing was as valuable as direct observation of the scenes he wanted to depict. Having to describe in *L'Education sentimentale* the sufferings of a child with diphtheria, he went to the Hôpital Sainte-Eugénie, planted himself in front of a little three-year-old patient who was coughing and choking on the verge of asphyxia, questioned an intern, and finally murmured, "I have seen enough; please deliver him." Only then did the operation begin. But Flaubert decided that in his novel the disease would take a turn it rarely did in real life: the false membrane would be expelled spontaneously. He went home horrified by what he had seen and impatient to recount it in his book. Now he had it, his chapter on the disease. "It is abominable," he wrote Caroline, speaking of his visit to the hospital. "I came away in the greatest distress, but art before everything! . . . Fortunately, it's over; now I can write my description."[4]

His current enthusiasms were Emile Zola's novel *Thérèse Raquin*, "remarkable, no matter what they say," and old Hugo's verse collection *Les Châtiments*, the poetry of which he thought "tremendous," "although the content of the book is stupid."[5]* To George Sand, who was insisting that he come at last to Nohant, he replied: "I would be *ruined* if I went anywhere between now and the end of my novel. Your friend is a wax figure of a man: everything imprints itself upon him, becomes ingrained, penetrates. When I came back from your place I would no longer think of anything but you, your family, your house, your landscapes, the appearance of the people I had met, etc. It takes great effort for me to collect my thoughts. . . . That is why, dear good adored master, I deprive myself of the pleasure of going to your home to sit down and dream out loud."[6] Accustomed to the calm and silence of the country, he found the noise of the capital hard to bear. It seemed to him that the whole city was conspiring to prevent him from working or even sleeping. "Having come home Sunday night at half past eleven,"

---

* *Les Châtiments* [Punishments] was a satirical denunciation of Napoleon III. —Trans.

he wrote the Goncourts, "I went to bed promising myself a deep sleep, and blew out my candle. Three minutes later, a blaring of trombones and beating of drums! It was a wedding at Bonvalet's. The said tavernkeeper's windows being wide open (because of the heat of the night), I didn't miss a single quadrille or a single shout. . . . At six in the morning the masons started up again. At seven I moved to the Grand Hôtel. . . . Scarcely was I there when they began nailing up a crate in the next apartment. In short, at nine I left and went to the Hôtel du Helder, where I found a wretched closet, black as a tomb. But the peace of the grave did not reign there: shouts of guests, rumbling of carriages in the street, clanking of tin pails in the courtyard. . . . From four to six tried to sleep at Du Camp's, Rue du Rocher. But I had reckoned without other masons, who were building a wall alongside his garden. At six I betook myself to a bathhouse on the Rue Saint-Lazare. There, children playing in the yard, plus a piano. At eight I returned to the Rue du Helder, where my man had laid out on my bed everything I needed to go to the Tuileries ball that night. But I hadn't dined, and thinking that hunger was perhaps weakening my nerves, I went to the Café de l'Opéra. I had scarcely entered when a gentleman vomited beside me."[7]

Exasperated, he went back to Croisset to receive George Sand, who had promised to visit. She arrived on May 24, 1868, and noted in her diary under that date: "Flaubert was waiting for me at the station and obliged me to go pee so that I shouldn't get to be like Sainte-Beuve.* It was raining in Rouen, as always. I found the mama not so deaf, but she can scarcely walk, alas! Had lunch, chatted while we strolled beneath the arbor, which the rain didn't penetrate. For an hour and a half I slept in an armchair and Flaubert on a couch. More talk. Dinner with the niece and Mme. Frankline.† Afterward, Gustave read me a religious farce. Went to bed at midnight." Next day, splendid weather. They took advantage of it to

---

* Who suffered from a bladder ailment. —Trans. (FS)
† A friend of Caroline's.

drive out into the surrounding countryside. That evening, after dinner, Flaubert read aloud some passages from *L'Education sentimentale*. "Three hundred excellent pages that charmed me," she wrote in her notebook. They went to bed at two in the morning.

After George Sand left, Flaubert went back to what he referred to as his "priestly calling." The closer he came to the end of his novel, the more he realized how daring it was politically. He was afraid he was going to offend everyone by proclaiming the truth about the events of 1848. "I've been slaving away furiously for the past six weeks," he wrote her. "The patriots won't forgive me for this book, nor the reactionaries either! Too bad: I write things as I feel them—that is, as I think they are. Is that foolish of me?"[8] Actually, his political convictions were as vague as they were virulent. He considered democracy, founded on universal suffrage, an aberration, because the majority of citizens were imbeciles and it was dangerous to ask half-wits their opinion on public affairs. Besides, in a democracy the people, flattered and swindled, possessed not one ounce of the power they had delegated to their representatives and remained in their wretched condition. But autocracy, he thought, whether despotic or paternalistic, was likewise to be condemned. He scoffed at Napoleon III, his self-importance and his ostentation. While he appreciated the delicate hospitality of Princess Mathilde, he considered her cousin a detestable, comical puppet. Tyranny was no better than demagogy. The artist could look upon any form of government only with contempt.

Having worked hard in Croisset, Flaubert gave himself a vacation, took a trip to Fontainebleau (again for his novel), stayed with the Commanvilles in Dieppe, and then spent a memorable week, from July 30 to August 6, at Princess Mathilde's in Saint-Gratien. The château did not awake until eleven in the morning. The princess would appear at eleven-thirty, shortly before lunch, and her guests would come in turn to kiss her hand. "At that morning hour she is generally gay, lively, with renewed health," noted the Goncourts. After lunch the company would gather on the veranda, and that was the great time for talk, when the princess would charm her listeners with ironic observations "in the style of

Saint-Simon."* At about one o'clock she would retreat to her painting studio and work there until five. Then there would be group excursions in the valley of Montmorency or boat trips on the lake. And always, crackling conversation. Each guest would try to shine before the mistress of the house, who reigned over her little circle, congratulating this one, criticizing that one. On Flaubert's last day there, she gave him a tart lecture on the subject of his visit to the salon of Jeanne de Tourbey. "Speaking with all the pride of rank and respectability, she complained this morning, almost wittily, that she had to share the company and thoughts of her friends with women of that sort," wrote the Goncourts. She resented Flaubert's stealing twenty minutes from herself "to go and present them to that trollop."[9] As he seemed crushed by this reproach, she made him the gift of a statuette.

He returned to Croisset toward the middle of August and immediately resumed his research for *L'Education sentimentale.* He called upon Jules Duplan for details regarding his home town of Lyons: "Describe for me, in a few lines, the living quarters of a family of Lyons workers. The *canuts* (as I think the silk weavers are called) work in very low-ceilinged rooms, don't they? In their own homes? Their children work too? I find the following in my notes: the weaver working at a Jacquard loom is continually struck in the stomach by the shaft of the roller on which the cloth is being wound as it is completed. Is it the roller itself that strikes him? Clarify, please."[10] And again: "I had made the trip to Fontainebleau and back by train when a doubt struck me and I became convinced, alas! that in 1848 there was no railroad between Paris and Fontainebleau. This means I have to scrap two passages and begin afresh. . . . So I need to know: (1) how, in June 1848, one went from Paris to Fontainebleau; (2) perhaps a section of the line had been built and was already in operation? (3) what coaches did one take? (4) and what was their terminus in Paris?"[11] He queried Ernest

* In spite of the duc de Saint-Simon's aristocratic snobbery, his memoirs of the court of Louis XIV are remarkable for their keen observation and psychological insight. —Trans.

Feydeau too: "You'd be very kind if you could answer these two questions: 1) In June 1848, where were the posts of the National Guard in the Mouffetard, Saint-Victor and Latin quarters? 2) During the night of 25–26 June (the night of Sunday–Monday) was it the National Guard or the regular army that occupied the Left Bank of Paris?"[12] Another concern: his hero, who came from Nogent, was called Frédéric Moreau. But there might still be some Moreaus in Nogent. So much the worse for them. He could not unbaptize his Frédéric at this point: "A proper name is an extremely important thing in a novel, a fundamental thing," Flaubert wrote his cousin Louis Bonenfant. "You can no more change a character's name than you can change his skin; it's like trying to turn a Negro white."[13]

Turgenev came to see him one Sunday in Croisset: "There are few men who are better company and have a more delightful wit," Flaubert wrote Princess Mathilde. Then again, solitude. His mother was living in the Caux region of Normandy with her granddaughters. Holed up in his den, he slaved away. Once more he refused to go to Nohant (for the baptism of George Sand's granddaughters) and wrote his old friend begging her to excuse him: "I am working tremendously hard and am basically delighted by the prospect of the end, which is beginning to be visible. To make it come faster, I have resolved to stay here all winter, probably until the end of March. . . . I shall turn to the Beautiful again when I am liberated from my hateful bourgeois, and I'm not about to have any more of *them*."[14] A brief escape to Paris to celebrate Christmas with the Goncourts and talk with them about "the baseness of the times, the shabbiness of character, the moral decay of men of letters,"[15] and on New Year's Eve he was back in Croisset again writing to George Sand: "In Paris I was told I looked 'as fresh as a girl,' and people ignorant of my biography attributed my healthy appearance to the country air. So much for conventional ideas. Each has his own regime of what's good for him. . . . A man who has no common sense shouldn't live according to the rules of common sense. As to my mania for work, I'll compare it to an itchy rash. I keep scratching myself and screaming. It's a pleasure and a torment at the same time." Soon the need for more information for his book brought him back to the capital. Dinner at Jeanne de Tourbey's with Gautier, Girardin, the Goncourts. "A real carnival of guests," noted the latter. "We played little word games, both innocent and dirty."[16] The atmosphere at Princess Mathilde's was very different. At his niece's instigation, Flaubert had the presumption to write and ask the princess for an unusual favor: "Ernest Commanville, merchant of Dieppe, dealer in wood from the North, owner of a mechanical sawmill and of extensive property in the same city, requests the post of vice consul of Prussia in Dieppe. The head clerk of his establishment speaks all the languages of the North."[17] The affair dragged for a few months and in the end, thanks to Princess Mathilde's support, Commanville was suddenly appointed vice consul not of Prussia but of Turkey. The princess watched jealously over her little court of writers, and one day, overhearing George Sand saying *"tu"* to Flaubert, whereas she herself addressed him formally as *"vous,"* she slid a mischievous glance at the Goncourts. "Was it the *tu* of a lover or just playacting?" they wrote in their *Journal.*[18]

It was in Paris, on Sunday morning, May 16, 1869, "at four minutes to five," that Flaubert finished *L'Education sentimentale.* He immediately wrote Jules Duplan: "Finished, old man! Yes, my book is finished! . . . I've been at my worktable since eight o'clock yesterday morning. My head is bursting. No matter—there's a tremendous weight off my stomach!"[19] A few days later the Goncourts, who had come to visit him, remarked nastily: "We saw the manuscript on his green baize table, in a cardboard box made specially for the purpose and bearing the title which he stubbornly insists on: *L'Education sentimentale,* with the subtitle: *L'Histoire d'un jeune homme.* He is going to send it to the copyist; for, with a sort of religious piety, ever since he began writing he has kept in his possession those immortal monuments, his original manuscripts. The man attaches a rather ridiculous solemnity to the least things he has brought forth with so much difficulty. . . . Decidedly, we don't know which is greater, our friend's vanity or his pride!"[20]

Princess Mathilde insisted that Flaubert read her parts of his work. Both flattered and embarrassed, he did so on May 22: the first three chapters would be enough, he thought. "Whereupon," he wrote Caroline, "enthusiasm from the Areopagus impossible to describe, and I *have* to go on and read her the whole thing—which means (amid my other occupations) four sessions of four hours each."[21] This encouragement, coming from the princess, filled him with joy. "You would not believe," he confessed to her, "how it 'flattered my pride (that weakness of my heart),' as the great Racine would have said."* And to Caroline he reported: "My last reading to the Princess attained the supreme limits of enthusiasm. . . . A good part of the success must have been due to the way I read. I don't know what got into me that day, but I delivered the last chapter in such a way that I was dazzled myself."[22]

In the midst of this triumph, he found himself short of money and decided to give up his apartment on the Boulevard du Temple, which was too expensive, and move to a smaller one at 4 Rue Murillo (fifth floor), with a view of the Parc Monceau. The rent was fifteen hundred francs a year. While waiting to make the move he went back to Croisset and, although he had only just been liberated from *L'Education sentimentale*, returned to his old project, *La Tentation de Saint Antoine*. "I've gone back to an old infatuation of mine, a book that I've already written twice and that I want to do all over again. It's totally absurd, but it amuses me. So now I am lost in the Church Fathers as if I meant to become a priest!"[23]

While he buried himself in religious texts, he was nevertheless waiting impatiently for Louis Bouilhet to come back to Paris so they could go over *L'Education sentimentale* together "sentence by sentence." He had so much confidence in his friend's judgment that he couldn't consider publishing anything without his approval. There was more than affection between them—an almost telepathic communication of heart and mind. They needed each other so intensely that acquaintances said they had come to resemble each other. At last Bouilhet returned. He had read his latest play, *Mademoiselle Aïssé*, to the directors of the Théâtre de l'Odéon, who had asked him to make some important changes in the second act. This

* The line quoted is spoken by Agamemnon in the opening scene of Racine's *Iphigénie*. —Trans. (FS)

distressed him greatly. He was so depressed, even, that Flaubert hesitated to ask him to work on his manuscript. "I'm troubled about my poor Bouilhet," he wrote George Sand toward the end of June 1869. "He is in such a nervous state that he has been advised to take a little trip to the south of France. He is overwhelmed by an unconquerable depression. It's so odd! He who used to be so gay!" On July 7 he told Caroline: "The Monsignor left for Vichy a week ago; after that he will go to Mont-Dore. They don't know exactly what's wrong with him. His terrible depression must have an organic cause. But maybe not! The last two times I saw him it was *heart-breaking*. His illness, apart from the fact that it grieves me very much for his sake, makes a problem for me in my own little affairs, because we were to go over my novel together. When will he be in condition to undertake that task?"

By early July Bouilhet's health was deteriorating seriously. He was suffering from albuminuria. Flaubert went to visit him at the Hôpital Sainte-Eugénie, where he had been taken. The patient had to struggle against his sisters, who wanted to make him see a priest. And on July 18, 1869, the end came. "I have to announce to you the death of my poor Bouilhet," Flaubert wrote Princess Mathilde. "I have just buried a part of myself, an old friend whose loss is irreparable." And to Jules Duplan, four days later: "Your poor giant has had a hard knock from which he will never recover. I say to myself: 'What's the use of writing, now that he's no longer there?' It's all over—the good shouting matches, the common enthusiasms, the dreaming together about the works we were going to write. . . . A commission has been formed to erect a monument to him. . . . I have been appointed chairman of this commission. I'll send you the first list of subscribers." The next day, July 23, he recounted the events to Maxime Du Camp:

No priest set foot in his house. His anger against his sisters was still sustaining him on Saturday. . . . At five o'clock on Sunday he became delirious and began to compose aloud the plot of a medieval drama on the Inquisition. He kept calling for me, to show it to me, and was enthusiastic about it. Then he was seized with trembling, stammered 'Adieu! Adieu!' burying his head in Léonie's breast, and died very peacefully. . . .* D'Osmoy and I took charge of the funeral. There was a large crowd at the cemetery, at least two thousand people! The Prefect, the public prosecutor, etc.—the whole lot. Would you believe that as I followed his coffin I relished most keenly the grotesque aspect of the ceremony? I kept hearing remarks he was making to me about it. Inside me, somewhere, he was speaking to me. It seemed to me that he was there beside me and that together we were attending the funeral of someone else. The heat was terrible; there was a storm brewing. I was drenched with sweat, and the climb to the cemetery finished me. . . . I leaned on the railing to catch my breath. The coffin was resting on poles, over the grave. The speeches were about to begin (there were three). At that point I gave up. My brother and someone I didn't know took me away.

Henceforth he felt he had been given a sacred mission: to serve his friend's memory. Thanks to his insistence, *Mademoiselle Aïssé* was produced at the Théâtre de l'Odéon and another play, *Le Coeur à droite*, at the Théâtre de Cluny. In addition, he planned to have a collection of Bouilhet's unpublished poems printed under the title *Dernières Chansons*. These struggles on behalf of a shade delayed the last revisions of his own novel. He nevertheless took time to read a few books, including a number of Turgenev's short stories, which had just been translated into French under the title *Les Nouvelles moscovites* and which he liked immensely. "You manage to be true to life without being banal, to be sentimental without being insipid, and comic without being in the least vulgar," he wrote the author.[24] At last he delivered the manuscript of *L'Education sentimentale* to Michel Lévy, but the publisher was hesitant and the negotiations dragged on; George Sand intervened as a friend, and at the end of August the contract was signed for eight thousand francs per volume (the work was to appear in two volumes).

* Léonie was Bouilhet's mistress.

Now he had to think about moving. On the Rue Murillo, the painters were followed by the paperhangers. When he saw his furniture being taken to the new apartment, Flaubert felt a pang of regret: "You wouldn't believe the sadness that came over me on Monday when I saw my big leather armchair and my couch being taken away," he wrote Caroline. "I feel bad to be abandoning my Boulevard du Temple, where I leave very fond memories."[25] Would he ever become accustomed to these lodgings where Louis Bouilhet had never set foot? The memory of his friend was a constant obsession. And now the directors of the Théâtre de l'Odéon were making difficulties about producing *Mademoiselle Aïssé* because Bouilhet had not had time to rework the second act before he died. Maybe it would only be possible to publish the play as a book or in a periodical. As for the collection of poems, Lévy agreed to print it, but not to pay anything for it. "The material success of the posthumous works of our poor old friend seems very problematical to me," Flaubert observed bitterly to Philippe Leparfait.[26]★

On October 13, more bad news: Sainte-Beuve died at half past one in the afternoon. It so happened that Flaubert arrived at his house five minutes later and found a corpse still warm instead of the living man with whom he had come to talk. "Another one gone!" he wrote Maxime Du Camp. "The little band is diminishing! The few survivors on the raft of the Medusa are disappearing.† Who is there to talk about literature with now?"[27] And to Caroline: "I'm none too cheerful! . . . . I had written *L'Education sentimentale* in part for Sainte-Beuve. He died without seeing a line of it! Bouilhet never heard the last two chapters. . . . The year 1869 will have been a hard one for me! It seems I must go on prowling the cemeteries."[28]

On November 17, 1869, the novel appeared in the bookshops, and the critics immediately began ripping it apart. The most rabid of them was Barbey d'Aurevilly, who wrote in *Le Constitutionnel*:

★ Philippe was Léonie's son and had been adopted by Bouilhet.

† The raft bearing survivors from the *Méduse*, wrecked off the coast of Africa in 1816, had been made famous by Géricault's painting of the subject, which was exhibited at the Salon of 1819. Géricault, incidentally, was, like Flaubert, a native of Rouen. —Trans.

"The author of *L'Education sentimentale* must have, for the works to which he gives birth so slowly and painfully, the feelings of a mother who idolizes her child all the more because of the length and difficulty of the pregnancy. . . . The principal characteristic of the novel, which is so unfortunately titled *L'Education sentimentale*, is above all vulgarity—vulgarity found in the gutter where it dwells, and under everyone's feet." That set the tone: most of the other papers echoed it. "Your old troubadour is being heavily criticized in the press," Flaubert wrote George Sand. "Read last Monday's *Constitutionnel* and this morning's *Gaulois*: they mince no words. They call me a fool and a knave. Barbey d'Aurevilly's piece is a model of the genre, and the one by our friend Sarcey, though less violent, is equally fine. These gentlemen protest in the name of morality and the Ideal! I have also been blasted in *Le Figaro* and in *Paris*, by Cesena and Duranty. I couldn't care less! Still, I *am* surprised at all the hatred and dishonesty."

On the other hand, he was supported by *La Tribune* (the review was by Emile Zola), *Le Pays*, and *L'Opinion nationale*. Their measured praise, however, was drowned out by the shouts of the opponents. "As for my friends—people who received copies adorned with my signature—they are afraid of compromising themselves, and speak to me about everything except the book," Flaubert commented in the same letter. "Instances of courage are rare. . . . The bourgeois of Rouen are furious with me. . . . They think it should be forbidden to publish books like that (I quote), that I am on the side of the Reds, that I am much to be condemned for stirring up revolutionary passions, etc. etc."[29] When he claimed that no one was coming to his defense, George Sand wrote a generous and insightful review that appeared in *La Liberté*. She praised the subtlety of the plot, which was "many-sided, like living reality," the skill with which the characters were presented—each one, from scene to scene and from speech to speech, progressively revealing his true nature—and the modesty of the writer, who never appeared behind his heroes. Flaubert regained confidence. Let the public and most of the critics speak ill of *L'Education sentimentale*. That was the price he had to pay for the work's hidden virtues. In his heart of hearts he knew that he had written what he wanted: a novel about weakness of will and failure. In no other book, perhaps, had he put so much of himself. His hero, Frédéric Moreau, was the incarnation of his own youthful desires and ambitions. Like him, Frédéric was in love with a married woman whom he respected. Mme. Arnoux was Elisa Schlésinger, the woman he had met when he was a boy on the beach at Trouville, whom he had met again as a young man in Paris and whom, while he adored her, he had never dared to make his mistress. For that matter, in his outline for the book, she is indicated by the letters *Sch.:* "Mme. Sch., me." For Frédéric, this ethereal passion is succeeded by a carnal affair with Rosanette, who was modeled on Mme. Sabatier, *"la Présidente."* Along the way, Flaubert describes, with fascinating power and precision, the events of 1848 in Paris. The third liaison, which unites Frédéric with Mme. Dambreuse, is motivated purely by ambition. To portray this last incarnation of his hero, Flaubert recalled certain character traits of Maxime Du Camp: the cynicism, the social climbing. . . . Thus Frédéric acquires his "sentimental education" through three women, representing Platonic love, sensual love, and self-interested love. At the end of these different trials, he comes to know the bitterness of a failed life, a life that is absurd and without real significance. But in the penultimate chapter he meets Mme. Arnoux again, now showing the signs of age, and faced with this white-haired ghost, he is torn between the memory of his former desires and a repulsion "like a fear of incest." Frédéric and Mme. Arnoux part, disappointed in each other but rich in their past.

With this book, Flaubert wanted to trace not only the story of an aborted love, but the humble drama of every man who, as he advances through life, is forced to accommodate his dreams to everyday reality. Even the most fiery spirits may be defeated in the long run by the surrounding mediocrity. This pessimistic philosophy is reflected in a dry style and gray tones. The figures are less colorful than the ones in *Madame Bovary,* which presented a gallery of types. Here, nuance is everything, events follow each other with a calculated slowness, psychological subtlety replaces dramatic turns of plot. And thanks to a prodigious effort to recreate the setting, in the midst of this broad painting of a society each character appears in his relation to the historical events without his presence at that moment ever seeming artificial. The words and deeds of the fictitious characters seem as authentic as those of the real actors of the period. Thus for the reader, *L'Education sentimentale*, apart from its emotional value, has the interest of a historical document. When he depicts the revolutionary days, the author, always determined to be impartial, is equally hard on the folly of the rampaging people and the egotism of the conservative bourgeois. This impassive coldness adds to the spellbinding power of the work. Less showy than *Madame Bovary* or *Salammbô*, *L'Education sentimentale* creates an extraordinary impression of sobriety, honesty, and psychological depth.

In spite of the book's obvious strong points, the readers, who had pounced on *Madame Bovary* and *Salammbô*, were not interested. Even the fellow writers to whom Flaubert had given autographed copies hesitated to congratulate the author. The truth was that people were not prepared to appreciate a novel in which there seemed to be nothing exceptional about either the plot or the characters. The intentional monotony of the account, the absence of color, the minute description of the failure of ambitions and hopes, the whole dreary fog that enveloped Frédéric's emotional life was disconcerting to readers in 1869. On the the whole, they thought the author was losing his talent. But Flaubert had never been more in control of his means. He was a century ahead of his audience.

Hurt by the book's failure, he took consolation in the thought that he was going to enjoy himself like a solitary, surly old bear when he went back to his *Saint Antoine*. Then, having celebrated his forty-eighth birthday, he agreed to join George Sand in Nohant for the Christmas holidays. He arrived by stagecoach on December 23, at half past five. Embraces, dinner, chat around the fire, and bed at one. Next day, rain and snow; they stayed in, and Flaubert gave the little girls the presents he had brought: a doll for Aurore and a punchinello for Gabrielle. After lunch, rambling conversation in the blue bedroom of the mistress of the house. In the evening the whole company, with the addition of George Sand's three grandnephews, trooped into the puppet theater. After the performance, a game of lotto. "Flaubert enjoyed himself like a child," noted his hostess. "Christmas tree on the stage. Presents for all. . . . We had a splendid Christmas Eve. I went upstairs at three o'clock. . . . Lunch at noon. From three to half past six Flaubert read us his big fairy play, which we enjoyed very much but which is not destined for success." The next day, Sunday, they went for a walk in the snow. Flaubert visited the farm, admired the ram that bore his name, Gustave, and when they returned to the house, "split his sides laughing" at a puppet show. On December 27, his last day at Nohant, he dressed up as a woman and danced the cachucha, provoking much merriment. He was sorry to leave this jolly company. Why did he have to? For no reason. Unless it was the desire to be alone again in front of a blank sheet of paper.

When he got back to Paris he thanked George Sand for her hospitality: "Those were the best moments of 1869, a year that was not kind to me."[30] She replied that everyone at Nohant "adored" him. But she could not refrain from passing on to him the opinion of certain readers of his latest book: "The youngest say that *L'Education sentimentale* made them sad. They didn't recognize themselves in it, they who have not yet lived. But they have illusions, and they say: 'Why does this man, who is so good, so kind, so gay, simple, likable, want to discourage us from living?' It's not well thought out, what they say, but since it's instinctive, it should perhaps be taken into account."[31] He bristled up at once: "What's the good of making concessions? Why force oneself? On the contrary, I am quite resolved to write from now on for my personal satisfaction and without any constraint. Let come what may!" And he admitted: "In losing my poor Bouilhet, I lost my *midwife*, the one who understood my thoughts more clearly than I did myself. His death has left a void of which I am more aware every day."[32] While he was thus mourning his friend, he was struck by yet another loss: Jules Duplan died. "I am deeply grieved by your misfortunes," George Sand wrote Flaubert. "It's too much, one blow after another."[33] He was increasingly tired and nervous. "No matter how hard I work, I can't make any progress," he replied. "Everything irritates me and wounds me; and since I control myself in the presence of others, I am sometimes seized by fits of weeping during which I think my end has come. In short, I'm experiencing something quite new: the approach of old age."[34] This "black melancholy," as he put it, was aggravated by money worries. Michel Lévy offered to make him an interest-free loan of three or four thousand francs, on condition that he keep his next novel for him. Flaubert smelled a trap and refused: "From now on, I mean to be perfectly free," he declared proudly.[35]

When he had settled into his flat on the Rue Murillo, he retreated to Croisset to sort through Bouilhet's papers and write a piece on his friend's life and work to serve as an introduction to the book of poems. This project plunged him back into a happy past and made him even more painfully aware of his unbearable loss. Would he ever find the courage to undertake another new work? "I no longer feel the need to write, because I wrote especially for one sole being who is no more. That is the truth," he confided to George Sand. "And yet I will continue to write. But the taste for it is gone, the enthusiasm has vanished. There are so few people who love what I love, who are concerned with the things that are my chief care. . . . I feel I'm becoming a fossil, a being unconnected with the life around me. . . . Almost all my old friends are married, with positions in life, thinking all year round about their little concerns, about shooting during their holidays and whist after dinner. I don't know a single one who is capable of spending an afternoon with me reading a poet. They have their worldly involvements: I have none. Note that I am in the same position as regards company as when I was eighteen years old. My niece, whom I love as though she were my daughter, does not live with me, and my poor old mother is growing so old that any conversation with her (except about her health) is impossible."[36]

Indeed, Caroline seldom came to Croisset. The Commanvilles traveled a great deal for her husband's business or for pleasure. They had purchased a townhouse in Paris, where a room was set aside for Mme. Flaubert. But it was very small. Would the old lady be offended? She was almost deaf, and they had to shout to make her hear them. Flaubert thought sorrowfully that she too would leave him one day soon. Meanwhile another close friend disappeared: Jules de Goncourt, having lost his mind, died on June 20, 1870, in the arms of his elder brother, Edmond.* Flaubert went to the funeral on June 22 and a few days later wrote Caroline: "What a funeral! I have rarely seen anything so moving. What a state poor Edmond de Goncourt was in! Théo [Gautier], whom people accuse of being heartless, wept buckets. I didn't keep a very stiff upper lip either: the ceremony combined with the heat had exhausted me."[37] And to George Sand he wrote: "From the seven that we were when the dinners at Magny's began, we are reduced to three! . . . I am choked with coffins like an old cemetery! Frankly, I have had enough. And in the midst of all this I go on working. Yesterday I finished, for whatever it's worth, the piece on my poor Bouilhet. I'm going to see if there isn't some way to revive one of his comedies in prose. After which, I shall set to work on my *Saint Antoine*."[38] He needed the *Saint Antoine*, he said, as "something fantastic to get my poor head going again."[39]

But he had hardly immersed himself again in his hero's delirious visions when he was distracted by external events. The tension between France and Prussia was increasing day by day. Although King William I of Prussia had given up the notion of placing a German sovereign on the throne of Spain, the ministers of Napoleon III were demanding guarantees for the future. King William politely refused, but Bismarck, sure of his superior strength, reported to the press a version of the facts that was damaging to the French ambassador. At the Tuileries, it was felt that such an affront could not go unpunished. The people, worked up by clever propaganda, took to the streets in anger. On the evening of the fourteenth of July, Bastille Day, on the boulevards of Paris a huge crowd shouted

---

* Jules de Goncourt—like Baudelaire, Maupassant, and, according to some sources, Flaubert himself—died of syphilis, a disease of epidemic proportions at the time. —Trans. (FS)

"To Berlin!" They sang *La Marseillaise* and *Le Chant du départ*. On both sides of the frontier troops were mobilized, and on July 19, 1870, France declared war on Prussia.

Flaubert was appalled: "I am nauseated, heartbroken, by the stupidity of my compatriots," he wrote George Sand. "The incorrigible barbarism of mankind fills me with black gloom. This enthusiasm [for war], unmotivated by any idea, makes me long to die, that I might witness it no longer. The good Frenchman wants to fight (1) because he thinks he has been provoked by Prussia; (2) because man's natural condition is savagery; (3) because in war there is an inherent mystical element that enraptures the crowd. . . . The frightful butchery now being prepared for lacks even a pretext. It's a craving to fight for the sake of fighting. . . . I have begun *Saint Antoine*. And it might go well if I could stop thinking about the war."[40]

As always, he could see only one way to escape from the criminal absurdity of the world: to bury himself in his hole, bow his head, and write, write. . . .

Chapter 17

WAR

At the outbreak of hostilities, Flaubert wanted to be impartial: he refused to give in to patriotic madness. He condemned this war in the name of culture. And once again, he blamed the people and their representatives. "The reverence, the fetishism people have for universal suffrage revolts me more than the infallibility of the Pope," he wrote George Sand. "Do you think that if France, instead of being governed, in effect, by the crowd, were ruled by the mandarins, we'd be where we are now?" To him, salvation lay not in trusting the lower classes but in granting freedom of decision to an elite. In any case, he foresaw nothing good. "Black darkness" lay ahead. "Perhaps we were too accustomed to comfort and tranquility. Perhaps we were sinking into materialism. We must return to the great tradition: no longer cleave to life, to happiness, to money, to anything. . . ."[1]

But while he took refuge in a lofty philosophical position, he still read the newspapers with the keenest interest. On August 7 the government announced major defeats at Froeschwiller and Forbach. The people were so alarmed that on August 9 the chambers were called into session. Premier Émile Ollivier was ousted and replaced by a right-winger, the comte de Palikao. A battle was expected any day now at Metz. Panicked by these events, Caroline returned from the warm springs of Luchon, visited Croisset briefly, then went to London. Ernest Commanville, in the meantime, landed a big government order that would start his lumber mill humming again. He, for one, had no reason to complain about the war.

Too impatient for news to sit still any longer, Flaubert took the train to Paris. He stayed in the capital only three days, however, soon becoming exasperated by the attitude of his fellow citizens, who were torn between illusion and despair, courage and fear, shame and pride. "Such stupidity! Such cowardice! Such ignorance! Such presumption! My compatriots make me want to vomit. . . . This people *deserves* to be punished, and I fear it will be."[2] In spite of this categorical judgment, he was revolted to think that Prussian boots were already trampling the sacred soil of France. He could not remain above the battle, as he had claimed to do at first. Notwithstanding his age and fatigue, he wanted to take part in the defense of the country. "If Paris is besieged (which I now believe will happen)," he wrote Caroline, "I am finally resolved to clear out of here with my rifle on my back. The idea of it almost puts me in good spirits. Better to fight than to eat my heart out with sorrow, as I am doing now."[3]

On August 26 four hundred wounded were brought to Rouen, and on the thirtieth the Bonenfants—Flaubert's cousins from Nogent-sur-Seine—showed up in Croisset, fleeing the advancing enemy. The house was full to bursting. Sixteen persons under one roof. Flaubert was provoked beyond measure by the noise the newcomers made. His mother spent her time arguing with the servants. And in the morning he was awakened by "poor Bonenfant with his perpetual spitting." Flaubert, buried under the covers, would hear him coughing in the garden. "If such a life were to continue, I'd go mad or collapse into idiocy," he informed his niece. "I have stomach cramps and a permanent headache. And no one, you realize, *absolutely no one*, even to talk to! Your grandmother complains endlessly about the weakness of her legs and her deafness. It's all dreadful! . . . The National Guard of Croisset (a very important organization) is finally meeting, next Sunday. Indirectly, I have had news of Prince Napoleon: he has really *fled*! Fine fellows we had to govern us."[4]

In early September he was working as a nurse at the Hôtel-

Dieu in Rouen. He was now convinced that the Prussians wanted to "destroy Paris" and that to force the capital to surrender they were going to "ravage the surrounding countryside." In Rouen people were preparing for desperate resistance. In anticipation of the fighting, Flaubert was named lieutenant of a company of the National Guard. He took his role very seriously, drilled his men, and went to Rouen to attend courses in the art of warfare. But while he swaggered in public, when he was alone in his study he collapsed. The news from the front was disastrous. On September 1, 1870, a French army commanded by Marshal MacMahon and accompanied by the Emperor himself was crushed at Sedan. The surrender, signed the next day, delivered into the hands of the enemy eighty-three thousand men and a large quantity of matériel. Napoleon III surrendered his sword to the victor and was immediately taken to Germany.

On learning of this terrible defeat, Paris rose in revolt. Gathered in front of the Palais Bourbon, a menacing crowd demanded a change of regime. The republic was immediately proclaimed at the Hôtel de Ville. The Empress fled to England. A hastily formed Government of National Defense announced that electors would be summoned to a Constituent Assembly. The empire had lived out its last days. A new era was beginning under the emblem of democracy. Paris, rejoicing, wanted to believe that faced with the enemy hordes, the motherland was going to be resurrected. But Flaubert was skeptical. He had no sympathy for republican principles and doubted that the political upheaval could have a favorable effect on the conduct of the war. While George Sand, an ardent socialist, was exulting in her corner, he wrote her: "Here we are, 'at the bottom of the abyss'; a shameful peace will perhaps not be accepted. . . . *I am dying of grief.* What a house this is! Fourteen people, all groaning, all driving me crazy. I curse women: they are the cause of all our woes. . . . * At times I fear I'm going insane. *The sight of my mother's face,* when I turn my eyes toward her, drains me of all energy. . . . We'll become another Poland, then another Spain. Then it will be

* Probably an allusion to the Empress Eugénie.

Prussia's turn—she'll be devoured by Russia. As for me, I consider myself *finished*. My brain will never recover. One cannot write when one has lost one's self-esteem. I ask but one thing—to die, so as to be at peace."[5]

Wearily, he went back to his *Saint Antoine*, but he soon found it impossible to work. The Germans had advanced as far as Paris without meeting any resistance. Flaubert said that he had "a grim, stupid, animal desire *to fight*." "Scholar though I am, the blood of my forefathers, the Natchez or the Hurons, is seething in my veins. . . . * The idea of signing a peace now infuriates me, and I'd rather see Paris burned, like Moscow, than occupied by the Prussians."[6] The capital, where there was a large concentration of troops, was preparing for a long siege. The French government proclaimed a "war to the death," which delighted Flaubert. "Since Sunday, when we learned the conditions that Prussia wants to impose on us just for an armistice, everyone's attitude has suddenly changed," he wrote Caroline. "Now it's a duel to the death. As the old saying goes, we must 'conquer or die.' The worst poltroons have become brave. . . . Today I begin my night patrols. Just now I made a fatherly speech to 'my men,' informing them that I would run my sword through the belly of the first one who retreated and urging them to shoot *me* if they saw me run away. . . . What a weird thing brains are, especially mine!"[7]

As the war went on, hunger set in. Poor, starving people spread over the countryside, gathered outside the garden in Croisset, shook the gates, and uttered threatening cries. Flaubert bought a revolver. He was convinced that sooner or later the National Guard of Rouen would have to fight. The military situation was deteriorating day by day. The capitulation of Metz made the German army that had been besieging the city available for use elsewhere. "I have no good news for you," Flaubert wrote his niece. "The Prussians are at Vernon

---

* Flaubert liked to maintain that he had Indian blood in his veins, a claim based on the fact that in the seventeenth century one of his ancestors on his mother's side had gone to Canada and was supposed to have taken a wife there before returning to France.

on the one side and in Gournay on the other. Rouen will not resist. . . . As for Paris, it will continue to resist for a while; but they say they will soon run out of meat, and then there will be no choice but to surrender. The elections for the Constituent are to take place on the 16th. . . . In a month it will all be over—that is, the first act of the drama will be over; the second will be civil war. . . . Whatever happens, the world to which I belonged is no more. The Latins are finished! Now it's the turn of the Saxons, who will be devoured by the Slavs."[8]

The Bonenfants and Mme. Flaubert had gone to Rouen and moved into the Commanvilles' empty apartment on the Quai du Havre, thinking to be safer there than in Croisset. Flaubert saluted the courage of Gambetta, who had flown out of Paris in a balloon "in the midst of bullets" to join the government in Tours. But he was afraid that the army of the Loire was not strong enough to repel the invader. "Never in the history of France has there been anything greater and more tragic than the siege of Paris," he wrote Caroline. "That word alone makes one's senses reel, and what visions it will summon up for future generations!"[9] The poor came in increasing numbers to beg for bread at the gates of the house. Each of them was given something, but Flaubert had the shutters closed in broad daylight so as not to see them. He was also furious at the Croisset militia's lack of discipline. Impossible to drum any sense into these demons who refused to behave like soldiers. On October 23 he resigned as lieutenant. He was astonished by the ferocity of the Germans: "How they hate us! and how they envy us, those cannibals! Do you know that they take pleasure in destroying any works of art and *objets de luxe* that they come across? Their dream is to annihilate Paris, because Paris is beautiful."[10] What worried him even more than the war was the consequences of the terrible bloodletting. "We are going to enter into an era of darkness. People will no longer think about anything but the art of warfare. They will be very poor, very practical, or very limited. Elegance of any sort will be impossible."[11]

After the surrender of Metz, the besieging army marched on Compiègne, then on Normandy to occupy the lower reaches of the

Seine. The maneuver was clear. Rouen would not escape seizure by the enemy. "For six weeks now we have been expecting the Prussians to arrive any day," Flaubert wrote George Sand. "We keep listening, thinking we hear the sound of cannon in the distance. They have encircled the department of the Seine-Inférieure at a radius of fourteen to twenty leagues. . . . What horrors! It makes one blush to be a man. . . . There's no lack of ready-made phrases. 'France will rise again!' 'We must not despair!' 'It is a salutary punishment!' 'We were really too immoral!' Etc. Oh, eternal poppycock! No! One does not rise again after such a blow. As for me, I feel stricken to the marrow of my bones. . . . Literature seems to me a vain and useless thing. Will I ever be in a condition to write again? . . . Oh, if I could flee to a country where one doesn't see uniforms and hear the sound of drums! Where there's no talk of massacres, where one doesn't have to be a *citizen*! But the earth is no longer habitable for us poor mandarins!"[12]

On December 5 Rouen, having declared itself an open city, was occupied by the Germans. Flaubert left Croisset at once to go live in town with his mother. Before leaving, he had his servant Émile bury his most precious papers, including the manuscript of *La Tentation de Saint Antoine,* at the foot of the garden. Seven soldiers, three officers, and six horses were billeted at his house. "So far, we have no reason to complain of these gentlemen," he wrote Caroline, "but what humiliation, my poor Carol what ruin! what sadness! what misery! . . . When we are not running errands for the Prussians (yesterday I was on my feet for three hours getting them hay and straw) we spend our time asking each other for news or weeping in a corner."[13] In Rouen he slept in his niece's old bedroom, where he could hear the snores of two German soldiers camped in the dressing room next door. His mother, who was increasingly frail, had to lean on the furniture and the wall when she walked. She was calling for her granddaughter, who was still in London. Ernest Commanville too was insisting that his wife return. Achille was now a member of the Municipal Council, which meant more work and more worry for him. And now Prince Mecklenburg's troops were coming to relieve Manteuffel's. To Flaubert, it was "like a second invasion." He went back to Croisset, found that there had not been too much damage, but was pained to see spiked helmets lying on his bed. "How will I find my poor study, my books, my notes, my manuscripts?" he wrote Caroline. "All I was able to put in a safe place were my papers relating to *Saint Antoine*. Emile has the key to the study, but they keep asking for it, and go in and take books. . . . We have come to the beginning of the end. . . . Poor Paris will not be able to hold out for long under the terrible shelling."[14]

In the meantime, the government, which felt threatened in Tours, had moved to Bordeaux, the two armies of the Loire had been beaten, and the army of the north had been put to flight. On January 18, 1871, the King of Prussia was proclaimed Emperor of Germany in the Hall of Mirrors in the Palais de Versailles. And on the twenty-eighth Paris, exhausted, bombarded, starving, resigned itself to accepting the conditions of the conqueror. An armistice was concluded pending the definitive peace. Flaubert was stunned and, with his usual tendency to excess, furious with the entire country for having let itself be conquered. "The capitulation of Paris, even though it was to be expected, had plunged us into an indescribable state," he wrote his niece. "I could hang myself from rage! I regret that Paris wasn't burned to the last house, leaving only a great black void. France has fallen so low, is so dishonored, so debased, that I wish she might disappear completely. But I hope that civil war will kill a lot of people for us. Would that I might be included in the number! In preparation for that event, there is to be an election of deputies. What bitter irony! Needless to say, I shall abstain from voting. I no longer wear my cross of the Legion of Honor, for the word honor is no longer French, and I feel so strongly that I am no longer French either that I am going to ask Turgenev (as soon as I can write to him) what one has to do to become a Russian."[15]

The elections for the National Assembly took place on February 8. It was the candidates in favor of peace who obtained the majority. On February 12 Thiers was named head of the executive power of the French Republic and charged with conducting the negotiations with Bismarck. On March 1 the National Assembly, meeting in

Bordeaux, confirmed the fall of Napoleon III and of his dynasty and accepted the draconian conditions posed by the enemy for signing the peace: Alsace and part of Lorraine were abandoned to Germany, the French were to pay war reparations of five billion francs, and the Prussians made a triumphal entry into the capital. In the meantime, the soldiers had left Croisset. But Flaubert still hesitated to go back to his house. Ever since it had sheltered the enemy, he had felt it was soiled. He would have liked to throw into the river all the objects which "those gentlemen" had handled. He was sorry he couldn't demolish the walls that had been profaned. "Oh, such hatred! Such hatred! It's suffocating! I, who was born so sensitive, I'm choking on gall. . . ."[16] On March 12 Prince Frederik Karl of Prussia reviewed his troops in Rouen. The inhabitants immediately hung out black flags. The shops put shutters over their windows with big signs reading CLOSED ON ACCOUNT OF NATIONAL MOURNING. The Prussians were exasperated by this insolence and became doubly demanding in their relations with the civilian population.

When he did go back to Croisset, Flaubert was somewhat reassured to find that the familiar setting had not changed, but he decided to leave at once for Brussels, going by way of Paris. Alexandre Dumas *fils* went with him. They had to be careful, for the Germans were "behaving abominably." The officers, he said, "smash your mirrors with white-gloved hands . . . fling themselves on your champagne . . . steal your watch and then send you their visiting card."[17] Flaubert considered them "civilized savages," more horrifying than cannibals.

In Paris the presence of the Germans seemed even more intolerable to him than in Rouen. "It's over. We have swallowed our shame, but not digested it," he wrote Princess Mathilde. "All day I saw the bayonets of the Prussians flashing in the sun on the Champs-Elysées and heard their bands, their hateful bands, playing under the Arc de Triomphe! The man who sleeps in the Invalides [Napoleon I] must have been turning in his grave with rage."[18] He hurried on to Brussels, checked into the Hôtel Bellevue, and had an emotional reunion with Princess Mathilde, who had taken refuge in Belgium. However, on March 18 Paris was rocked by a spontaneous revolt. Drunk with humiliation and rage, a crowd of citizens, including women and children, tried to stop the regular troops from seizing the cannons of the National Guard. As the insurrection spread, Thiers ordered the ministers, the government officials, and the army to leave Paris for Versailles. A Central Committee of the National Guard took the place of the government and set up a revolutionary power in Paris. "I greatly regret having left," Flaubert wrote Caroline. "Now one can't go back to Paris, and at the French border the Republican authorities give you a hard time over any trifle. So I am taking ship at Ostend tomorrow for London, whence I expect to return via Newhaven."[19]

Having made this detour to England, which enabled him to see Juliet Herbert again, he went back to Neuville, near Dieppe, where he was happy to be reunited with his mother and niece. But the news from Paris, which was abandoned to the fury of the rabble, moved him to new heights of indignation: "Those wretches make you turn your hatred in another direction. One no longer thinks about the Prussians. A little more and one would love them! There will be no shame we have not tasted."[20] And again: "Now we have the Paris Commune, which takes us right back to the Middle Ages. It's perfectly plain. . . . Many conservatives who, for love of order, wanted to preserve the Republic, are going to miss Badinguet, and in their hearts they call for the return of the Prussians. . . . * It seems to me that we have never been lower."[21] In the same letter he informed George Sand that he intended to leave his mother and niece in Neuville, where they were safe, and return to Croisset: "It is hard, but I must do it. I'm going to try to take up my poor *Saint Antoine* again and to forget about France."

When he was back in the house in Croisset, which was at last empty of its hateful occupants, his first concern was to make a survey. He found with relief that his study had been respected and that the Prussians had taken only small items of no value: a dressing case, a cardboard box, an assortment of pipes. . . . Little by little the warmth of the nest penetrated him. He immersed himself with

---

* "Badinguet" was another nickname for Napoleon III. —Trans.

delight in his old habits of reading, writing, and dreaming, in the midst of the furniture and bibelots that had been his lifelong companions. "Contrary to my expectations, I find myself *very comfortable* in Croisset, and I think no more about the Prussians than if they had never come here," he wrote Caroline. "It was a very sweet feeling, to be back in my study and see all my little belongings once again. My mattresses have been beaten and remade, and I sleep like a dormouse. Saturday night I went back to work again. . . . The garden is going to be very beautiful: the buds are forming, there are primroses everywhere. Such peace! I'm quite dazed by it."[22] Memories of the distant past came back to him: Bouilhet arriving on Sunday morning with his notebook of poems under his arm, Caroline in her little white apron running over the lawn in front of the house. . . . He thought nostalgically about bygone days and then was suddenly seized with anger again. The Commune's follies drew cries of hatred from him. He fulminated because the government was slow to act against the insurgents, whose insolence now knew no bounds: "What throwbacks!" he wrote George Sand. "What savages! How like they are to the men of the League and the Maillotins!★ Poor France, which will never emerge from the Middle Ages, still crawling along on the Gothic idea of the commune."[23] Or, again to George Sand: "I hate democracy (at least as it is understood in France) . . . that is, the exaltation of mercy at the expense of justice, the negation of right—in short, everything that is antisocial. . . . The Commune rehabilitates murderers, just as Jesus forgave thieves, and the homes of the rich are looted. . . . The only rational thing (I keep coming back to it) is a government of mandarins. . . . The people never come of age, and they will always be at the bottom rung of the social scale because they represent number, mass, the limitless. . . . Our only salvation now lies in a *legitimate aristocracy*,

---

★ The League (or Holy League) was a Catholic organization founded by the duc de Guise in 1576, during the Wars of Religion in France, to combat Protestantism and to seize power from Henri III. The Maillotins—so called because they were armed with *maillotins* [war hammers] seized from the armory—were insurgent Parisians who, in 1382, during the minority of Charles VI, rose in protest against oppressive taxes. —Trans.

by which I mean a majority composed of something other than mere numbers. . . . Paris is completely epileptic. That's the result of the stroke she suffered during the siege."[24]

In spite of his hostility toward universal suffrage, on April 30 he went to Bapaume on foot "to deposit my ballot." He pitied George Sand, who, shattered by the events in Paris, had written him a despairing letter. "She realizes that her old idol was hollow, and her Republican faith seems to me completely extinguished," he told Princess Mathilde.[25]

While the Versailles troops were beginning to besiege Paris, Mme. Flaubert returned to Croisset, and her extreme fatigue and mental weakness worried Flaubert. "My sole distraction is now and then to see the Prussian gentlemen march by under my windows on some military excursion, and my only occupation is my *Saint Antoine*, which I'm working away at without pause," he wrote in the same letter. "This fantastic work keeps me from thinking about the horrors of Paris. When we find this world too evil, we must take refuge in another." At this point he learned that Maurice Schlésinger had died, and he imagined for an instant that his beloved Elisa, she who had been the inspiration for *L'Education sentimentale*, would come back to live in France with her son. But she disabused him, and he was grieved: "I had hoped that the end of my life would be spent not far from you. As for seeing you in Germany, that is a country where I shall never voluntarily set foot. I have seen enough Germans this year to wish never to see another, and I don't see how any self-respecting Frenchman could deign to spend so much as a minute with one of those gentlemen, charming as they may be. They have our clocks, our money, and our land: let them keep those things and let's hear no more about them! . . . Ah, I have suffered horribly for the last ten months—suffered enough to go mad and kill myself! But I have gone back to work; I try to intoxicate myself with ink, the way others intoxicate themselves with brandy, so as to forget the public disasters and my private sorrows."[26]

In Paris, meanwhile, the regular troops entered the city by the ill-guarded Porte de Saint-Cloud. Barricades went up in the streets at once, and the Communards burned public buildings to slow the advance of the Versaillese. On both sides, prisoners were shot after a pretense of interrogation. But at the end of a week the insurgents succumbed. The last of the fighting took place in the Faubourg du Temple. Tricolor flags floated from all the windows now. The repression was terrible: deportations, executions. Flaubert breathed a sigh of relief. This stupid fratricidal struggle had completed his demoralization. As soon as communications with the capital were reestablished, he went to Paris to take stock of the damage, see a few friends, and do some research in the libraries. Edmond de Goncourt noted in his *Journal* for June 10, 1871: "Dinner this evening with Flaubert, whom I had not seen since the death of my brother. He has come to Paris to look for some information for his *Tentation de Saint Antoine*. He is still the same, a writer first and foremost. This cataclysm seems to have passed over him without distracting him in the slightest from the imperturbable composition of his book." It was a hasty condemnation, for Flaubert had been profoundly shaken by the war and the disorders that had followed the defeat. If he had nevertheless continued his work, it was in order to survive spiritually in the midst of the disaster. What he saw and heard in Paris was overwhelming and nauseating: "The smell of the corpses was less disgusting to me than the miasmas of egotism exhaled from every mouth," he wrote George Sand when he returned to Croisset. "The sight of the ruins is as nothing compared to the immense folly of the inhabitants. With very few exceptions, they all seemed to me to be raving mad. Half the population wants to strangle the other half, which would be happy to reciprocate. That is plain to see in the eyes of the passers-by. And the Prussians no longer exist! People excuse them and *admire* them!"[27]

Paris had made such an impression on him that he found it hard to go back to work. It seemed to him that the house in Croisset still smelled of Prussian boots. The rooms where the soldiers had lodged were repapered; Caroline had chosen the pattern. In addition, Flaubert was annoyed by countless domestic details. He wrote his niece: "Did you add up all the bills to be paid? Have you paid some of them? I don't know what I should do. What are the wages of the two maids?"[28] Then his inspiration would return and for a few hours he would forget his ill temper, his bitterness, his sorrow. There were even moments when, lost in Saint Anthony's hallucinations, he could believe that France had not been conquered. "It felt good to be back home again, in the midst of my books," he wrote Princess Mathilde, "and I go on turning out sentences as before. It's just as innocent and as useful as turning out napkin rings."[29]* And, to Mme. Roger des Genettes: "My sole diversion is, twice a day, to offer my arm to my mother and drag her out into the garden, after which I go back up to Saint Anthony. . . . The good man, after having had his head deranged by the spectacle of heresies, has just been listening to Buddha and is now witnessing the prostitutions of Babylon. I'm getting ready to put him through worse."[30]

Meanwhile, in a formidable burst of national solidarity, the French subscribed en masse to the bonds issued by Thiers to raise the sum demanded by the Prussians to end their occupation. Flaubert, however, had money worries of his own. It was Ernest Commanville who managed Mme. Flaubert's fortune, and he hardly seemed to be doing it very well. "As for me, who have received only fifteen hundred francs from your grandmother since January, in about ten days I would need three thousand francs," he announced to his niece.[31] Of course he found it a little humiliating to be begging the young woman for help. But all his life he had hated money matters, and he was now a grown-up child incapable of handling himself in the world of affairs. As soon as he rose from his writing table he was lost. Fortunately, around him France seemed to be at peace again. "The political horizon seems calm for the moment!" he wrote again to Mme. Roger des Genettes. "Ah, if one could only accustom oneself to things as they are, that is, to living without principles, empty phrases, and formulas! This is, I believe, the first time in history that such a thing has presented itself. Is it the beginning of positivism in politics? Let's hope so."

On July 22, 1871, the Prussians evacuated the region of Rouen.

---

* An allusion to Binet, the tax collector in *Madame Bovary*, whose hobby is making napkin rings on a lathe in his attic. —Trans.

Chapter 18

TOWARD GREATER SOLITUDE

From now on Flaubert's life was ruled by Saint Anthony. He worked on the manuscript at Croisset and went to Paris to read in the libraries. In town he saw few people, looked out his windows on the Parc Monceau, went to bed early, and took a rest from the constant fussing of his mother, whom he adored but who wore him out. For diversion he went to Versailles to attend the trial of the Communards by the Council of War. The harsh sentences passed on the troublemakers seemed to him a manifestation of the national common sense. He also allowed himself a few visits to Saint-Gratien to see Princess Mathilde, who had come back to France after the peace treaty had been signed. But these were only brief interludes. Already his mother was demanding that he return to her side. "I find it strange that your grandmother is putting so much pressure on me to go back," he wrote Caroline on August 9, 1871. "It does seem to me that at my age I have the right to do what I want, once a year. The last time I came here, in June, I didn't accomplish everything I wanted to, thanks to the fine habit I have acquired of setting a date for my return in advance, as if it were important!" In spite of this feeble rebellion, he went back to Croisset like a good son, as planned, in the last half of August and observed that the war had aged his mother "by a hundred years." As she could not stay alone any longer, he gave up the idea of going to Trouville to join Elisa Schlésinger, who was now there to settle her late husband's estate. But he begged his friend to visit him in Croisset: "So come, we have so many things to say to each other, the sort of things that cannot be said, or can only be said badly, in writing. Who is there to stop you? Are you not free? My mother would be very pleased to receive you, in memory of the good old days."[1]

More and more he felt the need to immerse himself once again in the affections of the past. The loves and friendships of former days consoled him for the horrors of the present. It was George Sand who was the preferred recipient of his political outpourings: "We are floundering in the afterbirth of the Revolution, which was a miscarriage, a failure, a gross blunder, no matter what people say," he wrote her. "If France is to rise again, she must pass from inspiration to Science, she must abandon all metaphysics in favor of critical inquiry—that is, the examination of reality. . . . I defy anyone to show me one essential difference between those two terms ["republic" and "monarchy"]. A modern republic and a constitutional monarchy are identical. No matter: there's great squabbling over it anyway—shouting, fighting. As for the good People, 'free and compulsory' education will be the end of them. . . . The first remedy would be to abolish universal suffrage, that insult to human intelligence. As it is constituted, one single element prevails to the detriment of all the rest: number dominates over mind, education, race, and even money, which is preferable to number."[2] Or else: "I believe that the poor hate the rich and that the rich are afraid of the poor. It will be ever thus. It is as futile to preach love to the one as to the other. The most urgent thing is to educate the rich, who after all are the stronger."[3] Or again: "In my opinion the entire Commune should have been sentenced to hard labor. The blood-stained fools should have been chained by the neck like common criminals and made to clean up the ruins of Paris. But that would have wounded *humanity*. There is plenty of sympathy for the mad dogs but none for the people they have bitten. That won't change so long as universal suffrage is what it is. . . . In an industrial enterprise (a joint-stock company), the number of votes each shareholder has depends on the value of his contribution. That's the way it should be in the government of a nation. I am easily worth twenty electors from Croisset. Money, intelligence, and even race should be taken into account—in short, all factors. But so far, I have seen only one: number."[4]

This last letter was dated from Paris, where Flaubert had gone in haste to persuade the Théâtre de l'Odéon to produce Louis Bouilhet's play *Mademoiselle Aïssé*. This time, the affair seemed well under way. A date had even been set: January 1872. Happy to have been able to serve the memory of his friend at last, Flaubert was about to take the train back to Rouen when he ran into Edmond de Goncourt. "He was carrying under his arm a minister's portfolio with a triple lock, in which he had his *Tentation*," noted his friend. "In the carriage he talked to me about his book, about all the ordeals to which he was subjecting the hermit of Thebaid and from which he emerges victorious. Then, at the Rue d'Amsterdam he confided to me that the saint's final defeat is due to the *cell*, the scientific cell. The curious thing is that he seemed surprised by my surprise."[5]

Flaubert returned to Croisset filled with happiness by the announcement of a forthcoming visit from Elisa Schlésinger, who was arriving from Trouville. But there she had had painful discussions with her children, who were their deceased father's only heirs, and when she saw Flaubert again, she was hardly in the mood for romantic reminiscences. If to him Trouville was the paradise of his adolescent love affairs, to her it was only the scene of family quarrels and humiliations. As soon as she left, he returned to Paris to look after *Mademoiselle Aïssé* again. On December 1, 1871, he read the play aloud to the actors of the Odéon. And that evening he wrote Philippe Leparfait: "The reading to the actors took place just now amid the greatest enthusiasm. Tears, applause, etc." Three days later, he turned over to the printer the manuscript of Bouilhet's *Dernières Chansons*, subtitled *Poésies posthumes*. He was also actively pursuing the question of the monument he wanted to have erected in Rouen to the glory of his friend: a fountain with a bust, at the foot of the Rue Verte. He had already collected subscriptions in the amount of twelve thousand francs. But on December 8, 1871, the City Council of Rouen rejected the project, on the ground that Bouilhet was not sufficiently famous to deserve such an honor. Flaubert was furious and sent the council a scathing letter that was immediately published in *Le Temps*. He hoped that the success of *Mademoiselle Aïssé* would make up for this failure and that when the citizens of Rouen heard that Louis Bouilhet was the rage of Paris, they would want to kick themselves for having been so niggardly with their esteem.

At the Odéon on January 6, 1872, the play was given an enthusiastic reception by the friendly first-night audience. Flaubert was there, of course, clapping to bring down the house. He thought his friend would have his revenge. But the next night's performance was a disaster. "House almost empty," he wrote George Sand. "The press, in general, was stupid and base. I was accused of having tried to make propaganda by inserting an incendiary tirade. I am considered a Red. You see how things stand. The management of the Odéon has done nothing for the play. Quite the contrary. On the day of the première, it was I who with my own hands brought over the props for the first act. And at the third performance I led the extras. . . . In short, Bouilhet's heir will earn very little money. Honor is saved, but that's all."[6] Seeking consolation, he took advantage of being in Paris to read 115 pages of his *Saint Antoine* to Turgenev. The "good Muscovite" was jubilant with admiration. "What a listener!" wrote Flaubert. "And what a critic! I was dazzled by the depth and clarity of his judgment. Ah, if all those who take it upon themselves to judge books could have heard him, what a lesson they would have had! Nothing escapes him. . . . He gave me two or three suggestions regarding very fine points in *Saint Antoine*."[7] Meanwhile, he had written a preface to Bouilhet's *Dernières Chansons*. To his astonishment, this posthumous homage to his friend elicited an insulting letter from Louise Colet. "I have received an anonymous letter from her, in verse, in which she represents me as a charlatan banging the big drum over his friend's tomb, a toady who debases himself before the critics after having 'fawned on Caesar'!" he wrote George Sand. "Sad example of the passions, as

Prudhomme would say."[8]★ He went to pay his respects to Victor Hugo, whom he found "charming," not at all the "great man" or "pontifical"; wrote Alphonse Daudet to express his enthusiasm for *Tartarin de Tarascon*, which he considered "a masterpiece"; and had a quarrel "for life" with the publisher Michel Lévy, who had gone back on his word regarding an advance he had promised to cover the printing costs of *Dernières Chansons*. Edmond de Goncourt, who saw him during his stay in Paris, observed: "Flaubert is so ill-tempered, curt, irascible, and ready to explode over everything and nothing that I am afraid my poor friend is suffering from the morbid irritability that marks the onset of a nervous disease."[9]

A new worry for Flaubert: he absolutely had to find a companion for his mother. "We need someone who can read aloud and who is very gentle," he informed George Sand. "She would also be asked to take some charge of the household. This lady would not have to provide much physical care, since my mother would keep her maid. . . . Religious principles are not required."[10] Mme. Flaubert could hardly keep her feet, and her mind was wandering. Back in Croisset, Flaubert found it increasingly hard to put up with her idiosyncrasies. Her chief concern was to eat to regain her strength, and she had the usual mealtimes advanced. "The house is so dirty and dilapidated, and the household affairs are so complicated that I haven't been able to do anything since my arrival," Flaubert wrote Caroline. "All these concerns, and above all being alone in the pitiful society of your grandmother, completely wipe me out. I feel that I would be incapable of writing, for I have trouble understanding what I read. My dream is to go live in some monastery in Italy and not be involved in anything anymore. . . . When will I be bloody well left alone? When will I not have to be eternally worrying about *other* people? I alternate between roaring and prostration."[11] He waited impatiently for the arrival of the companion who had at last

---

★ Joseph Prudhomme, a character created by the contemporary writer and cartoonist Henri Monnier, was the personification of the self-satisfied, narrow-minded petty bourgeois full of solemn platitudes. —Trans.

been engaged and who was to present herself at the beginning of April.

But on April 6, 1872, Mme. Flaubert passed away after a death struggle of thirty-three hours. Although Flaubert was prepared for the event, it shook him to his roots. It was his whole childhood that was suddenly torn from him. Now he was alone in the world. He wrote to his intimate friends—Maxime Du Camp, Edmond de Goncourt, Laure de Maupassant, George Sand—sending each a cry of despair: "My mother has just died. Since Monday I have not closed my eyes. I am shattered."[12]

Le Journal de Rouen published an obituary:

Madame the widow Flaubert was a person of very distinguished mind. She was a relative of M. Laumonier, the celebrated surgeon whom M. Flaubert succeeded as chief surgeon of the general hospital. She was the granddaughter, the wife, and the mother of doctors. The sorrow of Madame Flaubert's family will be keenly shared in Rouen. All those whose sufferings have been alleviated by the father and son, all those who have witnessed their devotion to humble people, will join in the same feeling of respect and affection. The interment will take place tomorrow, Tuesday, in Croisset, at ten o'clock in the morning.

After the funeral Flaubert had to go through the ordeal of drawing up an inventory of the property left by his mother. "It was grim!" he wrote Edmond de Goncourt. "I felt as if my mother were dying all over again and as if we were robbing her."[13] According to the last will of the deceased, the house at Croisset went to her granddaughter, Caroline, but Flaubert was to continue living there. By way of compensation, he received a farm at Deauville, the income from which would help him to live. Once the hateful administrative formalities were over, he tried to accustom himself to his new status as a fifty-year-old orphan. "Today at last I'm beginning to hear the birds sing again and to see the fresh green of the leaves," he wrote George Sand. "I've stopped resenting the sunshine, and that's a

good sign. If only I could feel like working again I'd be saved."
And he added: "Will I have the fortitude to live absolutely alone
here, in solitude? I doubt it. I'm growing old. Caroline cannot live
here now. She already has two places of her own, and the Croisset
house is expensive to maintain. I think I'll give up my apartment
in Paris. I have no reason to go to Paris anymore. All my friends
are dead, and the last of them, poor Théo, isn't long for this world,
I fear. Ah, it's hard to grow a new skin at fifty! I have realized for
a fortnight now that my poor dear mother was the being I loved
most. It's as though part of my entrails had been torn out."[14]

When all the details of the inheritance had been settled and
Caroline had left Croisset to return to Dieppe, Flaubert, faced with
the sudden emptiness of his existence, had a moment of panic. But
he got a grip on himself and wrote his niece: "My heart was very
heavy when I saw you leave, and I felt even less cheerful in the
evening, when I sat down to dinner. But one must be philosophical.
I have gone back to work. With persistence, I shall manage to take
an interest in poor *Saint Antoine* again."[15] And a few days later:
"You can't imagine how calm and lovely *your* Croisset is! Everything
is suffused with an infinite sweetness, and there is a kind of as-
suagement in the silence. The memory of my poor old lady never
leaves me: it floats around me like an enveloping mist."[16] The hardest thing was the solitary meals, served by his manservant, Emile.
Everything around him reminded him of the dead woman; it was
as if he were visiting in her house. He had to restrain himself to
keep from accosting a ghost: "The meals I take all by myself at an
empty table are hard," he wrote Caroline. "Tonight at last, for the
first time, I had a dessert without tears. I may get used to this
solitary, unsociable existence. Anyway, I don't see that I have the
means to lead any other. I force myself to work as much as I can.
But my poor brain rebels. I write very little, and what I do write
is poor."[17] Meanwhile, the division of the furniture in Mme. Flaubert's estate posed new problems. As was his habit, Flaubert yielded
on every point, partly from a spirit of sacrifice, partly from weariness. "What misery!" he confided to Princess Mathilde. "My in-
competence in money matters, or rather the aversion I feel for them,

has reached such a point that it borders on imbecility or lunacy. I am speaking very seriously: I would rather let myself be stripped to the bone than defend myself, not because I am disinterested but because it makes me furious to have to concern myself with such deadly work."[18]

Grumbling and complaining, he nevertheless went on with his *Saint Antoine.* "It's been a lifelong work," he said, "because the first idea for it came to me in 1845, in Genoa, when I was looking at a Breughel painting, and since that time I have never stopped thinking about it and reading things related to it." But he added at once that he was disgusted with publishers and had no thought of having this strange work printed: "I shall wait for better days; and if they never come, I am consoled in advance. One must practice art for oneself and not for the public. Had it not been for my mother and my poor Bouilhet, I should never have published *Madame Bovary.* In that respect I am as little like a man of letters as possible."[19] Although he rejected the title for himself, he followed with interest the careers of his fellow writers who, for their part, persisted in publishing. Victor Hugo's *Année terrible* made Flaubert exclaim in admiration: "What jaws he has yet, that old lion! He knows how to hate, which is a virtue, one that is lacking in my friend George Sand."[20]

On June 12 he was in Paris to attend the wedding of Elisa Schlésinger's son: "I am subject to waves of tenderness and fits of anger like an old man. . . . During the Schlésinger lad's wedding mass, I began to weep like an idiot."[21] He met George Sand, who was "not changed in the least," went to Saint-Gratien to visit Princess Mathilde, and on June 21 dined at the Café Riche with Edmond de Goncourt, who that evening noted in his *Journal:* "We dined, of course, in a private room, because Flaubert would have no noise, nor any people sitting next to him and, in addition, wanted to take off his jacket and shoes to eat." Over the hors d'oeuvres they were already talking about Ronsard, for Flaubert had been invited to the unveiling of a statue of the sixteenth-century poet in his native Vendôme. In spite of Flaubert's loathing for official functions, he had promised to attend the ceremony. Now he regretted it. As they left the restaurant, he and Goncourt ran into the publicist Aubryet, who told them that the important critic Saint-Victor was among the celebrities who were to be present at the festivities. Whereupon Flaubert went into a fit of cold anger: "Well then, I won't go to Vendôme," he cried. "No, really, I have become so morbidly sensitive, I am so shaken, that the idea of having the face of a disagreeable man opposite me on the train is hateful, unbearable! . . . Here, let's go into a café, I'm going to write my man that I'm coming back tomorrow." In the café he went on: "No, I am no longer capable of putting up with any vexation. . . . The notaries of Rouen think I'm crazy. You can imagine, for the division of the property I kept telling them to take whatever they wanted but not to talk to me about anything. I'd rather be robbed than aggravated. And it's like that for everything, for publishers. . . . Action? As for action, I am now lazy beyond words. Absolutely the only action I have left is working." Having written and sealed the letter to Émile, he said with a sigh: "I'm as happy as a man who has just done something silly." And he confessed to Edmond de Goncourt that he no longer wished for anything but death, so as to be "rid forever of his self." Goncourt, who was in the same frame of mind, approved of him and concluded: "Ah, what a fine physical disorder the intellectual life produces in even those who are strongest, most solidly built. It's a positive fact, we are all sick, half mad, and ready, all of us, to become wholly so."

On June 23, 1872, while they were waiting for Flaubert in Vendôme in front of the statue of Ronsard, he was back in Croisset. "I did not go to Vendôme because I was too depressed to tolerate a crowd, and especially because I wanted to avoid the company of my dear confreres," he wrote Princess Mathilde on July 1. "I would have traveled in the company of Saint-Victor, a gentleman for whom I have a profound dislike." And he informed his correspondent that he had just finished *La Tentation de Saint Antoine*. His nerves were so on edge that he agreed to go with Caroline to Bagnères-de-Luchon, where they would take the cure together. But far from calming him down, this stay in a spa filled with "bourgeois" soon became intolerable to him. The local doctor attributed his irritability to the abuse of tobacco. He resigned himself to smoking less, took baths, swallowed glasses of water, and waited impatiently to return to his beloved Croisset.

On August 16 he was back in his solitary retreat with a new project in mind. Or rather, a very old project that had surfaced again. As had been the case with *L'Education sentimentale* and *La Tentation de Saint Antoine*, it was a dream of his adolescence that came back to him in his mature years and made him want to write again. It was as if all the essence of his works had been given to him in his youth and now—tired, worn out, disillusioned—he was only obeying the merry demons of former days. "I am going to begin a book that will occupy me for several years," he wrote Mme. Roger des Genettes. "When it's finished, if the times are more propitious, I shall have it published at the same time as *Saint Antoine*. It's the farcical story of those two characters who copy a kind of critical encyclopedia. . . . One has to be insane, mad three times over, to undertake such a book!"[22] He had already outlined the plan of the book, which he thought "splendid," and found the title: *Bouvard et Pécuchet*. But how much reading he would have to do ("chemistry, medicine, agriculture . . .") before he could begin writing! To launch into this "overwhelming, appalling enterprise," he wanted to be completely certain of his income. But he was obliged to beg a thousand francs at a time from Ernest Commanville, who was managing his fortune, after a fashion. "Nothing is more annoying to me than to be perpetually asking him for money," he confessed to Caroline. "But how can we arrange it? I am impatient to have everything settled in such a way that I receive the small amounts that are due me at fixed intervals, without having periodically to pester that good fellow Ernest."[23] Fortunately, he had a new friend, Edmond Laporte, an estimable man in his forties who lived across the Seine in Grand-Couronne and whose visits were a comfort and diversion. Laporte kept insisting that Flaubert should get a dog to keep him company. He had even selected one for him, a puppy named Julio. Flaubert hesitated. "Last Thursday at Laporte's I saw my dog, who is not at all curly as I expected," he wrote Caroline. "He's a plain greyhound, iron gray in color, but will be very big. I hesitate to take him, especially as now I'm afraid of rabies. This foolish idea is one of the symptoms that I am going soft in the head. But I think I shall get over it."[24]

Although he was immersed in background reading for *Bouvard et Pécuchet*, he took time out for a trip to Paris to have a clean copy made of the heavily rewritten manuscript of *La Tentation de Saint Antoine*. Six days later the arduous task was finished. "You cannot imagine the bewilderment and exhaustion on the faces of the copyists," he informed Caroline cheerfully. "They told me the job had made them physically sick and that it was too much for them."[25]

The publisher Charpentier offered to buy from Michel Lévy all the rights to Flaubert's works. But the author did not know the exact terms of the contract he had signed with the "son of Jacob," as he called him. Furthermore, he wanted Charpentier to publish also the complete works of Louis Bouilhet. The negotiations seemed to be going well. Flaubert went home to Croisset with the feeling that he had been a clever bargainer.

He was hardly settled in again when Laporte brought him his dog, Julio. "I think I'm going to like him very much," Flaubert told Caroline.[26] And a little later: "My only distraction is embracing my poor dog, whom I talk to at length. What a happy mortal! His calm and beauty make you jealous."[27] And again, to Mme. Roger des Genettes: "I have been given a dog, a greyhound. I go for walks with him, watching the play of sunlight on the yellowing leaves, thinking about the books I'm going to write and ruminating on the past, for I am an old man now. For me, the future holds no more dreams, and the days of the past are beginning to flicker softly in a luminous mist. Against that background, a few beloved faces stand out, dear phantoms reach out to me. Dangerous daydreaming that must be thrust aside, delicious as it is."[28]

Among the "dear phantoms," his favorite was still Elisa Schlésinger. No matter that she was an old woman now: he still saw her as she had been in the happy days of the past, in her radiant, unalterable youth. In love with the love he had had for her, he wrote: "My old friend, my old beloved, I can never see your handwriting without being stirred. . . . I should like so much to welcome you to my home, to have you sleep in my mother's bedroom! . . . For me the future holds no more dreams, but the days of the past seem as though bathed in a golden mist. Against that luminous background where dear phantoms reach out to me, the face that stands out most splendidly is yours!—Yes, yours. Oh poor Trouville!"[29]★

The more pleasure Flaubert took in dwelling upon memories of the distant past, the more he came to hate all manifestations of the present. His abhorrence of public affairs, of the bourgeois mentality, of the false glories of art and literature was turning into misanthropy. He wanted to take revenge for the stupidity and ugliness of the world around him by producing an explosive book. *Bouvard et Pécuchet*, he hoped, would be that bombshell. "I am planning a thing in which I shall give vent to my anger," he announced to Mme. Roger des Genettes. "Yes, I shall rid myself at last of everything that is choking me. I shall vomit over my contemporaries the disgust they inspire in me, even if I burst my chest in the process. It will be big and violent."[30]

On October 23, 1872, when his wrath was at its height, he received word of the death of his dear Théophile Gautier. He had been expecting it for a long time, but it was a crushing blow just the same. Now more of his friends were dead than were living. He wondered by what injustice of fate he himself had escaped from so many shipwrecks. "The death of my poor old Théo, expected though it was, has laid me low, and yesterday I spent a day that I'll remember," he wrote Caroline. "I thought continually of the love my old Théo had for art, and felt as though I were being submerged in a tide of filth. For he died, I am sure, of prolonged asphyxiation caused by the stupidity of the modern world."[31] And to Turgenev: "I know only one man in the world whom I can talk to now, and that is you. . . . Théo died poisoned by the putrefaction of the

---

★ The almost word-for-word repetition in the last two letters cited of the phrases about the future without dreams and the dear faces of the past bears witness to Flaubert's obsession with these thoughts toward the end of his life. It is to be noted that the letters were written on the same day.

modern world. People like him, who are exclusively artists, have no place in a society dominated by the plebs."[32] Lastly, to George Sand: "Believe me, he died of disgust with the 'putrefaction of the modern world.' That was his expression, and he repeated it to me several times last winter. 'I'm dying of the Commune,' etc. . . . He had two hatreds. In his youth, hatred of the Philistines. That gave him his talent. In his maturity, hatred of the rabble. That killed him. He died of repressed rage, of fury at being unable to speak his mind. . . . To sum up, I don't pity him: I envy him. For frankly, life is not much fun."

Since George Sand, worried about Flaubert's despairing moods and his isolation, was suggesting that he take a wife, he expressed astonishment at the idea: "As for living with a woman, marrying, as you advise, it's a prospect I find fantastic. Why? I have no idea. But that's how it is. . . . The feminine being has never fitted in with my existence. And then, I'm not rich enough. And then, and then . . . I'm too old. And then, too decent to inflict my person on another as a life sentence."[33] The truth was that even if he had been rolling in money he would still have recoiled in horror from the mere idea of marriage. He could only tolerate a woman's presence at a distance. The only companion of his days and nights was creative imagination. All he needed to live was solitude, ink, and paper.

The work of writing brought him a satisfaction so complete that he no longer even felt the necessity of offering the fruit of his meditations to the public. "Why publish in these abominable times?" he asked George Sand. "Is it to earn money? What a farce! As if money were, or could be, the reward for work! That will be when speculation has been eliminated, not until then. And then, how can one measure work, evaluate effort? So we are left with the commercial value of the book. For that, one would have to abolish all intermediaries between producer and buyer, and even so the problem in itself is insoluble. Because I write (I am speaking of an author who has some self-respect) not for the reader of today but for all the readers who may present themselves, as long as the language lives. My merchandise, therefore, cannot be consumed now, because it is not made exclusively for my contemporaries. So my service remains indefinite and, consequently, without price. . . . All this is to tell you that until better times (which I don't believe in), I am keeping *Saint Antoine* in the bottom of an armoire. If I do have it published, I'd rather it were at the same time as another book that was entirely different. I'm working on one now that might go with it. Conclusion: the wisest thing is to lie low."[34]

He was so determined on this point that even though on January 1, 1873, he recovered the rights to *Madame Bovary* and *Salammbô*, he had no thought of reprinting the two books.* "As for me," he wrote Philippe Leparfait, "I am so disgusted with all publication that I have declined the offers of Lachaud and Charpentier. I could sell *Bovary* and *Salammbô* now, but the vomiting spell such negotiations bring on is too much! I want only one thing: to die. I don't have the energy to kill myself. I am so outraged over *everything* that I sometimes have palpitations that almost suffocate me."[35] In politics, having been infuriated by the democrats, he was now railing at the conservatives: "I am so exasperated by the Right that I wonder if the Communards weren't correct in wanting to burn Paris, because raving madmen are less abominable than idiots. Besides, their reign is always shorter."[36]

Amid the turmoil of all these feelings of rancor, indignation, and regret, he received a little comfort, in Paris, from a newcomer, a young man who was the son of Laure de Maupassant and the nephew of his great friend Alfred Le Poittevin, who had died in 1848. Guy de Maupassant was twenty-three years old and a clerk in the Ministry of the Navy. He wrote verse, dreamed of a literary career, and fervently admired Flaubert, who was touched by such youthful, naive veneration. "For a month now I've been meaning to write you to make a declaration of affection for your son," he wrote Laure de Maupassant.

You can't believe how charming I find him, how intelligent, good-natured, sensible, and witty—in short (to use a fash-

* According to the contract, Michel Lévy retained the rights to *L'Education sentimentale* for another seven years.

ionable term), *sympathique*. Despite the difference in our ages I consider him "a friend," and then he reminds me so much of my poor Alfred! Sometimes I am even startled by the resemblance, especially when he lowers his head when reciting poetry. What a man Alfred was! In my memory he remains beyond compare. Not a day passes that I don't think of him. For that matter, I am obsessed by the past, by the dead (*my* dead). Is that a sign of old age? I think so. . . . The times we live in and existence itself are a horrible weight on my shoulders. I am so disgusted with everything, and particularly with polemical literature, that I have given up all idea of publishing. There is no more joy in life for people of taste. Nevertheless, we must encourage your son in his predilection for poetry, because it is a noble passion, because literature is a consolation for many misfortunes, and because he may prove to have talent—who knows? So far, he hasn't produced enough for me to be able to cast his poetic horoscope. . . . I should like to see him undertake something long and ambitious, even if it turned out execrable. What he has shown me is certainly as good as anything being published by the Parnassians. . . .* With time he will acquire originality, an individual manner of seeing and feeling (that's the whole thing). As for the result, as for success, what does it matter? The principal thing in this world is to keep one's soul aloft, high above the bourgeois and democratic sloughs. The cult of Art gives one pride; one can never have too much of it. Such is my morality.[37]

During his stay in Paris he also saw Turgenev, and both solemnly swore to go to George Sand's, at Nohant, on April 12, the

---

* A group of poets who, in the reaction against romanticism, strove for objectivity, impersonality, and perfection of form and defended the theory of art for art's sake. (The name was taken from a first collection of their poems, published in 1866, titled *Le Parnasse contemporain*.) Théophile Gautier, Leconte de Lisle, and Catulle Mendès, whom the reader has already met, were all members of this group, as were also François Coppée, Théodore de Banville, and notably José-Maria de Heredia, who will appear later. —Trans.

day before Easter. On the appointed day Flaubert arrived at his friend's house alone. The next day, Easter Sunday, they walked in the park, went to see the animals on the farm, and Flaubert poked about the library "where he found nothing which he didn't already know." After dinner there was dancing. "Flaubert put on a skirt and tried the fandango," George Sand noted in her diary. "He was very funny, but after five minutes he was out of breath. He is really older than I. Still, I think he is not so fat as he was and he doesn't look so tired. Always the brain too active at the expense of his body." On April 14 Flaubert read *Saint Antoine* aloud to the assembled family, from three in the afternoon until six and from nine to midnight. "Splendid!" decreed George Sand. On Tuesday the fifteenth everyone gathered for conversation in the garden. And on the sixteenth George Sand's son Maurice led them all out onto the heath to show them a geological discovery he had made with his daughter Aurore. They went back to dress for dinner, and it was then that Turgenev arrived. George Sand found him "sprightly and rejuvenated." On the seventeenth it was raining and the whole company stayed indoors. George Sand chatted pleasantly with Flaubert and Turgenev. "Afterward," she wrote, "we jumped about, danced, sang, shouted, much to the annoyance of Flaubert, who always wants to stop everything and talk literature. He was overwhelmed. Turgenev likes noise and gaiety; he is as much a child as we are. He danced, waltzed. What a good, kind man of genius!" The following day George Sand was somewhat annoyed by Flaubert's booming voice that was always trying to dominate the conversation. "Talk by Flaubert, animated and funny, but he monopolized the conversation. Turgenev, who is much more interesting, could hardly get a word in. This evening it was a contest until one in the morning. Finally we all said our good-byes. They are leaving tomorrow." She placed her carriage at their disposal to drive them to Châteauroux, where they would take the train. And as soon as they were off, she confided to her diary: "I am tired, all worn out by my dear Flaubert. Still, I love him very much, and he is an excellent man, but his personality is too exuberant. He exhausts us. . . . We miss Turgenev, whom we know less well, for whom we have less affection, but who is graced with real simplicity and charming goodness of heart."

No doubt Flaubert too had been a little disappointed by his stay in the bustling, noisy family atmosphere of Nohant. In his view, as soon as the conversation strayed from literature, it was a waste of time for the mind. He left with a thousand profound thoughts in his head that he had not had the opportunity to express. Nevertheless, he wrote his hostess: "It is only five days since we parted and already I miss you like anything. I miss Aurore and the entire household. . . . One is so happy at your house! You are all so kind and so amusing."[38] But now George Sand herself came to Paris. Flaubert immediately organized a dinner for her at the restaurant, to which he also invited Turgenev and Goncourt. They were to meet at Magny's at half past six on May 3, 1873. "I am there at the appointed time," George Sand wrote her son Maurice. "Turgenev arrives immediately after. We wait for a quarter of an hour. Comes de Goncourt, all in a fluster: 'We're not dining here. Flaubert is waiting for you at the Frères Provençaux.' 'Why?' 'He says he can't breathe here, the private rooms are too small, he didn't sleep all night, he's tired.' 'But I'm tired too.' 'Scold him, he has no manners, but come!' " In the end, it was at the Restaurant Véfour that the little group found Flaubert, dozing on a settee. "I told him he was a pig," George Sand continued. "He asked forgiveness, got down on his knees, the others were holding their sides with laughter. Finally, we dined very badly, on a kind of cuisine I detest, in a room much smaller than the ones at Magny's." Flaubert told his friends that he had just read the outline of Louis Bouilhet's play *Le Sexe faible* [The Weaker Sex] to the director of the Théâtre du Vaudeville, Léon Carvalho, and that the latter had responded with the greatest enthusiasm and had engaged him to rewrite the work so it could be performed as soon as possible. "He bellowed with joy, he was enchanted, nothing else existed for him in the universe," concluded George Sand. "He never stopped talking and didn't let Turgenev get a word in, much less Goncourt. I escaped at ten. I shall see him again tomorrow, but I shall tell him that I'm leaving on Monday. I have had enough of my little comrade. I love him, but he wears me all out with his incessant din. He dislikes noise, but the noise he makes himself doesn't bother him."[39] That same evening when Edmond de Goncourt came home from the restaurant he wrote in his *Journal*: "The older Flaubert gets, the more provincial he becomes. And really, if you subtract from my friend the ox in him, the plodding, toiling animal, the manufacturer of books at the rate of one word an hour, you find yourself faced with a creature of such ordinary talent, endowed with so little originality! . . . Heaven knows he conceals the bourgeois resemblance of his brain to everybody else's—a resemblance which, I am sure, makes him furious at heart—by means of truculent paradoxes, horrifying axioms, revolutionary bellowings, and a brutal, even ill-bred way of maintaining the opposite of all received and accepted ideas. . . . The poor fellow's blood rushes to his head when he talks. The result, I think, is that with a mixture of one-third boasting, one-third empty verbalism, and one-third congestion of the brain, my friend Flaubert manages to intoxicate himself almost sincerely with the untruths he spouts."

Unaware of how irritated his friends were by his flow of words, his sophisms, and his outbursts, Flaubert returned to Croisset on May 17 with a big project in mind. After his recent conversation with Carvalho he was in a fever to get to work on the revision of Bouilhet's *Sexe faible*, setting everything else aside so that his friend's play should at last be produced on the stage. Nevertheless, the first thing he did on reaching home was to visit his mother's bedroom. Looking around at the pieces of furniture, still in their old places, he felt as if he himself were an unwanted article. After he had unpacked his suitcases, he wrote Caroline: "I have nothing more to tell you, my dear Caro, except that the house seems very big and empty to me! And that I long to see my poor girl to whom her Nanny sends a little kiss from afar."[40]

Chapter 19

THE ILLUSION OF
THE THEATER

This time, Flaubert had really succumbed to the lure of the footlights. There was no question now of beginning *Bouvard et Pécuchet:* he had shelved that project for the time being. His attention was entirely taken up by *Le Sexe faible,* the first scene of which he finished on May 21, 1873. That day he wrote Caroline: "So far as style is concerned, I am aiming for the ideal of natural conversation, which is not too easy when one wants to make the language firm and rhythmic. I hadn't written anything for a long time (almost a year), and it feels good to be turning out sentences again." And a few days later: "Your old Cruchard, your old Nanny, is lost in the dramatic art.* Yesterday I worked eighteen hours (from half past six in the morning until midnight!). That's the way it is, and I took no nap all day. Thursday I had been at it for fourteen hours. Monsieur has worked himself up into quite a state. But so far as that goes, I think that once the outline has been drawn up, a play should be written in a kind of fever. It makes the action move faster; one can revise afterward."[1]

When the publisher Alphonse Lemerre paid him a thousand francs for a special edition of *Madame Bovary* in Elzevir type, he hastened to buy curtains, napkins, sheets, an oilcloth for the table,

---

* The Reverend Father Cruchard, a fashionable Jesuit, was a persona invented by Flaubert, originally for the amusement of George Sand. (FS) It can scarcely be coincidental that in colloquial French *cruche* [jug] means "ass" or "ignoramus" and that in Flaubert's correspondence the word is often so used. —Trans.

and a kitchen cupboard, because the Croisset house was, he said, "grievously run down." By the end of May he had been "slaving and super-slaving" so hard over *Le Sexe faible* that he hoped to wind it up in three weeks. In any case, he didn't consider that this work had any esthetic value: "What an awful way of writing is required for the stage!" he wrote George Sand. "If you want things to move you have to be lavish with ellipses, interrupted thoughts, questions, and repetitions, and all of that is very ugly in itself. I could be deceiving myself, but I think I'm doing something now that goes very fast and will be easy to act."[2] And he confided to Mme. Roger des Genettes that if he hoped this minor work would be a success, it was for only two reasons: "(1) to earn a few thousand francs; (2) to irritate a few imbeciles."[3]

On June 20 he received a visit in Croisset from the publisher Georges Charpentier, to whom, after some hesitation, he sold the rights to *Madame Bovary* and *Salammbô*. Early in July, it was Léon Carvalho who came to seek him out in his hermitage. Flaubert read him *Le Sexe faible* and the theater manager applauded: "He seemed very pleased with it," Flaubert reported to George Sand. "He thinks it will be a success. But I have so little faith in the judgment of all those clever fellows that personally, I doubt it. I am exhausted, and I'm sleeping ten hours a night now, in addition to two hours a day. It rests my poor brain."[4] But he couldn't resign himself to intellectual inactivity. When George Sand spoke in one of her letters about "the pleasure of doing nothing," he protested: "As soon as I am no longer working on a book or thinking about writing one, I am seized with such boredom I could scream. It seems to me that life is tolerable only if one evades it." And he revealed to his friend that, his appetite having been whetted by the verbal fencing of stage dialogue, he intended to write a play of his own now: "Since over the last six weeks I have gotten into the habit of seeing things from the theatrical point of view, of thinking in dialogue, what have I done but started plotting out another play, to be called *Le Candidat*."[5] In his mind, this play was to be a satire of political life. He would attack all parties: both the supporters of the comte de Chambord and the Orléanists, both the reactionaries and the republicans.

The Illusion of the Theater

His hero, M. Rousselin, would be an idle bourgeois who was dying to be elected to office. "I shall be torn apart by the populace, banished by the authorities, and cursed by the clergy," Flaubert prophesied.[6] And the mere idea of it spurred him on.

At this time, all of France was breathlessly watching an attempt at "fusion," or reconciliation between the comte de Chambord (grandson of Charles X) and the comte de Paris (the Orléanist pretender, grandson of Louis-Philippe). Flaubert, for his part, wanted the republic to be maintained in order to escape the "nightmare" of monarchy and clericalism. He thought "fusion" would be "a folly from the practical point of view and a piece of stupidity from the historical point of view." While he was castigating third-rate politicians in *Le Candidat,* he took time out to make a few short field trips in search of a setting for *Bouvard et Pécuchet.* He thought he had discovered in Houdan just the house for his two characters. With that question off his mind, he poured all his energy into his play again. A fine fit of rage on learning that Michel Lévy—that traitor, that swindler, that "son of Jacob"—had just been decorated with the Legion of Honor. A brief sadness on hearing that Ernest Feydeau had died, on October 29: "So much the better for him, anyway." A profound sense of relief when, because the comte de Chambord refused to return to France without the fleur-de-lis banner of the Bourbon royalty, the plan for a restoration of the monarchy collapsed. One more reason to put some backbone into *Le Candidat.* He hoped to finish the play by the end of the year. After which, he would go back to "serious things"—that is, the novel. "The theatrical style is beginning to get on my nerves," he wrote George Sand on October 30, 1873. "These short little sentences, this continual bubbling irritates me like Seltzer, which is pleasing at first but soon begins to taste like water that has gone bad." However, three weeks later, in a letter to Caroline, he gave a shout of victory: "I've finished *Le Candidat!* Yes, Madame, and I think the fifth act is not the worst. But I am totally exhausted and am looking after myself. It was high time I stopped: the floors of rooms were beginning to move under my feet like the deck of a ship, and I had such a weight on my chest at all times that I could hardly breathe."[7]

In the meantime, the National Assembly had passed a law making MacMahon president of the republic for a term of seven years. "I don't think this hypocritical solution will improve matters any," Flaubert declared. "The same people who have been groaning for two years over the 'provisional nature of the situation' have just decreed a provisional situation for seven years. . . . What seems certain to me is that a permanent Republic is going to be constituted, by a slow transition."[9]

But now that passions seemed to have calmed down, he thought the time had come to launch his play. And just at this moment, Carvalho announced that he was coming to Croisset. He arrived on a Saturday at four in the afternoon. "We embraced, after the fashion of theater folk," Flaubert wrote Caroline. "At ten minutes to five began the reading of *Le Candidat*, which he interrupted only with praise. What struck him most was the fifth act, and in that act, a scene where Rousselin has religious—or rather superstitious—feelings. We had dinner at eight and went to bed at two. Next day we went back to the play, and then the criticisms began. I was exasperated—not that most of them weren't very judicious, but the idea of reworking the same subject gave me a feeling of revulsion and unspeakable pain." Until two in the morning he defended his text, with rage in his heart, accepted a few changes of detail, agreed to collapse the fourth and fifth acts into one, but refused to add violent tirades, in particular "against the little newspapers of Paris." "It's outside my subject!" he cried. "It's anti-esthetic! I'll do nothing of the sort."[9] And the same day he told Mme. Roger des Genettes: "No success could repay me for the annoyance, the irritation, the exasperation that the criticisms of the said *sieur* Carvalho have caused me. Note that they were reasonable. But I am too nervous to go through that sort of exercise again. Palpitations, tremblings, tightness in the throat, etc. Oh, I've had the lot! I prefer to devote myself to works that are longer, more serious, and more calm."

In any case, the decision had been made: no more talk about *Le Sexe faible*—the production was postponed indefinitely. As for *Le Candidat*, it must be put into rehearsal at once. At the beginning of December 1873, with a complex feeling of anxiety and triumph,

The Illusion of the Theater

nervous tension and pride, Flaubert went to Paris to settle the details of this worrisome enterprise. The young Anatole France came to visit him in his little flat on the Rue Murillo. It was Flaubert himself who opened the door. "Never in my life had I seen anything like him," wrote Anatole France. "His figure was tall, his shoulders broad; he was enormous, dazzling, resounding; he was wearing a kind of loose-fitting brown coat with a hood, a real pirate's costume; breeches as wide as a skirt came down over his heels. With his bald crown, long hair, wrinkled forehead, clear eyes, red cheeks, and drooping, colorless mustache, he was the incarnation of everything one reads about the old Scandinavian chieftains whose blood flowed in his veins, although by no means unmixed. . . . He held out to me his beautiful hand, the hand of a chieftain and an artist, said a few kind words to me, and from that moment on I had the sweet satisfaction of loving the man I admired. Gustave Flaubert was very kind. He had a prodigious capacity for enthusiasm and sympathy. That is why he was constantly in a rage. He was always charging off to war over something, always having some insult to avenge. It was with him as with Don Quixote, for whom he had such esteem."[10]

The reading of *Le Candidat* to the actors of the Théâtre du Vaudeville was set for Thursday, December 11, 1873. Flaubert felt very confident as he went to the theater. "I began the reading as calm as a god and as imperturbable as Baptiste," he wrote Caroline later that day.* "To fortify himself for the occasion, Monsieur had slipped down his gullet a dozen oysters, a good steak, and a half bottle of Chambertin followed by a glass of brandy and another of chartreuse. I read *on* the stage, by the light of two oil lamps, before my twenty-six actors. Starting with the second page, laughter from the audience, and the whole first act was found extremely amusing. Less favorable reaction to the second act. But during the third (in

* The reference is to Jean-Baptiste-Gaspard Deburau, the most celebrated mime of his day. In order to draw attention to the Théâtre des Funambules where he was performing, Baptiste would sit at the entrance in his Pierrot costume, as motionless and unresponsive as if carved in stone. —Trans. (For this charming explanation of an obscure allusion I am indebted to Professor Andrée Demay.)

273

Flore's drawing room) the laughter never stopped, I was interrupted at every word. And the fourth won unanimous approval. . . . In a word, they all think it will be a great success."

More good news, arriving just in time for his fifty-second birthday: Charpentier had decided to publish *La Tentation de Saint Antoine*, which would appear after Victor Hugo's *Quatre-vingt-treize* so as to avoid damaging competition. Also, thanks to the diligent efforts of Turgenev, a Russian magazine had agreed to publish a translation of the said *Saint Antoine*, which would bring the author three thousand francs. "At last I think I'm going to become practical!" Flaubert exclaimed. "I only hope I don't become idiotic, which is often the consequence!"[11] Mme. Charpentier, who had read the manuscript of *La Tentation* with great enthusiasm, asked him to be the godfather of the child to whom she was about to give birth and whom she wished to name Antoine. "I refused to inflict on this young Christian the name of so troubled a man, but I had to accept the honor done me," wrote Flaubert to George Sand. "Can you see my old puss next to the baptismal font, beside the baby, the nurse, and the parents?"[12]*

The play having been passed by the censor, there were no more obstacles to its performance and rehearsals went forward apace. On February 6, 1874, Flaubert signed off on the final proofs of *La Tentation de Saint Antoine*. As usual, he felt a pang at the idea of turning over to the judgment of the public a work that he had nursed so long in solitude. He felt that it was both a provocation and a profanation, that he was both launching into foolish combat and abandoning a child. "It's finished, I don't think about it anymore," he wrote George Sand. "To me, *Saint Antoine* is no more than a memory. Still, I won't deny that I spent a very sad quarter of an

---

* In this connection, the reader may recall Renoir's group portrait of Mme. Charpentier and her children painted about five years later and now in the Metropolitan Museum of Art in New York. (The lady has one little daughter on the couch beside her and another is sitting on the large family dog stretched patiently at their feet.) It is clear from the correspondence that Flaubert had very affectionate relations with the Charpentier family—in his own words, "children and dog included." —Trans.

hour when I beheld the first proof. It's hard to part from an old companion."[13]

He had a moment's anxiety when Carvalho left the Vaudeville, but his successor, Cormon, was likewise "full of zeal," and the actors proved excellent in their respective roles. The prospect of a success in the theater softened Flaubert's disappointment when he learned that the czar's censors had forbidden the publication of the Russian translation of *Saint Antoine* and that they would not even allow the French text to be printed in *La Revue de Saint-Pétersbourg*. So now he was deprived of some thousands of francs of income. Would the Vaudeville's receipts make up for the loss? The opening was set for March 11, 1874. Tickets were selling rapidly. Flaubert had the flu: "I cough, blow my nose, spit, and sneeze without letup, to the accompaniment of fever at night," he wrote Mme. Roger des Genettes. "In addition, a lovely pimple is blooming in the middle of my forehead between two patches of red. In short, I am becoming extremely ugly and I disgust myself. Despite all that, I have a good appetite and am in excellent spirits. I think I shall conduct myself well on the day of the premiere."[14]

Of course, that night all his friends were in the audience, ready to applaud. But they were present at a disaster. Edmond de Goncourt described what had happened:

Yesterday, at the performance of *Le Candidat*, it was funereal, a kind of icy chill falling gradually over an audience fired with sympathy for the author, an audience waiting in all good faith for sublime speeches, marvelous flashes of wit, words that would become battle cries, and confronted with nothingness, nothingness, nothingness! At first, on every face there appeared an expression of pity and sadness; then, after being long restrained by respect for Flaubert's person and talent, the spectators' disappointment took revenge in a sort of jeering chorus of "shhhs," a smiling derision of the whole pathetic business. . . . And the ill-concealed amazement grew from one minute to the next at the lapses of taste, of tact, of invention. For the play is nothing but a pale reflection of

Prudhomme. . . . After the performance I went backstage to shake Flaubert's hand. . . . Not a single member of the cast was left on the boards. Everyone was deserting the author, fleeing from him. The stagehands, who were still at work, were finishing up in a mad rush, with their eyes fixed on the exit. A troop of extras came tumbling down the stairs in silence. It was both sad and slightly fantastic, like a stampede, a rout in a diorama viewed at twilight. When he saw me, Flaubert gave a start as if he were waking up, as if he wanted to resume his official countenance, the mask of the strong man. "Well, that's it!" he said to me, with an angry gesture of the arms and a contemptuous laugh intended to give an impression of total indifference.[15]

The day after the performance, Flaubert confirmed to George Sand that *Le Candidat* was a complete failure: "If ever there was a flop! People who want to flatter me insist that the play will catch on with the general public, but I don't believe it for a minute. I know the defects of my play better than anyone. . . . I must say too that the audience was detestable, all fops and stockbrokers who had no understanding of what words *mean*. Anything poetic they took as a joke. . . . The conservatives were annoyed because I didn't attack the republicans, and the Communards would have liked me to throw a few insults at the legitimists. . . . I never even saw the head of the claque. It's almost as though the management of the Vaudeville had set me up for a failure. Their dream came true. . . . The 'bravos' of a faithful few were immediately silenced by 'shhhs.' When my name was mentioned at the end, there was some applause (for the man, not the work), accompanied by two lovely catcalls from the top gallery." And putting up a good front under the insult, he added: "As for Cruchard, he is calm, very calm. He had dined very well before the performance, and supped even better afterward. Menu: two dozen Ostend oysters, a bottle of chilled champagne, three slices of roast beef, truffle salad, coffee, and liqueur."[16] Three days later he withdrew the play, although five thousand francs' worth of tickets had been sold in advance: "Too bad, but I won't have my actors hissed and booed," he wrote George Sand. "The second night, when I saw Delannoy come off the stage with tears in his eyes, I felt like a criminal and decided that was enough. . . . I'm being flayed by all parties—*Le Figaro* and *Le Rappel*, it's unanimous. . . . Well, I don't give a damn, and that's the truth. But I regret the several thousand francs I might have earned. My little jug of milk is broken.* I wanted to buy some new furniture for Croisset. Not a chance!"[17]

Fortunately, *La Tentation de Saint Antoine* was off to a good start. The first edition of two thousand copies was sold out in a few days, a second was immediately launched, and the publisher was looking for paper for a third. Actually, this fantastic prose poem was baffling to the public. They were overwhelmed by the avalanche of visions that haunted Saint Anthony and staggered by the author's wealth of invention. For Saint Anthony is really Flaubert in search of fundamental truth and incapable of choosing between faith, which he denigrates, and science, which does not fully satisfy him. His hero, like himself, is attracted sometimes to a basic skepticism, sometimes to an instinctive trust in the forces that rule creation. And the intellectual and moral conflict that tears him apart is expressed in dizzying, shimmering dialogue. But once again, the contemporary critics rose up in arms against a work that defied the rules of current literary production. Some reviewers admitted that they "didn't understand a word" of this hybrid work. Others said they were "appalled" by it. Barbey d'Aurevilly, the relentless adversary, declared that readers of *La Tentation* would experience "sufferings and obstructions" comparable to those which Flaubert must have had "after having swallowed this dangerous erudition, which killed all ideas in him, all feeling, all initiative. . . . The punishment for all that," he went on, "is boredom, implacable boredom, a boredom that is not French but German, the boredom

---

* An allusion to La Fontaine's fable *La Laitière et le pot au lait*. This is a version of Aesop's familiar story of the milkmaid who, on her way to market with a jug of milk on her head, becomes so absorbed in imagining what she will do with the money it will bring (counting her chickens before they are hatched) that she lets the jug fall. —Trans.

of Goethe's second *Faust,* for example. . . ." Edmond de Goncourt himself noted in his *Journal* for April 1: "Read *La Tentation de Saint Antoine.* Imagination composed of notes. Originality always reminiscent of Goethe." Every day brought Flaubert its load of venomous articles. "The insults are piling up!" he wrote George Sand. "It's a concerto, a symphony, with all the instruments playing full blast. I've been torn to pieces by everything from *Le Figaro* to *La Revue des deux mondes,* including *La Gazette de France* and *Le Constitutionnel.* And it's not over yet. Barbey d'Aurevilly insulted me personally, and the worthy Saint-René Taillandier, who declares I'm 'unreadable,' ascribes to me ridiculous expressions I have never used. . . . What comes as a surprise is the hatred underlying much of this criticism—hatred for me, for my person—deliberate denigration, and I keep looking for the reason. I don't feel hurt, but this avalanche of abuse does depress me."[18]

As always, he knew only one remedy for disappointment and disgust: work. "This summer I'm going to set to work on another book of the same sort. After which I'll go back to the novel pure and simple. I have two or three in mind that I'd really like to write before I die. Right now I'm spending my days in the library, amassing notes. . . . In July I'm going to decongest myself on a Swiss mountaintop, following the advice of Dr. Hardy, who calls me 'a hysterical woman'—an observation I find profound."[19] It seemed to him that Victor Hugo's *Quatre-vingt-treize* was being treated better than his own *Tentation.* And yet, he thought the old master's latest novel very uneven: "What gingerbread men his characters are! They all talk like actors. He's a genius but he lacks the gift of creating human beings. If he had had that gift, Hugo would have surpassed Shakespeare."[20] On the other hand he greatly admired Zola's *Conquête de Plassans:* "You're a talented fellow," he wrote the author, "and your latest novel is a terrific book!"[21]

In spite of the bad reviews, *La Tentation* continued to sell. On May 12 Charpentier proposed a new, in-octavo edition of the book with a printing of twenty-five hundred copies. Could it be that the readers were more insightful than the critics? On the other hand, after the fiasco of *Le Candidat,* the management of the Vaudeville gave up the idea of producing *Le Sexe faible*. Flaubert tried in vain to interest other theaters in the play. Actually, he no longer had much hope in that direction. He had recovered from footlight fever and had turned his energies to *Bouvard et Pécuchet*. Not satisfied with his earlier geographical investigations, he went to Lower Normandy to look for the ideal setting for his two characters. "I need a silly place in the midst of beautiful countryside, a countryside where one can go on geological and archaeological expeditions," he wrote Mme. Roger des Genettes. "So tomorrow I shall go spend the night in Alençon, then from there I'll explore all the surroundings as far as Caen. Ah, what a book! It exhausts me in advance; I am overwhelmed by the difficulties of this work for which I have already read and summarized 294 volumes."[22]

The little journey, in the company of Edmond Laporte, was a success. "I shall place *Bouvard et Pécuchet* between the valley of the Orne and the valley of the Dives," Flaubert decided, "on a stupid plateau between Caen and Falaise."* "We roamed around in rattletrap carriages, ate in country taverns, slept in classic inns. I introduced my companion to apple brandy and he took a bottle home with him. One couldn't find a better or more considerate fellow."[23] On the way back he stopped in Paris and received a visit from Emile Zola. The younger novelist was disappointed when they met: "I was looking for the man who had written his books," he wrote afterward, "and I found a terrible old man with a paradoxical turn of mind, an unrepentant romantic, who bewildered me for hours with a deluge of stupefying theories. That night I came home sick, utterly exhausted, dazed, saying to myself that the man in Flaubert was inferior to the writer." Flaubert, for his part, was convinced he had charmed his interlocutor. In any event, he had little time to give to his friends. Switzerland awaited him.

Following doctor's orders, he went to Kaltbad Rigi, where the pure air was supposed to restore order to his thoughts. He was oppressed by "immense boredom." "I am not a man of nature,"

---

* The valley of the river Dives (rich dairy country) is commonly known as the *vallée d'Auge*, and Flaubert so refers to it here. —Trans.

he wrote George Sand, "and I simply don't understand countries that have no history. I'd give all the glaciers for the Vatican Museum. That's where one can dream."[24] And to Turgenev: "The Alps are out of scale with our little selves. They are too big to be useful to us. . . . And then my companions, my dear fellow, the foreign gentlemen living in this hotel! All Germans or English, equipped with walking sticks and binoculars. Yesterday I was tempted to kiss three calves that I met in a meadow, out of sheer humanity and a need to be demonstrative."[25] Idling away his time in this picturesque desert, he received a piece of good news: the manager of the Théâtre de Cluny was delighted with *Le Sexe faible* and was thinking of producing the play. "Once again I am going to expose myself to the insults of the populace and the hack journalists," Flaubert announced to George Sand. "But I recall Carvalho's enthusiasm, which was followed by an absolute chill. . . . It's strange how the imbeciles like to muck about in other people's work, cutting, correcting, playing schoolmaster."[26]

Back in Croisset, after a return trip via Lausanne, Geneva, Paris, and Dieppe, he learned that his old servant, Julie, was in the hospital. His brother Achille had recently operated on her. "Julie will have the sight of both eyes, according to Achille's intern," Flaubert wrote Caroline. "She has one that is still inflamed. That's why they are keeping her at the Hôtel-Dieu, where she seems to be growing weaker, although she is not sick. I'm not cheerful, not in the least. . . . Maybe it's because I'm too full of my subject and the stupidity of my two characters is overcoming me."[27]

On August 6, 1874, he finally set to work seriously on *Bouvard et Pécuchet* and, at his niece's request, sent her the first sentence of the novel: "The temperature was 91, and the Boulevard Bourdon was absolutely deserted." "Now you won't know another thing for a long time," he added. "I'm floundering, scratching out, feeling generally desperate."[28]

At the end of August he went back to Paris to attend to *Le Sexe faible*. He took advantage of his stay in the city to have a few friends over to the Rue Murillo on Sundays, wearing a brown dressing gown, red-faced and booming. On September 2 he attended the funeral of the mother of the poet François Coppée. "The poor fellow was pitiful to see," he wrote Caroline. "I nearly had to carry him going down the main avenue of the Montmartre Cemetery. As soon as he saw me he almost clung to me, although we are not intimate friends. It was there that I saw . . . my enemy Barbey d'Aurevilly for the first time: he's unbelievable!"[29] And Juliette Adam noted in her *Souvenirs*: "The good giant [Flaubert] drew himself up to his full height, and Barbey d'Aurevilly did the same. We wondered whether the two cocks were not going to fly at each other." But they had too much respect for the solemnity of the place and merely exchanged murderous looks.

On September 26 Flaubert wrote George Sand from Croisset: "Everyone criticizes me for letting my play be performed in such a dump [the Théâtre de Cluny]. But since the other theaters will have none of it and I really want to have it produced so that Bouilhet's heir can earn a few sous, I have no choice. . . . Once you are in that world ordinary conditions are changed. If you have had the (slight) misfortune not to be a success, your friends turn from you. You are greatly discredited. People no longer greet you! I swear to you on my word of honor that that has happened to me because of *Le Candidat*. . . . Anyhow, I don't give a damn, and I am less concerned about the fate of *Le Sexe faible* than about the least sentence in my novel."

Notwithstanding this declaration of indifference, he rushed back to Paris again in November to confer with Weinschenk, the manager of the Cluny. "This regular running back and forth between Paris and Croisset is getting to be a nuisance," he confessed to Caroline. In the end, he was so disappointed by the actors and the conditions for launching the play that it was suggested he beat a retreat. "I have withdrawn my play (or rather, our play) from the Cluny," he wrote Philippe Leparfait. "The cast Weinschenk was offering me was impossible. I was setting myself up for a spectacular flop. Zola, Daudet, Catulle Mendès, and Charpentier, to whom I had read it, were in despair at the prospect of seeing me performed on such a stage. . . . But as I'm not giving up, *Le Sexe faible* is now at the [Théâtre du] Gymnase. I'm waiting for a reply from Montigny."[30]

On December 2, at a dinner at Princess Mathilde's, Edmond de Goncourt, who was seated next to Flaubert, whispered to him: "I congratulate you on withdrawing your play. When you've had a failure . . . the next time around you have to make sure you're performed by real actors." Flaubert seemed embarrassed for a moment and then murmured: "I am at the Gymnase now. . . ." And by way of apology for having turned to another second-rate company, he added: "There are five dresses in my play, and there, the women can afford to buy them." By mid-December, still no word from the Gymnase. The hope of staging *Le Sexe faible* was abandoned. One satisfaction, however: after having been pestered by Flaubert for eight months, Ernest Renan agreed to write a laudatory article on *La Tentation de Saint Antoine*. As for the new novel, it was lurching along according to the usual rhythm. "I am now working as hard as I can, so as not to think about myself," Flaubert wrote George Sand. "But since I have undertaken a book so difficult to execute that it is absurd, my feeling of impotence adds to my sorrow." And he admitted: "I am becoming too stupid, I bore everyone to death. In short, thanks to his intolerance, your Cruchard has become an intolerable fellow himself. And since there's not a thing I can do about it, out of consideration for other people I have to spare them my ranting and raving. . . . Especially for the last six months, I don't know what's wrong with me, but I have been feeling profoundly sick, although I can't be more specific than that."[31] At times, having set himself the task of telling the story of two mediocrities who pass in review the so-called wisdom of all the sciences, he wondered whether he would have the strength to carry the inventory of human imbecility through to the end. Sometimes he wrote in a burst of rage against the world around him; sometimes he was seized with a gloomy foreboding in the face of the immensity and futility of his task. Suddenly, an agonizing doubt crossed his mind, and he wrote his publisher Charpentier: "*B. et P.* is leading me very quietly, or rather relentlessly, to the abode of the shades. It will be the death of me!"[32]

Chapter 20

TROIS CONTES

Each day brought Flaubert a new reason for despair. His physical deterioration and mental disarray were such that his letters were now only one long groan. "Abnormal things are going on inside me," he wrote George Sand. "My depression must have some hidden cause. I feel old, worn out, disgusted with everything. And I am as bored with other people as with myself. However, I am working, but without enthusiasm, the way one works at a thankless chore, and it may be the work that is making me ill, for this book is an insane enterprise. I lose myself in memories of childhood like an old man. . . . I expect nothing more from life but a series of blank pages to scrawl over with black. I feel that I am traversing an endless solitude, going I know not where. And I myself am at one and the same time the desert, the traveler, and the camel."[1] And to Mme. Roger des Genettes: "As for me, I am *worse*. What is wrong with me I have no idea, and neither does anyone else, the term 'neurosis' expressing both a number of different phenomena and the ignorance of the physicians. I am advised to rest—but what's the good of resting?—to get some relaxation, to avoid solitude, etc., a lot of things that aren't feasible. I believe in only one remedy: time. . . . Judging from the way I sleep—ten or twelve hours a night—I have probably done some damage to my brain. Is it beginning to soften, I wonder? I am so filled with Bouvard and Pécuchet that I have become them. Their stupidity is mine, and I'm dying of it. Maybe that's the explanation. One has to be under a curse to think up books like this! I've finally finished the first chapter and prepared the second, which will include chemistry, medicine, and geology, all in thirty pages! And with some secondary characters, for there has to be some semblance of action, a kind of continuous story so the thing doesn't seem like a philosophical dissertation. What makes me despair is that I no longer believe in my book."[2] In Paris Flaubert's friends were surprised at his growing hypochondria. He confided to them that often, after spending hours bent over his papers writing, when he raised his head he would be "afraid of finding someone behind him."[3] Sometimes, for no apparent reason, he would be choked by a flood of tears. "When we left Flaubert's," noted Edmond de Goncourt, "Zola and I spoke of our friend's condition: he had just confessed that he had periods of black melancholy followed by fits of weeping. And while we were talking about the literary reasons which are responsible for this condition and which are killing us all one after the other, we expressed surprise that there is not more of a circle around this famous man. He is celebrated, talented, kindhearted, and very hospitable: so why, at these Sunday gatherings that are open to all, is there no one except Turgenev, Daudet, Zola, and myself? Why?"[4]

Flaubert had left his flat on the Rue Murillo and was now living in an apartment next to one the Commanvilles had rented on the sixth floor of a building on the Rue du Faubourg Saint-Honoré at the corner of the Boulevard de la Reine-Hortense (now the Avenue Hoche). It was there that he received his usual visitors on Sundays. When Goncourt informed him of the death of Michel Lévy, he put back in his buttonhole the rosette of the Legion of Honor, which he had not worn since the publisher had received his. "No, I did not rejoice at the death of Michel Lévy," he wrote George Sand, "and I even envy him so painless a death. No matter! that man did me much harm. He hurt me deeply. It is true that I am absurdly sensitive; things that only scratch other people tear me apart." And he concluded: "A wandering gout, pains that show up all over, an unconquerable melancholy, a sense of universal futility and great doubts about the book I am doing—that's what's wrong with me!

Add to that money worries and melancholy reflections on the past. . . . Ah, I have eaten the best part first, and old age doesn't present itself in the gayest of colors!"[5] He interpreted the smallest mishap, the most commonplace incident as an ill omen. He recognized this irrational tendency in himself and mentioned it to his niece: "Yesterday when I left your place [in Paris], the front door *refused* to close behind me. Something was holding it back; no matter how I pulled, it resisted: it was your concierge who wanted to go out at the same time as I. No matter! Notwithstanding this perfectly simple explanation, I saw a kind of symbolism in the phenomenon. The past was holding me back."[6]

However, he had had a very real reason to be worried of late. Ernest Commanville, who managed his inheritance, had engaged in some risky speculation. His business consisted of cutting up at his sawmill in Dieppe timber that he bought in Sweden, Russia, and central Europe. But he had gotten into the habit of selling the wood before he had paid his suppliers. In 1875 a sudden drop in the price of lumber unbalanced his accounts and brought him to the brink of bankruptcy. "If your husband could get out of his difficulties," Flaubert wrote in the same letter, "if I saw him earning money again and confident about the future as he used to be, if I could make an income of ten thousand francs from [the farm in] Deauville so that I no longer needed to fear destitution for two, and if I were satisfied with Bouvard and Pécuchet, I think I would not complain about life anymore." A storm breaking over Croisset, where he had taken refuge in his study, was enough to persuade him of impending catastrophe. When he learned the magnitude of Ernest Commanville's debts, he was left reeling: one million five hundred thousand francs. Where could one find a sum like that? Would not Caroline, faced with ruin, be obliged to sell Croisset, which she owned, to pay her husband's creditors?

"I have spent my life depriving my heart of the most legitimate nourishment," Flaubert wrote his niece. "I have led an existence of hard work and austerity. Well, I can't take any more! I'm at the end of my rope. Pent-up tears are choking me and I'm opening the floodgates. And then, the thought of no longer having a roof of my own, a *home*, is unbearable to me.* I look at Croisset now the way a mother looks at her consumptive child, thinking: 'How much longer will he last?' and I cannot get used to the possibility of a permanent separation.''[7] Croisset was attached to him by so many sensitive fibers that he thought if its protective shell were torn from him he would die. He gazed at the walls, the furniture permeated with memories of his mother, and the question presented itself to him with tragic intensity: what was the point of going on? Yet he could not demand that Caroline refuse to sell the place. His niece's happiness was ample justification for abandoning it. "What breaks my heart, poor Caro, is your ruin! Your present ruin and the future. It's no joke to come down in the world! All the great sayings about resignation and sacrifice don't console me in the least, not in the least! . . . I won't say anything about your move. Do as you like. Whatever you do will be right.''[8]

From letter to letter his anxiety became more explicit. When would the bankruptcy be pronounced? How would they all live, afterward? "Are you really telling me the whole truth?" he asked his niece. "Forgive me, but I have become suspicious. I am afraid that you are trying to spare my feelings and that you want me to learn of the disaster by degrees. . . . How much longer can Ernest hold out? It seems to me that the final catastrophe is going to arrive and I expect it from one minute to the next. . . . Ah, what cups of bitterness I am swallowing! And you too, poor pet, for whom I had dreamed of a happier fate.''[9] Reluctantly, he informed a few friends of his plight. On July 30 he admitted to Turgenev: "My nephew Commanville is absolutely ruined! And I myself am going to be very seriously affected. What drives me to despair in all this is the position of my poor niece. My (paternal) heart suffers cruelly for her. Sad days lie ahead: lack of money, humiliation, life turned upside down. I've had the lot now, and my brain is wiped out. I feel that from now on I won't be capable of anything whatever. I shall never recover

---

* The word *home* is in English in the original. There is no real equivalent in French. —Trans.

286

from this, my dear friend. I am stricken to the core." And on August 13, to Emile Zola: "My nephew is completely ruined, and I have had heavy losses as a consequence. . . . My life is now turned upside down. I shall still have enough to live on, but under other conditions. As for literature, I am incapable of any work." To satisfy the most pressing creditors, he sold his farm in Deauville: two hundred thousand francs. Then, worn out with humiliation and distress, he went to Concarneau in Brittany for a rest. Although he had promised himself not to do anything there, a week after he had moved into the Hôtel Sergent he was thinking about writing a little story, the legend of Saint Julian the Hospitaler, "to see if I can still make a sentence, which I doubt."

On October 1, 1875, they escaped the worst, "honor was saved": Ernest Commanville's assets would be liquidated without his having to declare bankruptcy. "My grief is less acute . . . my heart is not in such a knot," Flaubert wrote Turgenev. But he was still preoccupied with his financial position. Since under the terms of the marriage settlement Caroline's property had to be preserved intact, she pledged part of her income to pay a debt of fifty thousand francs, an operation that required a guarantee from two of Flaubert's friends: Edgar Raoul-Duval and Edmond Laporte. Then they borrowed again right and left to appease a few more creditors. George Sand was alarmed and offered to buy Croisset, leaving her "old troubadour" to spend the rest of his days there. Flaubert thanked her but refused the generous proposal, describing the family situation as follows:

> My nephew has devoured half my fortune, and with the remainder I indemnified one of his creditors who wanted to put him into receivership. Once the liquidation is completed, I hope to recover approximately the amount I have risked. From now until then, we can keep going. Croisset belongs to my niece. We have definitely decided not to sell it except in the last extremity. It is worth a hundred thousand francs (which would bring an annual yield of five thousand), and it brings in no income, as the upkeep is expensive. . . . My

niece's marriage contract contained a dowry stipulation, and therefore she cannot sell a piece of land unless she immediately reinvests the proceeds in real estate or securities. Thus, as things stand, she cannot give Croisset to me. To help her husband, she has pledged her entire income—the only resource she has. As you see, the situation is complicated. To live, I need six or seven thousand francs a year (at least) *and* Croisset. . . . It will be a great grief to me if I have to leave this old house, so full of tender memories. And your goodwill would be powerless, I fear. Since there is no urgency at the moment, I prefer not to think about it. Like a coward, I dismiss, or rather would like to dismiss, from my mind all thoughts of the future and of business.[10]

At Concarneau he swam, went for walks, watched the fish in the aquarium at the laboratory of marine zoology, and from time to time wrote a few lines of his tale, which had been inspired by a stained-glass window in the cathedral of Rouen. His companion, Georges Pouchet, a doctor and a naturalist, was conducting experiments in the aquarium. The hotel was peaceful, the meals, based on seafood, abundant. But it began to rain: "The rain is coming down in buckets and I sit woolgathering by my fireside in my room at the inn, while my companion dissects little creatures in his laboratory," Flaubert wrote Mme. Roger des Genettes. "He has shown me the insides of several fish and mollusks; they are curious but do not suffice to bring me happiness. What a good life scientists have, and how I envy them!"[11]

At the beginning of November, Georges Pouchet had to return to Paris and Flaubert decided to do the same. In spite of his crying fits, fatigue, and disgust, the stay in Brittany had done him good. He was thinking about resuming his Sunday gatherings with friends. But henceforth he wanted young Guy de Maupassant, whose talent and pleasant disposition he appreciated, to join them. "It's understood, I trust, that you are lunching at my place every Sunday this winter," Flaubert wrote him imperiously.

Settled in Paris in his new apartment in the Faubourg Saint-

Honoré, he went on writing his "little piece of medieval nonsense which will come to no more than thirty pages," and at the same time began thinking about a contemporary novel: "But I am hesitating among several embryonic ideas," he wrote George Sand. "I should like to do something compact and violent. But the string of the necklace (that is, the main thing) is still missing."[12] His Sunday regulars—Ivan Turgenev, Emile Zola, Alphonse Daudet, Edmond de Goncourt, and Guy de Maupassant—showed him an affection, a deference, and a loyalty that were a comfort to him. At fifty-four he could say to himself that for all his disappointments, he enjoyed the flattering admiration of some of his fellow writers. George Sand, however, was always reproaching him for not intervening in his novels with his own personal convictions. "It seems to me that your school [of writing] is not concerned with fundamentals and that it dwells too much on the surface," she wrote him. "By emphasizing the search for form, it places too little value on content. It addresses itself to educated people. But we are not just 'educated people.' We are human beings, first and foremost. At the heart of every story, of every deed, we want to find the man."[13] He promptly protested: "As for my 'lack of convictions,' alas! I am choking on convictions. I am bursting with suppressed anger and indignation. But according to my ideal of Art, one should not reveal any of these personal feelings, and the artist should no more appear in his work than God does in nature. The man is nothing, the work everything! . . . Speaking of my friends, you call them 'my school.' But I am killing myself trying *not* to have a school! I reject all schools a priori. The writers whom I see often and whom you mention strive for everything I despise and trouble themselves very little about the things that torment me. . . . Above all else, I strive for *beauty*, which my companions are not greatly interested in. When I am devastated by admiration or horror, I see that they are unmoved. Phrases that make me swoon seem very ordinary to them. . . . In short, I try to think well *in order* to write well. But it is to write well that is my goal, I don't deny it."[14]

He came back to this basic idea a number of times in his letters to George Sand: "As for revealing my personal opinion of the people

I bring on stage, no, no, a thousand times no! I don't acknowledge that I have the right to do that. If the reader doesn't draw from a book the moral it should contain, either the reader is an imbecile or the book is *false* because it is inaccurate. For the moment a thing is true, it is good. . . . And note that I detest what is commonly called *realism*, even though I'm made out to be one of its high priests."[15] Or again: "This concern with external beauty that you reproach me for is *a method* for me. When I discover a disagreeable assonance or a repetition in one of my sentences, I can be sure that I'm floundering around in something false. By dint of searching, I find the right expression, which was the only one all along, and at the same time the harmonious one. The word is never lacking when one is in possession of the idea."[16]

The year 1876 began inauspiciously. Flaubert was worried about Caroline's health. Consumed with care, she was wasting away, anemic to the last degree, and had to give up painting for the time being. Like her uncle, she was advised to take hydrotherapy. Then on March 10 he learned that Louise Colet had died two days before. He was very moved by the news, in spite of the hatred his former mistress had shown for him in later years. His thoughts went back to the good times of the old days, to the pleasures they had shared in their youth, to the lovers' quarrels, and he became even more keenly aware how lonely and empty his life was now. "You understood very well all the feelings aroused in me by the death of my poor Muse," he wrote Mme. Roger des Genettes. "This revival of her memory made me go back in time to an earlier period of my life. But your friend has become more stoical over the past year. I have trampled on so many things, in order to go on living! In short, after an afternoon spent plunged in days gone by, I determined not to think of them anymore and went back to work."[17]

The "work" was the drafting of another short piece, *Un Coeur simple* [A Simple Heart]. Having finished *La Légende de Saint Julien l'Hospitalier*, Flaubert could not resign himself to going back to *Bouvard et Pécuchet*. He was put off by the technical difficulties of the heavy novel and preferred to postpone such exhausting labor in favor of a story whose delicacy and compassion seemed restful by comparison. He described the new project in a letter to Mme. Roger des Genettes: *"L'Histoire d'un coeur simple* is just the account of an obscure life, the life of a poor country girl, who is pious but mystical, quietly devoted, and as tender as fresh bread. She loves successively a man, her mistress's children, a nephew, an old man she is taking care of, then her parrot. When the parrot dies she has him stuffed, and when she herself is dying, she confuses the parrot with the Holy Ghost. It's not at all ironic, as you suppose, but on the contrary very serious and very sad. I want to arouse people's pity, to make sensitive souls weep, since I am one myself."[18] To establish the character of the humble, faithful Félicité, he mingled reminiscences of the Léonie who had been the servant of his friends the Barbeys in Trouville with certain features of his old Julie, who still waited on him in Croisset. Returning to the nostalgic world of his childhood, he resuscitated under other names uncles, aunts, acquaintances in Honfleur or Pont-l'Evêque. The little girl and boy in the story were himself and his sister Caroline whom he had so loved. The marquis de Grémanville was his great-granduncle, Charles-François Fouet, better known as Councilman of Crémanville. Even the parrot, Lou-lou, had really existed, in the Barbey family. In April, to immerse himself again in the setting of his story, Flaubert took a trip to Pont-l'Evêque and Honfleur. During this pilgrimage he intensely relived his early years, visited the places where his mother's ancestors had lived, measured the painful depth of the past, and took notes. "This excursion filled me with sadness, for inevitably it plunged me into a bath of memories," he wrote Mme. Roger des Genettes. "How old I am, dear Lord! How old!" But he didn't let that discourage him, because in the same letter he announced: "Do you know what I want to write after that? The story of Saint John the Baptist. Herod's nastiness toward Hérodias excites me. It's still only a vague idea in my head, but I'd really like to go into it more deeply. If I do do it, that will make three tales, enough to publish a rather amusing book next fall. But when will I go back to my two old copy clerks?"[19]

At the end of May he was back in Croisset and learned that George Sand was ill: an intestinal obstruction that was giving her terrible pain. He sent a telegram to the novelist's son Maurice, asking for news. On June 8, 1876, George Sand died. Overwhelmed with grief, Flaubert hastened to the funeral. "That loss is added to all the others that have piled up for me since 1869," he wrote afterward to Mlle. Leroyer de Chantepie. "It was my poor Bouilhet who began the series; after him, Sainte-Beuve departed, then Jules de Goncourt, Théophile Gautier, Feydeau, and an intimate friend named Jules Duplan, who was less famous but no less dear, not to mention my mother whom I loved tenderly!"[20] And to Princess Mathilde: "This death of my old friend is a great sorrow to me. My heart is becoming a necropolis: how the empty space is expanding! It seems to me that the earth is becoming depopulated."[21] Finally, to Maurice Sand: "I felt as if I were burying my mother for the second time! Poor dear great woman! What genius and what heart!"[22]

He made the trip to Nohant in the company of Prince Napoleon, Alexandre Dumas *fils,* and Ernest Renan. One thing he felt good about was that, true to her convictions, George Sand "received no priest and died perfectly unrepentant." But her family asked the Bishop of Bourges to authorize a Catholic burial. After the religious ceremony, the funeral procession went to the little cemetery of the château where George Sand's grandparents and her granddaughter, Jeanne Clésinger, were already laid to rest. A gentle rain was falling. The country people standing around the open grave wept and murmured prayers. Flaubert could not keep from sobbing when he saw the coffin lowered into the hole, or again when he kissed Aurore.

On June 13 he was back in Croisset and happy to be home after so many painful emotions. "Emile was waiting for me," he told Caroline. "Before unpacking my bags he went to draw me a pitcher of cider which I emptied completely, to his great terror, for he kept repeating: 'But Monsieur is going to make himself sick!' It did me no harm whatever. At dinner I was glad to see the silver soup tureen again and the old sauceboat. The silence that surrounded me seemed pleasant and soothing. While I was eating I looked at your paintings of country scenes over the doors, at the little high chair you had as a child, and I thought of our poor old lady, but without sorrow, or rather with sweet regret. I never had a less painful return."[23]

The next day he went back to work on *Un Coeur simple* with an enthusiasm that he himself found surprising. "Things are not marvelous, but they are tolerable after all," he wrote Mme. Roger des Genettes. "I have gotten my mast up again, I feel like writing. I am hoping for a fairly long period of peace. That's all we can ask of the gods! So be it! And to tell you the truth, dear old friend, I am delighted to be home again, like a petty bourgeois, in *my* armchairs, amid *my* books, in *my* study, with a view of *my* garden. The sun is shining, the birds are cooing like lovers, the boats glide noiselessly over the smooth surface of the river, and my story is progressing. I shall probably have finished it in two months."[24] To build up his strength and refresh his will to work, he took walks and went for a daily swim in the Seine. But one day when he was trying to "swim against the tide," he made a violent movement that produced a pain in his left hip. This incident led him to moderate his "natatorial exercises" but didn't slow down his work in the least. "As for me, I am working furiously, seeing no one, reading no newspapers, and shouting in the silence of my study like a man possessed," he wrote Guy de Maupassant. "I spend all day and almost all night bent over my worktable and pretty regularly I admire the dawn coming up. Before dinner, around seven o'clock, I disport myself in the bourgeois waves of the Seine." He would have liked his young "disciple" to be, like himself, wholly dedicated to writing, instead of wasting his time with easy women. "I urge you, in the interest of literature, to be more moderate," he wrote in the same letter. "Take care! Everything depends on the goal one wants to reach. A man who has become established as an artist no longer has the right to live like other people."[25] Yet there were times when he regretted not having followed the usual path. His manservant Emile having married Caroline's maid Marguerite, the couple had a baby boy. The child was to die a few days later, but on learning of his birth, Flaubert was overcome with a strange feeling of tenderness: "Emile is in raptures over having a son, a joy which I understand, which I used to think very ridiculous and which now I envy," he wrote Caroline.[26]

While he sometimes thought wistfully of the pleasures of family life (a sign of senility, in his opinion), he was more often angry over the Paris press. When *La République des lettres* published an article on Renan that was full of nasty personal remarks about the author of *La Vie de Jésus*, he asked Catulle Mendès, the editor of the magazine, to remove his name from the list of contributors and to cancel his subscription. "If people don't agree with Renan, fine!" he wrote Zola. "I don't agree with him either! But to take no account of the work he has done, to blame him for his red hair, which he doesn't have, and for his poor family background by calling him the servant of princes, that is what I cannot tolerate! My decision is firm, I am abandoning those little gentlemen joyously and forever. Their base democratic envy is nauseating to me."[27] And to Guy de Maupassant: "Conclusions: stay away from the newspapers! The hatred of those outfits is the beginning of the love of Beauty. They are essentially hostile to any personality that is a little above the others. Originality, in whatever form it is displayed, is infuriating to them."[28] In the meantime, he had asked Dr. Georges Pennetier, the director of the Museum of Natural History of Rouen, to lend him a stuffed parrot. Now he was writing under the glassy eye of one of the emerald-plumaged fowl. "For the last month I have had a stuffed parrot on my table so as to be able to paint from nature," he reported to Mme. Roger des Genettes. "His presence is beginning to be tiresome. Never mind! I shall keep him in order to fill my soul with parrot."[29]

On August 7 he was laboring over the last pages of the story: "I continue to scream like a gorilla in the silence of my study, and today I even have a pain in my back, or rather in my lungs, which has no other cause," he wrote Caroline. "Someday I shall make myself explode like a shell; they will find the pieces of me on the table. But above all, I have to make a splendid end for my *Félicité*."[30] Three days later, another bulletin on his health: "The fervor with which I am going at this task borders on mental derangement. The day before yesterday I put in an eighteen-hour day! Very often now I work before lunch; or rather I never stop working, for even while I'm swimming I roll phrases around in my head, in spite of myself. Shall I tell you what I think? I think that (without knowing it) I was profoundly and secretly ill ever since the death of our poor old lady. If I am mistaken, how is it that I have felt a kind of brightening of late? It's as if a fog were lifting. Physically, I feel rejuvenated. I have given up my flannels (height of imprudence!) and right now I'm not even wearing a shirt."[31]

Finally, on August 17 he sent Caroline a shout of victory: "Yesterday, at one in the morning, I finished my *Coeur simple* and I'm copying it over. Now I realize how tired I am, I'm breathing hard, with as much difficulty as a big ox that has done too much plowing." One copy of the text was going to Turgenev, who had already translated *La Légende de Saint Julien l'Hospitalier* into Russian and had promised to take on the new story as well.

Two weeks later, with a great weight off his shoulders, Flaubert was in Paris, where he met his usual friends. He recounted to them in detail the agonies of creation he had gone through for two months, working fifteen hours a day, in the worst heat of summer, his only recreation being a plunge in the Seine at evening. "And the product of those nine hundred hours of work is a thirty-page novella," concluded Edmond de Goncourt with mingled irony and pity. Flaubert had only one regret: that George Sand had died before she could read this story. She had always reproached him for the clinical coldness of his writing. This time she would have been moved to see the influence she had had on the style of her "old troubadour." It was too bad.

Nevertheless, he was in excellent spirits again. Far from exhausting him, his work on *Un Coeur simple* had whetted his appetite. "Now that I've finished with Félicité," he wrote Caroline, "Hérodias presents herself and I *see* (as clearly as I *see* the Seine) the surface of the Dead Sea sparkling in the sun. Herod and his wife are on a balcony from which one can see the gilded tiles of the Temple. I am impatient to get started on it and to grind away furiously this fall."[32] As was his habit, he began by reading a vast number of historical works to prepare the ground. He continued his research in Paris, in the libraries. He was consumed by a need for documentation. But he also gave some time to the demands of friendship—went to the opening of Alphonse Daudet's play *Fromont jeune;* recommended Guy de Maupassant to Raoul-Duval for a "dramatic serial" to appear in *La Nation;* gathered his customary companions for a reading of *Un Coeur simple;* thanks to Turgenev, sold his two stories to the Russian review *The European Messenger.* . . . He found the company of his old comrades invigorating. However, he refused to approve of Zola's latest novel, *L'Assommoir:* "I think it's wretched, absolutely," he wrote Princess Mathilde. "To be truthful does not seem to me to be the first requirement for art. The main thing is to aim for beauty, and to attain it if you can."[33] He was equally disappointed with Daudet's *Nabab:* "It's made up of disparate elements. It's not just a question of seeing; you have to arrange and combine the things you have seen. Reality, in my opinion, should be only a *springboard.* . . . This materialism makes me furious. . . . After the Realists we have the Naturalists and the Impressionists. What progress! Bunch of frauds. . . ."[34]

At this point, a sweet face from the past reappeared in his life: the little English girl Gertrude Collier, now Mrs. Tennant. Moved by their reunion, he wrote her afterward from Croisset: "I miss you! That's all I have to say to you. The good impulse that led you to see me again, after so many years, must have further consequences. It would be cruel now to forget me again. . . . How can I express to you the pleasure your visit, your reappearance gave me? I felt as if the intervening years had vanished and I was embracing my youth. It is the only happy thing that has happened to me for a long time."[35] Another "happy thing" was the publication in *La République des lettres* of a very admiring article about him signed Guy de Valmont, the temporary pseudonym of Guy de Maupassant. Flaubert was deeply touched and wrote to thank his disciple: "You have treated me with filial affection. My niece is enthusiastic about your piece. She thinks it is the best thing that has been written about her uncle. As for me, I think so too, but I dare not say so."[36] This encouragement came just when he needed it for his work on *Hérodias.* He had already expressed his anxiety about it to Mme. Roger des Genettes: "As the time to write the story of Hérodias draws near, I am going into a funk of Biblical proportions. I'm afraid of repeating the effects produced by *Salammbô*, for my characters are of the same race and the setting is quite similar."[37]

In the last days of October he finished taking notes, and early in November he threw himself feverishly into the writing of the story—a story that he said was of "overwhelming" complexity and "might very well be a failure." While he was in the midst of his creative ferment, an unfortunate incident occurred: "My man [Emile], who I thought was devoted to me, has left me after ten years of service and for no reason," he wrote Princess Mathilde. "But one must be philosophical about small misfortunes as well as great ones."[38] In any event, he soon found a replacement for Emile in the person of one Noémie, who turned out to be a pearl: "She makes a very agreeable servant," he wrote Caroline. "She is lively, thrifty, and knows all my little idiosyncrasies."[39] So his peace of mind was restored. His friend Laporte often came to visit him in the country. As the younger man was thinking about "marrying a rich lady," Flaubert did his best to dissuade him, stating with authority that celibacy was the only conditon that enabled a decent man to live according to his own inclinations without taking other people's opinions into account. Yet he admitted that there were evenings when he was overcome with loneliness. Although it had been four years since his mother died, he was haunted by her memory. His obsession was turning into fetishism. He was always rummaging in armoires to find and touch the dead woman's dresses. He felt as if he were reunited with her through the garments she had so often worn. At the age of fifty-five, half bald, with a drooping mustache, protruding eyes, and shortness of breath, he dreamed of melting once more in his mother's warmth and odor. One evening, being unable to put his hand on certain items that had belonged to the deceased, he panicked and imagined that in his absence Caroline had moved them or taken them away. "What have you done with my poor mama's shawl and garden hat?" he wrote her. "I looked for them in the bureau drawer and didn't find them, because every now and then I like to look at these objects again and muse over them. With me, memories never fade."[40] Six days later, having received no answer from Caroline, he returned to the charge: "What has become of, where have you put my poor mama's shawl and garden hat? I like to see and touch them from time to time. I don't have so many pleasures in the world that I can afford to refuse myself that one!"[41] Finally, on December 20, an apology: "I was mistaken: it wasn't the shawl I was looking for but an old green fan that mama used on our trip to Italy. It seems to me that I had set it aside, with her hat, which I went to visit as soon as I found out where it was." On Christmas Day, the same fixation on the past drove him to write Gertrude Tennant: "I thank you for detesting the modern Trouville. (How well we understand each other!) Poor Trouville! the best part of my youth was spent there. Many a wave has rolled over the beach since we were there together. But no storm, my dear Gertrude, has erased those memories. Are things enhanced when we see them in retrospect? Was it really as beautiful, as good as I remember? What a lovely corner of the earth and of humanity it was, with you, your sisters, mine! Oh unfathomable depths! If you were an old bachelor like me, you would understand much better. But no, you understand me, I feel that you do."

Despite the intensity with which he was working on *Hérodias*, he had doubts about the result. "Something is missing," he wrote Caroline, "I don't know what. The truth is, I can't tell anything anymore. But why am I not *sure* of it, as I was with my other two stories? How much trouble it's costing me!"[42] For relaxation from the daily struggle with vocabulary and syntax, he read the works of his fellow writers. Renan's *Prière sur l'Acropole*, published in *La Revue des deux mondes*, moved him to heights of praise. On the other hand, he was not impressed with Balzac's *Correspondance*. "It shows that he was a fine man whom one would have loved," he wrote Edmond de Goncourt. "But what a preoccupation with money, and so little love of Art! Did you notice that he doesn't speak of it *once*? He strove for Fame, but not Beauty. And he was a Catholic, a legitimist, a landowner, nursing ambitions for the Chamber of Deputies and the Académie; above all, ignorant as a pot and *provincial* to the marrow of his bones, dazzled by luxury. The writer for whom he had the greatest admiration was Walter

Scott. All in all, for me a tremendous figure, but of the second rank. His end was lamentable! What an irony of fate! To die on the very threshold of happiness!" And he concluded: "I prefer the *Correspondance* of M. de Voltaire: the compass spreads a little wider there."[43] On New Year's Day he went to dinner in Rouen "so as not to be too unsociable," and, when he reached the corner of the garden of the house where he was born, had to keep from sobbing. His brother received him with gloomy looks. After which, Flaubert visited the cemetery. But his mother was more present at Croisset than under the gravestone.

Another reason for sadness: good old Laporte was ruined too. When he announced this to Flaubert, he added fraternally: "It's one more thing we two have in common." Fortunately, he was not thinking of moving away. "If he doesn't find anything, he is determined to stay on in Couronne just the same and to get by any old way so as not to leave his house, which I understand perfectly," Flaubert wrote Caroline. "At a certain age, a change of habit is death."[44] He himself was so comfortably ensconced in his retreat that he took pleasure in listening to the stories of old Julie, who no longer did much work about the house but still took her ease there, last witness of a radiant era. "Talking about the old days, she reminded me of a host of things, portraits, images, that gladdened my heart. It was like a fresh breeze."[45] He became increasingly interested in family history, rescued portraits of his ancestors that were moldering in the attic, and hung them in the hall. As for the miniature of grandfather Fleuriot, "head of the armies of the Vendée," from now on it had the place of honor over the mantelpiece. Too bad if Caroline, who had small interest in genealogy, didn't approve of the arrangement! He also informed her that he expected to finish his *Hérodias* soon and that he was getting ready to leave for Paris, where he hoped to find "good wines, pretty liqueurs, amiable company, pocket money, mirthful countenances, and blithe discourse."

In preparation for his stay in Paris, he ordered himself a dressing gown, a pair of velvet slippers, and some white ties, and commissioned Caroline to buy two "sponges for a giant," some eau de

Cologne, mouthwash, pomade, "or rather oil that smells of hay (Rue Saint-Honoré)," four pairs of pearl-gray gloves, and two of suede with two buttons. And on February 1 he sent his friends a comic invitation card reading:

> Monsieur Gustave Flaubert has the honor to inform you that his drawing rooms will be open as from next Sunday, February 4, 1877. He looks forward to your visit. Ladies and children will be admitted.

As soon as he arrived, he fulfilled some social obligations, but without abandoning his manuscript. And on February 15 he could announce to Mme. Roger des Genettes: "Yesterday, at three in the morning, I finished recopying *Hérodias*. One more thing done! My volume can be published on April 16. It will be short, but amusing, I think. I worked frantically this winter, so I arrived in Paris in a lamentable state. Now I'm recovering a little. In the last week I had slept a total of ten hours (sic). I sustained myself with cold water and coffee."

While in the admirable *Un Coeur simple* he had gone back to the sober style of *Madame Bovary*, while in *Saint Julien l'Hospitalier* he had reinvoked the legendary and religious world of *La Tentation de Saint Antoine*, in *Hérodias* he returned to the ferocity, lechery, and barbaric colors of *Salammbô*. Three main characters, strongly drawn: Herod Antipas, cowardly and cruel, who trembles for his position as tetrarch; Hérodias, his wife, ambitious and treacherous, who will stop at nothing to preserve her power; and Salome, a graceful, immodest girl who is unaware of the effect she has on men and who innocently serves her mother's criminal designs. The dance of this virgin, inspired by Kuchuk Hanem's lascivious hip-swaying in front of Flaubert, seals the tragic fate of Saint John the Baptist. The author's tour de force consists of bringing a biblical universe to life, in a few pages and with fascinating precision. Thus each of the three tales, so different in treatment, demonstrates an absolute mastery of theme and language. The extraordinary economy of the narration, the swift, accurate portrayal of the characters, the presence of the setting, described in a few touches—it is all perfect. The clarity and purity of a diamond. Yet Flaubert was not sure of what he had done. As usual, he sought the opinions of his friends. Most of them were favorable. But after attending a reading of *Hérodias* to Princess Mathilde, Goncourt noted sourly in his *Journal:* "Without question there are colorful scenes in the story, delicate epithets, some very good things; but how much clever contrivance there is too, as in a stage farce, and what a lot of little modern feelings stuck into that gaudy mosaic of archaic details! For all the reader's bellowing, the whole thing struck me as a harmless exercise in archaeology and Romanticism."[46]

Flaubert was hard on his friends too. Thus, irritated by the success of *L'Assommoir*, he never missed an opportunity to attack in public the doctrines of naturalism that Zola was always professing. On one such occasion Zola replied imperturbably: "*You* had private means that liberated you from a good many things. I, who have earned my living with nothing but my pen, who have had to make my way by writing all sorts of shameful stuff, by journalism, I have come out of all that with—how shall I put it?—a little charlatanism. . . . Yes, it's true I make fun of the word *naturalism* just as you do, but I shall keep repeating it all the time because you have to give things new names if you want the public to think they're new."[47]

In March, *Trois Contes* [Three Tales] was in the hands of the printer. Before publication, *Un Coeur simple* and *Hérodias* were to appear separately in *Le Moniteur*, bringing the author a thousand francs each. *La Légende de Saint Julien l'Hospitalier* was promised to *Le Bien public*. One encouraging sign was that more and more young authors were sending their works to Flaubert. And Victor Hugo, "that immense old man," wanted him to present his candidacy for the Académie. "He's driving me crazy with his eternal Académie Française. But I'm not going to fall for that one!" sneered Flaubert.[48] He was disappointed in the books of his friends: "Do you know [Edmond de Goncourt's] *La Fille Elisa?*" he asked Mme. Roger des Genettes in the same letter. "It's short and anemic, and *L'Assommoir* looks like a masterpiece beside it. For after all, in Zola's long dirty pages there is real power and undeniable individuality.

Coming after those two books, I'm going to look as if I wrote for young ladies' boarding schools." When he had finished the chore of correcting proof, he reread the letters of his youth and burned most of those he had exchanged with Maxime Du Camp. Then, in a gesture of generosity and trust, he made Edmond Laporte a gift of the manuscript of *Trois Contes*, bound in leather: "You saw me writing these pages, my dear fellow; accept them and may they remind you of your giant, Gustave Flaubert."

On April 16 six young writers—Paul Alexis, Henry Céard, Léon Hennique, Guy de Maupassant, J. K. Huysmans, and Octave Mirbeau—gave a dinner at the Restaurant Trapp for Flaubert, Zola, and Goncourt and officially declared them "the three masters of our day." "This is the new army in process of formation," Goncourt noted with satisfaction. But Flaubert hadn't the slightest desire to take command of an "army." He was too individualistic to accept the role of spiritual guide. Realism, naturalism—none of those labels corresponded to his conception of the novel. Zola made him furious with his literary pseudo-theories. Alone in his life, he wanted to be alone in his art as well. So from start to finish of this dinner that was supposed to anoint him as the leader of a school, he loudly proclaimed his rejection of all schools.

Trois Contes was published by Charpentier on April 24, 1877. Unlike *La Tentation de Saint Antoine*, this work was immediately given an enthusiastic reception by the press. Edouard Drumont spoke of "marvels"; Saint-Valry, in *La Patrie* of "an admirable combination of precision and poetry"; Mme. Alphonse Daudet (who signed herself Karl Steen) in *Le Journal officiel* called the book "a unanimous and well deserved triumph"; and Théodore de Banville in *Le National* said the tales were "three absolute and perfect masterpieces, created with the power of a poet sure of his art, who must be spoken of only with the respectful admiration due to genius." This last critic even went so far as to advise the members of the Académie Française to go in a body and "lay down a red carpet" for Gustave Flaubert. Only Henri Brunetière of *La Revue des deux mondes* dared to attack the author, saying that *Trois Contes* was "the weakest thing he had written" and that the book betrayed a "flagging invention." This harsh judgment was drowned out by the acclamations of the "young men."

The public was more reserved. In any case, the launching of the book was overshadowed by political events. All attention was focused on President MacMahon, who had just sent Jules Simon, the president of the Council of State, a letter disavowing the latter's republican views. A crisis ensued, resolved on May 16 by the installation of a conservative interim cabinet headed by the duc de Broglie. But people were very agitated over the affair. It was rumored that the Chamber of Deputies was going to be dissolved and new elections held. "The frolics of our modern-day Bayard are having a damaging effect on business of every sort, the business of literature among others!" Flaubert wrote a friend.* "The Charpentier bookshop, which ordinarily sells three hundred volumes a day, last Saturday sold five! As for my poor book, it's completely demolished. All I can do now is tighten my belt![49] Indeed, Flaubert had been counting on a big sale to restore his fortunes. He hardly had enough to live on, and Commanville's "affairs" were not being straightened out as readily as had been hoped. So for all his growing prestige with the critics and contemporary writers, he ended his letter on a melancholy note: "The deterioration of public affairs is added to the sad state of my personal affairs. Everything on my horizon is black." As always, there was only one consolation: work. Bouvard and Pécuchet were waiting for him in Croisset. Once again, he would try to forget the world in their company.

* "Our modern-day Bayard" is a sarcastic reference to MacMahon: Pierre du Terrail, seigneur de Bayard, was a sixteenth-century military hero whose exploits earned him the sobriquet of *le chevalier sans peur et sans reproche* [the fearless and perfect knight]. —Trans.

Chapter 21

BACK TO BOUVARD ET PÉCUCHET

The new season in Croisset opened on a note of happiness: "Yes, my pet," Flaubert wrote Caroline, "I was delighted to be back in my poor old study. . . . Last night, I finally got back to work on *Bouvard et Pécuchet*. A number of good ideas came to me. The whole part about medicine can be done in three months, if I'm not disturbed. Our business affairs seem to be on the right track, and perhaps we shall soon put our penury and anxiety behind us. . . . I feel sorry for you, poor kitten, for being in Paris. It's so nice in Croisset! So peaceful! And then, no more frock coats to put on! no more stairs to climb."[1] And a little later: "For the last two days I've been doing excellent work. There are times when I'm dazzled by the vast scope of this book. How will it turn out? Unless I'm completely mistaken, and instead of being sublime it's just foolish? But I think not! Something tells me that I am on the right road. But it's all either one or the other. I repeat what I've said before: 'Oh, I will have known them, all right, the agonies of literature!' "[2] In July 1877 Caroline came to join him in Croisset. There she went into a "frenzy" of painting. Having taken lessons with Bonnat, she wanted to persevere in that line and maybe earn her living with her brush as her uncle did with his pen. Flaubert encouraged her without having too much faith in her success. In spite of his niece's presence in the house, he went on working at the same pace. "My life (which is austere at bottom) is calm and

305

tranquil on the surface," he wrote Princess Mathilde. "It's the existence of a monk and a workingman. All the days are alike, I read
one thing after another, my white paper becomes covered with black,
I put out my lamp in the middle of the night, a little before dinner
I play salamander in the river, and so on."[3]

A juicy piece of news caused him much merriment in his retreat:
he learned that the former imperial prosecutor Ernest Pinard, who
had presented the case against *Madame Bovary* for outrage to morality and religion, was himself the author of obscene poems. "I'm
not surprised," Flaubert exclaimed, "nothing being filthier than
magistrates (their genius for obscenity comes from their habit of
wearing gowns). . . . And when I think how indignant Pinard was
over the descriptions in Bovary!"[4]

The oppressive heat of August awoke vaguely lascivious memories in him and he wrote to his dear Mme. Brainne: "As we are
far apart, in the absence of caresses I am going to give you compliments, which is a cold way of caressing. . . . Well, then, I think
you are beautiful, kind, intelligent, witty, sensitive. I love your eyes,
your brows, your good laugh, your lovely legs, your hands, your
shoulders, the way you talk, the way you dress, your black hair that
always looks as wet as that of a naiad emerging from her bath, the
hem of your dress, the tip of your foot, everything. . . ."[5] On August
20, when his niece left to take the waters at Eaux-bonnes, he gave
himself a vacation and went to visit Princess Mathilde in Saint-
Gratien. There he rested, went to bed early, rose late, took long
naps in the afternoon, and wound up being bored to death. "I am
not enjoying myself in the least in Saint-Gratien, not in the least!"
he confessed to Caroline. "As soon as you take me out of my study,
I'm no good for anything anymore."[6] But he didn't go back to
Croisset just yet. Paris tempted him, even though he denied it. For
the last few months he had been growing hard of hearing, he had
lost many teeth, and when he spoke, a little whitish saliva, caused
by the mercury treatments, appeared at the corners of his lips. He
was aware of these physical failings, and they only made him more
contemptuous of his fellow men. "Is it I who am becoming unso-

ciable, or the others who are growing stupid?" he asked. "I have no idea. But at present I can't stand to be with people."[7]

Nevertheless, he made the effort to attend Thiers's funeral, lost in a crowd of notables. "I witnessed Thiers's funeral," he wrote Caroline. "It was splendid and incredible. A million men bareheaded in the rain! From time to time there were shouts of *'Vive la République!'* then 'shhh! shhh!' so as not to create a provocation."[8] And to Mme. Roger des Genettes he explained: "I had no liking for that king of the Prudhommes, but no matter! Compared to the other men around him, he was a giant. And then, he had one virtue: patriotism. No one has epitomized France as he did."[9] He was worried about the political situation, concerned that at the next elections the fear of Gambetta might drive many bourgeois to vote for "that idiot of a marshal" [MacMahon]. On the local level, at any rate, he couldn't complain. After eight years of hearing representations on the subject, the City Council had been convinced, and Louis Bouilhet was to have his fountain and bust against the wall of the new library in Rouen.

Flaubert's spirits were lifted by this victory over administrative stupidity, and he decided to take another field trip to Lower Normandy, with Laporte, to complete his research for *Bouvard et Pécuchet*. Armed with a horse trader's cane and wearing a fedora and a big red scarf around his neck for protection from the chill mists of September, he felt rejuvenated by the prospect of this expedition with his friend. They hurried from town to town, from village to village, visited châteaux, churches, and inns, gorged themselves on seafood, drank, laughed, took notes. "We get up at six in the morning and go to bed at nine," Flaubert wrote his niece. "The whole day is spent in excursions, generally in little open carriages where the cold cuts our faces. . . . We are in excellent health and are not wasting our time. Our only debauchery at table is over fish and oysters. Laporte is always fussing over me: what a good fellow he is!"[10] And five days later, again to Caroline: "It's Bouvard and Pécuchet's country. . . . I saw some things that will be very useful to me. In short, all goes well. I look well and have an appetite that frightened Valère.* The only accident I had was that I broke my pince-nez."

As soon as he was back in Croisset, he put his travel notes in order and confided his main concern to Emile Zola: "I live in fear and trembling over this damn book. It will have no meaning except taken as a whole. No *showpiece*, nothing brilliant, and always the same situation that has to be varied in some aspect. I'm afraid it's going to be a deadly bore."[11] But he was also worried about the future of the country. What a catastrophe if MacMahon won the upcoming elections! But the provinces weren't showing much enthusiasm for him. "The Bayard of modern times, this man illustrious for his defeats, is the object of universal disapproval," Flaubert said in the same letter. "In Laigle ([department of the] Orne), where I was the day before yesterday, the posters of his candidates had been covered with shit."

In the general elections of October 14, 1877, the republican opposition obtained a majority of one hundred and twenty seats. MacMahon had been repudiated, but he remained in office. "Universal suffrage (a lovely invention!) has really had splendid results," exclaimed Flaubert. After this political excitement, he plunged back into work. He asked Guy de Maupassant, who had grown up on the coast of Normandy, for certain detailed geographical information he needed, read more works on science and history ("enough to ruin my eyesight"), begged Laporte to help him classify his notes, and on the eve of his fifty-sixth birthday concluded: "What a grind! At times I feel crushed under the sheer mass of this book."

No tonic like a stay in Paris. One of his friends, Agénor Bardoux, deputy from the department of the Puy-de-Dôme, had been appointed Minister of Education in the Dufaure cabinet that had been formed on December 14, 1877. Flaubert lunched at the ministry several times, with the ribbon of the Legion of Honor in his lapel. But on January 18, 1878, he met someone even more impor-

---

* Flaubert's nickname for Laporte.

tant. At a dinner at the Charpentiers', he struck up a conversation with Gambetta. Edmond de Goncourt, who was also among the guests, recorded the incident: "When dinner was over, Flaubert carried Gambetta off, so to speak, into a drawing room, closing the door behind them. Tomorrow he will be able to say: 'Gambetta is my intimate friend.' It is really astonishing, the effect any celebrity has on that man, the need he has to get close to him, rub up against him, violate his privacy." When Mme. Roger des Genettes asked what he thought of the great republican tribune, Flaubert admitted, not without some fatuity, that a friendly rapport had been established between them: "Gambetta (since you ask for my opinion of the said *sieur*) seemed to me at first grotesque, then reasonable, then agreeable, and finally charming (the word is not too strong). We chatted together in private for twenty minutes, and we know each other as well as if we had met a hundred times. What I like about him is that his thinking is never conventional, and I believe he's a humane man."[12]

On the other hand, he couldn't find harsh enough words in which to denounce the absurdity of the war in the Middle East. "I am indignant over England, indignant enough to turn Prussian! For what does she want, after all? Who is attacking her? The nerve of her to defend Islam (which is in itself a monstrosity)! It's infuriating. In the name of humanity, I ask that the Black Stone be ground up and its dust scattered to the wind, that Mecca be destroyed, and that the tomb of Mohammed be desecrated.* That would be the way to discourage Fanaticism."[13]

In Paris he was disgusted by the Exposition, although he admired the view from the heights of the Trocadéro. He was invited to the festivities organized for the centenary of the death of Voltaire but, despite his veneration for the author of *Candide*, refused to attend for fear of meeting people he didn't like. Right now his dream

---

* The Black Stone, greatly venerated by adherents of Islam, is embedded in the wall of the Kaaba, the sacred building that is the goal of the pilgrimage to Mecca. —Trans.

was to write a novel set in the time of Napoleon III. "I think I can feel it. Until I change my mind, it will be called *Un Ménage parisien*. But I have to get rid of my two chaps first."[14] And for that he needed the solitude of Croisset.

"Here I am, back at last with my lares and penates," he wrote Caroline on May 29, 1878. Thank God, but *I'm ready to drop!!* I arrived home at half past eleven . . . the weather was terribly cold. My lunch was ready. Julio came bounding to meet me and overwhelmed me with caresses. From one to three I spent putting things away, then I slept until five. Now I can go back to work." Deep in his labors, he was surprised to learn that Taine and Renan both coveted a seat in the Académie Française. "In what way can the Académie bestow honor on them? When you are somebody, why should you want to be something?"[15] He had developed a pimple on his forehead, and to get rid of it he was taking Fowler's solution "like an anemic girl" and bicarbonate of soda. Always short of money, he envied Zola, whose books were selling so well that he had just bought a house in the country. He himself was still struggling with the intellectual explorations of his two imbeciles. Not a chance that such a book would be appreciated by the public. For one chapter that he had in mind he needed a description of a priest's dining room. He asked Laporte to inquire into the matter. Would there be "a crucifix, a religious picture, a bust of the Holy Father"? Laporte carried out the assignment. Despite his duties as a member of the county council, he was always entirely at Flaubert's disposal. Thanks to him, Caroline obtained a commission to execute copies of the portraits of Corneille by Mignard and Lebrun. These canvases were destined to hang in the restored birthplace of the most famous of Rouenese writers, in Petit-Couronne. Another influential friend was the Minister of Education, Agénor Bardoux. Flaubert was counting on his support to have his "fairy play," *Le Château des coeurs,* staged at last, even though it had been refused by all the theater managers, and to have Zola awarded the cross of the Legion of Honor. When the minister did not immediately comply with these requests, Flaubert exploded: "As for my comrade Bardoux, he's a *khon* (Chinese spelling).* I have promised myself to tell him so."[16]

In August, as usual, the return of torrid weather made him attentive to the charms of the ladies. At such times it was always the figure of Mme. Brainne that preoccupied his fevered mind. "It occurs to me that it would be very pleasant to go for a dip with you, in secluded waters somewhere," he wrote her. "Which leads to daydreams, poetic tableaux, desires, regrets, and in the end sadness. . . . I imagine (since you are taking the waters) a great room at the baths, vaulted in Moorish style, with a pool in the center. You appear at the edge, wearing a long chemise of yellow silk—and with your bare toes you test the water. In a flash, off with the chemise, and we swim side by side—but not for long, because in the corner there's a lovely divan whereon my dear Beauty reclines—and to the plashing of the fountain . . . your Polycarp and his lady friend spend a delicious quarter of an hour."† He used cruder language in preaching abstinence to his disciple, Guy de Maupassant: "You complain that women's asses are 'monotonous.' There's a very simple remedy, and that is not to use them. . . . You *must*—do you hear me, young man?—you *must* work more than you do. . . . Too many whores! too much rowing! too much exercise! . . . You were born to write poetry: write it! 'All the rest is vanity,' starting with your amusements and your health: get that through your head. . . . What you are missing is 'principles.' Say what you will, one has to have them; it remains to find out which ones. For an artist there is only one: sacrifice everything to Art. An artist should consider life as a means, nothing more, and the first person he shouldn't give a damn about is himself."[17]

But while he professed a hearty contempt for the artist's material circumstances, he felt bad that his books were not selling well. Charpentier was not planning more printings, and the deluxe edition

---

* The French word Flaubert is playing with is *con* (literally: "cunt"), an ancient obscenity still widely used in the sense of "idiot," "jerk," "stupid bastard," etc. —Trans.

† Ever since he was a young man, Flaubert had claimed that his true patron saint was Polycarp, the martyr who had been wont to cry: "In what times, O Lord, hast thou caused me to be born!"

of *Saint Julien* which was to come out the next winter wouldn't bring the author much return. To reduce expenses, the Commanvilles were forced to give up their apartment in Paris and keep only Flaubert's little flat. "It's over," he wrote. "The 'For rent' sign is hanging on the door."[18] He was hoping that Agénor Bardoux would get Caroline an important commission and even expected the obliging minister to come up with an honorific and lucrative position for Laporte. But for himself he asked nothing. He would have felt it a terrible comedown to accept any other means of livelihood than the irregular one of writing. The grim tenacity with which he worked irritated Edmond de Goncourt, who noted in his *Journal:* "It is not the length of time, as Flaubert imagines, that makes the superiority of a work, but the quality of the passion one brings to the writing of it. What difference does the repetition of a word or an error of syntax make if something new has been created, if the concept is original, if, here and there, there is an epithet or a turn of phrase which by itself is worth a hundred pages of impeccable, commonplace prose?"[19] The two men debated this question a hundred times. In spite of Goncourt's arguments, Flaubert would passionately defend the necessity for perfect form, which alone was capable of ensuring the balance, beauty, and enduring appeal of the work. But often the discussion over their friendly dinners was of a less elevated nature: "This evening, conversation about the bad smells of feet, noses, and mouths, a conversation that greatly interested Flaubert and made him beam with delight," wrote Goncourt. "Flaubert, on condition that one leaves the center of the stage to him and resigns oneself to catching cold from all the windows he keeps throwing open, is a very pleasant companion. He has a jovial gaiety and a childlike laugh which are contagious; and everyday contact develops in him a certain bluff affectionateness which is not without charm."[20]

In October Flaubert, still tormented by his concern for faultless documentation for *Bouvard et Pécuchet,* made a field trip to Etretat on the English Channel. There he met his old friend Laure de Maupassant, Guy's mother, and was distressed to find her worn out, ill, half blind: "She cannot stand the light, she is obliged to live in shadow. The ray of a lamp makes her cry out in pain. It's horrible!

What poor pieces of machinery we are!"[21] The bad news piled up: Charpentier was delaying publication of the deluxe edition of *Saint Julien;* in spite of Agénor Bardoux's efforts, no theater or publisher wanted to take on *Le Château des coeurs;* and potential buyers for Commanville's sawmill were so few and reluctant that it would probably have to be sold at a considerable loss. "When you're at the bottom of the abyss, you have nothing more to fear," Flaubert wrote Princess Mathilde. "I have managed my affairs badly, through an excess of idealism; I am punished for it, that's all there is to the mystery."[22] And Edmond de Goncourt, worried about his friend's financial straits, noted on December 10: "Heartbreaking details about poor Flaubert. It seems that he is completely ruined, and that the people for whom, out of affection, he has ruined himself begrudge him the very cigars he smokes. His niece is supposed to have said: 'He's a strange man, my uncle, he doesn't know how to bear adversity!' "

Actually, Caroline was by no means insensitive to her uncle's distress. But she herself was on the verge of a nervous breakdown. The two of them were in the same boat and, through the fault of Ernest Commanville, it was listing heavily. "I grieve because I see those I love suffering beside me and because my work is disturbed," Flaubert wrote Princess Mathilde. "Snow covers the earth and the roofs in spite of the sun. I live like a bear in his den! Not a sound reaches me from outside, and to forget my sorrows I work without respite. The result is that I have done three chapters in the last four months, which is amazing, considering how slow I am usually."[23]

For the new year, Mme. Brainne, his "dear Beauty," sent him a box of chocolates, and he was very touched by the gesture: "You love me, I feel that you do, and I thank you for it, from the depths of my soul." But in the letter accompanying the gift she had suggested that he look for an honest job that would bring in some money. He protested at once: "I beg you, dear Beauty, don't speak to me anymore about a job of any sort! I find the very idea of it distressing and, to speak plainly, humiliating; do you understand?"[24] A few days later, since she returned to the question, he expressed himself even more strongly: "As for a job, an official post, my dear friend, never! never! never! I refused one that was offered me by my friend Bardoux. It's like the cross of an officer of the Legion of Honor, which he also wanted to give me. If worse comes to worst, it's possible to live in a country inn on fifteen hundred francs a year. That's what I'll do rather than take one centime of the government's money. . . . Besides—am I capable of filling a position of any sort? After a single day I'd be kicked out for insolence and insubordination. Misfortune doesn't make me more compliant—quite the contrary! More than ever I'm a wild idealist, resolved to die of hunger and fury rather than make the least concession."[25] But he confessed to Alphonse Daudet: "My life is a heavy weight to bear. I must be strong as an ox not to have died of it a hundred times over."[26] He was sorry that his doctor, Fortin, refused to give him opium to help him sleep. In the evening after dinner, he would call in Julie, who was wearing an old black-and-white-checked dress that had belonged to Mme. Flaubert. Looking at her, he fancied that his mother had come back to earth and was going about her little household tasks. "Then I think about the good woman until the tears rise in my throat," he confided to Caroline. "That's what I do for amusement."[27] On January 21, the sale of the sawmill having been postponed, he wrote his niece again: "We can't say anything or make any plan even for the short term until this sale has taken place! I long for it to be over! When it's done, I'll have at least a few thousand francs that will tide me over until I've finished *Bouvard et Pécuchet*. I'm increasingly irritated to be so hard up, and this constant uncertainty drives me to despair. In spite of gigantic efforts of will, I feel that I am succumbing to sorrow. My health would be good if only I could sleep. I have persistent insomnia now: whether I go to bed late or early, I can't fall asleep until five in the morning. So I have a headache all afternoon. . . . There's no point in complaining! But there's less point in living! What future do I have now? Who is there to talk to, even? I live all alone like an outcast." He would have liked to go to Paris to complete his research, but the Commanvilles were living in his apartment and it was physically impossible for three people to stay there at the same time. "Here, at least, there's nothing to annoy me; it wouldn't be that way in Paris," he concluded.

On January 25, four days after Flaubert had sent this letter, on his way to the garden gate he slipped on a patch of ice and injured his leg. His first thought was to reassure Caroline: "I'm afraid *Le Nouvelliste* might carry a short item that would alarm you: Saturday I slipped on the ice, gave myself a nasty sprain, and cracked my fibula; but the leg is not broken. Fortin (for whom I had to wait forty-eight hours) is giving me admirable care. Laporte comes to see me very often and sleeps over. Suzanne [a young servant] looks after me very well. I read and smoke in bed, which is where I shall have to stay for six weeks. . . . When I have had a proper board made so that I can write in bed, I'll send you more details."[28] The devoted Laporte watched over him, slept at Croisset sometimes, and even wrote letters to his dictation. Touched by such faithfulness, Flaubert nicknamed him the "Sister of Charity." Many messages of sympathy arrived at Croisset, and he was both pleased by them and annoyed: "Yesterday I received fifteen letters, this morning twelve, and I have to answer them all, or have them answered. What an expenditure of stamps!" But what really disgusted him was that *Le Figaro* printed an announcement of his accident: "Villemessant [the editor] may have thought he was doing me an honor and a service, and that I would be pleased. Far from it! I am hhhindignant! I don't want the public to know anything personal about me: 'Conceal thy life' (maxim of Epictetus)," he wrote Caroline.[29]

When the swelling in his leg had gone down, he hoped that in a couple of weeks he would be able to sit in an armchair. Dr. Fortin made him a "dextrin boot," a kind of cast that itched so much he couldn't sleep. And while lying awake he could think of nothing but that "damned business." "It's so far from the way in which I was brought up," he wrote his niece. "What a difference of milieu! My poor old father couldn't do a simple sum, and until his death I had never seen a stamped legal document. What contempt we had for trade and money matters! And what security, what comfort!"[30] When he did close his eyes at last, he had nightmares: "I was crawling on my stomach and Paul [the concierge] was insulting me. I was trying to preach religion to him (sic) and everyone had abandoned me. I was in despair at being powerless. It's still in my mind. The view of the river, which is splendid, is gradually calming me."[31]

Flaubert's friends were greatly distressed over his plight. A few weeks before, Taine had had a generous idea: having learned that the Academician Silvestre de Sacy, librarian at the Bibliothèque Mazarine, was dying, he had thought that with the support of Agénor Bardoux, Flaubert might succeed him in that post. This solution would have provided Flaubert with a decent salary and handsome official lodgings. But Flaubert hesitated, turned up his nose at the prospect, and when Bardoux left the ministry in January following a change of government, the opportunity seemed to be disappearing. In February Flaubert's close friends decided to take the matter up again. The conspirators—Ivan Turgenev, Edmond de Goncourt, Alphonse Daudet, and Juliette Adam—held one secret meeting after another. They alerted Jules Ferry, the new Minister of Education, and also Gambetta, the new president of the Chamber of Deputies. On February 3 Turgenev went to Croisset and solemnly exhorted Flaubert to be reasonable: "Gambetta asks whether you want M. de Sacy's post: eight thousand francs and living quarters. You must give me your answer at once."[32] Flaubert was stunned by the proposal and spent a sleepless night weighing the pros and cons. In the morning, worn out and fed up, he told Turgenev to go ahead. Turgenev left Croisset satisfied. But he had hardly returned to Paris when he sent his friend a panicked telegram: "Forget about it. Definitive refusal. Letter gives details. —Turgenev." The truth was that Gambetta had made no promises whatever. He had even indicated to Turgenev, whom he had met at Juliette Adam's, that he was hostile to the proposed appointment. *Le Figaro* of February 15 published an ironic account of this interview between the president of the chamber and the Russian novelist. When Flaubert read the article, he was in despair—especially since he had learned in the meantime that the post had been promised to his boyhood friend Frédéric Baudry, librarian at the Bibliothèque de l'Arsenal and son-in-law of the barrister Sénard, who had defended *Madame Bovary* years before. Sénard, now a deputy and member of the republican majority, was doing everything in his power to win the appointment for his daughter's husband. On February 17 he succeeded.

Flaubert, tied to his bed of pain, was choked with shame and rage. Not because he had lost out on an enviable post (he was rather relieved not to have to consider himself a civil servant), but because through their clumsy intrigues, his friends had revealed his distress and isolation to the world. "To have my penury publicized, and to be pitied by those wretches, who talk about my 'goodness of heart'! That's hard, that's really hard! I didn't deserve it! Cursed be the day when I had the fatal idea of putting my name on a book! Had it not been for my mother and Bouilhet I would never have published. How I regret it now! All I ask is to be forgotten, to be left in peace, never to be spoken of again. I'm getting to hate myself. When will I be dead so people will leave me alone? . . . My heart is bursting with rage, and I'm sinking under the weight of insults. . . . Well, I had it coming after all. I was a coward. I abandoned my principles (because I too have principles), and now I'm punished for it. . . . The dignity of my entire life is lost. . . . I consider myself disgraced. . . . Besides, I often think I shall never be able to write again. My poor brain has received so many blows that the mainspring is broken. I am dead tired, all I want is to sleep, and I can't sleep because my skin itches abominably. . . . In addition, I have a toothache, in the one upper tooth I have left. Comical! comical! but not in a way that makes me laugh."[33]

Emile Zola was aware of the blunders that had been made in this imbroglio, and he sent Flaubert a letter of apology: "All of us here have been clumsy in this business concerning you. . . . I beg you once again: don't be sad. Rather, be proud. You are the best of us all. You are our teacher and our father. We do not want you to grieve in solitude. I swear to you that today you are as great a man as you were yesterday. As for your life, I know you are somewhat harassed at this moment, but a solution will be found, you can be sure. Get better quickly, and you'll see that everything will be all right."[34] "Nobody could be a better chap than you," Flaubert replied.[35]

At last he could get up, but he hesitated to use crutches: he thought he was too heavy to entrust his weight to two pieces of wood, and preferred to move about by leaning his knee on a chair. It would be another good six weeks before he risked going downstairs. And he dared not dream of a visit to Paris. Besides, he couldn't afford the trip.

In March 1879 Ernest Commanville's sawmill was sold. But the sum realized on the operation was so small that it enabled him to pay off only a few privileged creditors. The factory and land, evaluated at a total of six hundred thousand francs, brought only two hundred thousand. And there were other creditors to satisfy, including Raoul-Duval and Laporte. "It's no joke, poor darling!" Flaubert wrote Caroline. "But it could be worse, and I prefer it this way! It's over, we know where we stand! Here we are at the bottom of the abyss! Is it the bottom? The problem now is to get out of it, that is, to be able to subsist. . . . There is one economy we can make, and that is for me to give up living in Paris entirely. I have already made the sacrifice in my heart. Sometimes it won't be much fun, but at least here I am at peace. Oh peace! rest! absolute rest!"[36] He turned his brain inside out and still couldn't make head or tail of these real estate transactions. Clearly, the other creditors had had guarantees while he did not. He had blindly trusted Commanville. His reward was to be stripped of everything. But could he have behaved any differently, when his niece's happiness was at stake?

At the end of March the second brace was removed from his leg and he took a few steps in his study. Learning that some good souls in Paris were still plotting to obtain a sinecure for him, once again he responded with anger: "I want no such alms, and I don't deserve them anyway," he wrote a friend. "It is those who have ruined me who have the duty to support me, and not the government. Stupid, yes! Self-seeking, no!"[37]

Nevertheless, under pressure of necessity, he resigned himself to accepting, if it were offered, a temporary pension, which he would pay back as soon as he came into some money again. One condition in any case: that there be no mention of it in the press. "If *Le Figaro* takes it up or friends congratulate me, I shall be in despair," he wrote Maupassant, "for after all, it's no joke to be living on public welfare."[38] And to Caroline: "I have every reason to believe that I'm going to be offered a pension, and I shall accept it, even though it humiliates me to the marrow of my bones (for which reason I want it to be kept the most absolute secret). Let's hope the press keeps out of it! I feel guilty about this pension (which I have in no way deserved, whatever people may say). The mere fact that I haven't looked after my own interests properly is no reason why the country should provide for my keep! To allay these scruples and live in peace with myself, I have thought of a way that I'll tell you about and that I'm sure you will approve of. . . . If it works out as I hope, I shall be able to await death in peace. . . . In short, I'd rather live in the most wretched, sad, and solitary conditions than to have to think about money. I'd give up everything, if only I can have peace, that is, my freedom of mind."[39]

As for the brief visits he expected to make to Paris, he assured his niece that he would manage very well in a bed set up in some corner of her flat; his doctor had examined him and judged that he could undertake the journey in May. He immediately wrote to inform Princess Mathilde that he would visit her and took advantage of the occasion to ask her to speak about Caroline's paintings to the members of the jury of the annual salon. Caroline's work was accepted and would be hung "in a place of distinction." Limping about the house, Flaubert was very worried about the health of his dog Julio, who was visibly wasting away. "They are giving him enemas of wine and bouillon and they're going to blister him again," he wrote Caroline. "The veterinary would not be surprised now if he survived. The day before yesterday, his extremities were cold and we watched him, thinking he was going to die. He's just like a person."[40] Julio recovered, but he remained very weak. Flaubert watched over him lovingly.

The dog, at the end of his strength, reminded Flaubert of himself. But he still forced himself to take notes, classify them, and read books of philosophy for his *Bouvard et Pécuchet*. And he was periodically disturbed with business papers drafted in the style of a bailiff or a notary. "Here is the receipt signed and initialed," he told Caroline. "This act of a tradesman, which I perform regularly every month without understanding what it means in practice, is increasingly exasperating to me. One doesn't remold one's character."[41] His hatreds were exacerbated by his solitude. On learning of the death of Villemessant, founder and editor of *Le Figaro*, he was exultant: "Its inventor has croaked: so much the better! That's what I really think," he declared to Princess Mathilde.[42] And to Caroline: "Don't be concerned about my coming to Paris. Society attracts me less and less, and I don't know when I shall resign myself to boarding a train. The mere idea of crossing my threshold is disagreeable to me."[43] He could walk now, but he had to wear a binding around his ankle. "Plus, I've had one of my last molars pulled. Plus, I've had lumbago. Plus, blepharitis. And now, since yesterday, I rejoice in a boil right in the middle of my face."[44]

These ailments did not prevent him from inviting his "two angels," Mme. Pasca and Mme. Lapierre, to lunch one Sunday. To his great surprise, they fell asleep after the meal, one on her divan, the other in an armchair. He took advantage of the situation to sit down at his writing table "like a calm little father confessor." Age, he thought, had made him virtuous. A few days later he went to dine at Mme. Lapierre's to celebrate Saint Polycarp's day.* His servant, Suzanne, went with him in the carriage, to look after him in case he felt ill. "I was extremely uncomfortable in the carriage," he reported to Caroline. "The motion of the wheels and the jolting hurt my foot, and the open air made me dizzy. If I had been alone, I wouldn't have gone on." To receive him gaily, Charles Lapierre had dressed up as a Bedouin, Mme. Lapierre as a Berber, and Mme. Pasca's dog had been tricked out in ribbons. A garland of flowers surrounded the illustrious visitor's place setting. Mme. Pasca read

* The saint's feast day, now celebrated on January 26, was then observed on April 27. —Trans.

aloud verses in his praise. Toasts were drunk in champagne. "My hosts were very kind, but . . . the shrimp weren't fresh," Flaubert noted. "You know that I stuff myself with them every day, since I can't eat meat anymore. Fortin calls me more than ever 'a big hysterical girl.' " And he concluded: "I'm correcting proof on *Salammbô* for Lemerre. Well, frankly, I still like it better than *L'Assommoir*."[45] He also detested *Les Soeurs Vatard* of Huysmans, "a student of Zola's," but he found Anatole France's *Chat maigre* and Edmond de Goncourt's *Frères Zemganno* charming: "I am *delighted* with your book," he wrote Goncourt. "Several times I had to hold back tears, and last night it gave me a nightmare."[46] His illness had slowed down his own work, but he reassured Charpentier: "A year from now we'll be nearing the end of the whole thing, and when you read the manuscript, you will see that I've worked fast."[47]

One night he decided to sort over his old letters and burn those that were not worthy to be passed on to posterity. Guy de Maupassant assisted in the nocturnal auto-da-fé. He sat paralyzed with respect while Flaubert glanced over a few old pages, set some aside, and threw the others into the fireplace with a profound sigh. The flames leaped up, iluminating the heavy silhouette, the deeply lined face with the bald crown and big, moist eyes. Flaubert lingered over a note from his mother. "He read me parts of it," wrote Maupassant. "I saw tears shining in his eyes, then coursing down his cheeks. . . . The clock had struck four; suddenly in the midst of the letters he found a small packet tied with a narrow ribbon, and having opened it slowly, he revealed a little silk evening slipper, inside which was a faded rose rolled up in a lady's handkerchief, all yellow in its lace border. . . . He kissed these three relics with sorrowful groans, then burned them and wiped his eyes. Then he stood up: 'That,' he said, 'was the pile of things that I hadn't wanted either to file away or to destroy; now it's done. Go to bed. Thanks.' "

On June 2, having finally made the trip to Paris, he learned that thanks to the good offices of Victor Hugo, who had recommended him to Jules Ferry, he was going to obtain a post of "honorary" librarian at the Mazarine, which would entail no duties, would not even require him to show up at the library, and would bring him three thousand francs a year. This time he was in a quandary and couldn't afford to turn up his nose at the offer. With rage and shame, he capitulated. "It's done! I've given in!" he wrote a friend. "My obstinate pride had held out until now. But alas! I am on the brink of starvation, or almost. I therefore accept the position in question, three thousand francs a year, with the promise that I shall not be made to perform any duties whatever, for you understand that if I were obliged to live in Paris I would end up even poorer than before."[48]

In Paris he had the opportunity to meet his brother Achille, whom he had not seen for a long time and who was passing through the capital. Weakened by a stroke, Achille had retired and was living for much of the year in Nice. Flaubert had no great liking for his pious, bourgeois sister-in-law, but he remained very fond of Achille. He believed Achille to be rich and, in the course of their interview, told him about his own financial straits. Achille immediately promised to help: three thousand francs a year. But he forgot his offer at once. He was no longer in full possession of his faculties. "An incurable softening of the brain," noted Flaubert. Nevertheless, on June 8, when Flaubert was lunching with Edmond de Goncourt, he told him of the improvement in his financial situation. "He added that it had really pained him to be forced to accept this money, and that, for that matter, he had already made arrangements for the state to be reimbursed one day," wrote Goncourt. "His brother, who is very rich and who is dying, is to give him an allowance of three thousand francs a year; with that and what he makes from his books, he will get back on his feet. . . . His face is more brick red, more glowing like a Jordaens painting than ever; and a lock of his long hair at the back of his head brushed up over his bald crown reminds one of his Indian forebears." Two days later Flaubert, Zola, and Goncourt were gathered for an intimate dinner at the Charpentiers'. During the meal Flaubert questioned his host about the deluxe edition of *Saint Julien l'Hospitalier,* for which he wanted no other illustration than a reproduction of the stained-glass window in the cathedral of Rouen. "But," Charpentier protested, "with only your window, the publication has no chance of success! You'll sell twenty copies. . . . Anyway, why are you being so stubborn about something that you yourself admit is absurd?" With a theatrical gesture, Flaubert replied: "Just to throw the bourgeois off balance!"

He took advantage of his stay in Paris to go every afternoon to the Bibliothèque Nationale, where he took notes on mountains of books. "Work is the only thing that still amuses me," he wrote Caroline. He even bristled when people were solicitous about him. If they made so bold as to express sympathy over his broken leg, he testily cut the conversation short. "Yes, my fracture is getting to be a crashing bore," he wrote Mme. Roger des Genettes. "It's like *Bovary*, which I can't stand to hear about anymore; its very name is exasperating to me. As if I had never written anything else! . . . Literature is becoming increasingly difficult. I must have been mad to undertake a book like this one."[49]

In spite of this admission of discouragement, he was already thinking about another book. A book so brilliant and so erudite that it would eclipse all the preceding ones. "Do you know what I'm obsessed with now?" he wrote Caroline. "A longing to write the battle of Thermopylae. It's taken hold of me again."[50] In the midst of this new plan, a disappointment: Laporte, "the good Valère," the "Sister of Charity," had just been appointed divisional factory inspector in Nevers. His departure from Grand-Couronne would deprive Flaubert of a devoted friend who from time to time enlivened the solitude of Croisset. No matter: he had grown accustomed to watching all the people who were dear to him disappear from sight. Deaths and departures—he was doomed to be perpetually alone.

As soon as he had settled back into his house on the banks of the Seine, he began badgering Charpentier to hurry up a new edition of *L'Education sentimentale*, the rights to which, according to Flaubert's contract with Michel Lévy, were to revert to him on August 10 of that year. "I need to have the aforementioned book come out as soon as possible," he wrote Mme. Charpentier. "This is very serious. The novel was strangled at birth by Troppmann and Pierre

Bonaparte.★ It would be simple justice to rehabilitate it. It didn't deserve to be a flop."[51]

Thus, in spite of his fatigue and his disgust for the games played in the literary world, he was increasingly absorbed in plans for publishing, correcting proofs, writing. Whatever he did or said, he could not escape from the inferno of paper and ink which he had entered in childhood and whose agonies and joys had become, in the end, his only reasons for living.

★ An allusion to two famous murder trials that riveted the attention of the public shortly after the book was published at the end of 1869.

Chapter 22

THE UNFINISHED
MANUSCRIPT

 In Croisset, Flaubert was suffering from a summer without sun, which was not good "for vegetables, pears, or people." But the bad weather, which he pretended to deplore, inspired him to stay home and work with renewed energy. "I've pushed all the books aside and I'm writing," he informed Mme. Roger des Genettes on July 15, 1879, "that is, I do nothing but splash about in the ink. I am now in the hardest (and maybe the most elevated) part of my infernal book—the part about metaphysics. To take the theory of innate ideas and make people laugh over it! Do you see the task ahead of me?" He had even less time to dream because he also had to correct the proofs for a new edition of *Salammbô* to be brought out by Lemerre, and for *L'Education sentimentale*, which was being reprinted by Charpentier. Lemerre also intended to publish the complete poems of Louis Bouilhet.

The author was on such friendly terms with his publisher that at the end of August, Charpentier came to visit Flaubert in Croisset along with his wife and children. Flaubert received them with joy and bounty and immediately afterward rushed off to Paris, with the manuscript of *Bouvard et Pécuchet* in his suitcase. On September 3 he spent the afternoon rereading "in the silence of his study" the last three chapters he had written. He was pleasantly surprised: "It's very good, very firm, very strong, and not boring in the least. That's my opinion."[1] Lifted on a wave of optimism, he authorized Camille du Locle to write the libretto for an opera based on *Salammbô* for which Ernest Reyer was to compose the music. Another piece of good news: *Le Château des coeurs,* if it could not be performed, was at least going to be published, and Caroline had been approached about illustrations for the play. On September 20 Edmond de Goncourt came to visit his old friend and found him just closing his trunk. Flaubert was preparing to leave Paris for Croisset. He was in a great state of excitement: "Yes, I still have two chapters to write," he announced in his booming voice. "The first will be finished in January, the second by the end of March or April. . . . My book will appear at the beginning of 1881. . . . Right after that I'm going to start a volume of short stories. . . . It's not a very popular genre, but I'm tormented by two or three ideas for short pieces. After that, I want to try something original. I want to take two or three Rouen families before the revolution and bring them up to our own time. . . . Then my big novel on the Second Empire. . . . But before everything else, old chap, I need to get rid of something I'm obsessed with. . . . It's my battle of Thermopylae. . . . I'll take a trip to Greece. . . . I see these Greek warriors as a troop of men dedicated to death, going to it gaily, ironically. . . . This book has to be a kind of lofty *Marseillaise* for all peoples!"[2]

So he went back to Croisset in a euphoric and energetic mood. But he was soon plunged into gloom by a serious incident that came between him and his dear friend Laporte. In 1875 Laporte had stood surety for Ernest Commanville's debts to save him from bankruptcy. That guarantee was no longer sufficient, and he was asked to renew it. But the information about Commanville given by the bankers Laporte talked to was deplorable. According to them, Commanville continued to live on a grand scale with no concern for the future. Furthermore, Laporte had financial worries of his own and was in no position to act as guarantor for someone else. Lastly, he was a civil servant (a factory inspector) and a county councilman. He couldn't afford to risk his double position in a shady business. To the fury of the Commanvilles, he accordingly refused. Caroline, who was dominated by her husband, demanded that Flaubert break off all relations with the man who had been his best friend. She explained to her uncle that Laporte's defection was due to avarice and ingratitude. This attitude, she said, was more of an offense to Flaubert than to herself and her husband. Torn between his love for Caroline and his affection for "Valère," in the end Flaubert sided with his niece. He had complete confidence in her. How could he imagine that she and Ernest were deceiving him? "This is just what I was afraid of, my good Giant," Laporte wrote him sadly. "You are being involved in a discussion in which you should have had no part. . . . If we [your nephew and I] lay all our grievances and justifications before you, what will be the consequence? You will have to decide against one of us, and your affectionate relations with that one could be spoiled. . . . Be assured, my dear Giant, that I shall always love you with all my heart."[3] Flaubert was distraught by this letter, especially when its writer returned to Grand-Couronne for a few days. Laporte would surely try to come and see him in Croisset. "This waiting is veritable agony for me," he wrote Caroline. "What am I to say to him? I am perplexed and greatly distressed. When will I ever be at peace? When will I be left alone, once and for all? This business about Laporte fills me with such bitterness and so utterly spoils my life that I haven't the strength to enjoy a bit of good news that has come my way. Jules Ferry . . . wrote me yesterday that he was granting me an annual pension of three thousand francs, retroactive to the first of July. His letter is ultra-amiable. This free thinker has his good side. I should be pleased, no? Well, not a bit of it! For after all, it's charity he's offering me, and I feel humiliated to the marrow of my bones. When will I be able to return it, or to do without it?"[4]

In spite of his reluctance, he asked Maupassant, who was going to Paris, to call at the ministry on his behalf, pick up the money, and bring it to him in Croisset. He also asked Charpentier to send him his royalties on the new edition of *L'Education sentimentale*. Trying to understand why the book was not more of a success, he wrote Mme. Roger des Genettes: "It's too true and, esthetically speaking, *it lacks the falseness of perspective*. Because the plan was well conceived, the plan disappears. Every work of art should have a peak, a summit, make a pyramid, or else the light should strike some one point on the sphere." And still tortured by his break with

Laporte, he confided to his correspondent: "A man I considered my *intimate* friend has recently behaved toward me with the most contemptible selfishness. This betrayal has been very painful for me. Your old friend has had plenty of bitter cups to drain."[5]

On November 18 Dr. Georges Pouchet, "a charming man, so learned and so simple," came to visit Flaubert, and the two men talked about the possibility of making an expedition to Greece. "We dreamed of journeying to Thermopylae together, when I am finished with *Bouvard et Pécuchet*," Flaubert wrote Caroline. "But at that time, that is, eighteen months from now, won't this old fellow be too old?" He had come to detest all intrusions from the outside world and was even irritated by his fame, which meant that he received many letters from young writers hoping for encouragement. "Really, my reputation is a nuisance!" he declared to his niece. "This week I've had three authors send me their works. With the reading I have to do (and the scratching out), I'm at the end of my rope. My mind is turning numb from theology. What a chapter! I don't think I'll be able to finish by New Year's. Difficulties arise in every line. Since Tuesday evening I have seen no one, not a living soul."[6] As a distraction from his writing, he would count the boats that passed under his windows: "I counted twenty-three yesterday. Good-bye, poor darling. Your nanny kisses you." He shared his paternal affection now between his niece Caroline and his disciple Guy de Maupassant, whom he wanted to have indisputable success. He recommended the young writer to Juliette Adam, who had just founded *La Nouvelle Revue:* "First, I believe he has a great literary future; and then, I love him dearly because he is the nephew of the most intimate friend I ever had—whom he greatly resembles, incidentally—a friend who died almost thirty years ago, the one to whom I dedicated my *Saint Antoine*."[7] At Flaubert's urging, Maupassant sent Juliette Adam his collection of poetry, *La Vénus rustique*. She rejected it and advised the young author to follow the example of the novelist André Theuriet, a recommendation that aroused Flaubert's wrath: "That's the press for you! Theuriet cited as a model! Life is hard, and this isn't the first time I've noticed it."[8]

The December snow covered the still countryside. The world

of the living retreated into the distance. "So long as I'm working, it's all right," Flaubert reported to Caroline, "but the times when I take a rest, the intermissions between bouts of literature, are not always filled with glee. What weather! what snow! what solitude! what silence! what cold! Suzanne has made a coat for Julio out of an old pair of my trousers. He never budges from the fireside. . . . I still think very often of my ex-friend Laporte. That's a business that has been hard for me to swallow."[9] And to Princess Mathilde: "Here, it's impossible to set foot outdoors. Not a boat on the water, not a passerby on the road. It's like a totally white tomb in which I am holed up, buried. I'm taking advantage of this absolute solitude to push on with my interminable book."[10] Turgenev came to Croisset to celebrate Flaubert's fifty-eighth birthday with him and stayed for two days. They talked literature late into the night. "He has put some heart back into me for *Bouvard et Pécuchet,* which is something I sadly need, because frankly, I'm ready to drop," noted Flaubert. "My poor brain is exhausted! I must get some rest! (After all these years that I've been working without respite!) But when will that be?"[11] It was so cold that Suzanne was always on the stairs bringing up wood and coke for the fireplace. "This morning, a fog you could cut with a knife. In spite of my advanced age, I have never seen such a winter."[12]

Suddenly, between Christmas and New Year's, there was a thaw. It rained. Flaubert, shivering, compared himself to a "fossil." On December 31 he wrote his niece: "May 1880 be kind to you, my dear girl! Good health, triumphs at the Salon, success in business! . . . We are drowned in mud. It's very difficult to go to the privy because of the puddles of water and patches of ice. Just now I almost broke a leg again. Another nuisance: the poor (the bell rings all the time, which greatly disturbs me). Anyway, Suzanne turns them away with charming impassivity. . . . To cheer himself up, Monsieur looks after himself in the food department. Turgenev's caviar and my niece's butter form the basis of my lunches, and Mme. Brainne has sent me (not counting a pot of ginger) a Strasbourg pâté that is something to shout about." Presenting his best wishes for the new year to Maupassant, he hoped that his "much beloved disciple" would find a good subject for a play that would earn him a hundred thousand francs and concluded: "Wishes relating to the genital organs come only in last place, since nature provides for them by herself."[13] He wrote Mme. Charpentier to enlist her aid in persuading her husband to publish the young author's volume of poems: "I insist. The said Maupassant has a lot of talent—but a *lot!* I'm the one who's telling you so, and I think I'm a pretty good judge of horseflesh. . . . If your old man doesn't yield to all these arguments, I shall hold it against him, that's certain."[14]

On the other hand, he gave up trying to do anything for the other beginners who asked for his help: "I'm overwhelmed. My eyes are no longer good enough for my work and I don't have enough time for it either. I am obliged to tell the young men who send me what they've written that I can't pay attention to them anymore, and of course I make myself just so many enemies."[15]

He did take time, however, to read the three volumes of Tolstoy's *War and Peace*, which had been published in French by Hachette and which Turgenev had just sent him. He was profoundly impressed: "It's a first-rate novel," he wrote Mme. Roger des Genettes. And to Turgenev: "What a painter and what a psychologist! The first two volumes are *sublime*, but the third falls down badly. He repeats himself and philosophizes. You finally see the man, the author, the Russian, whereas up to that point you see only Nature and Humanity. Sometimes he reminds me of Shakespeare. I cried aloud with admiration as I read—and it's long! . . . Yes! it's strong, very strong!"[16] A few days later he had another reason for happy excitement when he read the proofs of a story by Maupassant: "*Boule de suif* [Ball-of-Fat] is a masterpiece," he announced proudly to Caroline. "I stand by the word: a masterpiece of composition, humor, and observation."[17] On the same day he wrote the author: "I consider *Boule de suif* a *masterpiece*. Yes, young man! No more, no less: it's the work of a master. It's very original in conception, well constructed from beginning to end, and written in excellent style. One can see the countryside and the characters, and the psychology is penetrating. In short, I'm delighted. . . . This little story will *endure,* you can be sure of that. . . . No, really, I'm pleased. I enjoyed it and I admire it."

To thank him for this unreserved approval, Maupassant came to spend three days in Croisset. He was followed by another distinguished admirer: Jules Lemaître, professor of rhetoric in Le Havre, who read *Madame Bovary* aloud to his students. Shortly afterward, *La Vie moderne,* an illustrated magazine edited by Émile Bergerat and published by Charpentier, printed *Le Château des coeurs,* embellished with drawings that Flaubert thought were wretched. "My poor fairy play has been brought out in a dreadful edition," he wrote Princess Mathilde. "My sentences are interrupted with childish illustrations. That will stay with me as part of my hatred for the press."[18] But Charpentier had also just published Zola's *Nana.* And this time, forgetting all literary jealousy, Flaubert was jubilant: "If I were to mention everything in it that is rare and strong, I would have to make a comment on every page," he wrote the author. "The characters are wonderfully truthful. It's full of expressions that are absolutely true to life; in the end, the death of Nana is Michelangelesque! . . . A tremendous book, my lad! Nana becomes a mythic figure without ceasing to be real. This creation is Babylonian."[19]

It was all the more to his credit that he rejoiced in Zola's success because at that very moment he was seriously worried about the future of Guy de Maupassant. The latter was threatened with prosecution before the tribunal of Etampes over his poem *"Le Mur,"* which was held to be an outrage to morality. The idea that his beloved disciple might have to appear, as he himself had done, before imbecilic judges made his blood boil. Especially since the young man had recently obtained a job with the Ministry of Education and a scandal might cost him his place. Determined to fight back, Flaubert drew up a list of influential persons whom Maupassant should visit—senators, members of the Council of State—and wrote many letters himself trying to have the affair dropped. Of all the potential protectors, Raoul-Duval, of the City Council of Rouen, proved the most understanding. He promised to intervene in high places. "Thanks to Raoul-Duval, the public prosecutor will put a stop to things and you will not lose your job," Flaubert wrote triumphantly to Maupassant.[20] Two days later he elaborated on the peril that had been averted:

> When one writes well, one has two enemies to face: first, the public, because style forces it to think, obliges it to do some work; and second, the government, because it senses a force in us and power loves not another power. Governments may change—monarch, empire, or republic—it makes no difference! The official esthetics never changes. By virtue of their position, the agents of government—administrators and magistrates—have a monopoly on taste. . . . They know how one ought to write, their rhetoric is infallible, and they possess the means to convince you. . . . While your lawyer is signaling to you to restrain yourself (a single word could mean your ruin), you will vaguely sense the presence behind you of the whole police force, the whole army, the whole public power pressing on your brain with an incalculable weight. Then there will rise in your heart a hatred that you didn't know you felt, accompanied by plans for vengeance, immediately abandoned out of pride. But once again, that can't happen. You will not be prosecuted. You will not be convicted.[21]

And indeed, the legal proceedings were quickly dropped.

But Flaubert's indignation was soon aroused again by another event. Maxime Du Camp had just been elected to the Académie Française, to fill the seat of Saint-René Taillandier. "Du Camp's election to the Académie has plunged me into endless musings and increases my disgust for the capital!" Flaubert wrote Caroline. "It only strengthens my principles. Labiche and Du Camp, what authors!* But after all, they are worth more than many of their colleagues. And I repeat to myself this maxim of my own invention: 'Honors dishonor, titles degrade, official posts numb the mind.' Commentary: impossible to carry pride any further."[22] And to Max-

---

* Eugène Labiche was the prolific author of comedies and farces, some of which are still successfully revived. —Trans.

ime Du Camp, who wrote to inform him of his election, he replied: "Why would you think I'd be 'irritated'? Since it gives you pleasure, it gives me pleasure too. But I am surprised, astonished, stupefied, and keep asking myself: 'Why? To what end?' Do you remember a skit that you, Bouilhet, and I once acted out in Croisset? We officially welcomed each other into the Académie Française! . . . Which inspires me with curious reflections."[23]

On March 8 he learned with relief that Ernest Commanville had at last succeeded in finding a business venture that he thought would be profitable. He was starting up a sawmill again and leaving for Odessa in search of timber. "How pleased I am, or rather happy!" Flaubert wrote his niece. "I wish I were in Paris to rejoice with you. So it's over. . . . In the beginning things may not be magnificent. But there will, after all, be a flow of metal that will get us out of our present straits. And the future is bright. Hosanna!"[24] He was already reorganizing their joint occupancy of the Paris flat. The last time he had gone there, he had found the place cluttered with Caroline's clothes and furniture. It had to be set to rights. He posed conditions: "I ask to be liberated from my enemy, the *piano*, and from another enemy, which hits me on the forehead—the *stupid hanging lamp* in the dining room. It is very inconvenient when one has something to do at the table. . . . Free me also of *all the rest*— it will be simpler!—the sewing machine, the plaster casts, your *beautiful* glass-front bookcase, your chest. . . . Store this superfluous furniture at Bedel's until your next move. But arrange things so I'll feel a bit at home and have some elbow room."[25]

For some time now he had had a great plan in mind: to bring together in Croisset, on Easter Sunday, Zola, Goncourt, Daudet, Charpentier, Jules Lemaître, and Maupassant for "a little rustic feast." He offered them four beds and the promise of a few hours of delightful camaraderie. They all accepted. The only one missing would be the gentle giant Turgenev, who had returned to his remote and politically dangerous Russia. In preparation for the festivities, Suzanne "scrubbed and rescrubbed mightily." "She has never worked harder," Flaubert wrote Caroline. He himself, he said, was attacking his manuscript again: "What a book! I've run out of turns of phrase, words, and effects. Only the idea of coming to the end of the book sustains me, but there are days when I weep with exhaustion; then I pull myself together, and three minutes later I collapse again like a worn-out old horse."[26]

On Easter Sunday, March 28, 1880, Goncourt, Zola, Daudet, and Charpentier got off the train at the Rouen station. Maupassant, who had preceded them, was waiting on the platform to drive them to Croisset. "Flaubert welcomed us wearing a broad-brimmed hat like an Italian bandit's and a short jacket, with his big behind in pleated trousers and his kind, affectionate face," wrote Goncourt. "It is really very beautiful, his place—I hadn't remembered it too well. The enormously wide Seine, with the masts of invisible ships passing by as though against a backdrop in a theater; the splendid tall trees, their shapes tormented by the sea winds; the park with its espaliers, the long terrace-walk facing full south, a walk suitable for philosophical meditations: these all make it a fit dwelling for a man of letters—for Flaubert. . . . The dinner was excellent. There was a turbot in cream sauce that was a marvel. We drank many wines of all kinds and spent the whole evening telling broad stories which made Flaubert burst into laughter that bubbled over like a child's. He refused to read aloud from his novel, saying he was exhausted, done in. And we retired to chilly bedrooms peopled with family busts."[27] The next morning the guests rose late, spent the morning chatting lazily, had lunch, and departed. Solitude closed in again on Flaubert.

On April 18 he received a copy of *Les Soirées de Médan* [Evenings in Médan], a collection of short stories, with an affectionate inscription from the authors, Zola, Céard, Huysmans, Hennique, Alexis, and Maupassant. The volume contained, among others, Zola's *L'Attaque du moulin* [The Attack on the Mill] and Maupassant's *Boule de suif*. When he had read all the stories, Flaubert decreed: "*Boule de suif* dwarfs the rest of the volume. The title of the book is stupid."[28]* His dear Guy, whom he now addressed with an af-

---

* It was a reference to Zola's house in Médan, between Paris and Rouen, which was a regular gathering place for the young writers in question. —Trans.

fectionate "*tu*," had also sent him his volume of poems. The work was dedicated "To Gustave Flaubert, the illustrious and fatherly friend whom I love with all my heart, the faultless master whom I admire above all others." Flaubert, much moved, answered the author: "My young man, you are right to love me, for this old man cherishes you. . . . Your dedication stirred up in me a whole world of memories: your uncle Alfred, your grandmother, your mother; and for a while this old fellow's heart was full, and there were tears in his eyes."[29] He was not far from believing that Guy de Maupassant was the incarnation of the son he had always refused to have.

Other friends tried to show him their affection as well. As they had done in preceding years, on April 27 the Lapierres organized a comic celebration in honor of the writer and his mystical protector, Saint Polycarp. "The Lapierres outdid themselves!" Flaubert reported to Caroline. "I received nearly *thirty* letters sent from different parts of the world, and three telegrams during dinner. The Archbishop of Rouen, several Italian cardinals, some cesspool cleaners, the floor-waxers' guild, the proprietor of a shop selling religious articles, and so on, all sent me their greetings. As presents I was given a pair of silk socks, a silk neckerchief, three bouquets, a wreath, a portrait (Spanish) of Saint Polycarp, a tooth (relic of the saint); and a box of flowers is on its way from Nice! . . . I almost forgot a menu composed of dishes all named for my books. Really, I was touched by all the trouble they had taken to give me a good time. I suspect my disciple of having had a large hand in all these amiable pranks."[30]

After the merriment of Saint Polycarp's day, he had trouble getting back to work on *Bouvard et Pécuchet*. "When will the book be finished?" he wrote in the same letter. "If it is to appear next winter, I haven't a minute to lose between now and then. But there are times when I feel as if I were liquefying like an old Camembert, I'm so tired." He was all the more worried about what would happen to the novel because he had lost confidence in his publisher. In his magazine *La Vie moderne*, Charpentier had dared to cut short a scene of the unfortunate *Château des coeurs* to insert an article on sports. Flaubert was choking with rage. "I regard this publication as a dirty trick you pulled on me," he wrote Charpentier. "You deceived me, that's all. . . . I can't get over it. Of all the insults I have endured over *Le Château des coeurs*, this is the worst. The others rejected my manuscript; they didn't shit on it."[31] Money worries adding to his wrath, he wrote Maupassant: "If the house of Charpentier does not immediately pay me what it owes me and fork over a large sum for the fairy play, *Bouvard et Pécuchet* will go somewhere else." And he observed with a pang: "Eight printings of the *Soirées de Médan? Trois Contes* had four. I'm going to be jealous."[32] Which didn't prevent him from writing Théodore de Banville: "Guy de Maupassant doesn't dare ask you for a little trumpet flourish in *Le National* for his volume of poems."

Actually, the success of his "disciple" was more important to him than his own. He had gone beyond the stage of literary ambitions. When he analyzed himself, he was obliged to observe that he was a strange animal, bristling with contradictions. His loathing for the bourgeois was all the stronger because he felt himself to be bourgeois to the bone, with his love of order, comfort, and hierarchy. He condemned all governments but couldn't stand the excesses of the rabble when they dared to defy them. Curled up in his downy nest in Croisset, he dreamed of journeys to distant lands and had made a few that bore witness to his courage and endurance. The sworn enemy of priests, he was attracted by religious problems. Obsessed with feminine charm, he refused to become attached to any woman. A revolutionary in art, he was conservative in daily life. Hungering for friendship, he lived most of the time apart from his fellow men. And these perpetual conflicts made him a profoundly unhappy man. When he looked back over his past—which he did more than ever now—he could see only work, bereavements, and solitude. In his eagerness to write he had forgotten to live: hadn't that been a mistake? But no, the love of art excused everything, justified everything. A life sacrificed to the passion for literature could not have been lived in vain. He had not wasted his opportunities, since from earliest youth he had marched straight toward the goal he had set himself.

The Unfinished Manuscript

For a moment he was sunk in doubt and despondency; then he shook off his somber thoughts. Paris was waiting for him. Suddenly, he was impatient to go there. He would stay in the flat in the Faubourg Saint-Honoré and finish *Bouvard et Pécuchet*. He looked forward with joy to the reunions with his friends, with dear Guy, with Caroline. She had recently become infatuated with a priest, Father Didon, and was carrying on an edifying correspondence with him. Flaubert recognized that the Dominican clergyman, who was also Mme. Roger des Genettes's spiritual adviser, was lacking neither in erudition nor in high moral standards. Religion gave Caroline the strength to bear her reverses. But without criticizing her openly, her uncle regretted that she was unable to draw the necessary fortitude from the lofty practice of skepticism. He was also worried about his niece's disappointments in her career as a painter. He meant to talk to her about all that, in Paris.

On Saturday, May 8, 1880, his trunks were packed. He planned to leave the next day. Around half past ten in the morning, following a very hot bath, he suddenly felt unwell. A golden yellow cloud that was very familiar to him obscured his sight, suffused his brain. The blood suddenly rushed to his face. Alarmed, he called to his maid, and as she was slow in coming, he shouted to her from the window to go fetch Dr. Fortin. When she arrived, he added: "I think I'm going to have a kind of fainting fit; it's a good thing it's happening today—it would have been a great nuisance tomorrow, on the train." Then he opened a bottle of eau de Cologne and rubbed some on his temples. But his legs gave way under him. Despite the tumult that filled his head, he tried to speak. Incoherent words escaped his lips: "Rouen . . . we're not far from Rouen . . . Eylau, go . . . look on Avenue . . . I know it . . ." In a letter from Caroline that he had received that morning, she had informed him that Victor Hugo was probably going to move to the Avenue d'Eylau. But perhaps he was trying to summon Dr. Hellot of Rouen? A few moments later he lost consciousness. Dr. Fortin of Croisset being out, they ran to get Dr. Tourneux in Rouen. By the time he arrived, it was noon. Flaubert lay motionless on the couch. His heart had stopped beating.

The doctor hesitated between two hypotheses: cerebral hemorrhage or an apopleptic attack. Maupassant, who was informed at once, arrived in Croisset shortly after the event. "I saw in the failing light, stretched out on a wide divan, a great body with a swollen neck and red throat, as terrifying as a colossus who had been struck down," he wrote. A sculptor took a mold of the dead man's face. "The eyelashes remained caught in the plaster," Maupassant also noted. "I shall never forget that pale mask that retained, over the closed eyes, the long hairs which until then had flickered over his gaze." It was Maupassant who laid out the corpse, sprinkling it with eau de Cologne, dressing it in a shirt, shorts, and white silk socks. Kid gloves, peg-top trousers, a waistcoat, jacket, and tie completed the costume. Flaubert was ready to receive his friends.

They were all shattered by the news. "For some time I was in such a state of agitation that I did not know what I was doing or in what city I was driving," wrote Edmond de Goncourt. "I felt that a bond, sometimes loosened but always inextricably knotted, secretly attached us to one another. And today I recall with a certain emotion the tear trembling at the end of one of his eyelashes when he embraced me to say good-bye, on his doorstep, six weeks ago."[33] When Laporte came to pay his respects to the dead man, Maupassant, on strict instructions from the Commanvilles, forbade him to enter the room where the body lay. Caroline was not one to forget an injury. She could not forgive the visitor for having refused to stand surety for her husband's debts. Bustling about with dry eyes, she overrode the wishes of the deceased and decided that it would be a religious funeral. Goncourt arrived and not long after had a conversation with Georges Pouchet on one of the garden walks. "He didn't die of a stroke," Pouchet said to him. "He died of an epileptic attack. . . . In his youth, you know, he had had such attacks. . . . His journey to the Orient had cured him, so to speak. . . . He didn't have any more for sixteen years. But the worry over his niece's affairs brought them on again. . . . And on Saturday he died from an attack of congestive epilepsy. . . . Yes, with all the symptoms, foam at the mouth. . . . Listen, his niece wanted them to make a cast of his hand, but they weren't able to, it was still so tightly clenched. . . ."³⁴*

Early in the afternoon of May 11 the funeral procession got under way. The mourners were led by Ernest Commanville and Guy de Maupassant. A little dusty road led up a hill to the church of Canteleu, which had served as the model for the one where Mme. Bovary had gone to make confession to Father Bournisien. On the way, Flaubert's friends took turns holding the silver tassels of the coffin. Neither Hugo, nor Taine, nor Renan, nor Dumas *fils*, nor even Maxime Du Camp had bothered to come. But Zola, Daudet, Goncourt, and the young poet José-Maria de Heredia were there. Also present were a representative of the prefect, some journalists, the mayor of Rouen, a few city councilmen, some pharmacy students, and, to do the honors, a detachment from the second regiment of the line. From time to time a drumroll startled the countryside drowsing in the bright sunshine.

After the religious service, they took the road to the cemetery. In the crowd winding along behind the coffin, Edmond de Goncourt was indignant to hear plans developing for a little celebration to follow—there was talk of duckling *à l'orange* and brill *à la normande* and even mention of a brothel. The procession reached the cemetery, "full of the scent of hawthorn and overlooking the city that lay shrouded in violet shadow." Flaubert was to be interred beside the tombs of Dr. Flaubert, Mme. Flaubert, Caroline Hamard, and various other members of his family. Consternation, as the gravediggers had miscalculated: the giant's coffin was too long for the hole they had dug. They handled the box clumsily and it got stuck on a slant, head down. They could neither raise nor lower it—the same grotesque, macabre misadventure as had occurred at the burial of Flaubert's sister thirty-four years before. The ropes slipped on the sides of the coffin, the gravediggers strained and swore over their task, Caroline wrung her hands and groaned, Zola cried: "Enough, enough!" They left it at that. They would do the necessary later, after the family had gone. A priest sprinkled holy water on the bier.

* In fact, according to the most recent medical studies, Flaubert's death was caused not by an epileptic attack but probably by a cerebral hemorrhage.

No speeches. Flaubert would not have wanted any. A few embraces of mutual condolence, then a general rout. "The whole thirsty crowd made off down the hill toward the city, with eager, merry faces," wrote Goncourt. "Daudet, Zola, and I, refusing to join in the carousing to take place that evening, left to go back to Paris and came home talking reverently about the dead man."[35]

Three days later Goncourt completed his impressions, adding a severe judgment: "The nephew-in-law who ruined Flaubert is not just a dishonest businessman, but a crook. . . . As for the niece, Flaubert's *little darling*, Maupassant says that he cannot make up his mind about her. She has been, is, and will go on being an unwitting tool in the hands of her scoundrel of a husband, who has the power over her that rogues always have over decent women. Well, this is what happened after Flaubert's death. Commanville talked all the time about the money to be made from the works of the deceased and kept making such peculiar references to the amorous correspondence our poor friend had received as to suggest that he was capable of blackmailing the surviving ladies." The evening of the funeral, Ernest Commanville dined heartily, cutting himself seven slices of ham, and after the meal took Maupassant into the little summerhouse in the garden to justify himself in the young writer's eyes and win his sympathy. Caroline, meanwhile, tried to charm José-Maria de Heredia with her sorrowful looks. "The woman took off her glove and draped her hand over the back of the bench so close to Heredia's mouth that it seemed to be soliciting a kiss," wrote Goncourt. He interpreted this flirtation, on the evening of a funeral, as "a sort of playacting in which the wife was engaging at her husband's behest in order to gain ascendancy over an honest young soul who might be induced, by the exciting prospect of possession, to take a hand in swindling the other heirs." And he concluded: "Ah, my poor Flaubert! Around your corpse there are machinations and human documents out of which you could have made a fine novel of provincial life!"[36]

A few months after Flaubert's death, Caroline turned over to Juliette Adam the unfinished manuscript of *Bouvard et Pécuchet* to be published in *La Nouvelle Revue*. Lemerre brought the text out in book form in the spring of 1881. When the dead man's friends read it, they were disoriented at first but hailed it as the apotheosis of the master. For Maupassant it was an "extraordinary critique of all scientific systems, set in opposition to each other, destroying each other by the contradictions between facts, the contradictions between undisputed, recognized laws. It is the story of the weakness of human intelligence, of the eternal, universal stupidity." The novel was to be accompanied by a "survey of stupid notions," a kind of "dictionary of accepted ideas" which would have justified the entire enterprise. Flaubert's intention had been to ridicule the whole body of ideas on which his contemporaries had been nourished and which ruled their lives. Thus, the story of these two self-taught men in search of truth was a book that fell into no known category. By the encyclopedic range of its subject, the constant mockery of its commentary, and the seriousness of the questions it posed, it was related to the imperishable *Don Quixote*. In these pages of caricature there was so much knowledge, so much negation, so much derisive laughter, and so much sadness that they became a trap for successive commentators. Some denigrated the book, others praised it to the skies. But the author had been used to that. Over his grave the war continued with the same fierceness and the same fervor. But while his work grew in stature after his death, the material traces of his stay on earth were effaced. Gentle Caroline, steeped in piety, sold the Croisset property for one hundred and eighty thousand francs. The house would be demolished, except for the summerhouse at the entrance, and replaced by a factory. In this sacred place there would stand successively a distillery for grain alcohol, a chemical works, a paper mill. . . .

In the same year the house was sold, 1881, Maxime Du Camp published his *Souvenirs littéraires* in *La Revue des deux mondes*. The pages dealing with the friend of his youth revealed that Flaubert had epilepsy and that Du Camp regarded him with a condescension tinged with jealousy. Caroline expressed shock. Henceforth she considered herself charged with a mission: to defend the memory of her uncle. His fame reflected upon her. Puffed up with importance, she undertook the publication of the complete works of Flaubert.

First she published the letters to George Sand and fragments of *Par les champs et par les grèves*. Then she attacked the correspondence as a whole. But Father Didon, her spiritual director, felt the letters were too intimate and strongly advised her to expurgate them. "You are responsible before God and before men for the moral consequences," he told her in 1888. Two years later she lost her husband and, as a widow, devoted herself with even greater ardor to her role as champion of Flaubert's reputation.

On November 23, 1890, a monument to Flaubert, by Henri Chapu, was unveiled in Rouen in the garden of the museum. Edmond de Goncourt attended the ceremony, along with Zola and Maupassant. It was raining; the band was blasting away with fairground music; all the local officials had turned out. At last, in a strong voice but with his legs trembling with emotion, Goncourt began to speak: "After our great Balzac, the father and teacher of us all, Flaubert was the inventor of a reality perhaps as intense as that of his precursor and undeniably more artistic, a reality that seemed to have been obtained by a perfect objectivity, a reality that might be defined as a picture painted strictly from life and rendered by the prose of a poet. . . . Now that he is dead, my poor great Flaubert, he is being granted as much genius as his shade could wish. But do people today know that during his lifetime the critics were somewhat reluctant to acknowledge that he even had talent? . . . What was the reward of this life filled with masterpieces? Negation, insults, mental crucifixion. . . . Well, under these attacks Flaubert remained generous, without bitterness toward more fortunate men of letters, never losing his hearty, affectionate, childlike laugh." As he pronounced these words of respect and affection, the speaker felt himself carried back ten years in the past. Had not he himself often been unjust toward Flaubert? As he came to the end of his address, he felt his legs giving way under him and stiffened himself so as not to fall. The rain redoubled in force. An icy wind blew over their heads. In the squall, Chapu's monument struck him as "a pretty bas-relief in sugar, in which Truth looks as if she were relieving herself in a well."[37] That evening the journalists and writers dined at a local restaurant. On the menu was the inevitable "Rouen duck." The conversation was gay and sprightly. Flaubert was forgotten amid the latest Paris gossip. At twenty minutes to nine, having eaten, drunk, and laughed their fill, the little band caught the express train back to the capital.

In the course of the few years that had preceded the inauguration of the monument, some important witnesses to Flaubert's life had disappeared. His brother Achille had died insane in January 1882; the servant Julie in 1883; Louise Pradier in 1885; Elisa Schlésinger in 1888, in an advanced state of mental derangement. In February 1890 Reyer's opera *Salammbô* was created in Brussels; in 1892 it was revived at the Paris Opera. Another two years and the name of Gustave Flaubert was given to a street in the capital, a new street on the site of the former Ternes gas works. Guy de Maupassant sank into madness and breathed his last in 1893. The following year it was Maxime Du Camp's turn to leave the literary scene. And the hecatomb continued: Edmond de Goncourt in 1896. Alphonse Daudet in 1897. . . .

Only Caroline seemed indestructible. In 1900 she married again, and in the glow of conjugal happiness with Dr. Franklin Grout softened her policy with regard to posthumous publication. Forgetting, to an extent, the instructions of Father Didon, she allowed the publication of Flaubert's early works, the first *Education sentimentale*, the first *Tentation de Saint Antoine*, the *Notes de voyage*, and finally the *Correspondance*, expanded with new letters. In 1926 she even gave permission for the letters to Louise Colet to be made public. France was amazed to discover a Flaubert who was no longer severe and tightly controlled as in his novels but relaxed, ribald, irascible, generous. Reading the letters of this man who had always maintained that an author should be absent from his works, people could hear and see him. The public was suddenly confronted not with a literary creation but with the living writer himself. Long admired for the books over which he had labored so patiently, he was now admired for angry pages he had scribbled in haste, without any thought of publication. Some critics even went so far as to place the letter writer above the novelist.

Living in retirement in Antibes, in the Villa Tanit, Caroline followed the extraordinary rise of her uncle's reputation with satisfaction, deference, and profit. Conscious of having fulfilled her duty, she was serene. She died on February 2, 1931, at the age of eighty-five. After her death, the manuscripts in her possession were divided among the libraries of Rouen, the Institut de France, and the city of Paris. The rest of the papers she had left would later be dispersed at auctions.

Meanwhile, the work of the analysts was beginning. The keenest minds of modern criticism have studied the illustrious writer. The few books he wrote have inspired an avalanche of sententious commentary. Both the man and his work have been examined in the light of assorted philosophical, political, neurological, and psychoanalytic theories. No doubt he would have been pained by this relentless effort to understand him, he who tried to preserve his privacy by living aloof from his fellow citizens and excluding from his writings all personal opinion. But the price of genius is, after one's death, to reveal to the curious crowd the secrets one has jealously guarded throughout one's life. And the good fortune of genius is that in most cases, those who seek to track down the truth get nothing for their pains and that, despite the most learned explications, the mystery of the artist remains inviolate.

NOTES

1. The Cocoon

1. Letter to Louise Colet of July 7, 1853.
2. Letter of February 4, 1832.
3. Letter of early September 1833.

2. First Writings, First Stirrings of Love

1. *Mémoires d'un fou.*
2. *Novembre.* [The quotations from this work are taken from Frank Jellinek's translation, *November* (London: Michael Joseph, 1966). —Trans.]
3. Letter of September 11, 1833.
4. Letter of August 29, 1834.
5. *Mémoires d'un fou.*
6. Letter of 1837.
7. *Mémoires d'un fou.*
8. Ibid.
9. Ibid.

3. Studies and Daydreams

1. Letter of April 15, 1845.
2. Letter of March 24, 1837.
3. *Mémoires d'un fou.*
4. Ibid.
5. Letter of October 11, 1838.

6. Letter of September 13, 1838.
7. Letter of December 26, 1838.
8. Letter of November 19, 1839.
9. *Souvenirs, notes et pensées intimes.* [The quotations from this work are taken from Francis Steegmuller's translation, *Intimate Notebook 1840–1841* (Garden City, New York: Doubleday & Company, 1967). —Trans.]

4. Eulalie Foucaud

1. *Souvenirs, notes et pensées intimes.*
2. Letter to his sister Caroline of September 29, 1840.
3. *Novembre.*
4. Letter of March 28, 1841.
5. Letter of November 14, 1840.
6. Letter to Ernest Chevalier of November 30, 1841.
7. Letter of January 10, 1841.
8. Letter of December 31, 1841.
9. Letter of January 22, 1842.
10. Letter of January 8, 1842.

5. Elisa

1. Letter of February 24, 1842.
2. Letter of March 15, 1842.
3. Letter of June 25, 1842.

4. Letter of July 3, 1842.
5. Letter of July 9, 1842.
6. Letter of September 6, 1842.
7. Letter of November 16, 1842.
8. Letter to Caroline of December 10, 1842.
9. Letter to Caroline of December 21, 1842.
10. Letter to Louise Colet of December 2, 1846.
11. Letter to Ernest Chevalier of February 10, 1843.
12. Letter of March 15, 1842.
13. Letters of July–August 1842 and March 18, 1843.
14. Letter of December 3, 1843.
15. Letter to Mlle. Amélie Bosquet of November or December 1859.
16. Letter of the end of April 1843.
17. Letter of May 11, 1843.
18. Letter of July 17, 1843.
19. Letter of September 2, 1843.
20. Letter of December 20, 1843.

6. The Break

1. Letter of February 1, 1844.
2. Letter to Ernest Chevalier of February 9, 1844.
3. Letter of April 26, 1884.
4. Letter of June 7, 1844.
5. Letter to Alfred Le Poittevin of May 13, 1845.
6. Letter to Louise Colet of August 31, 1846.
7. Letter of April 1846.
8. Letter of July 1844.
9. Letter of April 2, 1845.
10. Letter of July 1845.
11. Letter of October 31, 1844.
12. Reported by Maxime Du Camp, who was present at the scene, in his *Souvenirs littéraires*.
13. Letter to Emmanuel Vasse-de-Saint-Ouen of January 1845.

7. Bereavements

1. Letter of April 2, 1845.
2. Ibid.
3. Ibid.
4. Letter to Alfred Le Poittevin of April 15, 1845.
5. Ibid.
6. *Notes de voyage*.
7. Letter of May 13, 1845.
8. Letter to Alfred Le Poittevin of May 26, 1845.
9. Ibid.
10. *Notes de voyage*.
11. Letter of July 10, 1845.
12. Letter of August 13, 1845.
13. Letter of June 17, 1845.
14. Letter of July 1845.
15. Letter of September 16, 1845.
16. Letter of January 1846.
17. Letter of the end of January 1846.
18. Letter of March 15, 1846.
19. Letter to Maxime Du Camp of March 25, 1846.
20. Letter to Maxime Du Camp of April 7, 1846.
21. Ibid.
22. Letter of May 31, 1846.
23. Letter of June 4, 1846.
24. Letter to Emmanuel Vasse-de-Saint-Ouen of June 4, 1846.

8. Louise Colet

1. Letter of August 4, 1846.
2. Letter of August 6, 1846.
3. Letter of August 6 or 7, 1846.
4. Ibid.
5. Letter of September 30, 1846.
6. Letter of September 2, 1846.
7. Letter of August 23, 1846.
8. Letter of August 24, 1846.
9. Letter of August 30, 1846.
10. Letter of September 4–5, 1846.
11. Letter of September 5, 1846.
12. Letter of September 6, 1846.
13. Letter of September 10, 1846.

14. Letter of September 30, 1846.
15. Letter of October 4, 1846.
16. Letter of September 15–16, 1846.
17. Letter of November 7, 1847.
18. Letter of August 8–9, 1846.
19. Ibid.
20. Letter of December 20, 1846.
21. Letter of December 16, 1846.
22. Letter of the end of December 1846.
23. Letter of March 7, 1847.
24. Letter of April 28, 1847.
25. Letter of April 13, 1847.
26. Letter of April 30, 1847.
27. *Par les champs et par les grèves.*

9. Travel and Travel Plans

1. *Par les champs et par les grèves.*
2. Letter of July 13, 1847.
3. Letter of July 14, 1847.
4. Letter of August 6, 1847.
5. Letter of August 16, 1847.
6. Letter to Louise Colet of September 1847.
7. Letter to Louise Colet of September 23, 1847.
8. Letter of October 1847.
9. Ibid.
10. Letter of November 14, 1847.
11. Letter of the end of December 1847.
12. Letter of March 1848.
13. Ibid.
14. Letter of April 7, 1848.
15. Letter of July 4, 1848.
16. Letter of August 25, 1848.
17. Letter of May 6, 1849.
18. Letter of May 5, 1849.
19. Letter to his uncle Parain of May 12, 1849.
20. Letter to his uncle Parain of May 18 or 25, 1849.
21. Maxime Du Camp, *Souvenirs littéraires.*

10. The Middle East

1. *Notes de voyage.*
2. Maxime Du Camp, *Souvenirs littéraires.*
3. Letter of October 30, 1849.
4. Letter of November 7–8, 1849.
5. Letter to his mother of November 17, 1849.
6. Letter of December 1, 1849.
7. Letter to his mother of December 14, 1849.
8. Ibid.
9. Letter of December 15, 1849.
10. Letter to his mother of January 5, 1850.
11. Letter of February 14, 1850.
12. *Notes de voyage.*
13. Letter to Louis Bouilhet of March 13, 1850.
14. *Notes de voyage.*
15. Letter of March 24, 1850.
16. Letter of April 15, 1850.
17. Letter of August 20, 1850.
18. Ibid.
19. Ibid.
20. Letter of November 14, 1850.
21. Letter of November 7, 1850.
22. Letter of November 14, 1850.
23. Letter of December 15, 1850.
24. Letter of December 19, 1850.
25. Ibid.
26. Letter of December 26, 1850.
27. Letter of February 9, 1851.
28. Letter to his mother of February 27, 1851.
29. Letter of April 9, 1851.
30. Letter of May 4, 1851.
31. *Notes de voyage.*
32. *Memento* of Louise Colet.
33. Letter of July 26, 1851.

11. Madame Bovary

1. Letter of September 20, 1851.
2. Letter of October 21, 1851.
3. Letter of October 23, 1851.

4. Letter of November 3, 1851.
5. Ibid.
6. Letter to his uncle Parain of January 15, 1852.
7. Ibid.
8. Ibid.
9. Letter of January 15, 1853.
10. Letter to Louise Colet of November 3, 1851.
11. Letter to Louise Colet of January 16, 1852.
12. Letter of January 31, 1852.
13. Letter of February 8, 1852.
14. Letter of April 3, 1852.
15. Letter of April 24, 1852.
16. Letter of December 31, 1851.
17. Letter of January 16, 1852.
18. Letter of March 20, 1852.
19. Letter of April 24, 1852.
20. Letter of April 3, 1852.
21. Letter of December 16, 1852.
22. Letter of June 26, 1852.
23. Letter of the beginning of July 1852.
24. Letter of July 3, 1852.
25. Letter of July 7, 1852.
26. Letter of July 22, 1852.
27. Letter of July 26, 1852.
28. Letter of September 1, 1852.
29. Letter of September 19, 1852.
30. Letter of September 25, 1852.
31. Letter to Louise Colet of November 16, 1852.
32. Letter of December 9, 1852.
33. Letter of December 11, 1852.
34. Letter to Louise Colet of December 16, 1852.
35. Letter to Louise Colet of December 27, 1852.
36. Ibid.
37. Letter to Louise Colet.
38. Letter to Louise Colet of July 2, 1853.
39. Letter of July 15, 1853.
40. Letter of July 15, 1853.
41. Letter of August 14, 1853.
42. Ibid.
43. Letter of August 24, 1853.
44. Letter to Louise Colet of August 21, 1853.
45. Letter to Louise Colet of August 26, 1853.
46. Letter of September 2, 1853.
47. Letter to Louise Colet of September 16, 1853.
48. Letter to Louise Colet of September 12, 1853.
49. Letter of October 7, 1853.
50. Letter of October 12, 1853.
51. Letter to Louise Colet of October 17, 1853.
52. Letter of October 28, 1853.
53. Letter of November 22, 1853.
54. Letter of November 25, 1853.
55. Letter of December 8, 1853.
56. Letter of December 14, 1853.
57. Letter of December 23, 1853.
58. Letter of January 13, 1854.
59. Letter of August 7, 1854.
60. Letter of January 9–10, 1854.
61. Letter of December 24, 1853.
62. Letter of February 25, 1854.
63. Letter of March 6, 1853.
64. Letter of September 30, 1855.
65. Letter of October, 1855.
66. Letter of October 10, 1855.
67. Letter of April 9, 1856.

12. *The Book, Publication, the Trial*

1. Letter to Louis Bouilhet of June 1, 1856.
2. Letter to Louis Bouilhet of June 16, 1856.
3. Letter to Louis Bouilhet of August 3, 1856.
4. Letter to Louis Bouilhet of August 24, 1856.
5. Letter to Jules Duplan of October 11, 1856.
6. Letter of October 2, 1856.

7. Letter of December 7, 1856.

8. Maxime Du Camp, *Souvenirs littéraires*.

9. Letter of December 12, 1856.

10. Letter of January 3, 1857.

11. Ibid.

12. Letter of January 4 or 5, 1857.

13. Letter of January 14, 1857.

14. Letter of January 16, 1857.

15. Letter of January 20, 1857.

16. Letter to his brother Achille of January 25, 1857.

17. Letter of January 30, 1857.

18. Letter of February 10, 1857.

19. Letter to Frédéric Baudry of February 10, 1857.

20. Letter to Maurice Schlésinger of February 11, 1857.

21. Letter of March 18, 1857.

22. Letter of March 30, 1857.

23. Letter of March 18, 1857.

24. Letter of the end of April 1857.

13. Salammbô

1. Letter of May 28, 1857.

2. Letter of June 24, 1857.

3. Letter to Louis de Cormenin of May 14, 1857.

4. Letter to Ernest Feydeau of the end of June 1857.

5. Letter to Ernest Feydeau of August 6, 1857.

6. Letter of August 14, 1857.

7. Letter of October 3, 1857.

8. Letter of October 8, 1857.

9. Letter to Jules Duplan of October 3, 1857.

10. Letter of November 17, 1857.

11. Letter to Ernest Feydeau of November 24, 1857.

12. Letter to Ernest Feydeau of the end of November 1857.

13. Goncourt, *Journal*, April 11, 1857.

14. Letter of January 23, 1858.

15. Ibid.

16. Letter of February 10, 1858.

17. Letter of April 6, 1858.

18. Letter of April 23–24, 1858.

19. Letter of May 8, 1858.

20. Flaubert, *Voyage à Carthage*.

21. Letter of June 20, 1858.

22. Letter of August 23, 1857.

23. Letter of June 20, 1858.

24. Letter of June 24, 1858.

25. Letter to Ernest Feydeau of August 28, 1858.

26. Letter to Ernest Feydeau of mid-October 1858.

27. Letter to Mlle. Leroyer de Chantepie of October 31, 1858.

28. Letter to Ernest Feydeau of December 19, 1858.

29. Letter of December 26, 1858.

30. Letter of the beginning of February 1859.

31. Goncourt, *Journal*, May 11, 1859.

32. Letter of May 1859.

33. Letter of August 7, 1859.

34. Letter of the end of September 1859.

35. Letter written during the first half of October 1859.

36. Letter of the end of October 1859.

37. Letter of November 12, 1859.

38. Letter of December 1859.

39. Two letters of March 15, 1860.

40. Letter to Louis Bouilhet of March 29, 1860.

41. Letter of April 21, 1860.

42. Letter of May 1860.

43. Letter of July 3, 1860.

44. Letter of July 1860.

45. Letter of July 4, 1860.

46. Letter of August 15, 1860.

47. Goncourt, *Journal*, November 29, 1860.

48. Letter of January 1, 1861.

49. Letter of January 15, 1861.

50. Letter of January 26, 1861.
51. Letter of January 1861.
52. Letter of the beginning of May 1861.
53. Letter written in the last two weeks of June 1861.
54. Letter of January 18, 1862.
55. Letter of January 19, 1862.
56. Letter to Alfred Baudry of February 7, 1862.
57. Goncourt, *Journal*, March 3, 1862.
58. Letter of April 24, 1862.
59. Letter of the beginning of May 1862.
60. Letter of May 19, 1862.
61. Letter of July 1862.

14. In Society

1. Letter to Jules Duplan of the beginning of June 1862.
2. Another letter to Jules Duplan from the same period.
3. Letter to Jules Duplan of June 10, 1862.
4. Letter of the beginning of July 1862.
5. Letter of July 26, 1862.
6. Letter to Mlle. Amélie Bosquet of the end of July 1862.
7. Letter of September 14, 1862.
8. Letter to Mlle. Amélie Bosquet of October 21, 1862.
9. Letter of December 22, 1862.
10. Letter of January 21, 1863.
11. Letter of January 28, 1863.
12. Letter of January 31, 1863.
13. Letter of January 31, 1963.
14. Goncourt, *Journal*, February 18, 1863.
15. Letter to Jules Duplan of the beginning of April 1863.
16. Letter to Mlle. Amélie Bosquet of the beginning of July 1863.
17. Letter to Mlle. Amélie Bosquet of October 26, 1863.

18. Goncourt, *Journal*, October 29, 1863.
19. Goncourt, *Journal*, November 2, 1863.
20. Goncourt, *Journal*, December 2, 1863.
21. Letter of December 23, 1863.
22. Letter of January 1864.
23. Goncourt, *Journal*, January 24, 1864.
24. Letter of February 29, 1864.
25. Letter of March 3, 1864.
26. Letter of April 11, 1864.
27. Letter of April 14, 1864.
28. Letter of April 19, 1864.
29. Letter of May 4, 1864.

15. A New Friend: George Sand

1. Letter to Mlle. Amélie Bosquet of July 1864.
2. Letter of October 6, 1864.
3. Letter of October 1864.
4. Letter of November 17, 1864.
5. Letter of February 5, 1865.
6. Letter of February 22, 1865.
7. Letter to Mlle. Leroyer de Chantepie of May 11, 1865.
8. Letter of May 1865.
9. Goncourt, *Journal*, May 9, 1865.
10. Letter to the Goncourts of August 12, 1865.
11. Letter of August 1865.
12. Goncourt, *Journal*, November 29, 1865.
13. Letter to the Goncourts of December 1865.
14. Letter of January 23, 1866.
15. Letter of February 1866.
16. Letter of March 12, 1866.
17. Goncourt, *Journal*, May 6, 1866.
18. Letter of May 19 or 26, 1866.
19. Letter of August 16, 1866.
20. Letter of August 20, 1866.
21. Letter of August 31, 1866.
22. Letter of the end of August 1866.

23. Letter of September 22, 1866.
24. Letter of September 29, 1866.
25. Letter to Mme. Roger des Genettes of November 12, 1866.
26. Letter of November 12–13, 1866.
27. Letter of November 27, 1866.
28. Letter of December 5, 1866.
29. Letter of December 15, 1866.
30. Ibid.
31. Letter of December 1866.
32. Letter of January 4, 1867.
33. Letter of January 23–24, 1867.
34. Goncourt, *Journal*, February 25, 1867.
35. Letter of the end of February 1867.
36. Letter of April 8, 1867.
37. Letter to George Sand of March 17, 1867.
38. Letter to June 7, 1867.
39. Ibid.
40. Letter of October 1867.
41. Letter to Jules Duplan of December 15, 1867.
42. Letter of November 1867.
43. Letter of December 18, 1867.

16. L'Education sentimentale

1. Letter of January 24, 1868.
2. Letter to Jules Duplan of March 14, 1868.
3. Letter of March 14, 1868.
4. Letter of March 1868.
5. Letter to Caroline of the end of March 1868.
6. Letter of March 19, 1868.
7. Letter of May 20, 1868.
8. Letter of July 5, 1868.
9. Goncourt, *Journal*, August 7, 1868.
10. Letter of late August or early September 1868.
11. Letter to Jules Duplan of October 1868.
12. Letter of October 27, 1868.
13. Letter of December 1868.

14. Letter of December 15, 1868.
15. Goncourt, *Journal*, December 24, 1868.
16. Goncourt, *Journal*, January 20, 1869.
17. Letter to Princess Mathilde of 1869.
18. Goncourt, *Journal*, May 12, 1869.
19. Letter of May 16, 1869.
20. Goncourt, *Journal*, May 23, 1869.
21. Letter of May 23, 1869.
22. Letter of June 9, 1869.
23. Letter to Princess Mathilde of June 1869.
24. Letter of July 1869.
25. Letter of September 8, 1869.
26. Letter of September 1869.
27. Letter of October 13, 1869.
28. Letter of October 14, 1869.
29. Letter of December 3, 1869.
30. Letter of January 3, 1870.
31. Letter of January 9, 1870.
32. Letter of January 12, 1870.
33. Letter of March 2, 1870.
34. Letter of March 15, 1870.
35. Letter to George Sand of April 29, 1870.
36. Letter of May 21–22, 1870.
37. Letter of June 28–29, 1870.
38. Letter of June 26, 1870.
39. Letter to Caroline of July 8, 1870.
40. Letter of July 20, 1870.

17. War

1. Letter of August 3, 1870.
2. Letter to George Sand of August 17, 1870.
3. Letter of August 26, 1870.
4. Letter of August 31, 1870.
5. Letter of September 10, 1870.
6. Letter to George Sand of September 28, 1870.
7. Letter of September 27, 1870.
8. Letter of October 5, 1870.

9. Letter of October 13, 1870.

10. Letter to Princess Mathilde of October 23, 1870.

11. Letter to Caroline of October 28, 1870.

12. Letter of November 27, 1870.

13. Letter of December 18, 1870.

14. Letter of January 16, 1871.

15. Letter of February 1, 1871.

16. Ibid.

17. Letter to George Sand of March 11, 1871.

18. Letter of March 4, 1871.

19. Letter of March 21, 1871.

20. Letter to Mme. Roger des Genettes of March 30, 1871.

21. Letter to George Sand of March 31, 1871.

22. Letter of April 5, 1871.

23. Letter of April 24, 1871.

24. Letter of April 30, 1871.

25. Letter of May 3, 1871.

26. Letter of May 22, 1871.

27. Letter of June 11, 1871.

28. Letter of June 14, 1871.

29. Letter of June 24, 1871.

30. Letter of July 1871.

31. Letter of July 3–4, 1871.

18. *Toward Greater Solitude*

1. Letter of September 6, 1871.

2. Letter of September 8, 1871.

3. Letter of October 7, 1871.

4. Letter of October 12, 1871.

5. Goncourt, *Journal*, October 18, 1871.

6. Letter of January 21, 1872.

7. Letter to George Sand of January 28, 1872.

8. Letter of February 26, 1872.

9. Goncourt, *Journal*, January 17, 1872.

10. Letter of early March 1872.

11. Letter of March 28, 1872.

12. Letter to Maxime Du Camp of April 6, 1872.

13. Letter of April 19, 1872.

14. Letter of April 16, 1872.

15. Letter of April 25, 1872.

16. Letter of April 29, 1872.

17. Letter of May 5, 1872.

18. Letter of June 5, 1872.

19. Letter to Mlle. Leroyer de Chantepie of June 5, 1872.

20. Letter to Mme. Roger des Genettes of May 15, 1872.

21. Letter to Caroline of June 23, 1872.

22. Letter of August 18, 1872.

23. Letter of September 1, 1872.

24. Ibid.

25. Letter of September 14, 1872.

26. Letter of September 24, 1872.

27. Letter to Caroline of September 27, 1872.

28. Letter of October 5, 1872.

29. Letter of October 5, 1872.

30. Letter of October 5, 1872.

31. Letter of October 25, 1872.

32. Letter of October 30, 1872.

33. Letter of October 28, 1872.

34. Letter of December 4, 1872.

35. Letter of January 1873.

36. Letter to Mme. Régnier of January 1873.

37. Letter of February 23, 1873.

38. Letter of April 24, 1873.

39. Letter of May 3, 1873.

40. Letter of May 18, 1873.

19. *The Illusion of the Theater*

1. Letter of May 24, 1873.

2. Letter of May 31, 1873.

3. Letter of June 18, 1873.

4. Letter of July 3, 1873.

5. Letter of July 20, 1873.

6. Letter to Mme. Roger des Genettes of August 4, 1873.

7. Letter of November 22, 1873.

8. Ibid.

9. Letter of December 2, 1873.

10. Anatole France, *La Vie littéraire,* First Series.
11. Letter to Caroline of December 15, 1873.
12. Letter of December 30, 1873.
13. Letter of February 7, 1874.
14. Letter of February 18, 1874.
15. Goncourt, *Journal,* March 12, 1874.
16. Letter of March 12, 1874.
17. Letter of March 15, 1874.
18. Letter of May 1, 1874.
19. Ibid.
20. Letter to Mme. Roger des Genettes of May 1, 1874.
21. Letter of June 3, 1874.
22. Letter of June 17, 1874.
23. Letter to Caroline of June 24, 1874.
24. Letter of July 3, 1874.
25. Letter of July 2, 1874.
26. Letter of July 14, 1874.
27. Letter of August 1874.
28. Letter of August 6, 1874.
29. Letter of September 4, 1874.
30. Letter of November 1874.
31. Letter of the end of December 1874.
32. Letter of December 1874.

20. Trois Contes

1. Letter of March 27, 1875.
2. Letter of April 1875.
3. Goncourt, *Journal,* April 25, 1875.
4. Ibid., April 18, 1875.
5. Letter of May 10, 1875.
6. Ibid.
7. Letter of July 9, 1875.
8. Ibid.
9. Letter of July 12, 1875.
10. Letter of October 11, 1875.
11. Letter of October 1875.
12. Letter of December 11, 1875.
13. Letter of December 18, 1875.

14. Letter of the end of December 1875.
15. Letter of February 6, 1876.
16. Letter of March 14, 1876.
17. Letter of March 18, 1876.
18. Letter of June 19, 1876.
19. Letter of the end of April 1876.
20. Letter of June 17, 1876.
21. Letter of June 19, 1876.
22. Letter of June 25, 1876.
23. Letter of June 13, 1876.
24. Letter of June 19, 1876.
25. Letter of July 23, 1876.
26. Letter of July 1, 1876.
27. Letter of July 23, 1876.
28. Letter of August 1876.
29. Letter of the end of July 1876.
30. Letter of August 7, 1876.
31. Letter of August 10, 1876.
32. Letter of August 17, 1876.
33. Letter of October 4, 1876.
34. Letter to Turgenev of November 1876.
35. Letter of October 19, 1876.
36. Letter of October 25, 1876.
37. Letter of September 27, 1876.
38. Letter of November 28, 1876.
39. Letter of December 9, 1876.
40. Ibid.
41. Letter of December 15, 1876.
42. Letter of December 31, 1876.
43. Letter of December 31, 1876.
44. Letter of January 17, 1877.
45. Ibid.
46. Goncourt, *Journal,* February 18, 1877.
47. Ibid., February 19, 1877.
48. Letter to Mme. Roger des Genettes of April 2, 1877.
49. Letter of May 21, 1877.

21. *Back to* Bouvard et Pécuchet

1. Letter of early June 1877.
2. Letter of June 6, 1877.
3. Letter of July 27, 1877.

4. Letter to Mme. Roger des Genettes of August 1877.

5. Letter of August 1877.

6. Letter of September 2, 1877.

7. Letter to Caroline of September 6, 1877.

8. Letter of September 11, 1877.

9. Letter of September 18, 1877.

10. Letter of September 24, 1877.

11. Letter of October 5, 1877.

12. Letter of March 1, 1878.

13. Ibid.

14. Letter to Mme. Roger des Genettes of May 27, 1878.

15. Letter to Princess Mathilde of June 13, 1878.

16. Letter to Emile Zola of August 15, 1878.

17. Letter of August 15, 1878.

18. Letter to Caroline of September 10, 1878

19. Goncourt, *Journal*, September 8, 1878.

20. Goncourt, *Journal*, September 19 and 21, 1878.

21. Letter to Princess Mathilde of October 30, 1878.

22. Letter of December 1878.

23. Letter of December 22, 1878.

24. Letter of December 30, 1878.

25. Letter of January 1879.

26. Letter of January 3, 1879.

27. Letter of January 16, 1879.

28. Letter of January 27, 1879.

29. Letter of January 30, 1879.

30. Letter of February 1879.

31. Ibid.

32. Letter to Caroline of February 22, 1879.

33. Ibid.

34. Letter of February 17, 1879.

35. Letter of February 18, 1879.

36. Letter of March 11, 1879.

37. Letter of March 1879.

38. Letter of March 12, 1879.

39. Letter of March 14, 1879.

40. Letter of April 6, 1879.

41. Letter of April 12, 1879.

42. Letter of April 16, 1879.

43. Ibid.

44. Letter to Edmond de Goncourt of April 24, 1879.

45. Letter of April 25, 1879.

46. Letter of May 1, 1879.

47. Letter of May 1879.

48. Letter of early June 1879.

49. Letter of June 13, 1879.

50. Letter of June 19, 1879.

51. Letter of June 25, 1879.

22. *The Unfinished Manuscript*

1. Letter to Caroline of September 3, 1879.

2. Goncourt, *Journal*, September 20, 1879.

3. Letter of September 30, 1879.

4. Letter of October 8, 1879.

5. Letter of October 8, 1879.

6. Letter of November 23, 1879.

7. Letter of November 25, 1879.

8. Letter to Guy de Maupassant of December 3, 1879.

9. Letter of December 6, 1879.

10. Letter of December 8, 1879.

11. Letter to Caroline of December 16, 1879.

12. Letter to Caroline of December 23, 1879.

13. Letter of January 2, 1880.

14. Letter of January 13, 1880.

15. Letter to Mme. Roger des Genettes of January 25, 1880.

16. Letter of January 21, 1880.

17. Letter of February 1, 1880.

18. Letter of February 13, 1880.

19. Letter of February 15, 1880.

20. Letter of February 17, 1880.

21. Letter of February 19, 1880.

22. Letter of February 28, 1880.

23. Letter of February 27, 1880.

24. Letter of March 8, 1880.

25. Letter of March 14, 1880.

26. Letter of March 23, 1880.

27. Goncourt, *Journal*, March 28, 1880.

28. Letter to Guy de Maupassant of the end of April 1880.

29. Letter of April 25, 1880.

30. Letter of April 28, 1880.

31. Letter of May 2, 1880.

32. Letter of May 3, 1880.

33. Goncourt, *Journal*, May 8, 1880.

34. Ibid., May 11, 1880.

35. Ibid.

36. Ibid., May 14, 1880.

37. Ibid., November 23, 1890.

BIBLIOGRAPHY

In writing this biography I have relied chiefly on Flaubert's vast correspondence and on the memoirs of his contemporaries. The reader will find below a list of some of the works I have consulted.

Albalat, Antoine. *Gustave Flaubert et ses amis*. Plon, 1927.

Bardèche, Maurice. *L'Oeuvre de Gustave Flaubert*. Les Sept Couleurs, 1974.

Barnes, Julian. *Le Perroquet de Flaubert*. Stock, 1984. [English original: *Flaubert's Parrot*. New York: Alfred A. Knopf, 1985. (Paperback by McGraw-Hill, 1985.) —Trans.]

Bertrand, Georges. *Les Jours de Flaubert*. Editions du Myrte, 1947.

Bood, Micheline, and Serge Grand. *L'Indomptable Louise Colet*. Editions Pierre Horay.

Brombert, Victor. *Flaubert*. Series "Ecrivains de toujours," Le Seuil, 1971.

Bruneau, Jean. *Les Débuts littéraires de Gustave Flaubert*. Armand Colin, 1962.

———. *Album Flaubert*. N.R.F., 1972.

Bulletin de la Société des Amis de Flaubert.

Chevalley-Sabatier, Lucie. *Gustave Flaubert et sa nièce Caroline*. La Pensée universelle.

Clébert, Jean-Paul. *Louise Colet, ou la Muse*. Presses de la Renaissance, 1986.

Commanville, Caroline. *Souvenirs intimes*.

Danger, Pierre. *Sensations et objets dans les romans de Flaubert*. Armand Colin, 1973.

Debray-Genette, R. *Flaubert*. Didier, 1970.

Digeon, Claude. *Flaubert*. Hatier, 1970.

———. *Le Dernier Visage de Flaubert*. Aubier, 1946.

Du Camp, Maxime. *Souvenirs littéraires*, 2 vols. Hachette, 1882–1883.

Dumesnil, René. *Gustave Flaubert, l'homme et son oeuvre*. Desclée De Brouwer, 1932.

Bibliography

_____. *Flaubert et L'Education sentimentale*. Les Belles Lettres, 1943.

_____. *Gustave Flaubert, son hérédité, son milieu, sa méthode*. Société française d'impression et de librairie, 1906.

Eaubonne, Françoise d'. *Les Plus Belles Lettres de Gustave Flaubert*. Calmann Lévy, 1962.

Flaubert, Gustave. *Oeuvres*. Conard.★

_____. *Oeuvres complètes*. Club de l'Honnête homme.

_____. *Oeuvres*, 2 vols. Gallimard, La Pléiade.

_____. *Oeuvres complètes* ("integral" edition). Le Seuil, 1964.

_____. *Correspondance et supplément*. Conard.

_____. *Correspondance*, 2 vols. (published to date). Edited by Jean Bruneau. Gallimard, La Pléiade.

_____. *Dictionnaire des Idées reçues*. Aubier, 1978.

_____. *Correspondance Flaubert-Sand*. Flammarion, 1981.

_____. *Carnets de travail*. Edited by Pierre-Marc de Biasi. Balland, 1988.

"Flaubert et ses héritiers," *Magazine littéraire*. February 1988.

Gérard-Gailly. *Le Grand Amour de Flaubert*. 1944.

_____. *L'Unique Passion de Flaubert*. Le Divan, 1932.

_____. *Flaubert ou les Fantômes de Trouville*. La Renaissance du livre, 1930.

Goncourt, Edmond and Jules. *Journal*, 4 vols. Fasquelle-Flammarion, 1959.†

Guillemin, Henri. *Flaubert devant la vie et devant Dieu*. Plon, 1939.

Henry, Gilles. *L'Histoire de monde est une farce, ou la Vie de Gustave Flaubert*. Editions Charles Corlet, 1980.

Lanoux, Armand. *Maupassant, le bel ami*. Fayard, 1967.

Leleu, Gabrielle. *Ebauches et fragments inédits de Madame Bovary*, 2 vols. Conard, 1936.

Mauriac, François. *Mes Grands Hommes*. Fayard, 1952. [English translation: *Men I Hold Great*, trans. by Elsie Pell. New York: Philosophical Library, 1951. —Trans.]

Maynal, Edouard. *La Jeunesse de Flaubert*. Mercure de France, 1913.

_____. *Flaubert et son milieu*. Editions de la Nouvelle Revue critique, 1927.

★ All of Flaubert's principal works have been translated into English, some of them a number of times. The largest selection of his letters is the two-volume annotated edition—in itself almost a biography—in Francis Steegmuller's masterly translation, published by Harvard University Press in 1980 and 1982. Separate volumes of Flaubert's correspondence with George Sand and Turgenev have also appeared in English. —Trans.

† Several collections of excerpts are available in English. The most extensive is the one admirably translated by Robert Baldick, *Pages from the Goncourt Journal*, published by Oxford University Press in 1962 (paperback by Penguin Books, 1984). —Trans.

Bibliography

Nadeau, Maurice. *Gustave Flaubert, écrivain*. Editions Lettres nouvelles, 1980. [English translation: *The Greatness of Flaubert*, trans. by Barbara Bray. New York: Library Press, 1972. —Trans.]

Pommier, Jean, and Digeon, Claude. *Du nouveau sur Flaubert et son oeuvre*. Mercure de France, 1952.

Poulet, Georges. *Flaubert, les métamorphoses du cercle*. Plon, 1961.

Sartre, Jean-Paul. *L'Idiot de la famille*, 2 vols. Gallimard, 1971. [English translation: *The Family Idiot: Gustave Flaubert, 1821–1857*, trans. by Carol Cosman. Chicago: University of Chicago Press, 1981. —Trans.]

Starkie, Enid. *Flaubert, jeunesse et maturité*. Mercure de France, 1970. [English original: *Flaubert: The Making of the Master*. New York: Atheneum, 1967. (Second volume in English: *Flaubert: The Master*. New York: Atheneum, 1971) —Trans.]

Suffel, Jacques. *Gustave Flaubert*. "Les Classiques du XXe siècle." Editions universitaires, 1958.

Thibaudet, Albert. *Gustave Flaubert*. Gallimard, 1935.

INDEX

Index

Index

Index

Index

Flaubert, Emile-Cléophas (brother), 3

Flaubert, Gustave
adolescent loves of, 11, 13–16
affair with Louise Colet, 67–79, 118–20, 130–36, 179, 203
on Art, 116, 146, 265, 289, 311
artistic control of, 139–40
baccalaureate exam for, 22
birth of, 3
booming voice of, 266, 267–68
on bourgeois, 215
brothels visited by, 38, 100–101, 105, 203
celebrity of, 190
childhood of, 4–10
contradictions of, 336
daily schedule of, 113–14
death of, 337–39
dual life of, 196
early physical descriptions of, 13, 26
early travels of, 25–26
early writings of, 6, 12, 17–20
elitism of, 205–6
on fame, 120–21
financial problems of, late in life, 285–88, 313–19, 321–22
and Franco-Prussian War, 236, 237–49
funeral of, 339–40
hypochondria, growing, of, 283–284
identification with Emma Bovary of, 139, 141
at law school, 29, 33–36, 40, 41, 43–44, 46
Legion of Honor awarded to, 209
literary anguish of, 117–18, 212
and *Madame Bovary*, beginning, 111, 114
and *Madame Bovary*, government concern over, 147–48
and *Madame Bovary*, prosecution of, 149–51

and *Madame Bovary*, publication of, 143–46
on marriage, 104–5, 263
and memories of past, 261–62, 265, 285, 297–98
Middle East expedition of, 94, 95–103, 105–6
monument to, 342
mood swings of, 159, 258–59, 272–73
morality of, 146, 265
need to occupy center stage, 196–97
nervous attacks of, 45–47, 82, 84, 89, 125, 141
personality of, 266, 267–68
political convictions of, 86–87, 89, 208, 216–17, 222, 252–53, 264, 272
posthumous reputation of, 341–44
in print, 18
protected solitary life begins for, 47–49
on reality, 296
reality vs. dream for, 106–7
and George Sand, friendship ripens with, 232–33
at school, 9–22
sexual experience, first, of, 26–27
social experiences of, 190, 195–97
and style, 84–85, 116, 140, 172–173, 269, 290
suffering of, while writing, 117–118, 212
vanity of, 155, 204
venereal disease contracted by, 38, 102–3, 109, 235n
on women, 57–58
work method of, in *Madame Bovary*, 142
as writer, perfectionistic strivings of, 117–18, 125–27, 129–30, 173
on writing well, 263–64, 289–90

Flaubert, Jules-Alfred (brother), 3

Index

Index

Index

Index